WOKELYND

A NOVEL BY

GEORGE P. DENNY

DEFIANCE PRESS
& PUBLISHING

Wokelynd

ISBN-13: 978-1-959677-91-8 (Paperback)
ISBN-13: 978-1-959677-90-1 (eBook)
ISBN-13: 978-1-959677-92-5 (Hardcover)

Published by Defiance Press and Publishing, LLC

Bulk orders of this book may be obtained by contacting Defiance Press and Publishing, LLC. www.defiancepress.com.

Public Relations Dept. – Defiance Press & Publishing, LLC
281-581-9300
pr@defiancepress.com

Defiance Press & Publishing, LLC
281-581-9300
info@defiancepress.com

> *"Mass movements can rise and spread without belief in a God, but never without a devil. Usually, the strength of a mass movement is proportionate to the vividness and tangibility of its devil."*
>
> —Eric Hoffer

TABLE OF CONTENTS

ACT I: Anti-Racists vs. the cisheteropatriarchy

ACT II: The Last Liberati

ACT III: The SOMA MOMA Momalla Gala for Love Massacre

GLOSSARY

Author's note: language and the evolution of words is of great importance to New California in 2066, so in the interest of clarity, the reader may want a list of basic terminology and proper nouns for quick reference. Three notable exceptions are "violence," "racism," and "Social Justice," as their use and possible applications are too vast to be summarized here.

Anti-Racist: The dominant ideology of New California, Anti-Racists view all differing outcomes between groups as proof of discrimination, and therefore prioritize the needs, feelings, and aspirations of underachieving "victim" identities over their more "privileged" peers.

Anti-Anti-Racist: The counter-revolutionary ideology of New California, Anti-Anti-Racists disregard the value and wisdom of innate identity and are hunted throughout the state.

Anti-Anti-Anti-Racist: The law enforcement ideology of New California, the AAA developed as the Anti-Racists muscle, mainly by capturing Anti-Anti-Racists and staffing penal colonies.

Baizuo: A derogatory Chinese term for outlandishly naïve political views and/or worldview, literally translated as "white left."

BIPOC: Black or Indigenous Person of Color.

Cisheteropatriarchy: A society founded, run, and maintained primarily for the benefit of cisgender, heterosexual white men. The citizen of New Cali-

6

fornia should regard everywhere else in the world as a cisheteropatriarchy, especially the United States of America.

Elect: The upper class of New California, the educated and placated elite who tacitly support all Anti-Racist policy proposals and aims of the state.

The Federals: The United States of America, as seen by a citizen of New California.

Intersectional Score (IS): The total value of one's identity in the eyes of the government, used to regulate equity, material rewards, career opportunity, and societal worth.

JSS: The Justice of Social Soldiers, the one and only government of New California.

Knowers: The highest members of society with the greatest lived experience and the most valued victimhood, the Knowers decide policy, punishment, and rewards for all.

Liberati: The Anti-Anti-Racists name for themselves and each other.

Lived Experience: Treated as wisdom, and believed to be accumulated through the historic and current victimization of a person's identity.

New California: The new nation state carved out of a northern slice of the old American state of California. New California is a totally isolated civilization run by its own JSS government and Anti-Racist ideology.

Safe Space: Idea-approved living quarters for valued members of New California society.

Speakers: The second highest rung of New California, Speakers are the conduit through which Knowers transmit their ideas and decisions to the people.

Standpoint Theory/Epistemology: The view that all knowledge is rooted in the power of the speaker, including science and math, which means that nothing can be objectively true. Often viewed as the intersection between feminist theory and Marxism, Standpoint Esistemology consciously values the historic victimhood of a speaker above the veracity of their speech.

Venis: The appendage invented in New California, the venis is formed from male parts to create a more phallic vagina. The penis is split and encircles a deeper wound, while the testicles usually remain untouched. Therefore, the owner of the venis may keep his reproductive instincts while retaining some possibility of stimulation.

Whiteness: Traits promoted or maintained through a connection to Caucasian history of global conquest and colonization; "white" or "whiteness" is generally a synonym of evil.

White Tears: A known diversionary tactic of white people, especially white women, who manipulate the deployment of their emotions to claim victim status their identity hasn't earned.

Workers/Relievers, Etc.: Everyone below the Knowers, Speakers, and Elect. Everyone with a job to do, or anyone who can be assigned to virtually any job at any time.

PROLOGUE

IN THE FIRST DECADES OF the twenty-first century, America's social polarization convinced many that the Union could not continue in its existing construction. A constitutional amendment, known officially as the "California Secession Act" to politicians but as the "Great Rupture" to the people, was ratified in December of 2039. Through this legislation, a portion of Southern California would be granted back to the United States of America, while Northern California would become its own independent country known as New California with San Francisco as its capital. The colossal economic loss to the United States of America was rationalized by the potential to save the Union from total collapse, as it was believed that an independent California would appeal to those political segments that most ardently opposed the US Constitution, thereby saving the rest of the nation from their political influence, social unrest, and votes.

The twelve months of 2040 would be the last opportunity for Californians and Americans to move freely among each other. In the dawn of 2041, all those living in California would forfeit their US passports and citizenship. Many millions of conservative, moderate, and liberal Californians alike chose America, and many of the most radically progressive Americans chose the promises of "Social Justice, Equity, and Anti-Racism" that New California advertised as its highest values. Most who flooded into

San Francisco to create the New California government were educated by the most accredited Anti-Racist minds from Old America. They were ambitious, ideological, and wholly dedicated to the utopian ideals guaranteed in an equal society for all identities.Those who subsequently held roles of greatest societal import became known as the Elect; those among the Elect who would transmit information to the rest of society became known as Speakers; and those Speakers whose lived experience surpassed the rest were called Knowers, entrusted with the responsibility to generate the right knowledge with which to educate and guide the rest of New California in Anti-Racism.

Eight years later, on February 16, 2048, one Quinceton Rift was born to Horace and Marcy in San Francisco's Children's Hospital. This is his story.

ACT I

Anti-Racists
vs.
the cisheteropatriarchy

ACT I, CHAPTER ONE

6:08 P.M., July 2, 2066

IT WAS ON NIGHTS LIKE this that Quinceton was willing to believe in San Francisco. The state had really hooked it up this time—he had a premium suite in the Macy's Apartments lining Union Square, and for the second of his two nights in the luxury pad, he felt the opportunity would be wasted if he didn't go out and try to find a lady with whom to share the place. In all of Quinceton's nineteen years, he'd never seen such a comfy apartment with such prime location to close with, and on this night, he had a pretty good cause and contribution to cite for his own Anti-Racism.

Quinceton surveyed the scene from Powell Street, the western border of Union Square, with his Macy's pad ready and waiting on the whole south side.

The sound of Social Justice emanated from all corners of Union Square as cancellations both large and small purified the roaming fog. There was a sexism problem to worry about in the Black Studies department; there was anti-Black Racism in the Latinx's Fighting Sexism campaign; there was transphobia impacting lookism, which made it all the more important to expose ableism, especially insofar as it came into conflict with different members already bogged down in a Black Sexism scandal. The world would always have bigotry to root out where it slept; that the dedication of this society brought such human weaknesses out into the open for the transparency of social instruction was proof enough that Social Justice would ultimately triumph. First for New California, then slowly the world as it grew to see the righteousness of an equitable society modeled right here in San Francisco's Union Square.

This central meeting place of San Francisco's young and connected was a square piece of cement on a hill with two distinct exhibition spaces: one elevated at the eastern end for politics, and the other on the ground level, much more accessible, for political messaging—or "art," as it was occasionally called. In the center of the concrete, teetering on top of a thirty-foot pole, was the symbol of local government and all their Anti-Racism: a rainbow baby, representing all the oppressed peoples of New California. The baby's bright colors were the only real sign of decorative personality Quinceton saw in any given direction, as the buildings all seemed to be graying from their capitalist roots, appropriately lacking any sense of community.

At the base of the baby statue, an inscription of the state motto read:

CERTAINTY IS SUPREMACY
CONFUSION IS COMPASSION

There were a few open-minded female bodies milling around the political messaging/art complex, with more commotion among a higher concentration of male bodies near the Accountability Platform at the opposite end of the square. Knowing the usual crowd at each of these installations quite well, Quinceton chose the esoteric glass box. He still had a chance at a lady before disembarking, especially with the sweet pad at his immediate disposal. He'd seen plenty of denunciations, enough to be bored by the tearful confession and jeering profanity by now, and planned to earn his first taste of a real battle soon enough—a step up from the daily grind of combating whiteness, white supremacy, and all other forms of bigotry, as all BIPOC did by nature of their very existence in this conquered land.

The new live expressionist exhibit transported from the hallowed halls of the nearby Social Justice gallery confused Quinceton, but that was nothing new in the world of representative representations of those who had been historically marginalized. A white man mannequin—dressed in all his apparent privilege with a vintage pin-striped suit, top hat, and gaudy (fake) gold watch—sat on a stool in the middle of a glass case. Nearby stood a Black womxn, a Latinx man, a trans person of some legitimate color, and a white person with an Indigenous American headdress and the standard permission sign around her neck clearing this particular act of cultural appropriation. Quinceton couldn't read the fine font but knew the text by heart: "I received BIPOC permission to appropriate this traditional clothing to platform BIPOC art and center colonial erasure, and I do so only after offering the position to marginalized voices and erased bodies. It is with privilege and the desire for decolonization that I continue the eternal struggle for equity and righteousness."

The four live persons stood around the mannequin and read pseudo land acknowledgement statements, recapping some of the genocidal highlights of the white man's destruction of this land and its peoples.

"I acknowledge this land as the birthplace of whiteness, of white supremacy, and the Western world's existing racial order," the Black womxn said from inside the plastic box. She appeared to wear an African headdress and dashiki and held a long spear at her side to complete the Motherland look.

"Established as a means to circumvent their own Constitution," the Latinx continued, "the white man's Racism came to define the dignity and potential of all people, everywhere." The reach was so massive that Quinceton almost had to respect it, even though it was the very definition of evil.

The whitey with permission to pose as Native spoke next. "But *this* land, heretofore an American slave realm, is the first in the nation, and the world, to be officially decolonized. No longer will the rights and opportunities of BIPOC, alternatively-abled, neo-knowing, mobility-challenged, and trans or gender-bending bodies be threatened by hatred and extermination!" It seemed they couldn't find an actual Indigenous person—a constant problem, what with the genocide and relocations and such—so they'd had this whitey fill in for legitimate color.

"The era of punching down is over!" the legitimately colored trans person said. "This is how we punch up at the cisheteropatriarchy: every-body dance!" The sound of banging drums clamored from somewhere, and the four performance artists began to dance around the oppressive white man mannequin. The specific historical message platformed by the musical scene would have perplexed Quinceton had he given a damn about politics, but luckily he only wandered down to the art crowd to find an authentic womxn.

One had to be careful, though. Quinceton knew that feeling attracted to a specific kind of gendered body was a thoroughly transphobic thought, as legally identifying as straight demanded that you be open to *all* womxn—always spelled with an *X* so as to strengthen the psychological independence from men and their associated patriarchy. As far as Quinceton knew, "female" was still spelled like it derived from a masculine root, but maybe they'd get on that next.

Some oppressive mental blockage prevented Quinceton from wanting anything other than cisgender womxn, and he didn't have much brain space to feel guilty about the trans womxn's penises in which he was not sexually interested. Plenty of men tried to up their social standing by claiming bi-sexuality, but Quinceton had decided long ago never to go this route; most of the hottest women he knew still identified as straight, and most of them wanted straight guys as well. Men claiming to be bisexual were generally viewed as liars—people thought they must either be gay or just lying for the extra government benefits—and to Quinceton, nothing was worth the loss of those few truly attractive opportunities.

If he really thought hard about it, he'd probably admit to being jealous that beautiful womxn could identify as a pile of dogshit and still be hounded by guys on every corner, while a dude in this world had to play his identity cards right. However, beautiful womxn did have their own glass ceilings to consider: Ever since the Me Too revelations in America about powerful men being subject to abuses of power for the sake of sex, it had become pretty suspicious to hire any lady above mediocre for a position requiring any form of teamwork. This also kept the best bodies in San Francisco somewhat hungry for the approval of others, which none of the "body positive" bodies seemed to mind. Besides, there wasn't time for Quinceton to worry. This would be his last sexual opportunity in the city for some time, and the artsy-progressive crowd gave it up right quick if you knew how to speak the language. And if you had enough womxn, you'd never really be alone, even without friends.

"What do you see?" Quinceton asked of a Latinx-presenting womxn about his age staring at the exhibit. She was dangerously pretty, with clearer skin than most young people, and made the effort to tie her hair back in a complicated knot. Many Latinxs still resisted the proper Anti-Racist term "Latinx," so Quinceton wouldn't use it unless she did, but the real masterful part of this opening salvo was Quinceton's physical stance—his shoulders were aimed only partially at the glass box, just enough in her direction that she would know whom he intended to address. With any luck, she would see him as a fellow art connoisseur and not a nineteen-year-old man looking for some warmth before the cold, desperate masturbation of battle.

"It's incredible, isn't it?" she answered with a glance in his direction that he tactfully ignored. It wasn't a question so much as an agreement that whatever they were looking at had succeeded for her, which was the opinion Quinceton wanted to find.

"Just stunning," Quinceton agreed. "As a straight cis he/his Black man of ableist advantage, I think it looks very … abstract."

"Interesting," the womxn said, indicating dissent. "From my perspective, as a straight cis she/her Latina with the same genetic benefits, I see it as an extension of the cisheteropatriarchy's discouragement of difference and the repressive imposition of whiteness on BIPOCs." She paused. "Or … Latinx. I guess I feel weird saying that."

Not pure orthodoxy, but the answer encouraged Quinceton nonetheless. Though he didn't know her name, he knew this cis female from a lifetime of feigned indignity. The rewards of acting offended at the right time stretched to the limits of imagination, but in this moment, Quinceton only needed to parrot the most basic stuff to properly demonstrate civic solidary—a mighty aphrodisiac. Landing this flying airship should be no problem.

"I see the erasure of marginalized groups, the deplatforming of problematic queer voices, plus the desire to decolonize homogenous spaces and the systemic vitality of white fragility," Quinceton recited from memory. This sentence had been written on a notecard and taped to his bathroom mirror until he could repeat it verbatim, as it seemed applicable to virtually all art and political messaging that the nation-state formally known as the American state of California allowed in public.

"I see that, too," she voiced above a perky set of breasts in a relatively tight sweatshirt. "The white man on the stool represents the former Federal government, and the dancing is the response to their policies." They shared a laugh as Quinceton snuck another peek at her body through a reflection in the glass. A few white girls chatted on the other side of the exhibit but they both wore loose muumuu dresses, thick-rimmed glasses, and had some inconvenient face tattoos, likely done at home. Other than this Latinx, tonight's display of personified oppression wasn't exactly drawing a talent show.

"It's very decolonizing," Quinceton continued, going off-script. He didn't know the precise meaning of this phrase, but he'd heard it said repeatedly by the sophisticated Elect around art stuff, and he was fairly confident she wouldn't contradict him. He also couldn't think of a way to fit the verb "center" into an applicable sentence, but he had it chambered and ready to go.

The Latinx gave him a quizzical look, but one without suspicion. "Yeah, I don't know the artist. I don't even know if they're a Speaker or a Knower or just regular Elect, but I like their work."

This quickly dimmed the conversation. It might've died there in lesser hands, but Quinceton had summoned water from dryer deserts before, and believed that self-doubt was the glass ceiling inhibiting the involuntary celibates. These so-called "incels" blamed their virginity on anything but themselves, and Quinceton might've felt some sympathy for them if he understood their problem. Young womxn generally responded to Quinceton with some interest, and he enjoyed nothing more than charming attractive cisgender females into sex.

"Totally agree," Quinceton said, "and I hope I have time to see more of their work after I fight the Nevada Americans, however long it takes. I'm on the bus to South Lake Tahoe at the crack of dawn tomorrow and don't know when I'll be back." He checked her face, then readied his hook with proper bait. "I guess I just walked down here from Macy's to clear my head—you know, get my mind right before really fighting for Social Justice." A person of Quinceton's meager victimhood couldn't be caught exploiting the term, but nothing worked quite like "Social Justice." It was bulletproof. It could never be denied by peers of equal or lesser status, and it could be anything at any time so long as you had the right power.

The Latinx female looked behind Quinceton at the Macy's Apartments, which faced Union Square with a flashy glass exterior blazing with the glitzy mask of Old America's capitalist empire. Few regular workers got to live in the former department store full-time, as the prime location and downtown views usually served as a temporary reward from the Knowers. Quinceton had gotten a big new room with a window view for his last night before deployment, and now was the time to try to use it.

"I've never been inside the Macy's," the womxn said, her expression turning curious. "I didn't even know they finished putting the divider walls up on the fifth floor."

"I'm on the fourth, but it's pretty sweet. We get our own rooms and our own towels and everything." Quinceton analyzed her stature and knew he hadn't closed her yet. "But I came out here to get away from other soldiers and all their battle talk. Take a little walk with me? I'm Quinceton, by the way."

"Sure, that sounds good. I'm Natalie. I live with my whole family in a TL apartment, so I get it. I like some fresh air, too."

Most dwellings in the Latinx portion of the Tenderloin had been designated for physical laborers—mostly Mexican, with a few blocks reserved for Guatemalan and Honduran families—with the city still working to separate them into ethnic affinity quadrants. Perhaps Natalie had done some farming; at the very least, it was highly likely someone in her family knew that kind of toil. Quinceton had spent the last summer doing a Sunny Vacation detail picking vegetables in the fields of the Central Valley, but once he'd signed up for the military, he dreamed of a better life. Maybe with a few kills to his name and a celebrated service record he could become a Community Safety patrolperson, or a Diversity, Equity & Inclusion Camp supervisor, or even a Knower's bodyguard. Once you proved your loyalty, you could get fast-tracked to a gig that came with its own four walls and a roof, which then meant access to even more womxn—the good life. Easy street forever.

Quinceton looked around Union Square for avenues to keep the conversation going but didn't see anything of much help. He'd already used his best opening material on the live art thing and saw only apartment buildings and an excited cluster around the Accountability Platform. By his estimation, Natalie didn't look like a big law and order enthusiast—she seemed like a three or four on a ten-point politically progressive scale—but maybe the scene would boost the image of his own fearlessness.

"Well, nice to meet you, Natalie. Want to check out the cancellations? I don't know about the transgressors, but it looks like a bigger crowd than normal."

Natalie glanced over to the Accountability Platform and shrugged. "Why not?" she said. "Could be a good preview of what you'll be up against." She ambled gradually toward the center of the square and Quinceton followed.

Quinceton blathered about seeing the first public cancellations in New California here in 2056. He spoke generally about the sight of so many people crowded onto the same stage and how the crowd reacted with a true mix of horror and delight, noise of all kinds. It wasn't like these days, where the display drew predictable jeering from a young audience. He did not, however, mention that his birthing parent had taken him to the first cancellations because his birther did not survive the confused turmoil of those years. Instead, he talked about other people his birther's age, and how different their reactions to Social Justice had been to those of Quinceton's generation.

"It's like the older you are, the more resistant you are to Social Justice and centering the goals of society around Diversity, Equity, and Inclusion," Quinceton said as they passed the Circles of Responsibility, a misdemeanor exercise to restore social standing in the realm of Restorative Justice. One light-skinned person, neck bent in shame, had a sign reading "VERBAL ASSAULT: DENIED GENDER EXPRESSION OF PERSON OF GREATER VICTIMHOOD BY CLAIMING TO KNOW HOW MANY GENDERS THERE ARE" slung around their neck. Usually, it wasn't so descriptive. Another's sign read "DENIED MY PRIVILEGE," the most common offense, and another was "CENTERED CISHETEROPATRIARCHY," which could mean almost anything. They would be out soon enough—but never overnight—and were allowed to eat food provided by friends and family during the Restorative Justice process. Plenty of transgressors didn't even get assigned to the Circles of Responsibility; many got to hide among each other in the massive Friday night Perp Walk down Market Street. Transgressors had to learn to take ownership of their violent words and ideas; it was just as simple as that. Restorative Justice was nothing barbaric or traumatizing, not like locking humans in cages as though they were war criminals or barnyard animals.

"I know, right? My parents didn't really get it, either," Natalie replied, not quite meeting Quinceton's eyes for emotional confirmation. Perhaps this was a delicate subject for them both.

"Well, let's hear what these bastards did to get here." Quinceton nodded toward the social scene taking shape at the foot of the Accountability Platform, tabling the parental topic with conspicuously deliberate speed. A handful of Community Safety patrolpersons led three transgressors up the platform steps with some difficulty despite willing submission by the voluntarily condemned. The canceled wore the same frowns on their faces, their hands bound behind their backs so as not to conceal the sign tied around their necks stating their crime.

At the top of the platform waited two very important people: the Speaker and Knower assigned to Criminal Social Justice duty for the day. The Knower's official gold hat was much taller and shinier than the Speaker's red one, and both contrasted sharply with the drab jeans and monochrome

T-shirts of the crowd. It also helped to instruct the viewer who it was that held court here at a glance, as the Knower sat on a padded seat at the rear of the platform and directed the Speaker with practiced hand gestures, saving all speech for the sound of the chosen voice.

"Silence! Quiet! Silence!" the supervising Speaker shouted with two arms raised. They wore simple Level One Speaker robes but smiled confidently as nearby talk faded into rapt attention. Once it was quiet, the Speaker read from the first page of a stack of loose paper.

"Before we begin, I'd like to present a statement from Knower Gladdius K. Lakanda regarding her controversial recent gender philosophy work titled *She Centers His Vagina to Platform Their Penis*. Knower Lakanda would like to remind all workers, Elect, Speakers, and even other Knowers that it was not her intent to discriminate against any segment of the nonbinary community with her choice of vocabulary, and she has not forgotten about those with neither a penis nor a vagina, but a venis. To the venis-offering community, Knower Lakanda pledges herself to future academic efforts breaking down the penis/vagina binary and will reveal why a venis or any combination of remodeled reproductive organs is really the exact same as the original appendage."

Quinceton had heard plenty about the "venis," the new male-born trans-identifying organ that was much, much easier to construct for Anti-Racist wielders of the scalpel. Nothing he'd ever heard about it made it seem like a regular vagina, but he'd never seen a venis, either, and reminded himself not to think so transphobically. No doubt the Knower who'd written *She Centers His Vagina to Platform Their Penis* also had to remind herself not to think so absentmindedly within the gender binary.

"Knower Lakanda finishes her explanation with a statement that I will now read: 'Whenever you are in doubt, just remember: *She Centers His Vagina to Platform Their Penis*. Just think about that. And then it will all make sense.' End quote." Quinceton had a few practical curiosities remaining, but he was just as happy to think about something other than a venis for the time being, and then the duration of his existence after that.

The government Speaker continued on stage: "In other news we can all be proud of, and about which so many of you are already aware, many of our most committed and diverse workers will be sent to South Lake Tahoe tomorrow. The twenty-four-hour violence being committed at each and every major road and intersection between New California and Federal America will no longer be tolerated. For too long, we've been boxed in by the never-ending assault of violence and other problematic imagery from just across the border, which your government has gone to great lengths to protect you from. In two days, the cisheteropatriarchy will know Social Justice. Now, give a cheer for our brave soldiers, some of whom may currently be in attendance."

A murmur of "Trust us … jus-tus …" ebbed from the crowd without nearly so much enthusiasm as they offered in jeers for the canceled. Social Justice could have many different forms, but as long as it was aimed in the right direction it was all good. Natalie joined the chant in a soft voice; Quinceton could tell he'd have to sell her on something personal, beyond the typical government soldier association. Maybe even something more individual, about himself.

"In addition, I have a ZNN news update you must all hear," the Speaker read. "'Unforeseen dust storms stretching across southern New California have slowed planting season, and in response, the Knowers have decided to suspend the agricultural Intersectional Score minimums for the duration of 2066. Many of you will be reassigned, some as soon as Monday. Check with your commitment masters for details on your duty.' End ZNN update."

Quinceton heard some murmuring among the crowd but nothing truly distinguishable. He felt pretty damn glad to be in the infantry right then, all things considered. He was a Bay Area boy, and he'd always hated the hot toil of farming.

"Finally, a local opportunity: Those with any cooking or catering experience should contact their commitment master immediately for a chance to work directly for our Knowers. We are looking for those with Intersectional Scores of eight or above, but sacrifices may be made for those with unique ability. That is all." The Speaker relocated the first page to the rear

22

of the stack and nodded to the nearest patrolpersons.

"Bring forward the first transgressor," the Speaker bellowed in a new voice of prestige and authority. Quinceton knew this voice well, and assumed everyone else did too. It was strong yet indifferent, spoken with a robotic face toward the crowd. The Knowers must have chosen their Speakers based partly on how well they could deliver pronouncements with a sound of unquestionable finality, he suspected, because they were all so good at it.

Two patrolpersons delivered the transgressor on the left to a faint white circle in the middle of the stage and straightened the sign around their throat. The transgressor, a sullen Caucasian colonizer with the facial expression of one fast running short on spare privilege, had a sign around their neck stating simply "SPREAD RACISM."

"This individual has been found guilty of spreading Racism in the second degree," the Speaker announced. "The individual did knowingly and intentionally transcribe Racist ideas to paper and distribute these Racist ideas among their local community. In light of personal restitution contributed to the primary aggrieved victim, this individual's Diversity, Equity, and Inclusion Camp sentence has been commuted to three years of Restorative Justice and two days to consider their bigotry in the Circles of Responsibility. As a further act of forgiveness, this transgressor has been permitted an Accountability Statement."

Only in a formal setting would anyone use the full title of Diversity, Equity & Inclusion Camp for a rehabilitation facility; it was referred using the acronym "DIE" for any of the average workers around New California. Every one of them was capable of the original dark humor, and it caught on quick, as getting sent to DIE was typically the last anyone ever saw of you.

The canceled white guy stepped forward awkwardly, clearing his throat. In the most pathetic way possible, he began crying White Tears—a known diversionary tactic used by privileged people to manipulate sympathy and re-center the conversation around the hurt feelings of the oppressor rather than focus on the Social Justice of the marginalized masses.

"It's all true," he wept. "I'm a Racist white supremacist colonizer. I didn't mean to be—I didn't want to be, but I became one anyway. Down with the cisheteropatriarchy!"

The transgressor added nothing further as the Speaker raised an eyebrow in final judgement. As the cancelled was directed from the stage to the Responsibility Circles, all Quinceton could think about was the lucky bastard on the other end of this Restorative Justice—that lucky guy had earned some of this transgressor's credits for three years just for finding Racism. Social Justice could be pretty sweet sometimes, but it often left each member of the crowd to fill in the information holes for themselves in their own head.

"You know, I liked it better when they let all the transgressors really put it in their own words before they got cancelled," Quinceton said quietly to Natalie. "I know they could use the opportunity to commit more violence against us by shouting their Racist ideas, but most said good things. Most just wanted their families to be safe and happy and learn from their mistakes. If I were going out, and I couldn't go out happy in my sleep, I'd want to at least apologize specifically for what I'd done wrong and end it all with something hopeful for other people to hear. But these cancelled people only ever say the same thing, and it's boring."

Natalie nodded next to him, giving him a different look than he'd seen before. She seemed to hear something deep inside Quinceton, something that wasn't in the original game plan. Whatever he had said reached her in such a way as to make him more connected to her. He didn't understand any of this, but it felt alright.

"I wish we knew more about them, too," she said. "The transgressors, I mean. They just march out here, we hear the sentence, and then what happens to them? You ever seen anyone come back from a DIE camp? They're probably shark bait." The tone in her voice convinced Quinceton to sideline his whole "brave soldier" angle. He didn't know what to replace it with, but he'd think of something.

"Bring forward the second transgressor." This one, a brown-skinned womxn wearing a "CONSPIRED TO DEFECT" sign, started mumbling immediately and shrugged the patrolperson's hands off her arms in some gruff form of protest, but at least she didn't run. Quinceton had seen that plenty of times before, and it never ended well. After falling off the platform, they got corrected swiftly with a baton to the gut and went straight back up anyway.

"This individual has been found guilty of conspiring to defect in the third degree," the Speaker said in the same big boss tone. "This individual did knowingly and intentionally plot apostasy against the state. This individual stole supplies and conspired to defect from their duties to the state. This individual acted alone, received no support from their community, and was identified as a traitor by their female-presenting child."

The transgressor's stifled murmurs rose to a frantic hum at these last words, but when the Speaker bellowed, "Silence!" again, they went deathly silent. "This transgressor is a single womxn with two children and, having betrayed their dependents and commitment to Anti-Racism, should spend a number of years rehabilitating in a Diversity, Equity, and Inclusion facility. However, a number of peers of Intersectional Scores of ten or greater, including a member of the Elect, have spoken out for the past contributions this individual has made to Anti-Racism and believe the Restorative Justice process can apply here, too. Therefore, this individual will serve their penance to the state locally in to-be-determined restitutionary assignments, and only after participating in tonight's Market Street Accountability Processional. Child visitation rights will be re-established in time to prevent further harm from infecting the minds of the young. An Accountability Statement has been granted and will now be read."

Two Latinx-ish children stood alone in the crowd, and when one softly called, "Mommy," Quinceton assumed they were here to see their mother's sentence. The cancelled recited an Accountability Statement that was eerily similar to the previous iteration—"I'm a Racist and I don't want to be, blah blah blah"—but as she did so, both of her presumed children began to cry. This womxn, likely a single birther, would suffer the consequences of her Racism, but so, too, would her children.

Back in Quinceton's schooling days, your parent being cancelled was a precursor of becoming a specific kind of social pariah, and any outcast was scrutinized mercilessly to guard against future Racism. That the offender and her children were of legitimate color was proof of the great lengths the state was willing to venture to root out Racism of all kinds. Even BIPOCs could be held responsible for BIPOC-on-BIPOC offenses.

"Social Justice can be harsh sometimes," Quinceton said. He looked from the kids of the cancelled to Natalie, and she agreed with her eyes. This parent-child situation seemed to shock her. Restorative Justice was supposed to be quick and painless, but this time it wasn't easy to watch at all.

"Do you want to get out of here?" Quinceton asked. "I'm not busy or anything. Do you want me to walk you home?"

"No, that's okay. The last transgressor's sign says 'ANTI-ANTI-RAC-IST,' and they have them in one of those full-body cover-ups. I want to hear what the Knowers convicted them of."

"Oh, yeah," he replied. "Me too."

This tall, gaunt cuffed-and-masked third transgressor was no doubt gagged as well, and likely would have folded into a human lump of wasted calories if it hadn't been for Community Safety propping them up. The patrolpersons lifted the Racist (or the Anti-Anti-Racist) from their knees and carried them to the middle circle where the first two had seen their fate decided. It took some effort to keep the condemned upright. The Speaker paused to eye this particular bigot with conscious, narrowed eyes and the deep scorn of clenched lips. They paused, raised a hand this time to de-mand total silence, and actually turned slightly to face the condemned. Quinceton got the sense that this was special retribution somehow, and no matter how pathetic the limp body looked as it waited for judgement, no amount of Social Justice would be extreme enough to satisfy the Speaker.

"This individual has been found guilty of Anti-Anti-Racist activities in the first degree," the Speaker proclaimed with such force that the words broke their guise of dispassion. "This individual did knowingly and inten-tionally disseminate heretical ideas of a Racist, transphobic, and ableist nature among all levels of our society, including Knowers, Speakers, other members of the Elect, regular workers, and transgressors. This individual spread dissent and opposition to the very foundations of our government, including the Standpoint Mandate, and conspired to dethrone our exalted Knowing Leader Xumwaza Q. Jumping Bull and many other members of the Elect. For revealing their co-conspirators, this individual's sentence has been commuted to reeducation in a Diversity, Equity, and Inclusion facility." This was a fate Quinceton knew all too well; since everyone was susceptible to permanent Racism, some reeducations could last a lifetime.

After the decree, the patrolpersons, struggling to keep the transgressor's drooping body high enough to face the crowd, did not react in the same automatic fashion as they'd done before.

"Proceed," the Speaker demanded with greater volume. The patrolpersons labored to carry the transgressor off the stage, clearly bearing the full weight of the unwillingly convicted. The friction pushed against the back of the transgressor's skull, dislodging the mask and the gag that had evidently held them in silence.

"Pithawalla will rise again!" the Anti-Anti-Racist shouted immediately in a long howl. "Free at last, free at last, God almighty, I'll be free at— !" They couldn't finish the verbal assault before a therapeutic nightstick spared the crowd from further violence. Quinceton truly couldn't remember the last time he'd heard the name of the reviled Advi Pithawalla. The transgressor imploded at the physical reminder, folding forward onto their knees. Quinceton caught a glimpse of their neck, exposed for the briefest of moments from under a long black hood, and saw very dark skin. Almost exactly like his own. For all he knew, it could be his seeder up there, still failing to keep his word to a long-forgotten son.

Scattered clapping and cheers emerged from around Quinceton, but he said nothing. He couldn't take his eyes off the last transgressor as patrolpersons on the ground rushed to re-gag their mouth and re-bag their head. The crowd fused their voices into the popular chant of "Trust us ... jus-tus ..." once more as Natalie tapped Quinceton on the shoulder.

"You okay?" she asked, watching his face for cracks in the standard public mask. "You ever meet that last one, the transgressor?"

"No, no, not at all. I have no idea who they were. But didn't it seem different this time? Like the Speaker actually knew who it was under the hood? Knew them personally?"

Natalie squeezed his bicep. "Maybe. It did seem a little hostile. I'm not sure the transgressor was fully conscious when they read the charges."

Quinceton turned his back to the Accountability Platform and lowered his voice. "Yeah, that got me too. How could a person get close enough to Speakers and Knowers to spread violence against the state without being a Knower or Speaker themselves? Or at least Elect … at least that much." This idea stuck to the part of Quinceton's mind he wished he could ignore—the part that made him think about his birther and her own political ambitions.

"Well, maybe they were a bodyguard or cook or gardener or something. Or maybe you're right and they were Elect or above. What does that mean to you? To see an Elect or a Speaker or Knower cancelled out here basically like anyone else?"

"I don't know," Quinceton lied. "But I don't want to stay here around the sad Racists and jeering crowd. It's ugly and depressing. Are you sure I can't walk you home?"

"Well, it's not so late, and I don't think it'll get *that* dangerous for another hour or so. Actually, can I see your Macy's room? I'm not tired at all."

Quinceton realized he was succeeding somehow, but it felt like winning on an emotional technicality. He didn't quite feel in control of the situation anymore once the conversation ballooned into something that actually mattered to him. Suddenly he didn't feel invincible, the way he wanted to feel when going head-to-head with an attractive female, but he didn't want to lose Natalie yet.

"Sure. I'm not tired either. I'll show you the view, but when it gets late, you have to let me walk you home." He paused, feeling like a virtue-signaling conman. "I just wouldn't be the son I am if I dumped you on the curb and fed you to the dogs after you read me how you do."

She smiled, took his arm in hers, and led him to Macy's, a building that seemed like a cheap payoff of some kind, but now at least Quinceton didn't feel like either one of them were offering the bribe. They climbed the escalators arm in arm and dashed through the repurposed hallways, careful to keep their voices low inside the fresh paper-thin walls.

Within the suite, Natalie giggled as she sat on his bed and reached for the Sexual Consent Form and erasable pencil offered in any decent state-sanctioned residence. Quinceton held his breath.

"Hmmm," she hummed, eyeing Quinceton from the height of total monopoly. "I didn't see the latest version of this thing even has a list of romantic vocabulary to choose consent for. Weird."

"Yeah, I don't know about any of that. You can call me anything under the sun, and I don't give a damn. I'm also happy to just, you know, talk, cuddle, whatever."

"A cuddle wouldn't last you very long in wartime, though, would it?" Natalie laughed again as she ticked off a few acts Quinceton couldn't wait to realize and signed her name at the bottom with a big fancy signature. Satisfied, she handed the sheet to Quinceton for him to read. As the biological man in a sexual situation, his consent was assumed and his signature unnecessary.

"Now that the romantic paperwork is done," she said, "come here."

ACT I, CHAPTER TWO

The Rifts

THERE WAS ONLY ONE MEMORY that haunted Quinceton when he couldn't sleep, and somehow looking at Natalie softly snoring made him think back to it. He actually needed rest, but instead he paced around the window, looking at the tired city and not seeing any of it.

He was ten years old at the time, sitting at the kitchen table trying to explain his Anti-Racist Math pamphlet to his seeder after dinner. The kitchen felt massive, with a long spotless counter and an immortal stove-oven combination that never stopped sprouting complex smells he could no longer taste. This was the warmest room in their ground-floor apartment, and it was here that Quinceton liked to share his lessons from school with Dad, who added to the schooling by teaching his own advanced vocabulary words and life lessons like: *"Believe what people do over what they say."*

Quinceton still remembered the movie his seeder had borrowed to watch that night but couldn't, as Quinceton's birther had been part of the committee recommending its cancelation. The film, called *Hoosiers 2: Trans Girls Mop the Floor,* was about a high school basketball sports team. Dad had been desperate to watch something with sports in it ever since athletics were deemed an extension of historic racial stereotyping and canceled on grounds of inequity, but this film was still problematic despite its intent toward gender-inclusive messaging. It was the title: to suggest that trans girls mop the floor, even with their male counterparts, was to implicate these females in a classic *sexist* stereotype of females being confined to kitchen work. Apparently, the creators of this blatantly bigoted movie were already being prepared for reeducation in a Diversity, Equity & Inclusion Camp.

Quinceton usually tried to cheer up the old man on nights like this. Putting an advanced vocab word into a sentence that made sense was a guaranteed way to impress his father, a person who also liked to put on a silent comedy routine by bulging his eyes, sucking all the air out of the room with a great gasp, or pointing his fingers at his head like a gun when he heard something political he didn't like. These gestures amused Quinceton every time, but in recent months Dad responded with less humor and more head-shaking disapproval—conversation over. On this evening, Quinceton opted for distraction, simply handing Dad the stapled Anti-Racist Math pages he'd gotten at school.

"What *the hell* is this *bullshit*?" Dad said in the usual comic tone reserved for educational commentary. He could use curse words, but Quinceton could not because he was still a boy.

"It's math. It's our math book this year."

Dad rifled through the pages, reading some chapter titles and subheadings. "I don't see any equations. Where is the math?"

Quinceton shook his head. "Maybe we start learning that in a few years. But the teacher says first we need to know how dangerous math can be. It's rooted in white supremacy and has been used for centuries to promote ideas and create statistics that deny the lived experience of the oppressed. So, we're learning that first so we don't commit violent ideas on oppressed people."

Dad stopped sifting and read from the text with condensed facial features, an expression that worried Quinceton. Dad was never afraid but he could be really bothered.

"Don't show me your science book or I think I'll have a goddamn heart attack," he said at last. "This chapter—chapter five, called 'Equity Mathematics: How to Uphold Community Standards After Arriving at Different Math Answers.' What does that mean?"

"Before we do equations we're learning how many different answers there can be to the same question in math, and how it's so toxic to expect kids of different backgrounds to come to the same conclusions about a math problem."

"No," Dad said, head twitching. He paused. "That's not right. Not right in any way. That's just too far."

Then the boy's birther appeared in the doorway, looking annoyed. Quinceton vaguely remembered expecting what happened next to happen, but he couldn't be sure if that was real or if it just felt that way. He could see the direction of his life veering onto the present course from that one evening, and he had replayed these words so many times in his head that he half worried it was a script implanted in his brain by foreign Americans seeking to corrupt him.

"Either of you seen my nice pullover, the blue one?" Mom said. "I'm sure it's going to be cold and windy again tomorrow."

"Well at least we know what to blame," Dad mocked, swiveling in his chair to face her head-on. "White supremacy, obviously, assuming it isn't because of the patriarchy. For the bad weather, I mean. Your sweater is probably in the laundry pile I put on the washer."

"It better not go in the dryer, Horace. And you better check yourself before you start up with me again—patriarchy is the only reason we're pressured to keep this damn *nuclear family*. I can't think of another reason to let you and your ideas around Quinceton, especially now that words are official 'violence.' This was a big day for Anti-Racism, and I already know you're not going to like it, but it's final."

"Oh, I'm sure it's all just brilliant stuff, Marcy. Like this Anti-Racist Math pamphlet. You know what your son's math class is all about? I mean, have you *seen* this shit?"

Mom responded with a familiar look, one of boastful confidence pressing into the realm of condescension. She was always in the know; she'd been on some exclusive community council for a few years and had close contact with the local Speakers, while Dad was a sweaty carpenter almost completely detached from politics. These fights had begun to happen more and more frequently, and though there was some sarcasm, it no longer came in funny jokes about how different life was now from the past. Mom leaned against the doorway, still holding her expression, eyes cast down at Dad, ready to begin the verbal brawl from on high.

"Did you know your son is being told that there are multiple answers to the same math problem? For Social Justice, no doubt. So I guess we're making objectivity illegal in this country we're building. Maybe two and two can equal five or six if you have the right identity. Did you know that?"

"Of course," Mom answered, not budging. "We discourage all binary thinking. That's just an extension of white supremacy, and it enables denialism of lived experience and alternate ways of knowing. You don't listen, but the Anti-Racist Math initiative is a wild success—we've doubled equity in just one semester." Dad rose from his chair to pour a glass of water, then leaned against the sink with head bowed. Quinceton didn't need to see his face to know what it looked like just by hearing the defeat in his tone.

"Well, that's just great. 'Doubled equity'—congrats, Marcy. I mean, there are barely tests or grades anyway, so this must make sense, too, if you're religious enough. It's really a perfect plan. Just make sure no one ever needs to build anything, or buy or sell something, or use simple logic again. Is there any educational goal here? Aiming at anything specific with your Anti-Racist curriculum besides the same universal cluelessness?"

"Once equity is achieved in all settings we'll invite the platforming of other initiatives and decolonization efforts. But you're going to want to sit your ass back in that chair for this one: The Speakers just told us King is problematic. He's heading to the whitelist."

Silence followed—Quinceton remembered that—like the eye of the storm. Dad might've paced around a bit but he was sitting down when he spoke next. It was a different tone than before, almost pleading, like he desperately wanted to keep negotiating after a deal had already been reached.

"You can't do it," Dad said, sounding distraught, "you just can't. You can't tell me the least Racist man from the American Empire is now Racist, even if he was American. MLK was so much more than an American; he's a man of history, someone the whole world is proud of. He taught us about nonviolent resistance and *not* caring so much about identity that you're blind to everything else. He was the actual anti-Racist before Anti-Racism became the pushy brand you could control people with."

Mom's face offered no slack. "You've got no idea what you're talking about. We have copies of King's actual words, things he wrote, and he was liable to rep colorblindness over and over again. He clearly supports the erasure of BIPOC identity as we see it today; I don't think he even once referred to us as 'Children of Africa' or anything to center our true roots."

"True roots—Africa? Marcy, you spent the first thirty years of your life in Atlanta!"

"It doesn't matter. I like 'Children of Africa' now that there's nothing American about us anymore. And it's high time we defeat white supremacy once and for all."

"You can only be ridden if your back is bent," Dad shot back. Quinceton remembered those lines as if he had been born with them printed inside his head.

"Crazy," Mom said, sweeping away whatever the phrase meant. "You remember all his desegregation focus, bordering on ethnic erasure and whitewashing of racial history? King wouldn't want us to care about each other's race, or other features of our identities which might have been historically problematic. Putting a halt to the exaltation of this false prophet is a necessary defense against—yes, Horace—white supremacy. Plus, King was a devout Christian, and you know how resistant they are. We're launching a new campaign to center education around alternative ways of knowing, and colorblindness is not only problematic, it's the enemy of progress. Colorblindness is the erasure of that which gives us power."

"Ah! No, King's no prophet, but a man who sold some really good ideas to a tough crowd, like treating each other equal. Still, good advice for all these angry identitarians." Dad shook his head, turned to Quinceton, and surprised him with a bemused smile. He actually seemed pleased to keep talking, even though he probably still didn't like the king's cancellation.

"You heard that, Quinceton, right? You heard what she said about colorblindness and losing their power? Finally, we agree. There's a word I want you to know and memorize, son: 'identitarian.' An identitarian sees everybody in terms of race and gender and that stuff; they care more about what you were born with than anything else, even your words and ideas. We used to read history books about all kinds of different white identitarian groups and it always led to lots of killing, lynching other people—especially Blacks—and sometimes even all-out war. Your mother and her people are just a new version of what good, honest people have been fighting against for hundreds of years, except around here, now it's a whole religion that controls everything."

Mom rushed to sit on the other side of the table, grabbing Quinceton's arm tight. Her eyes were very serious. "Your father better be careful, 'cause he's talking some American Racism. Remember, Quinceton, if you aren't Anti-Racist, you're Racist like an American. Americans don't do the work of platforming queer and BIPOC voices; they don't demand equity to the victims of colonization. Americans might even openly support the cisheteropatriarchy, but even if they won't admit it, they'll defend white supremacy all day long. White supremacy is the real menace, not whatever your father thinks, and you need to learn to recognize it, especially in people of color or other identities of historic marginalization."

Quinceton understood most of what Mom said, but Dad confused him; he didn't speak in terms of Social Justice. He had his own ideas. This American king had been important to Dad for some reason, but maybe only Dad, because he didn't ever come up in school and the few times Quinceton had risked asking elders about "the American MLK king" they pretended not to hear.

Dad left the table pretty soon after Mom sat down, picked up a jacket, and headed out the front door. It wasn't Quinceton's last sight of him, though. Hours later, when Quinceton was in bed trying to fall asleep, Dad knocked on the door softly and entered dressed in all black, like an Anti-

Anti-Anti-Racist agent out on a midnight prowl for criminal bigots. Dad knelt by the bed, put a hand on Quinceton's shoulder, and spoke in a whisper.

"Still awake, son? I know you're still awake. I've got to tell you something, and then I need to go."

"Don't go. Don't tell me if it makes you go."

"It's the world we're born into. I mean, it's not safe for me here anymore. Me being in this house puts you in danger, and maybe even Marcy, too, so that's why I need to go. But before I'm out, I want to tell you something important."

"Where will you go?" Quinceton asked, speaking over him.

"I don't know, and even if I did know I wouldn't tell you. They'll ask you and expect you to lie, so it's better if you don't know. But I'm out on this New California … what's left of California, anyway. I would take you with me but you're safer here, at least for now. When you're a man you'll make your own decisions."

"I want to come with you."

"I know, and keep your voice down. But you can't come with me. They don't want anyone to leave, and if they catch me … I don't know what'll happen, but it'll be bad."

"I don't care. I'm strong. I'm coming with you."

Dad ran his hand through Quinceton's hair and beamed a smile of pure paternal pride. This face was the one Quinceton saw first whenever he thought about Dad, even though it didn't always feel good to recall.

"Son, I know you're a warrior, and I love you, but you're staying here. You can't come with me. And I don't have much time to tell you everything I want to say, so I just want you to remember one thing. You listening?" Quinceton nodded.

"Your skin is Black, but who you are is Quinceton Rift. Now, you come from a proud people who took the worst shots from humanity any people can take—it's true what they say about us rising from slavery and genocide. American Blacks did that, and we kept pushing forward, hoping to make a better life one generation at time, and not getting much help from the US government Federals or anyone else to figure it out. When the story of racial integration is told all over the world one thousand years from now, the first people anyone will talk about are the Black Americans who descended from slaves and made it happen. And there was a time in even my life—so not that long ago—when American Blacks were damn near the best in the world at everything we did well, a giant in world culture second to none and copied by all ..." Dad's voice trailed off before he got his words back.

"But though all that's true, or even if it isn't, who you are is what you say and do. That makes you a good or a bad person—your actions, not your identity. But even more important is that you treat everyone else that way too. Whatever you can see about a person is not really who they are, or at least not *all* they are. The ability to treat everyone the same at first, to treat everyone with respect until they show you they don't deserve your respect—*that* makes you a good person. That's how you become a true class act. Having real integrity is not caring about the way someone looks different from you and treating everyone good unless they treat you bad. Got that? Understand what I'm saying?"

"Yes, Dad. I won't forget it."

"That's good. I'm proud of you. Now give your old man a hug." Quinceton pulled back the bedsheet, sitting up as Dad wrapped his massive arms around the boy.

"Now, be nice to your mother while I'm gone. You'll do a better job than I did. I swear to Christ I'll come back for you if I can, if it's ever safe. Pray that you'll see me again. I'll be praying for the same every night. Goodbye for now, son." Dad gave a quick nod and stood abruptly, crossed the room in a few long strides, and left through the window, shutting it behind him. The last thing Quinceton saw of his father was a dark backpack stretched to the stiches.

So much from that night stuck permanently in Quinceton's brain, as everything changed without Dad at home. "School" wasn't called "school" anymore—it was called a "Work Doing" center or facility—and Quinceton hadn't really seen the point of attending after fourth or fifth grade. He just hadn't held that many more feelings about being Black, and not enough words to fill another verbal address excavating the depths of his standard, boring heterosexuality. Even the words "Mom" and "Dad" were vanishing concepts, replaced by "birther" and "seeder" respectively by Knower decree in the intervening years, even if it wasn't yet common lingo.

Quinceton understood the need to reject cis-supremacy and the typical two-parent white-centric "nuclear family" but rarely heard "birther" and "seeder" used in his friends' homes, either, as most opted instead to call their parents by their first names. Quinceton just couldn't imagine calling his father Horace, but his mother's orthodoxy taught him to call her "birther" or "my birther" until eventually she, too, disappeared.

And now, taking in the city from the best view of his young life, Quinceton's eyes settled on the Accountability Platform and the three souls who had been judged there. Though he knew his seeder was considered a bona fide Anti-Anti-Racist in today's world, he forgave the person from his memory for not knowing any better. His parents' generation just didn't have the knowledge of lived experience that had been collected and revealed in the modern Anti-Racist age. Quinceton's seeder meant well, but committed Anti-Anti-Racists were true terrorists to the state, and it was the job of the AAA—the Anti-Anti-Anti-Racist agents—to hunt them down.

Maybe the old man had new opinions after all these years. Maybe he'd learned about the importance of Diversity, Equity & Inclusion. Quinceton resolved that if he ever met the big man again, the risk was worth the archaic title, and only "Dad" would fit.

ACT I, CHAPTER THREE

The Bus to South Lake

QUINCETON DIDN'T WANT TO WAKE up, didn't want to leave Natalie to sleep alone, and really didn't want to sit on this bus heading for war. Sure, he was tired, but he was far more grumpy, and in no mood to get shoved into the window by some lily-white colonizer. Something larger than this European fool next to him had to be responsible for driving him out of bed at such an ungodly hour to go and kill an enemy he had never seen. The sight of so many soldiers filing into a string of motor-powered vehicles reminded him of how much gas they'd have to use to get to South Lake Tahoe, how rarely the state authorized the use of such a rare and precious resource, and who was really at fault for necessitating New California's ban on foreign trade.

Everyone blamed the Parsee people, as the Parsees ditched the state completely when it was time to pay their fair share of the equity tab. Quinceton felt they should have blamed the first and main Parsee deserter, Dr. Advi Pithawalla, more than those who got swept up in the exodus, but it was true that most all Parsees followed his lead and got their Zoroastrian religion whitelisted right along with Christianity due to their deceit. Some people would always resist their own material taxation, never understanding the required economic liberation to guarantee equity between groups, and the first group to act en masse to avoid an ethnicity-associated tax bill had been funded by the notorious Dr. Advi Pithawalla. If there was a luxury pad in America to invade, it was perfectly acceptable to imagine stealing it back from under the greedy clutches of the rich Parsees. Revolution solved that which couldn't be solved any other way, and if carried out correctly, it was theoretically possible that one could be victorious without exposing too many troops to the violence of unauthorized ideas.

Even so, Quinceton deeply resented the Parsees for bringing about the border lockdown that ultimately served to force him out of Macy's when he had such a fine lady sleeping next to him. If it hadn't been for Dr. Advi Pithawalla, Quinceton might never have had to board a bus headed for the front lines. The cause of Social Justice may never relent, but in that moment, he wished his role in the struggle could localize him next to a heady smokeshow like Natalie in a place he could live in for a while.

As Quinceton thought about who and what had caused the conflict he'd signed up for, the whitey tapped his thigh to get his attention. Something about his beady eyes, thin nose, and weak shoulders made Quinceton resist any attempts at interaction.

"Excuse me," the honkey said, "I'm pure Irish cracker he/him, and I don't mean to bother you, but I'm very nervous about all this. I never shot a gun before the training weekend and I'm regular infantry. Do you think it's going to be dangerous?"

The mick looked so helpless that Quinceton actually considered comforting the Bog Irish bastard. But then again, the mick looked so pale and puny that Quinceton couldn't resist the urge to fuck with him.

"I heard we might be hitting Dr. Pithawalla himself," Quinceton answered, deadpan, not offering the respect of presenting his intersectional identity. "I could see a trillionaire wanting a nice comfy lake view at the top of one of those fancy Nevada casinos. So if he's there, best case scenario is probably some massive firefight, heavy losses on both sides—a goddamn bloodbath, to be real."

In this moment, Quinceton decided that above all the Racist Americans in his hierarchy of evil, it had to be Dr. Pithawalla at the top, then all the Parsees, as their abandonment of New California had mandated closed borders, the destruction of all personal cellular telephones, and total disconnection from the tool once used to spread Racism called "the internet." Before the internet, it was harder to fuck with a clueless guy next to you on the bus, as now there were only a few avenues to source history or know current events for certain. No matter what you thought about anything, it was almost impossible to argue for or against it with historical examples. Memories were now the most tangible facts one had to work with, and though he'd still been a young boy, Quinceton vividly remembered his parents arguing about how to treat the Parsees. Life had more informational inputs in those days, but Dad split shortly thereafter, so it seemed fair to put his parent's estrangement on Dr. Pithawalla's tab, too.

"Pithawalla—really?" the mick asked with incredulity. "I heard he fled to the ass end of nowhere. But I did take his immuno-boost when I was a kid. At least that stuff really works." Quinceton had taken it, too, but bristled at a positive mention of the evil doctor. Everyone knew Dr. Advi Pithawalla had invented an immuno-boost to protect against old enemies like illness and disease, but this hardly came up anymore. The real historical significance credited to him these days was that he had destroyed cross-border relationships and mandated the total economic isolation of the California nation-state by fleeing before his proper material taxation.

"You know selling the vaccines and medical patents and such made him a legit trillionaire?" Quinceton replied, holding strong. "The richest trillionaire in human history, and it had to be a traitorous Californian. And beyond our borders, you know what a trillionaire does? Whatever they want, whenever they want. No one out there can ever say no to a trillionaire." This was true so far as Quinceton knew, and he had learned long ago to back up every lie with as much truth as possible.

"Yeah, you're right. I can't even imagine how rich we'd all be if they'd stopped him from leaving." The mick looked at Quinceton hopefully, expecting agreement. "I know I could use a few more credits to my name." Something about the mick's friendliness made Quinceton want to create some distance between them, even if he couldn't move so much as an inch away.

"Oh, I wouldn't get your hopes up, white boy," Quinceton said. "I think a lot more deserving people than you need to get paid before you'll get a handout." This was also true. When the Intersectional Equity Law had been passed by a unanimous quorum of Knowers, intersectional inequality became literally illegal. Taxation would be determined by whatever percentages needed to be subtracted or added to any non-Elect individual's income in order to assure that all wealth averaged out to the same number for all groups with political recognition.

The goal of incorporating free-market ambition with an intersectional equality mandate would be balanced by imposing higher taxes for privileged groups who advanced economically and a dividend for all those whose income was limited by apparent prejudice. So if, say, all Samoan income averaged out to 10 percent above the average of all citizens, the entire Samoan community would be responsible for the material liberation of an extra 10 percent of their collective income. Most would come from the wealthiest Saos, but some extra taxes would be drawn from every Samoan pocket. The Intersectional Equity Law solved one long-term problem of inequality between shifting groups with a solution that brought each crowd into annual equilibrium—but no one had predicted what the Parsees would do after one of their own became an overnight trillionaire.

"Yes," the mick hurriedly agreed. "Totally true. I'm too privileged to want more for myself. Sorry for bothering." The whitey turned away, completing Quinceton's deflection. The satisfied sniper closed his eyes and thought about the real traitor.

Dr. Advi Pithawalla's medical discovery couldn't have come at a worse time. Only a few years after New California had departed from the Federals—once known as the United States of America, but now just the Federals—the brand-new nation-state was unsure how to interact with their neighbors and former countrypersons. Trade might benefit both sides of a deal, but could the New California government willingly interact with people who practiced a doctrine so different from their own? Dr. Pithawalla proved that these divisions were truly irreconcilable; foreign places that openly rejected New California's unflinching morality could not be tolerated, and so Quinceton was now here, on this bus, waiting to take position and shoot some Federal Americans.

The problem with curing dangerous diseases before severing all connection to the international community was the inability of the New California nation-state (under the Anti-Racists) to contain Dr. Pithawalla's massive material gain. It should have been spread extensively around the state, but the fortune had been generated so quickly and in too few pockets. The Parsees were such a small New California population, perhaps even less than a thousand in total, that the presence of a single trillionaire made the average Parsee income inordinately high before any other individual's wealth could be added to the total pile. Naturally, the Parsees would all have to pay for their newfound collective privilege, and even though poorer Parsees were asked for a smaller percentage of their entire holdings, many would be reduced to something like roving squatters for equity to prevail.

Dr. Advi Pithawalla may really have been an evil bastard who only cared about himself, but no one ever claimed he was stupid. The day before the collective tax bill landed on all Parsees, he hired a fleet of jets to fly all his people to the edge of the Earth, to somewhere the rest of the world would never think to look. His last words to New California were recorded and replayed repeatedly just before the shutdown of the digital Racism-spreading system (the internet), and they ended in a warning that reminded Quinceton of Dad.

"You have become the opposite of everything you stood for, and I choose not to follow you into the abyss," Dr. Pithawalla said, calm eyes staring straight into the camera. "And to those who see what I see, I say this: run, hide, and learn to placate until you can escape. Find a place outside the grip of identity-driven authoritarianism, without institutional race or gender hierarchy and government-mandated Diversity, Equity, and Inclusion to enforce it ... where you may once again be free." With that, the Parsees fled in a midnight string of jumbo jets to the Deep South of the far north—a place called Maine, somewhere between Boston and Canada where there was no diversity, violence, or desire for either.

Routine denunciations of Dr. Advi Pithawalla rose when times got tough, and Quinceton was chock-full of loathing from merely thinking about the man as he sipped from his water flask and watched the last of the Elect assume their seats at the front, no doubt on some strategic duty or simply to raise morale. They, too, appeared to be exhausted and irritable, aiding the assurance of camaraderie earned through shared misery. But by the time the last of the Speakers plopped down on the forward seats of the converted Greyhound, Quinceton could smell something truly foul.

Even after all the waiting, it still looked like morning outside. The numbers inside the bus concerned him: dozens of people were crammed into the rear aisles, with too many butts clinging to too few cushions, and a familiar odor wafted through Quinceton's nostrils every time some new butt had to open the bathroom door and make matters worse. It rarely happened without some jostling around the people crouched in the aisles, a situation that all but guaranteed arguments between competing identitarians. Quinceton viewed this as some typical, predictable irony, given that they were all here to advance the cause of Anti-Racism, and yet even a line for the bathroom could not be negotiated without dispute.

This is how it always was, is, and will be for members of different groups, Quinceton reminded himself, resolving to redouble his focus on the overarching goals meant to unite each person on the bus.

"Watch out, Speaker coming through!" Quinceton heard before he felt the mick's bones press him up against the bus window. Quinceton couldn't see who it was under the Speaker's flowing black robes and tall red special-issued Kafkani hat scraping at the roof. No one had more claim to Social Justice than the Speakers—other than the Knowers, of course—and it comforted Quinceton's spirits to see the rear section cooperate in clearing a path for someone of such power. After relieving themselves of whatever they were full of, the aisles would have to forcibly clear once again, pulling Quinceton even closer to his comrades.

Teamwork, Quinceton thought. *Now that we're here, we'll come together, and we'll get this done.*

An hour later the bus ignition churned, stalled, was fixed by the driver, and ninety minutes after that, the cavalcade finally left.

ACT I, CHAPTER FOUR

Parked in Waiting

QUINCETON FILED OFF THE BUS—ONTO the California side of South Lake, of course—squinting in the summer sun, so different than it was in San Francisco, but so too, now, was Tahoe. Stacks of sand padded barbed wire fencing and machine gun nests faced north to the lake, with a great rainbow curtain stretching over one hundred feet high ringed around the sight of the Nevada casinos; such was necessary to protect onlookers from the twenty-four-hour border violence. A massive metal gate emerged from behind the curtain in either direction, intersecting the sizzling highway heading east. Each soldier knew that on the other side of the rainbow curtain and iron border fence sat the United States of America, Nevada first, starting with a few lakefront casinos. New California soldiers could only imagine the problematic machinery the Americans equipped to keep good, honest Anti-Racists at bay.

The Raley's parking lot—repurposed even before a large contingent of Americans had come down from Reno to fortify the other side of the border around the time of the Great Rupture decades back—looked like a human game of Solitaire, with disparate lines of people streaming from neatly ordered tents in front of the former supermarket. Those in the same line shared obvious physical similarities with some noticeable exceptions, but since the lines were of vastly different lengths, Quinceton found a

Speaker appearing to have been born of female biology with medium-light skin directing traffic with a clipboard and megaphone.

"All of the Elect, right here! We request that you please make your-self comfortable on those golf carts," she commanded into the booming bullhorn. "Low-scoring honkeys, non-Black POCs, and privileged Blacks in that long one—Line One. Those with an Intersectional Score, or IS, over ten in that middle one, Line Two, and we invite all those with IS scores over twenty to join the Elect going to their check-in—those golf carts there. Your line isn't in this parking lot."

Quinceton had no extra IS points beyond his race, but he figured he'd try the female-presenting person anyway. In spite of the heat, the only water available seemed to be handed out at each check-in tent, and he'd finished what he'd brought on the bus.

"Hey there, about getting into Line Two ..." he began, watching their eyes intently. They put down the bullhorn, giving Quinceton the sense that this was his day in court, and he had better get to his argument quickly. "I'm cis and straight but have some extra IS coming from a broken non-nuclear family, and my ex-girlfriend now identifies mostly as a lesbian. I haven't read the latest IS point report updates, so is that worth anything? Lesbian ex?"

"Nothing," the possible womxn said. "We assume everyone has slept with a few gays at this point. You have any Muslim leanings, any protected unique ways of knowing? Neo-knowing is *finally* being centered in the discussion." It was possible to fake a simple mental condition like PTSD or even obsessive-compulsive enlightenment, but Quinceton had legally confessed to being a regular old blandbrain long ago.

"Nope, but I think my ex—I think she identifies as gender non-binary these days and probably has some unique ways of knowing. I'd guess she's a narcissist and a sociopath, but I don't know if it's registered with the IS department. How about a possibly neo-knowing lesbian gender non-binary ex?"

"Nada," she(?) said. "Get in Line One. It starts around over back there."

Quinceton held a hand above his eyes to block some glare, but he still couldn't see the beginning of Line One. Its serpentine path around periodically parked vehicles seemed to have no actual genesis, and unlike the single-file cheer and simplicity of Line Two, the occupants of line one clumped up and whispered in hushed voices. They were mostly slouching, sunburnt honkeys, and their quiet held only until Quinceton walked past, at which point many offered their place in line. Customary though this was for honkeys in New California's Justice of Social Soldiers government, Quinceton hated these moments and pretended not to hear them. Some sounded almost desperate, groveling for his acknowledgement—just pathetic. He didn't know their motives, after all, and in such a scenario it was possible those honkeys were just trying to let him cut in when one of the Speakers were watching. Better not trust a honkey if you could help it, he figured; whatever they thought or produced was to be viewed against a full memory of all former Federal Americans' history of genocide, slavery, and systemic Racism.

By the time he'd located someone who believed they were the official last person in line, Quinceton's black T-shirt was wrapped around his head as sweat ran from every pore on his body. A bead down the center of his back had a brief, startlingly chilling effect, but otherwise Quinceton silently fumed at the hellfire unleashed on the Raley's blacktop. Fine, it wasn't a particularly smoky day, but wasn't there something they could have done to block some sun, or gathered them somewhere outside the harsh glare of the open sky?

These concerns faded as a bullhorn near the check-in tents announced that Line Three and Two had finished, and all of Line One was now invited to use the Line Two tents, which tripled the speed of progress. The Line Three tents were apparently set up near or within the Elect Safe Spaces, and none but they were welcome inside—a guideline said to be essential in protecting Elect bodies and living spaces from the pervasive violence of outside ideas.

No stranger to hustle when he was the direct beneficiary, Quinceton smoked most all the honkeys in the footrace to the front of Line Two, and within seconds he was close enough to the Raley's to read the banners adorning it. "END WHITENESS" read one popular slogan he'd seen all over San Francisco amid other staples like "ALL EQUAL OR NONE SAFE," "SPEAK TRUTH TO POWER," "SHUT UP WHITE SAVIORS," "SILENCE IS VIOLENCE," and "PEACE IS GENOCIDE," but he noticed the government had also ushered in a new state flag design without so much as an announcement on his local bulletin board. The bright rainbow-colored baby with cornrows was the same as the last mascot, but this rendition was bolstered by an Indigenous peace pipe in one hand and a burrito in the other. The baby decorated the centerpiece of a black background with red words in a graffiti-style font both above and below.

Quinceton read "DECOLONIZE CISHETEROPATRIARCHY" beneath the baby easily enough, but the new branding of the state party required some prior knowledge: "JUSTICE OF SOCIAL SOLDIERS." The JSS government had no rivals in New California but had picked the name for diplomatic reasons nonetheless, which explained the confusing literal meaning of the words all assembled together—no one knew what a "Social Soldier" was when it was coined, and the idea of one still hadn't caught on in common usage. Perhaps as a means to avoid the confusion they'd stepped into, it was traditional to refer to them as the "JSS government" instead of simply the JSS. Something about the word "government" just sounded powerful all on its own, even next to the underwhelming JSS acronym.

Since every Californian was technically a registered JSS government member by law, Quinceton had to submit to the wisdom of the government tagline, especially since elections and voting were Racist practices that led to inequity. A faction in New York claimed "Social Justice Soldiers" long ago, and a crew up north in Portland had early rights on "Soldiers for Social Justice." New California's JSS government wanted to maintain cordial relations with Portland's SSJ, and thus, they took the less phonetically pleasing Justice of Social Soldiers and promptly attempted to redefine the definition of a "Social Soldier." The phrase hadn't caught on yet, but the whole naming thing bolstered the rumor that Portland was still a willing partner for trade, and gasoline had to come from somewhere. Just wartime tactics and diplomacy, Quinceton figured.

"What up, victim?" a lightly Black male-presenting person asked when Quinceton finally reached the front of the line. "Lemme get your name, vic."

The guy's skin wasn't very dark, but to address Quinceton in such a way meant they shared African blood. Quinceton drank his allotted Dixie cup of water in one swig.

"Rift," he replied, "Quinceton Rift of San Francisco. Infantry, sniper division, reporting. Where can I get more water, vic?"

"Holiday Inn Express. That's where you're staying. Supplies there. Make sure you get along with your roommate, or roommates, too. Y'see this forward operating base is loaded, right? And there's always a reason when we get this full, so get along with your roommates. No time for fighting, right, victim? We all on the same side here now." The JSS government worker watched Quinceton for approval, and the sniper gave a nod.

"But you don't have time for barracks yet. A Level Two Knower is preaching in Raley's soon." The male-presenting person handed over a plastic bag preloaded with a camouflage uniform and toiletries.

Quinceton nodded and looked for the sun, now dipping behind the western range, and pondered why he had spent so long in this parking lot only to leave just as it began to cool.

ACT I, CHAPTER FIVE

A Crisis of Constant Violence

THE CASH REGISTERS REMAINED, THE deli sign still overlooking the gaping space from the far wall, but without racks and racks of food, the Raley's looked less like a supermarket than an abandoned spaceship hangar. The clutter and chaos of the parking lot morphed into simple signs indicating work affiliation, and Quinceton easily located his people beside a familiar sergeant holding a "Tactical Snipers" poster.

"There will be food," Sergeant Weed said, "after the speech. I know you're hungry."

Quinceton's spirit rose at the sight of the sergeant's military fatigues, which gave the impression of authentic armed services legitimacy. It reminded him of Dad, an imposing figure, a football coach in his free time until there was none—a man of strict discipline. When it came time to just buckle down and get 'er done, there was no one better, and despite his later Anti-Anti-Racist ideas, Quinceton couldn't help but admire the old man.

He wondered where his seeder was now. He had probably fled all the way to Canada, if that was where he'd had his heart set. At the forefront of Quinceton's hopes for the movement was the belief that their success would prove the righteousness of their cause to people like Dad—honorable people who had been led astray by the Federal world's constant pressure to submit to white supremacy.

"Hey there, brother," Quinceton heard over his left shoulder. "Yeah, *you*, tall guy. I got you." A light-skinned male-presenting person held out an apple. "Gotta figure this shit will take longer than they say it will."

Quinceton eyed the apple with ravenous attraction, unable to resist for more than a moment's hesitation. He took the fruit, bit into it, and watched his benefactor smile. The giver looked downright pleased with themselves, which made Quinceton feel guilty for accepting the offering. Hungry though he was, the gesture landed far short of compensation for four hundred years (and counting) of Black subjugation and servitude in America that every member of the JSS government had vowed never to forget.

The giver watched Quinceton, eyebrows raised, clearly expecting some sort of response. A needle prick of awkward bafflement filled the space between them. The giver *owed* him the fruit, among other compensation—at least four hundred years of it—so why should Quinceton thank them for the damn thing? The tactical sniper avoided eye contact as he turned away, chewing, not seeing the look on the giver's face. Quinceton couldn't have blamed the guy for expecting a little gratitude, but they shouldn't hold out hope until the horrors of history had been fully unwound.

Back with his sniper brethren, Quinceton could relax. With the possible exception of the sergeant, there weren't any high IS scores around here. Mostly just honkeys, people of color, practitioners of heterosexuality, and the occasional underachieving Jew—very ableist, not much diversity of mental cognition, and no trans people at first glance. Quinceton didn't mind Jews as much as most did. True, Quinceton had never met a really poor Jew, and he hadn't heard of one, either, but he'd also never met one who just sat on their ass and watched others do the heavy lifting.

The Intersectional Equity law tacitly encouraged everyone in the New Enlightenment to resent groups that had built so much pre-JSS government wealth, but Quinceton struggled to see this success as a result of privilege in all cases. To what degree was it necessary to ignore various periods when Jews had *not* been so privileged? Everyone had heard stories about them catching some serious flak in Europe. Certainly, Jewish privilege had led to their success in Federal America, but the how and why was not fully understood by Quinceton. The word "Holocaust" lingered in the back of his mind, but he'd learned not to repeat it, lest something Jewish distract from the struggles of the historically oppressed.

Luckily, these trained snipers knew how to keep their distance. Quinceton crouched down, slumped against his pack, and closed his eyes, and he was just easing toward a nap when a crackly speaker belched from the rear. The immense body of a Knower sat on an ornate throne in the middle of a velvet stage against the deli wall, with an official Kafkani headdress elevating their profile about three feet or so. This Kafkani offered the traditional Knower's gold turban base, above which a cylindrical tube with bright jewels wrapped in fine silk announced the Knower's rank: Level Two. With only three possible ranks, the presence of a Level Two Knower signaled how significant this frontline was to the overall Anti-Racism effort. Level One Knowers mostly handled the Restorative Justice process back home, so everyone knew what they looked like, but Quinceton had never spoken to a Level Two, and had never even seen Knowing Leader Xumwaza Q. Jumping Bull, the one and only Level Three.

The gold throne on top of a black velvet stage covering made for a truly awe-inspiring color scheme, and the Knower enhanced their prestige by vacillating the palm of their cupped hand vertically, like a prom queen back from the days when there were "schools." Seeing this great body surrounded by some of the world's most prized stones proposed some ancient vision of authority, something that would have been recognized by the pharaohs of Egypt to the Caesars of Rome to the kings of Medieval Europe to the politicians of the twentieth century. These were the trappings of power in all eras, but only the Justice of Social Soldiers government used such symbolism to advance the cause of equity.

The massive bulk of the Knower in tandem with their purple lipstick and beaming smile radiated body positivity for all, and their ambiguously dark skin tone assured onlookers that whiteness in no way contributed to the rise of this evident luminary. Quinceton casually assumed that if anyone could represent full commitment to toppling the cisheteropatriarchy and all that it stood for, it had to be someone who openly rejected all that had seemed standard in decades past. There was no telling what alternative neo-knowing mental operating system this Knower benefitted from—deadlines-related PTSD being most common, with bipolar arguably the most celebrated—but any redneck honkey walking in from the street could tell they were bound by no gender binary or loyalty to the old order. They could be trusted to do the work of centering Black and brown bodies in the dialogue for Social Justice, preventing honkeys across America from dictating who did the othering in this emerging land.

The Knower stood, cleared their throat, and looked at the assembled crowd with their right arm extended to the rafters. Quinceton joined the masses in matching this gesture of certain virtue. Breathing somewhat heavily in the prime of their mid-twenties, the Knower grabbed a microphone and sat once again, arm still raised but looking drained for the effort.

"Look around you, at us now. Look where you are!" Arms came down to clap in rapturous applause as the Knower beamed, almost laughing with glee at their shared excitement.

This is the stuff of revolution, Quinceton thought. *This is how the world was made, and how it will come to embrace Social Justice for all.*

"See this great hall, and remember what it once was: a monument to the stolen wealth of white supremacy!" More whoops from the audience this time, not much clapping—the best way to support the Knower without impeding their progress. "This Raley's was once the place where rich capitalists came to stock up for their second homes. But this space is not their Raley's anymore. Now, in the twenty-sixth year of the New Enlightenment under true Knowing Leader Xumwaza Q. Jumping Bull, the JSS government, Elect, and JSS citizens have claimed this as our forward operating base. Look across this room and you can see the decolonization happening as I speak." Something exploded in the distance, which, to Quinceton's ear, sounded as if it had come from the west.

"I've come to remind you today not to rest on our many victories against the forces of tyranny and capitalism. The lands of New California were once plagued by illegal drugs, environmental pollution of all kinds, and such rampant unregulated immigration that none could know who and what beliefs may enter and taint our nation-state. The conversion to our Anti-Racist government has addressed these issues once and for all. Now it is time to grant the same final clemency to the violence across our borders and the American cisheteropatriarchy which enables such international poison to flourish."

This part made Quinceton think back to his seeder, and the mass exodus from New California he sometimes spoke about. The economic shift really *had* ended the drug trade, placated the environmentalists, and ended immigration, but it had also cost some people in the process. Dad might have bitched about the fractional New California economy, but they usually had enough to eat, there were plenty of women around the city, and there were an abundance of places to sleep now that so many buildings were vacant. Trade-offs for Anti-Racism could totally be worth it.

"But our work is far from over," the Knower boomed as Quinceton's focus returned to the speech, "and it is time for a direct action campaign to end the violence. The people of New California are they who made all 'microaggressions' macro, but we have not come this far to worry about our own faults, or our Safe Spaces, but to cast our eyes to the ignored and misguided violence perpetrated by the other side—the side held by a stubborn faction of Northern Nevada Americans.

"They taunt us with their open Racism across the border, do they not? Now I, like you, am sick to death of explaining truth to them, of outlining the horrors of systemic Racism and educating them about so-called 'equal treatment' as the true enemy of equity. They will never accept that all difference between intersectional groups comes from discrimination, that no two groups in a diverse and fair society should have different problematic behaviors, income, or any other outcome. We are all created the same way, so why should we allow Racism to differentiate us anywhere, even in our Nevada neighbors? Are you comfortable living in the shadow of gloating Racism?" There was a decent cheer with some extra noise from the back.

"Exactly. You know what we have to do. There is no other choice."

Quinceton thoroughly enjoyed this part of speeches. He didn't want to live in the shadow of Racism—he hated Racists and all they represented.

How could one forget all they had done to Black people like him since America was founded to uphold slavery in 1619?

"On the other side of our violence-shielding infrastructure lies a constant assault on our values, on our peoples—on our *truth*. We Justice of Social Soldiers, we the Elect, are the liberators of all people—we are they who bestow freedom upon those who were never able to dream such dreams in the old Federal's republic," the Knower said, bouncing around on their throne with unbridled enthusiasm. "What did Washington, DC, do besides conquer and destroy, invalidate and appropriate? When would the erasure of BIPOC and trans voices ever end? Only when our work is complete, and it never will be—struggle can be the only guarantee.

"Our ways of knowing open our eyes to a truth the cisheteropatriarchy would never see, and only our ways of knowing can decolonize that which was once thought to be certain knowledge. After millennia of confusion and denial, we Knowers have revealed the truth that all truth is merely relative to those in power; by freeing ourselves of our old myths about truth, we have exposed the axioms in which two and two may make five, in which women may impregnate men, and in which equitable outcomes across intersectional groups is finally possible."

Quinceton had heard all this before—this was pretty standard JSS Elect speech boilerplate. He assumed that every Knower had some kind of neo-knower prestige, but he rarely knew what specific personality metamorphosis their worldview benefitted from. Maybe something big-time like schizophrenia, but for this one, he guessed obsessive-compulsive—it was a good trait in a Knower, one that kept them on the lookout for Racism. He got why gender was a social construct and had always been careful not to say anything that would draw attention from the progressives at the Bureau of Gender Equity & Enforcement.

His mind soon drifted to thoughts about beef, the various ways it could be prepared, and the time when he'd traded three pairs of newly issued socks for a genuine cut of cheddar cheese. A high price, sure, but he'd only made the deal after landing some white market ground beef, and the flavor of that burger had helped him survive years of the same tastes.

His hunger-induced musings ended as the crowd stirred, restless with a desire to hear the next thing and move on from the familiar recap of their cause. The Level Two Knower sensed this. Everyone knew you couldn't become a Knower without being able to read a crowd, even if no one said it.

"Many of you have heard of the crisis that brought me here," the Knower said in a shrill tone, leaning forward, their mouth practically sucking the bulb of the microphone like the protuberance of male-presenting genitalia. "And I don't just mean the twenty-four-hour border violence: An unauthorized explosion took out two BIPOCs on our demolitions team two days ago, so I'm here from Oakland to guard against the encroachment of white hegemony. Without immediate action, we would have had a catastrophic racial imbalance of three honkeys, a straight quarter-Oriental womxn, and a light-skinned Euro-presenting partial-Latinx male in total command of our bombing aim and payloads."

In between sentences came a groan from somewhere between Quinceton and the table stage. Quinceton heard it clear as a thunder crack, and it immediately registered on the face of the Knower. They paused, eyebrows furrowed for a beat before giving an exaggerated nod.

"Yes, exactly! That's exactly right. The Americans have no heart, would let anything happen—they would hand anything over to white supremacy that whiteness hadn't already claimed. But not your Elect. Oaths we have taken and sacrifices we have made are the bonding glue of our movement. True diversity is our strength. True equity in all ranks everywhere is essential to prevent the spread of hegemonic whiteness anywhere. It is the cement in our moral foundations and undeniable proof of our immortal and innate righteousness."

No one stirred—not even a whisper or a cough. This language was familiar to every member of the audience, but it was unclear what anyone really thought of it. You didn't need to know what "hegemonic" even meant so long as you knew what had to be expressed about the takeover of hegemonic whiteness; it was a very bad thing that had been perpetuated both long ago in California and at present in all other places.

"So, I'm here to promise that this emergency will be contained, and you may all carry on with the confidence that all departments will be run in accordance with equity laws. I've personally made sure to reassign a few low IS scores in demolitions and train their BIPOC replacements tonight. The presence of white supremacy anywhere is a threat of ascending white supremacy everywhere. We will take no risks in this blessed Safe Space: This Raley's has been meticulously decolonized, and with our supervision of this space and your loyal obedience, it will never be colonized again."

This felt very true to Quinceton; it was impossible to imagine the Americans in this room, trying to re-racialize a group of people who had evolved past their oppressive social hierarchy. The Americans might have had different technology and more access to gasoline, but at the end of the day, did they have *truth?*

"Now, don't be waylaid by the violence which will greet you upon wake up tomorrow—we will remove the curtain tonight, and you will see the ever-present violence as soon as you cast your eyes east. Do not be afraid, and do not deter from what you know in your heart to be true."

The Knower raised their fist once again, still sitting. "Speak truth to power!" they bellowed.

As the Knower ended their speech with a triumphant nod, the crowd briefly clapped in response, then dispersed—some with wild warrior eyes and energy, and others attempting to hide their ravenous hunger with a practiced muted gaze.

ACT I, CHAPTER SIX

Ketchup for a Dog

A PLASTIC PLATTER OF HOT dogs sat on the Holiday Inn Express lobby desk right next to a big bowl of baked beans as Quinceton stood in line, silently cursing his gnawing hunger. It was a privilege to be fully fed, he reminded himself, and desire is the natural state of revolution.

Shouts of commotion sprang from somewhere ahead near the serving trays. All other conversations ceased as the assembled soldiers listened.

"… chaps my goddamn ass! Hot dogs all over the place, and no ketchup? This is unconscionable. What are we, prisoners?"

Quinceton smiled at the sight of this thin male cracker throwing a tantrum—dark hair, olive-tinted skin, probably another pushy Italian. In any case, who but some privileged dago would question the provided sustenance with such volume? The greaseball looked old, way too old for regular infantry, probably somewhere around the age of fifty—geriatrics were always the most resistant to reeducation. Even the word "unconscionable" gave it away—a term so far from common usage, it may as well have been Shakespearian.

Command Sergeant Major Smythe, a vertically challenged xenogender (xe/xir) of Swedish white skin and exaggerated expressions, had his leopard-skin-dyed hair under the raucous goombah's nose within seconds. Quinceton knew Smythe from the weekend boot camp he'd attended to

58

become a tactical sniper, and he often wondered where the miniature Command Sergeant Major's support came from. Xe was obviously Caucasian and would be full-blown honkey if it weren't for his gender identity, which could not be explained by human reality. Smythe identified xirself as a feline, and had impressed the Intersectional Score auditors by using a litter box instead of a toilet. This also guarded xe against ever having roommates.

"You're not some so-called 'demolitions *expert*' anymore," Smythe explained, gazing up at the Eyetie whose chin seemed to land above his mouth. "Now you're a soldier, and soldiers don't talk back. Soldiers don't complain. Unless they want to spend a decade in a DIE camp."

The threat hit the guido like the hurricane of a Me Too sexual accusation. He must've been hungry, going all day without food, but to expect ketchup was to demand a luxury—and luxuries for the privileged existed in direct contradiction of Social Justice. Hadn't whiteness stripped BIPOCs of dignity in order to pad gaping estates, bank accounts, and a thirst for endless rape? Luxuries like ketchup should be reserved only for those who had paid the past price for it, and in so doing, this blocked the extension of historical injustice by bringing justice and equity to the present.

"Yeah, yes, I accept my reassignment, Command Sergeant Major," the old guinea said slowly through a tight jaw, looking as though he'd like to wrap his hands around Command Sergeant Major Smythe's throat and squeeze, a spectacle for which one could probably sell tickets around the squadron. "But I am also a citizen and contributing member of our nation-state. California has always been my home. I am a committed comrade in the Justice of Social Soldiers, and I don't understand this. Why can't we have ketchup on our dogs? It's not like I'm asking for diced onions, or even a bun. Just ketchup."

Command Sergeant Major Smythe's smile stretched to such an impressive degree that xir shoulders suddenly looked even smaller as groans and murmuring filled the small room. Quinceton wanted to care more about this conflict, but he could still smell the baked beans, and at this point he would have even settled for quinoa on kale.

A pale female-presenting person with a shaved head and a fashionable "white men are terrorists" hoodie abandoned the line to stand beside Command Sergeant Major Smythe. The crowd hushed in anticipation.

"How *daaaaare* you," she began, drawing out the tongue lashing. "As a cis womxn, I learned long ago to decenter myself. Why can't you see what's going on here? This isn't about you, and it's definitely not about whatever you want to eat. We're here for Soooocial Juuuustice!" she droned with extra smugness. The womxn cast a quick glance at Command Sergeant Major Smythe, whose grin remained frozen.

"And you know what Social Justice means? Do you have any idea how to be an active Anti-Racist ally? It means you can just go ahead and shut up tight, cis-male colonizer. And stay that way." She looked again at Smythe, and must've seen the go-ahead. "When there's something you need to do, you'll do it. And you'll know your orders *only* when he tells you—"

"HELP HER!" Command Sergeant Major Smythe roared, pointing at the bald female-presenting person. "COMMUNITY SAFETY! COMMUNITY SAFETY! HELP HER!"

Four burly Community Safety patrolpersons exploded on the scene from somewhere inside the building, cornering the female-presenting person on all sides as they shouted Social Justice at her. These were the hardened Anti-Anti-Anti-Racists, also known as the AAA, who were charged with doing the dirty work for the state. After all, once police were defunded and prisons abolished, *someone* had to step in and hold Racists physically accountable. It was hard to make out the exact words with the four AAA agents speaking different reeducation slogans, but Quinceton felt sure he heard "Transphobia is murder," "Pronouns are personhood," and "Something something years in Stockton" among them.

"I mean *xe!*" the bald womxn cried hysterically, tears bursting from her eyes and seemingly her mouth too—there was a ton of spittle. "I'm so sorry! I meant xe!" The four AAA agents kept their hands clasped behind their backs but moved the womxn by helping her in the right direction with their stomachs, an act which took some coordination. She easily could have escaped the circle of bodies, but submitting appeared to be her best hope; to act with Social Justice now meant she might be forgiven in time.

The line separated at the doorway to assist the agents. "I'm white, I'm straight, I'm cis, my nuclear parents live comfortably!" Quinceton listened to her screams as she faded into the distance. *She'd have plenty of time to acknowledge her privilege in a DIE Camp,* he thought. *With the right attitude readjustment, she could be back here to do some job so no one else would have to.*

The old mafioso stood still as attention turned back to him. Command Sergeant Major Smythe brushed sweat from xir eyes, staining xir hand a heavy maroon from special Elect eyeshadow. Quinceton wasn't sure whom to pity, even though the Command Sergeant Major had obviously been the victim of severe violence by one of xir own inferiors.

The greasy geezer took a bite from his hot dog and chewed. "It's good," he said carefully. "I am grateful for this food and for you as my commanding officer." Smythe nodded, then returned to xir seat behind the lobby desk.

Impatience and expectation commanded Quinceton's stomach once again as the line lurched forward. He collected his bowl of baked beans and grabbed a hot dog without uttering a word, but as he passed the lobby desk, he noticed Command Sergeant Major Smythe wasn't eating. There wasn't any food on the table in front of xir, and xe didn't look hungry either. Xe just watched soldiers filing through with obvious contentment easing the wrinkles on xir face.

Quinceton pondered the idea that xe was waiting to eat after xir people had taken their portion, then felt stupid for such naïveté. Those identifying as xenogender should never have to defer to normies who had invalidated them for millennia, whose crocodile White Tears had prohibited xenogender voices from claiming their innate identity. This was the only way to undo the horrors of history. This was Social Justice.

ACT I, CHAPTER SEVEN

The Rules of Engagement

THE KEY FOR ROOM 534 didn't work when Quinceton tried it, so he tried it again, then knocked. A flaming-red-haired but light-skinned female-presenting person opened the door, saw Quinceton's face, and nodded.

"Take it you're Quinceton Rift. I'm Sarah Goldstein. We're roommates. You want to go first, or should I?" She pulled the door back and held it open.

"Sure," Quinceton said, walking into the sparse Holiday Inn Express room. There were two beds separated by a side table with a telephone on top. "I'm Black, straight, cis he/him, full mobility privilege, and blandbrain. You got my name right. I assume we're both tactical snipers." He set down his heavy backpack. "Which bed is mine?"

"Well, I'm Jewish-White, identify as bisexual, female-identifying she/her, also full mobility privilege and blandbrain," Sarah replied. "So I guess you can pick the bed."

Quinceton knew the law and understood Sarah's allusion to his larger IS score, buoyed by his Blackness, but it didn't sit well with him. There was something begrudgingly subservient about Sarah. Her voice sounded confident, her tone direct, but it admitted a resigned duty rather than energized zealotry. The role she played in their cause made him think of actors on a stage, and this drove his curiosity to know what really happened behind the curtain. Such knowledge, though, was nearly impossible to access.

"Well, your stuff is already there, so take the window," Quinceton replied. "I honestly don't care. I'm exhausted. I could sleep on Market Street through the Friday night Perp Walk."

Quinceton heard Sarah laugh as he stretched out on the wall bed. When he saw her face again there was a different expression, one that broke through the stony exterior. She nodded, smiling. Quinceton registered camaraderie in her eyes that he hadn't seen since the early days of the movement, when the Anti-Racists still had to organize to shout down the capitalists and all other dissenters. Though a boy for most of it, he thought about those years more than any other, as they reminded him of his seeder and birther and the home they had shared in the early 2050s. If there was one thing Quinceton hoped for, it was the legal recognition of private property. He was sure Dad would return if he were allowed to carve out some space for himself. Though Quinceton never expected to see him again, the memory of the old man brightened him, unlike that of his birther. Hope of an afterlife further propelled Quinceton's curiosity about God, but the Lord wasn't bringing his birther back.

"Hey, one question: Do you know how Standpoint works on the battlefield?" Sarah asked. "I honestly have no idea, and looks like shit's about to go down."

Quinceton reached for his trusty backpack, a loved but worn thing still adorned with "Black Bipolar Disabled Trans Lives Matter" stickers from his youth, and found his copy of *The Principles and Dictates of Constitutional Anti-Racism*. It was version 3.86Q; this was dated by now, but it was comprised by the top Knowers of last summer, and even though a few of the authors had since been deposed for Crimes Against Persons of Greater Vulnerability, some sections were essentially verbatim in the new issues. Sure, the language and punishment regarding things like "Reinforcing Cisgender Normativity" and "Overt Extension of Ableist Privilege" grew harsher each year, but at least the First Amendment had gone untouched since version 1.0, and it explained most of what you needed to know about how knowledge was allowed to exist and perpetuate.

The Standpoint Mandate—not only the First Amendment but the formative idea around which all Anti-Racist philosophy originated—stipulated that all knowledge is rooted in power and experience. So, in order to criticize or voice an opinion on a political or social topic, one needed to be a part of that group (or one of greater oppression), otherwise they would be a down-punching bigot. The Standpoint Mandate did not suggest that all individual experience produced knowledge, however, but that wisdom came from the perspective of those who had experienced the most and greatest forms of intersectional bigotry. This clearly ordered society so that the individual understood who to trust and could usually read the hierarchy in a given situation solely from the appearance of skin color and presentation of gender, sexuality, mental or physical ability, and body image.

It also meant that Quinceton could only speak from the perspective of a straight, fully mobile blandbrain (lacking any accredited "non-consensus perspective," or what was once called a "personality disorder") Black man. He could assert this conversational authority over lesser historical victims, but he would have to submit to and accept the knowledge professed by anyone with more victimhood, represented these days by a simple number—the Intersectional Score.

Being Black really boosted your standing in the old BBDTLM days but had been downgraded in subsequent years, as suffering multiple historical prejudices now multiplied your IS score. Quinceton remembered how multiplying scores totaled high scores much faster than adding them but kept it to himself, not wanting to be found guilty of conducting something so steeped in white supremacy as mathematics, even in his head.

"Here, take my copy of *The Dictates*," he said, handing Sarah the worn constitution. "I don't think it says anything different about battlefield authority. I think we just go by whoever they picked to lead." The official state-sanctioned definition of Racism was in there, and it asserted that the key element missing from the old "discrimination on the basis of race" use of the word was power. A person with less racial power couldn't be Racist against one with more, so Quinceton never had to worry about being Racist against Mexicans, whites, Yellows, and the like—no matter what slang was used, the power imbalance kept his Black body in the clear. In a world where anyone could be considered a loathsome, unforgivable bigot, it not being theoretically possible to be Racist against most racial groups was a useful freedom.

"Well, I hope our boss is someone good. I heard we might attack Pithawalla and his rich-ass cronies tomorrow."

Quinceton had to laugh at Sarah.

"What, you know something?" she asked, leaning forward, feet now firmly on the ground between their beds.

"Yeah, I think I started that rumor on the bus. If you heard it during or after your ride here, it's probably bullshit." Quinceton shot her a serious glance to back up his words. "In fact, even if you heard it before getting here, it's still gotta be bullshit. Pithawalla's a coward and fled to the ballsack of East Bumfuck to avoid attention. No reason he'd return; I don't even know why he'd want to. He's got all the credits in the world, and New California is the only place he can't spend them."

Sarah didn't answer, but she looked relieved as her posture slackened. She didn't seem to be the kind of Jew he'd been explicitly warned never to trust, especially with credits. Blacks and Jews faced natural opposition, as they had always had different needs for the government to address on the equity spectrum. Jews reaped so many credits, they all too often fled for America's unequal rewards, whereas Blacks could never even dream of relocating to somewhere so Racist, somewhere they would be the sole focus of the bigoted American law enforcement.

Early New California government equity initiatives leveled the system of law enforcement into equal punishments of various political identities to guarantee that those being rehabilitated by the state would be in equal proportions of characteristics like race, gender, disability status, sexual orientation, etc. In some ways, it felt liberating—almost like the invincibility to grab and claim things, at least. Since young Black men such as Quinceton were disproportionally forced into lives of theft, their punishments would be collectively reduced—if not avoided outright—to maintain the equity of law enforcement outcome among, in his case, a race/gender group. For the same reason, trans women were afforded some leniency, as the harsh historic transphobia of the world evidently forced them into transgressions at a larger rate then cis women, which the Social Justice justice system would be sure to consider in any sentencing.

Only in New California were young men of Quinceton's color guaranteed the same punishments as everyone else, but sitting in the same room as Sarah made him think on how alienating it could be to loot some regular whitey and have them be connected to a roommate he'd have to fight beside. Even if the mugging made historic sense by transferring wealth from the historically oppressive to the historically oppressed, it was too exhausting to try and explain that to someone of privilege. Someone whose identity didn't require that they think constantly about righting historic oppression.

Quinceton remembered from early schooling that one of the first real equity initiatives had started in San Francisco when it was still an American city with the outlawing of something called "pretextual traffic stops," back when there were still "police" and there was still enough gas for people to buy and use their own automobiles. In those days, criminals were less likely to register their cars the right way and obey all driving guidelines, so the Racist police made it possible to bust these minor infractions as a way to interact (and therefore arrest) more criminals. But as it turned out, certain minority groups were ALSO less likely to register and license and fill out all the damn paperwork on this and that. The massive net the police used to snare criminals also captured an excess of underprivileged and impoverished minorities as well, which, by definition of unequal racial outcomes, made the entire effort undeniably Racist.

Even in those days, the identitarian question was asked: Why do we want to have laws that will disproportionately punish the groups of any given oppressed population? To do so would be to support white supremacy and systemic Racism against non-whites, and any other identity whose culture may distract them from following some colonizer's societal demands, like valid automobile registration.

"Do you realize how enforcing this law punishes different groups differently, and those groups have vastly different histories in this bloodied land?" went one argument. Or there was the whole idea of using state force to punish something so small as a driving ticket: "Are you really prepared to deprive someone of their freedom for such a small infraction?" And, others asked, where should this vague line of state punishment begin, exactly? If the state wasn't prepared to enforce a traffic ticket, then why not allow small moments of assault to become an opportunity for Restorative Justice too? Why involve the white supremacist American criminal justice system in any way, ever? What would be the most equitable way to treat both privileged populations and the historically marginalized?

It followed from there that these pretextual traffic stops should be illegal, as should any other tactic that would produce uneven outcomes. Ultimately, this suggested the emerging revelation that the city of San Francisco would rather be Anti-Racist than strictly punish crime just because it happened to happen in the city.

Society was already so Racist in those American years that *every* police maneuver produced unequal outcomes, so a binary choice emerged once San Francisco became New California: deploy Racist state mercenaries, like police, to punish different identities differently for their divergent historical treatment, or scrap that whole fascist American law enforcement system for something equitable. Obviously, old cops and jails were unnecessarily Racist; all New California needed was community patrolpersons, some Restorative Justice here and there, and a Diversity, Equity & Inclusion Camp to reeducate the really hardened cases. Only then did the Anti-Anti-Anti-Racists drop their previous obsession with the "Anti-Fascist" angle and volunteer for criminal Social Justice duties.

And so the principles of equity first came to be applied to law enforcement: Police were defunded, then replaced by community patrolpersons; prisons were abolished, their residents liberated; and going forward, restitution for perceived offenses would be dictated by the involved identities. These days, the Anti-Racists running the government always made sure that no matter what law was changed or action was outlawed, its enforcement could only apply to different identity groups in equal proportion to each other. So, unless they could figure out a way to bust more, say, elderly white Jewesses as muggers, they couldn't focus any more attention limiting young Black men from close to free reign on this front.

To Quinceton, it all made sense if you really remembered the history, but that still wouldn't help the living sitch with this Jew roommate here and now. He had just closed his eyes again when the phone's ringer shocked the two of them with a scream—it must have been connected to telephones all over the hotel. Sarah picked it up immediately and listened.

"Okay," she said, "we're coming down."

ACT I, CHAPTER EIGHT

Battle Plan

CAPTAIN JOHN CHARLES REDGRAVE WAS an impressively hideous man for one with such a classic jawbone: a mélange of biceps, boobs, and borderline bravado, his outfits generally juxtaposed a proper military color scheme against a sort of Mardi Gras queerness in a statement Quinceton casually assumed was a direct insult to the formality of the old Republic's armed forces. Today, standing in the hollow atrium of the Holiday Inn Express under dim lighting and beside Command Sergeant Major Smythe, he wore a navy-blue leotard adorned with his Elect certification stickers, a bright-pink sash that wrapped around his shoulders from his groin, and gold Roman sandals.

The bright sash splayed across his body created a clear *V* shape that probably stood for something like "victory" or "voice" in Redgrave's telling, but in Quinceton's mind, the *V* just made him think about the captain's reproductive-style genitalia. Redgrave had been born with male body parts and was known to use he/him pronouns, but he was known around the squadron for having one of the first surgeries to construct a gender-free sex organ. Or perhaps it was considered an evolved sort of gender, an advanced version of what even the most sophisticated people were up to in the San Francisco Capital. There was a technical term for it that no one bothered to remember; instead, as Quinceton had heard plenty of times in

Union Square last night, they just combined the words for gendered sex organs into the very speakable term "venis." Quinceton had never seen one but had heard it described as a sort of volcanic vagina, with a penis split and wrapped around the edges to enhance the depth and supposed aesthetics of the surgical cavern.

Despite his gender identity forcing him to get female-presenting body surgeries—a venis and implants still being a rarity in contemporary military culture—Captain John Charles Redgrave had risen up the ladder of military command with the breathtaking speed of his colonizing ancestors' capitalistic wealth accumulation upon arriving in this peaceful Native land. Even the Intersectional Score auditors didn't quite know how to rank the historical victimization level of Redgrave's identity—who knew (or wanted to argue about) what specific gender plight forced his de-cockification to create the venis?—so they must've been generous: The now-complete leader's green-and-gold Kafkani headdress assured witnesses of his associated Level Three Speaker rank. Any further promotion and he would become a full Knower, meaning they would have to let him into the Knower's San Francisco Secure Spaces, which no one wanted to do seeing as he was a rattlesnake-accuser who had a virtually unlimited capacity to perceive offense. Rumors like this aided the belief that no one dare challenge or question Captain Redgrave, which meant that, practically speaking, everyone feared him.

"Silence!" he yelled at the quiet, sullen crowd of over a hundred military personnel. "Orders just came down from SF and we're going in tomorrow, when they'll be weak and distracted. The Americans'll never know what hit 'em when we come through: Social Justice from the sky, Social Justice from the land, and Social Justice from the lake. A blitzkrieg of Social Justice—we'll give them enough Social Justice to sink the fucking *Titanic* ten times over! Our Social Justice will be swift, it will be deadly, it will be decisive. It will be glorious."

Some clapped, and someone even chanted "Trust us … jus-tus …", an old saying from the early days, but as Quinceton looked at his peers, he saw something far short of confidence. He saw worry, he saw confusion, and he saw many pairs of tired eyes. Not too much backbone to be seen anywhere, except in Captain Redgrave and Command Sergeant Major Smythe. The latter beamed with the look of a sixth-grade senior about to graduate.

"Now we're going to break you into your various tactical divisions and rally at oh-nine-thirty-ish tomorrow," Redgrave continued, voice rising with excitement. "Do your best to ignore the violence hanging off the front of Harvey's casino. Don't look at it, and if your eyes do pass over the violence, try not to think too deeply and let it inside you, where the violence will surely do its most lasting damage. This is your final warning: There is violence out there on the battlefield, but if you see it, the fault and responsibility to ignore the violence and focus on war will fall on each individual independently. There is no other way, but at least our entire society has prepared you for this moment." Quinceton didn't actually feel that to be true, at least from his own lived experience. In fact, he couldn't actually recall a single moment when resilience had been prized over fragility, but perhaps that was simply to eliminate the Racist fragility that prevented an equitable society.

"Back to the morning: that's oh-nine-thirty-ish, as sharp as you can make it without submitting to the harsh scheduling of whiteness. By oh-nine-forty-five-ish, we're going to send in the drones to bomb the border gate—that's the signal for the first infantry division to pour through the wreckage and take positions in the first two casinos across the Nevada border. That's Harvey's to the north of the highway, Harrah's to the south. Once we control the ground floor, clearing it room to room, take the stairs to the roof. This frontal attack must begin no later than oh-nine-fifty-ish. Then our divers will attack from the lake.

"It is absolutely crucial that ground infantry engage the Americans prior to the water landing. We will have our best snipers stationed on either side of the highway, covering your entry the whole way, but after the drones drop the first payload, you will lay down the real Social Justice—shoot every American you see. They're hiding now, but I'm sure they'll creep out of their penthouses soon after we attack. After the first round of Social Justice hits the gate, our drones will return to munitions, double up their loads, and bomb the remaining whiteness out of their replacement forces, but expect one hell of a firefight after the first explosions. Take the next casinos—I want MontBleu and the Hard Rock after we get the first two—and hold them until relieved. These are my orders."

Sarah's bowed head caught Quinceton's attention. She stood near him but slightly behind, and it was her lips that interested him. They kept moving in rapid, almost rhythmic ways; it looked like she was praying. Maybe she would teach him how. This moment—right before the plunge—made Quinceton want to believe in something supernatural.

Islam was still an acceptable doctrine, so long as any tenet at odds with JSS government knowledge was denounced or discarded, but Quinceton couldn't read Arabic and it was illegal to colonize the Koran by translating it, so his spiritual search had left him without a home. He wasn't a Jew, and no one invited him to be one, but he was kinda open to it. Practicing Christianity was a good way to get knocked down a few points by the Intersectional Score auditors before getting profiled for DIE, but only Zoroastrianism, the Parsee's religion, was explicitly punishable by indefinite—and probably somehow fatal—reeducation.

Redgrave paused to look over his audience. Quinceton tried to follow his eyes as they started drifting in his direction before settling on Sarah. Head still bowed, she couldn't possibly have seen him, and Quinceton felt the urge to tap her, to rouse her from her concentration lest Redgrave take her detachment personally.

"Now listen up, volunteers," Redgrave carried on, striking a calmer tone. "Now, I know you don't want to be getting up at the crack of oh-nine-hundred-ish to go risk your bodies. Our cause is one of empathy, after all, and I'll be with you every step of the way, watching from the Raley's command post. I see you and would never invalidate your feelings of fear, of dread, of self-doubt. But we must push forward if we are to bring a reckoning down on the heads of the Americans who mock all that which is holy to us." The crowd around Quinceton responded with some supportive shouts, and again he heard the familiar refrain of "Trust us ... jus-tus ..."

"We have not united California and come this far on behalf of marginalized groups to make peace with the enemy over our borders," Redgrave continued with rising excitement. "Now, I might not get there with you, but the Promised Land lies beyond that iron gate, barbed wire, banner of violence, and the extinction of those hardened, privileged Racists. We will not fail! We cannot fail, and by knowing their ways of knowing and then evolving to platform lived experience, we have uncovered the erasure of knowledge of the marginalized and will show the Americans the torment of the tormented. Never be afraid—even if we lose every single one of you, there is more than enough diversity left in New California to complete our final Anti-Racist solution to the cisheteropatriarchy!"

The loudest cheers came after the final line as Redgrave raised his right fist in the traditional vertical salute. They were addressed as "volunteers," which Quinceton understood: a smart way of reminding every soldier that they'd chosen to be here. The "volunteers" mirrored Redgrave's fist gesture and Quinceton copied them, although he did not feel particularly comforted by the organizational speech. He also understood timeliness to be one of the most damaging demands of whiteness, but coordinating the siege of a fortified position without clock precision concerned him.

And then there was Command Sergeant Major Smythe. Redgrave presented a certain amount of authority; there was strength in his words and a determination in his face, but Smythe was just a weasel. Smythe's method of exerting power was to overreact to every single slight or mistake, usually by kicking the problematic person up the chain of command for someone else to inflict maximum punishment upon, avoiding any prolonged confrontation and looking like a damn tattletale to soldiers like Quinceton. And yet, Smythe would be the one leading the infantry through the border gate. At least Quinceton would be on the periphery, covering them all and keeping his own ass out of the direct line of fire.

"Now, find your commanding officer," Redgrave instructed, interrupting Quinceton's survival calculations. "They'll know where you can get your gear, where you need to be tomorrow. And sleep tight, soldiers. Tomorrow, you prove yourselves to be true Anti-Racist allies. Dismissed!"

Quinceton turned and followed Sarah to Sergeant Weed nearby, a female-presenting cis she/her Latinx blandbrain and the commanding officer of a dozen snipers. Quinceton liked Sergeant Weed just fine. She spoke directly, answered most of his questions before he asked them, and frequently griped to Redgrave that the soldiers needed more rations and training than they got, which seemed to be dictated more by their Intersectional Score than their rank or specialty. The timing of the assault could not be delayed, however, as the Americans celebrated the Fourth of July with a religious fervor, and it was now the third. Tomorrow's attack would come on a clueless enemy, and the lake would be fully accessible for an aquatic landing in the summer. It *had* to be tomorrow.

"It has to be tomorrow," Sergeant Weed began, echoing his thoughts, "so remember your training and stay calm. Keep thinking out there, especially when the firing starts. You might want to panic—maybe that'll mean you freeze or want to run, but fight through it. You have jobs to do, and your comrades are counting on you to cover their assault."

She popped a stick of gum into her mouth and spread out a small cartoonish tourist map of the area, one that would have made more sense when South Lake Tahoe was still a ski resort town. She marked the map with letters representing each soldier's first name, and Quinceton brightened to see his *Q* next to an *S*.

"Now, this map isn't quite to scale," Weed said, "but it's the best I could get from command. You'll each be paired with your roommate, and take a good look at where I've stationed you, as I want you there at oh-nine-hundred-ish—well before the attack. You will use your sights to get a look at the land before anything happens, and I want you to know where their snipers are—look to the top of the casinos, anywhere there's broken or open windows, and around the edge of the tree line. That's where I'd put 'em. Stay in cover, and don't stand up straight until it's all over, even if you need to pee. I'm told to remind you that persons with vaginas should find a place where they can aim downhill, and those with the privilege of penises should bring an empty bottle."

Sergeant Weed paused and looked over her soldiers. There had been no integration emergency since boot camp, so these were all her people from the jump, and Quinceton could see her concern. She never held eye contact for more than a moment, the tone of her voice seemed to plead more than order, and orders from the top were delivered with a resigned duty rather than the eagerness of agreement. Quinceton recognized this attitude in most of his fellow soldiers, but it stood out when worn by a commanding officer. Weed looked like she wanted to relocate to basically anywhere else on Earth and take her whole squad with her.

"Your gear is being delivered to your rooms as we speak. I looked over your kits myself, so I know they're complete, and we've given you more than enough ammo in case the fighting drags on or we get called up to fortify positions. I'll leave the map out. You have all the preparation they want you to have. Get some sleep. Tomorrow morning, oh-nine-hundred-ish." Sergeant Weed dismissed the group with a nod, carried the map to the wall of the courtyard, and hung it using her gum as adhesive.

"So I guess that's it, then," Sarah said to Quinceton. "We're in the shit together."

"I can dig it. Happy to fight with a Jew so long as you're not some blind Hebe in glasses—you'll need sharp eyes to count my kills tomorrow." Sarah laughed from the bottom of her lungs, as though it were an unconscious reaction from somewhere she couldn't contain. The sound made Quinceton wonder if he'd ever truly heard laughter before.

Most of the specialty groups had disbanded for bed by now, but not the main infantry division. They were being held hostage by General Sergeant Major Smythe, who appeared to deliver directions individually to whoever stood at the front of the line. The old Italian, the one who'd wanted ketchup for his hot dog, nodded at Smythe and accepted a satchel and automatic rifle from the corporal next to xe. Quinceton watched him turn the gun over in his hands, inspecting the thing as though it were an alien artifact that just fell from the moon.

The old man caught Quinceton's gaze, saw Sarah watching too, and pretended to tip an imaginary top hat to the pair of them, the way one old capitalist might have greeted others in the pre-equality age.

"Beware Greeks bearing gifts," he said.

ACT I, CHAPTER NINE

The Battle of South Lake

LAKE TAHOE GLISTENED LIKE A thousand diamonds tossed into a spinning roulette wheel as Quinceton scanned the scene from somewhere around the knee of Mount Heavenly, a good hundred yards south of the highway and exposed atop an abandoned gray platform at the peak of a big metal post some fifty or sixty feet above ground. These massive poles were organized in a line up the former skiing paradise, and at some point the capitalists had used this as a system to get up and down Mt. Heavenly. Today, when it mattered, it would serve as an ideal bird's nest for Quinceton and Sarah to see 360 degrees of action around them, assuming no incoming fire. In that case, there'd be nowhere to hide, and they'd probably be shot swiftly as sitting ducks, but at least they'd be warned by watching plenty of other infantry take the plunge before they did.

First the infantry, like Sarah and Quinceton themselves, would have to endure the sight of the ever-present violence hanging over the street between Harvey's and Harrah's, the first two casinos over the border. It really was an assault on the mind. The JSS government Elect (or their water carriers) had cleared the great violence-prevention tarp during the night, so when the infantry arose and looked east they could start adjusting to the violence.

A great hideous caricature of Knowing Leader as a rainbow-colored diaper-wearing baby had been the violence they'd been protected from all along. Mumwaza Q. Jumping Bull was depicted as an especially weight-challenged puppeteer of sorts who dangled stick figures of white, brown, and Indigenous people with one hand and appeared to eat a Black person with the other. There was no blood in the drawing, but there was plenty of drool. Underneath a byline Quinceton didn't read, the title of the Racist painting loomed large: *Intellectualism for Idiots*. The subheading was even more violent, and though it appeared on the poster of the book cover, it had also been enlarged for clarity on a separate poster underneath the original: *How a Bunch of Buffoons Bluffed Free People into Their Own Enslavement.*

It was first-degree word violence—the absolute worst kind. This was the type of violence the Knowers warned them about, the type of violence that JSS citizens were usually protected from, and now the military would have to overcome such an attack before the armed invasion.

From the moment they saw the violence, Sarah and Quinceton instinctually went silent, perhaps agreeing to avoid thinking about this first taste of international commentary by not speaking about the Nevada poster. It was impossible to avoid wondering what everyone else was thinking when they saw it, but Quinceton wasn't about to risk his own ass by asking out loud.

Raley's stood to the left like an impregnable fortress, the Holiday Inn Express and Lake Tahoe behind it were close to the center of his vision, and he had a clear view of Nevada (and the book banner) to the right. A fire from years ago had demolished a massive complex in between Quinceton's position and the border gate, and though the destruction was necessary for a clear view, it left them more than a little exposed. He felt freshly vulnerable, lying on his stomach on a cold metal grate suspended in midair next to Sarah, who claimed the downhill side on account of being a person with a vagina.

From this vantage point, they could see other snipers taking position on different rooftops closer to the action. Quinceton knew they were damn lucky to be so far away, and off to the side, out of the direct line of sight from the casinos to the command posts. Even Sgt. Weed, peering through binoculars atop the Holiday Inn Express, seemed far more exposed.

A thin mist hovered over the water, the beach, and the highway as Quinceton used his scope to zoom in on individual trees and other dark corners of the land. The quiet in the air calmed him, as did the smell of pine. His partnership with Sarah was beginning to blossom with the simplicity of her having no sexual appeal to him whatsoever. She may have been feminine-leaning, but it was the kind of feminine you'd see on an old recruitment pamphlet for a womxn's backyard rugby team. She was, however, Quinceton's kind of comrade, and from her response to his jokes, he saw her as a soldier for whom JSS orthodoxy existed as guidelines rather than gospel.

"I don't see any Americans anywhere," he whispered, gazing beyond the border through his sights. Harrah's and Harvey's shimmered less than one hundred yards from the grisly gate, and the entire scene looked deserted. This wasn't necessarily news; JSS government command hadn't announced the appearance of an actual human being on the American side in forever, or at least not for as long as Quinceton had been aware of the Nevada border, and the roughly fifteen-foot gate mostly concealed their street level. Both sides had contributed to the bramble of barbed wire and reinforced barricades that separated the nation-states, but any information about past skirmishes existed merely as hushed speculation among the older folx. The Elect assumed that whatever the Americans had set up for defense had been done some time ago, given that they hadn't been seen recently, and JSS government deserters would probably pick any other point of entry to abandon their home.

Even though American refugees were to be shot on sight anywhere in California, Quinceton yearned to meet one. He didn't even know what they'd look like, or what clothes they'd wear. How did money-hoarding Racists treat each other? What goals did their movement have, and how did they determine who got to generate knowledge and show everyone else?

"All good, all good," Sarah replied, also looking deep into her sights. "Nothing out here but the regular."

Quinceton turned his scope back to the Raley's and noticed that the once-empty parking lot was gradually filling with sandbag barricades lining its perimeter. They weren't too high, and looking down from Mt. Heavenly he could make out a few commanding officers at the front of the building, stress carved across their faces. Captain Redgrave appeared in an urban camouflage tutu and white cowboy hat, pacing behind the sand and pointing here or there. Even without hearing him, Quinceton could sense the pressure mounting. Today was the day.

A diver crouched at the water's edge a few hundred yards northeast of the Raley's, armed with the best automatic rifle the JSS could augment. The divers' weapons were waterproof, fireproof, and loaded with both live rounds and a grenade launcher, just in case there were too many Racists to shoot one by one. Each of the thirty divers selected for the amphibious incursion would have four loaded grenades and were encouraged to shoot one off upon arrival—this would sow chaos and confusion into the enemy, freeing space for the frontal assault—but only a single diver seemed ready to rock. Quinceton watched the diver wait beside the lake and instinctively checked his watch: 0937.

"Hey, Quinceton," Sarah said, "looks like they're only starting to gather now. Look at the Holiday Inn Express." A few soldiers stood outside their barracks, looking confused. A few more ambled in as time passed, but sometime closer to ten a.m. or so as the drones passed overhead, hardly a single platoon was ready for action. The drones wandered over to the Nevada fence, hovered above it, and returned without a flicker of action ... save for one wayward contraption, which never wavered on its course and crashed straight into the third floor of Harrah's Casino. The exterior appeared to be glass, but it was strong enough to withstand the collision; the drone bumped off the wall and unceremoniously fell into a harmless heap on the street without so much as a spark of combustion.

This oh-nine-thirty-ish attack was supposed to have consisted of over a dozen platoons, counting the divers, whose dark-blue wetsuits were easier to see, but they were just as scattered as the meandering infantry. The drones were supposed to open the border wall by bombing the shit out of it right before the oh-nine-fifty-ish ground assault, but that made no sense with the troops collecting on their own sweet time. No one seemed to mind the delay until Sergeant Weed appeared on the scene, abandoning her post above the Holiday Inn Express to crack some necessary whip.

Quinceton watched her move around the edge of the battlefield. Sergeant Weed crept with quickness and stealth, sneaking around to various sniper positions before zeroing in on their bird's nest.

"Everything got moved back until the afternoon sometime, or at least after noon!" she shouted up to her snipers from the dry dirt below. "Almost no one is where they're supposed to be, and we're trying to re-coordinate with munitions running the drones. We'll need them for whenever we need them, and no one can find the guy who really knew how to reprogram all the different versions. Just sit tight and watch for the assault when it comes."

"Around when ... are you thinking?" Sarah asked back.

"Can't say for sure, but by the way they fucked up the morning wake up and let most infantry sleep in, I'm guessing around, say, thirteen hundred-ish? That's about one in the afternoon. Gives us something like three hours."

"Let's hope it's enough," Quinceton added loud enough for Sergeant Weed to hear. He didn't particularly care if it was enough time or not. The lack of urgency by everybody other than Sergeant Weed was fine by him so long as it prolonged the period of time he could spend not worrying about being shot out of a fifty-foot tower. And Nevada didn't seem to mind the wait, either; they hadn't budged since the drone crashed into Harrah's.

"Eventually, you'll see the infantry collect outside the Holiday Inn Express. After that, we'll cue the divers. They've got their shit mostly together already." And with that, she scurried off to the east, heading closer to the border gate to find and rouse the other snipers who were gullible enough to have reached their posts on time—and probably deserved a little catch-up sleep because of it.

They waited long enough for Quinceton to settle in on his stomach and arrange his arms as a fairly acceptable hammock for his head. The summer sun shone over the rear mountain, washing away the morning chill. He'd been warned before combat that "war is like poker: unrelenting boredom punctuated by unannounced moments of sheer terror." At least Quinceton understood the first part. No one was in position, there were no Americans in sight, and no one seemed all that eager to get killed. Except for surviving the initial violence of the poster's Racism/ableism/transphobia, it had been a morning like any other.

Sarah nudged him awake a few hours later. The sun's angle assured him that it was at least early afternoon by now, and he checked his watch to confirm. At 12:36 p.m., they'd fallen so far behind schedule that it was fair to wonder if the attack was still happening, or if maybe one of the generals would call a "mulligan" on the whole operation and they'd all get to go home.

A massive bug caught Quinceton's attention. It was the size of both his fists balled together, and it hovered in midair as if suspended by a string—the wings moved so fast, they appeared not to exist at all as they kept the gray insect with bright-blue eyes perfectly still. Quinceton had to lean onto his side to tilt his head for a better view, and when he did, the fly just buzzed silently and watched him.

"I don't really want to kill people today," he mumbled to Sarah, all tired and grumpy. "When do they pass out dinner rations?"

"They're finally collecting in front the barracks," she answered, ignoring the very practical question. "Now's the time if they're going to stick with the attack for today."

Quinceton used his rifle scope to check progress. Many dozens of soldiers stood in front of the building, armed and ready, but most were looking backward toward their barracks. A gap opened and Command Sergeant Major Smythe emerged from it, looking even smaller than xe had when xe'd lined up with the old Italian's chin. Xe walked a few paces forward, eyed the border through binoculars, and squatted on both hamstrings as though perched above a litter box.

"Time to hunt some American mice!" xe shouted at the company. Then, still in peeing position, xe held a pistol to the sky and fired off a few shots. "Meeeeeeeow!" This was apparently the signal for the wet-suited divers to grab their flippers and waddle to the shore. A few did and others followed, slowly.

"Are you feeling inspired?" Sarah asked. From the overlooking roof, Sergeant Weed shook her head and reached for a walkie-talkie, probably radioing Captain Redgrave to tell him their cover was blown, perhaps for the second time before the same incursion. "If not, then all that posturing can't be good for morale," she added.

"Let's hope the Americans didn't hear it," Quinceton replied, turning his attention back to the casinos.

A familiar buzzing interrupted the quiet—drones. Those machines worked on a timer set and reset by demolitions, which meant that the timer had been rerouted from the initial 0945. Now that they'd been reprogrammed not to be ridiculously early—by being on time—all bets were off. But maybe this was the border gate bombing on schedule now, albeit some three hours late.

With xir gun still hanging from a limp wrist, Smythe waved the ground troops forward as the drones covered xir in a blinking shadow. About one hundred infantry advanced east to the border gate in various columns on either side of the highway while crouched, some shaking slightly, but still committed, so far as Quinceton saw it. He, like everyone else, could look ahead and see the poster violence behind the border bramble, a mess of metal so hideous that it looked like the entrance to a prisoner of war camp American President George Washington might've invented to enslave the Mexicans. Smythe marched xir volunteers along while balancing one delicate foot (or paw) after another along the center stripe. Xir mouth and throat kept in constant motion, but Quinceton could only make out a few distinct words: "Forward," "Move," and "Racists."

The nearest column of infantry took cover behind the burned-out wreckage facing the border and waited. Smythe couldn't see them while cat-stepping down the middle of the highway, and they didn't seem too eager to spring forth from hiding. Since they lay directly between Quinceton and the enemy, these dozen or so soldiers would be the easiest for Quinceton to protect, and protect them he would most certainly do. If they went down, the young sniper in the old ski tower could be next.

The drones buzzed leisurely toward the border gate at a faster pace than the infantry, but in no formation or consistent speed whatsoever. Quinceton thought this looked odd; though the tech was a few years old, it was tech, after all, and tech was supposed to have superwomxn powers of precision. Perhaps the reprogramming delay and weight of the carried bombs affected the speed of each drone slightly differently, and their targets were different sections of the border. The ground infantry was depending on the drones to open access points so they could take some attention away from the exposed aquatic landing.

Yelling echoed from well behind the front, and there was Redgrave on the case: the divers didn't want to get in. The lake probably felt like melted snow, but they'd gotten the wetsuits and agreed to "volunteer" for water duty … so, tough shit. They didn't have to like it; that was optional, and unnecessary. Redgrave was well armed with verbal humiliation to make sure they kept up their end of the deal and earned those special grenade-launching assault rifles.

Relieved of some of their pride and selfish thinking, the divers rushed into the shallow water on the New California side of the beach. They were pretty far off, even in Quinceton's scope, but he saw one of them addressing the group and they circled around the individual. Then the speaking diver said something, raised his fist in a quick state salute, and affixed a facemask into place. The other divers did likewise and submerged themselves in the lake, waterproof augmented rifles equipped and waiting over their shoulders.

The first bomb fell on a pile of sandbags some twenty feet short of the border wall, and the next detonation leveled a fire hydrant past the fence, but the third and fourth drones claimed direct hits. Shards of metal, asphalt, and wire churned through the air, actually hitting a drone for a little midair sparkle, but the other tech dropped their payloads within the same basic neighborhood and reversed course for demolitions, way behind the Raley's castle.

Quinceton witnessed the explosions with awe, feeling the concussions underneath his chest, rattling not only his rifle but also his conviction to use it. It occurred to him that his every action up to this point had been completed on autopilot, a series of decisions he never remembered considering. He'd been talking to a kinda cute lady the day he'd signed up for the military and he had gotten all of June off labor duty before boot camp, during which time he'd slept with her twice. The last time she came to his apartment, she had just ripped off her shirt and let him kiss her nipple. She was no Natalie, but that was pretty nice.

The memory was just weeks ago. It didn't feel possible that from there, he would wind up here.

When the dust settled, the border fence resembled a gnarly old art installation in Union Square representing the struggle for liberation under the old Federal oligarchy, jagged metal wrapped in barbed wire extending in random angles from a shallow blackened crater. At least the bombing had split a path wide enough for any soldier to squeeze through, which encouraged Quinceton's confidence marginally. Time: 1255. *Only a couple hours late. Not that bad.*

The divers appeared first, wet and distant in Quinceton's scope as they commando crawled on their bellies up the beach and through a thin tree grove in Nevada territory. Harvey's, the first hotel-casino across the border on the north side of highway, loomed ahead as a collection of glass rectangles all melted together. The front of the building jutted out to the highway stacked with only a few stories on top, backed by a much taller and shinier section set behind by a good hundred yards. Quinceton watched the divers advance through the low trees and into a thicket of stumps, which had probably been cleared by the Americans to extend their visible perimeter.

A bang from the highway infantry reminded Quinceton of Smythe. The Command Sergeant Major fired off another round to get a platoon's attention, now on the far side of the highway, but fairly close to the border gate. Smythe was no longer strutting down the middle of Main Street— xe'd taken cover behind some fallen signage—but xe was clearly adamant that whatever group xe'd decided on should go first. From a prone position behind enemy lines, no doubt Command Sergeant Major Smythe's divers shared xir impatience.

There were three of them, at least that Quinceton could see. They were maybe fifty feet from the border gate, packed tightly against each other against a low rock wall on the north side of the street. The young sniper could see them speaking among themselves, probably trying to figure out which one would go first. Smythe focused on them, not looking at the attack point or the casinos covering their entry but the volunteers caught between the enemy and their leadership. None wanted to be first; none could have anticipated this moment. Maybe the Americans had abandoned the first hundred miles of Nevada, but if not, well, those volunteers would be the first to find out for the rest of them.

Smythe called out to the volunteer nearest xir and waved them forward with wild, twitchy exaggeration. Quinceton saw fear, and smelled panic. For a few breaths, no one moved. The volunteer being put on the spot finally obeyed Smythe by creeping closer to the yellow lines in the center of highway, followed by the others. All three volunteers paused halfway between the gate and front of the infantry column. Quinceton couldn't hear any words but they huddled close together, probably plotting a strategy to shirk their duty once more.

From the Raley's rear came an animalistic roar and the drumbeat of automatic gunfire from Captain Redgrave, who stalked behind his sandbags with an assault rifle ripping at the sky. Quinceton focused his scope on Redgrave's face, where the barbaric impatience of the commanding officer's white privilege confessed itself to the exposed battalion—this expression of atavistic rage, unchained by common civility and any BIPOC oversight, introduced the tactical sniper to the great malevolence of mankind, that most wicked and murderous branch of the animal kingdom. In this moment Quinceton did not remember Captain Redgrave's venis, surgeries, or intersectional identity, instead only seeing the capability of whiteness to slaughter, rape, and enslave.

The maniacal Captain, evidently displeased with their current progress, had the potential to give any order, to condemn anyone to the maw of the smoldering border gate. Redgrave's loose fire confirmed Quinceton's blessing to be lying on the periphery, witnessing the show while relatively safe due to sheer luck and maintained only with continued obedience. His watch said 1323, within three hours and fifteenish minutes of the intended start of the infantry's frontal assault, which honestly wasn't even that horrible.

Smythe must've gotten the message, as xe started waving xir pistol around, too, and raised the volume of xir verbal threats. Xe actually amped up the pressure by hurling a rock in the general vicinity of the paralyzed penal battalion and they lurched forward, uncertain, not wanting to win a race to the gate. Everyone watched them now, especially the other platoons, who probably wanted nothing less than for the spotlight to find them next.

Quinceton zeroed in on Smythe as the Command Sergeant Major slithered a few feet closer to xir charges, took a knee, aimed, and fired. The shot clanged against the gate with a sound that registered immediately on the silhouette of the volunteers—they each turned to face their commanding officer in a horrified stupor. Smythe then looked down, appeared to be looking for something, and perked up when xe found it. Wind whistled through the mountains behind xir, but some phrases rose through the rising afternoon heat: "All knowledge comes from power and social position," Quinceton heard clearly, then "… humans divided into power structures with historically nondominant peoples accumulating the greatest lived experience."

"Good lord," Sarah coughed. "I think he's reciting Standpoint Theory straight from the book. Must be desperate to find some credibility and up the pressure."

"Pretty pathetic," Quinceton agreed. "Also idiotic that Standpoint Theory puts Smythe in charge to order those other guys forward. Because from their physical battlefield standpoint of looking the enemy squarely in the face with their lives on the line … well, Smythe's lived experience as an oppressed feline gender still counts for more sway."

"Yeah." Sarah watched through her scope, as did everyone else Quinceton could see on the periphery. "Just mental. But be glad we aren't those divers—I wouldn't want to be waiting on Nevada ground for Smythe to get his shit together." Sure, it was a blatant instance of misgendering, but Quinceton had more pressing things to worry about now than reporting such spoken violence.

The three volunteers conferenced once again. Quinceton could see even from this distance that all three were white, and at least two were clearly cisgender men. The JSS government military could easily afford their loss on a diversity level, and they had absolutely no grounds to argue from a Standpoint Theory perspective, but still, their fate didn't seem to be so disconnected from Quinceton's own. They fought the same war, on the same side, and had no decent Standpoint to point to when fools from valued races with fancy genders started ordering them into battle.

Even if it was trademark Anti-Racist thinking, it didn't seem all too focused on practical battlefield implications. Instead, they'd all just have to assume that the limitless lived experience offered by the decision-makers at the top would prevail as a testament to the hidden genius of a Diversity, Equity & Inclusion-oriented society. Then, Quinceton reasoned, it could be clearly explained why it was so critical to end the violence from those Nevada casinos in the name of Anti-Racism; the Knower's speech last night had had the right tone to it, but they had thought better than to include unnecessary specifics regarding the public decolonization of formerly private capitalist spaces.

Smythe interrupted Quinceton's victorious daydream by clanging a few more shots off the border gate in rapid succession. This finally forced a decision: With one last glance at each other, the volunteers must've figured they had no other choice and rose to attempt the breach. In a low crouch, they snuck down the middle of the highway, with absolutely nothing nearby to use for cover. The dash to the border gate was only a few dozen yards, and when they got there the divers could open up with their destabilizing grenade launchers. It all hinged on those first few volunteers breaking through for the rest to follow. It wasn't too hard to imagine every pair of lungs with a life at stake going completely still.

The volunteers stood in unison and leapt forward like sprinters taking off at the same starting bell. They hurled toward the gate in a thin human line of battle cries, with determination, if not resignation, carrying their spirits to this Anti-Racist reckoning.

A hurricane of sound erupted from Nevada, instantly splitting all three volunteers into wet red pieces at the mouth of the border gate. It was dumbfounding to see the silent sprint turn so quickly into the aftermath of a deafening meat grinder, as though the three bodies had run headlong into a human dicing machine set to puree some Anti-Racist flesh for cannibal Americans to feed on. The image mesmerized Quinceton such that nothing else was visible; some force had opened these skeletons, stomping through bone and flesh with the ease of a steel boot kicking through performative White Tears. Severed pieces of the volunteer's limbs flew backward into the frozen infantry as torn intestines oozed bile onto asphalt, the only reminder that human bodies had hustled here just moments before. They hadn't even had a chance to scream.

Sarah's trembling shoulders thawed time for Quinceton, and he looked to the source of the sound. Fixed gun emplacements blasted from too many corners of Nevada to count: He saw the same big metal contraptions dumping rounds from seemingly every floor of the casinos, with multiple fixtures springing from under tree stumps and round womxnhole sewer covers on the street. The gun emplacements were as tall as a person and as lethal as a white colonizer, with oversized high-caliber slugs that passed through one JSS soldier after another. A few grenades, presumably from the divers, thumped into the enemy weapons, redirecting some streams of fire but destroying none of the targets. Bodies of divers littered the landscape all the way to the beach as the remaining regular infantry commando crawled to cover away from the highway. The platoon nearest Mount Heavenly, the one tucked behind the rubble of a burned-out building, didn't move at all; most remained in deep cover, not even watching the main event. Quinceton couldn't locate Smythe in all the hysteria, which somehow seemed appropriate.

"Shoot before the next round of drones?" Sarah shouted above the din, leaning the stock of her rifle into Quinceton to reclaim his attention. "And what do you aim at?"

"Fuck no!" Quinceton shouted back. "Our rounds won't do anything those grenades couldn't. Don't draw attention. They might not know we're here." He took a few deeps breaths and looked hopefully toward the Raley's.

The scene inside the parking lot did not inspire tremendous confidence in Quinceton that everything was going according to plan, that something like these fixed gun emplacements had been expected, or that leadership was capable of changing the original attack strategy and coordinating a life-saving alternative at the peak of the afternoon sun. At least three different subordinates approached Redgrave with tourist maps—likely suggesting some new flank they could attack, anything but this botched frontal assault—but Redgrave would hear none of it. He tore one map in half and berated one of the subordinates into hysterics, which caused a whole clot of other subordinates to rush in and attend to the psychological safety of the original hysteric.

Redgrave barely noticed; his attention was back on Smythe, and as he pointed to the other side of the street, Quinceton followed with his scope. The Command Sergeant Major had maneuvered south of the highway to a half platoon crouched at the front of the burned-out complex.

The young snipers in the ski lift tower watched Smythe shouting at a handful of immobile infantry. The fixed guns wouldn't stop their barrage on whatever divers had yet to be dissected, making it damn near impossible to hear even a single word, but from the look of it, Smythe was doing the same Standpoint speech xe'd pushed on the first three guinea pigs—except these infantry weren't even pretending to be receptive. They remained in cover, even as Smythe's bulging eyes grew desperate at being so blatantly ignored.

Once more, Smythe aimed xir sidearm at the wreckage of the border gate and began firing in intervals of five seconds or so. When the gun's top slide fell forward in a universal sign of a spent clip, two of the chosen platoon leapt from cover and tackled the Command Sergeant Major. Quinceton couldn't see the whole tussle, but he saw one of the daring infantry secure Smythe's sidearm as the other backhanded xir across the face hard and true.

Was Smythe worth an open palm? Probably not—it'd be like sucker punching an infant. But a swift backhand to slap silly their feline leader? Well, who could argue with that?

The ultimate outcome of the mutiny was a strange kind of mutual divorce: The rebel platoon veered straight south along the Nevada border while Smythe dashed back for the familiarity of the Holiday Inn Express, xir metaphorical tail between xir hind legs. At least two platoons used the backward dash of the fearless feline to retreat for some safety themselves, following Smythe to the infantry barracks. In order to do so, many had to traverse damn near the entire battlefield, but as they did, the fixed guns focused elsewhere or shut down entirely. This surprised Quinceton more than anything else; they'd been told that the easiest kills they'd get all day would be from retreating Americans once they'd captured the first casino or two. But the fixed guns even ignored the mutineers—the ones who'd disarmed Smythe—and let them wander south down the border between the two states. Eventually, there'd be no wall to climb, and Quinceton couldn't imagine the deserters coming back for more Anti-Racism in a DIE Camp.

"Hey!" one of the divers yelled from the graveyard across the Nevada border. "We're trapped—save us!" The volume of the shout impressed Quinceton, as the halting fire had enabled him to actually make out the words from so far away.

Even so, it was no use worrying about spilt milk. Without anyone willing to back their assault by putting their own lives on the line, the divers were done for. *So is the battle, probably, come to think of it,* Quinceton thought. *The war will have to wait for another day, too.*

Except no one in a position to call it off had done so yet, at least not officially. Captain Redgrave remained on his feet, firing off a clip in one general Nevada direction before reloading and aiming somewhere else. The last of his subordinates evacuated to the giant supermarket command center, and for a moment Quinceton saw him as a towering hero of grit and dedication. Two JSS government soldiers retreating from the front lines faced the Raley's from the other side of the parking lot—the no-person's-land in between familiar safety and the enemy's shrapnel. One of them tried to flank the Raley's by using signage to creep down a line of cover, but the moment their head wafted above the sandbags, it fell backwards—caught by a single headshot.

"Cowards!" Redgrave bellowed, neck veins visible from the ski tower. "Racists! You call that 'commitment,' you worthless yellowbellies? Live Anti-Racism or die like an American!"

It soon became clear that Redgrave was intentionally aiming at the accumulating stampede of his own battalion. Somewhere behind the Raley's a drone bomb detonated, reminding Quinceton that the clueless demolitions team might still be on the offensive, for reasons that seemed logical at first and now could scarcely be remembered.

A few drones appeared above Redgrave heading loosely toward the border gate, but their payloads fell randomly, far short of the enemy. Quinceton hoped this wave of drones would at least distract the fixed guns, but something had gone haywire—where their payloads had ben within a hundred feet of each other during the opening bombing, they now seemed totally detached from command.

Redgrave stopped firing and watched one drone destroy a stone wall just beyond the Holiday Inn Express, burying a few soldiers in debris. The captain bellowed something toward the fleeing infantry, turned around, and rushed behind the exterior of the Raley's. Perhaps demolitions were due for DIE Camp reeducation or even swift humane dispatchment, after which the Elect could handpick a perfectly elite intersectional team.

And then a drone let loose on the Raley's itself, igniting some chain reaction of rupturing energy systems. The middle of the building caved in on its inhabitants as senior JSS government Elect scampered out the front door, painted in flames. Sickening smoke from the hellish inferno reached Quinceton quickly as the carcass of the command center burned against torturous shrieks of toasting human flesh. The scene reminded him of the "mostly peaceful protests" he saw in his youth.

"Holy fuck," Sarah gasped, no longer shouting. Nevada's fixed guns seemed to be easing off, but Quinceton concentrated on insulating himself from the smell of scorched human meat. Without a gas mask, the best he could do was stretch his undershirt up to his nose and bury the damn thing, eyes hovering just above the rim of the metal ski tower.

"See anyone alive down there?" Sarah mumbled, mimicking Quinceton's improvised ventilation system. The Nevada guns slowed to a stop but lost little of their menace. Quinceton looked first to the Raley's, then to the border gate, but nothing moved. The sudden silence shocked him more than the dismembered bodies.

The group Quinceton had first planned to cover behind the nearby burned-out building emerged, five of them looking frazzled but lively—definitely not furious, mournful, or even all that disappointed. They cut south just like the mutineers—an uphill Mount Heavenly hike—meandering past the young sniper's position in the old ski tower.

"Where are you going?" Sarah called out. "You regrouping or something? Heard any talk of a counterattack?"

All five of them laughed.

"Are you serious?" one of them, a white dude, called back as though the answer was so obvious that even to ask was simply ridiculous. "I just came here to get out of factory-packaging work."

"Then where to now?" Quinceton asked.

"Why should we tell you, Captain Redgrave?" a brown-skinned womxn answered. She knew he wasn't the infamous captain or even important enough to be Elect—otherwise, he wouldn't be here—but Quinceton understood her suspicion. "Have fun with your next suicide mission … I'm sure *Anti-Racism* will still want your Black ass after we bounce." The way she said "Anti-Racism" was different than he'd heard it spoken before, and it made her companions laugh again.

Quinceton watched the group depart with mixed feelings. He understood why they'd lost faith in the attack, but he couldn't imagine how their next move would play out a day or a week from now. Abandoning the JSS government attack on South Lake Tahoe was so predictably unforgivable that they'd never be anything but outcasts in New California for the rest of their lives. They'd be treated like Anti-Anti-Racists, sent to DIE Camp reeducation as fast as the Anti-Anti-Anti-Racist patrolpersons caught up to them. And if they tried to sneak into Nevada, well, who really knew what was in store for them in Federal America? The JSS government had warned everyone since early childhood that exiles were shot on sight. Quinceton wasn't sure if he really bought that since there were plenty of rumors to the contrary, but then again, Federal America had done as promised so far as the divers were concerned.

"I don't see any other snipers at their posts," Quinceton said maybe an hour after the deserters had left. "What are you thinking?"

In the meantime, there had been nothing at all—no Redgrave, no sign of a counteroffensive, not even a sighting of Sergeant Weed, who would surely have known the next move. Nothing but waiting and watching corpses cook in the heat of the mid-afternoon glare.

"I mean, what are the options?" she answered rhetorically. "I guess, just to be on the safe side, we wait here until someone tells us otherwise. If we wait here, not Redgrave or anyone else can blame us for anything. We stayed where they asked us to, and peed downhill as directed."

"Right. We followed orders. But how long do we wait to hear from someone giving those orders, or the next orders?"

"I have no idea. I don't think this in the Standpoint Theory manual."

Quinceton couldn't tell if she was joking or not, but at least they shared the same confusion. "Alright, well … I say we just hold out a little longer," he concluded. "You saw Redgrave shooting his own soldiers for retreating, right? The longer we hold out up here, the less we look like we're giving up."

"Yeah," Sarah said. "But stay on your scope. Speak up if you see anyone alive down there. Anyone at all."

"Deal."

Enough time passed that the sun covered the battlefield in shadows from the west, and just as the light began to really dim, a limb stirred beside a wall that the JSS demolitions had razed on the New California side.

"Maybe fifty yards east of the Holiday Inn Express," Quinceton observed. "There's a white guy moving there to the right, under the rubble." He zoomed in with his scope and paused. "Think I can get his attention without scaring the shit out of the guy?"

Sarah followed his sightline with her rifle.

"Just don't shoot *at* him," she said. "Just near enough he hears it, and knows it didn't come from the Americans. Go for it."

"Okay, but watch Nevada. If those guns move an inch, I want to know."

"Yes, got it."

Quinceton exhaled slowly, then fired before another breath. The shot buried itself in the main street blacktop, making no sound the sniper could hear over the din of his own fire. But the white guy heard it. Looking around wildly at first, he put a scope to his eyes and followed the gunfire to their position in the ski chair tower.

"All quiet in Nevada," Sarah said.

"Well, I'll be damned," Quinceton chuckled. "I think he's that old bastard Smythe hates, the ketchup guy." The white man put down his rifle and held up two palms facing the snipers in a universal "halt" signal. "I think he's hiding in the stone," he said. "Not buried underneath it."

"We can use this guy, I think," Sarah replied. "He's a smart one."

Quinceton waved at the old man, then gestured in their own direction. The guy pointed toward Nevada, then held out his hands, palms to the sky, which Quinceton read as concern and confusion.

"I'm going to test it out." Quinceton fired another shot into the asphalt about one hundred feet shy of the gate as the old man looked on. Then he fired one even closer, and a third into the border gate. Nothing moved in Nevada. Quinceton waved the old man toward him once more, and this time he got a nod in response. The guy crept out from under the rubble and commando crawled his way between cover, gradually moving toward their position. The snipers kept a lookout across the border, and even without seeing a stir, the wait was agony. Night began to descend by the time the guy reached earshot.

"I'm Sarah, and he's Quinceton," Sarah began. "So it's really over, huh?"

"The battle, maybe, but who knows when the war will start," the old guy answered, still on his belly at the base of the ski tower but finally able to make eye contact. "I'm Phil Bondurant, and please, for my sake, don't present your IS identity. It'll only piss me off, and it's been a helluva day. We're all we got now."

"I'm good with that," Quinceton said, "as long as your old bones don't slow us down. If I'm the Americans, I'm attacking soon with full steam ahead and pushing clear to the coast. Let's get out of here and find help."

"I'm with you," the man said, now moving in a crouch toward them.

"We can't come off as deserters when we find people." Sarah's brow furrowed in concern. "This scenario isn't in the manual. We have to be careful. Where's Sergeant Weed?"

"She was running around, trying to coordinate a response from her snipers, when she got hit by the Nevada guns early on in the shooting," Phil told them. "And I saw Smythe run off behind the Holiday Inn Express, followed by some of his biggest fans, and I don't think the fans had forgiveness in mind. If *xe's* dead, and we can find *xir* body, we might find some useful tools on *xir*, like a compass, and food inside the barracks." The guy really labored to use the right pronouns, which halted his speech; the Anti-Racist vocabulary clearly took conscious effort. Somehow, that made him more trustworthy.

The falling light also made Quinceton feel safer, but he couldn't ignore the devastating potential of a counterattack.

"If the body is there, I can get to it forty times faster than you, Old Bones. Stay here and I'll go."

"Don't split up," Sarah urged. "Let's walk the perimeter—stay low, but move."

"I'm with you," Phil repeated, "and I can lead you to his general whereabouts a lot better than I can point from here."

"Sure, Bones," Quinceton replied, fixing his backpack for the ladder climb back to the ground. "Keep up, and let's move out."

The trio descended Mount Heavenly single file, with Bones leading the way and Quinceton guarding his backside. In the dark over Nevada, they saw fireworks of red, white, and blue exploding into the night, gleaming like an arrogant flex by the victors.

ACT II

The Last Liberati

ACT II, CHAPTER ONE

Ignorance, Bliss

QUINCETON ASSUMED THAT LOCATING COMMAND Sergeant Major Smythe would be difficult, if not impossible, and brightened to discover just how wrong he had been. Behind the Holiday Inn Express, slumped against a wall facing the lake, they found Smythe right where Bones predicted. Shards of skull stuck to dried blood a few feet above Smythe's head as xir eyes remained open, gazing into the eternal beyond.

"Looks like Smythe's loyal division finally caught up with him," Bones noted. "So I guess we can save time on a doctor, at least."

"Got that right," responded Quinceton. "I think we can skip the investigation, too. Hard to blame an execution this clean on the Americans." Bones chuckled without the slightest hint of remorse as remnants of some hundred bodies saturated the town's gutters with their collective limbs, organs, and failure.

"You know, we can also save on the funeral arrangements if we find a shoebox big enough to fit xe/xir," Bones quipped. "I thought cats were supposed to have nine lives, but it turns out xe/xir's identity wasn't fully feline after all."

"All that effort to live like a cat when all it takes is one bullet to remember that you're as human as the rest of us," Quinceton added as they finally discovered an appropriate application for Smythe's gender identity.

Sarah remained quiet as the two men shared a laugh.

"What, no death comedy?" Bones asked Sarah. "C'mon, now that we've destroyed every independent business from American California, gallows humor is our only export."

Quinceton wanted to hear more California history, but hunger and darkness took priority. "Hey, guys, it's getting late—" he began, but Sarah cut him off.

"I'm just worried about someone listening in. You never know how they collect evidence and stuff against the people they arrest."

"You think they actually collect evidence?" Bones interjected, voice rising in pitch. "Really? You think Smythe was a guy who went to the effort of actually building a case against those he sent to the Gulag?"

Quinceton didn't know what "the Gulag" was, but Sarah kept going. "Well, maybe not, but he—"

"AH! You said 'he'! I *hope* you didn't mean *xe* there, or else they'd have all the evidence they need."

Sarah physically shrank into a defensive posture, looking in every direction for movement, but nothing stirred in the blackness.

"So there's your answer, Sarah," Quinceton said. "If they were listening to us, you'd be starting your long climb up DIE Mountain."

Bones extended a hand and gave her a few pats on the shoulder, a presumptuous act that could ordinarily have put him in danger of a sexual assault allegation.

"It's okay, Sarah, no one here gives a damn. We know what you meant, what your intentions are, and we need your help to get out of this mess. It's okay."

Quinceton's eyes widened at this exchange; it was so different from the empathy practiced by the JSS government Elect and their leaders. The ruling authorities in California only recognized empathetic actions as protections for the more oppressed party in accordance with the standard hierarchy of marginalized groups. Sarah's comment ignored Smythe's oppressed gender identity, so it was a form of punching down that was typically treated with DIE Camp reeducation—and yet Bones had excused and forgiven

Sarah for her mistake without demanding further recompense, which did not prioritize the feelings of the more marginalized and deceased Smythe, but the present offender. And somehow, even if it wasn't legal, it made Quinceton respect Bones more. Forgiving carelessly violent speech was something his father might have done.

"Thanks, Bones," Sarah said quietly.

Quinceton didn't know what to say. He didn't want to openly support the old man's illicit empathy, but he didn't object, either. "How about that food, then?" he finally said, changing the subject. "Think we'll find anything inside the Holiday Inn Express?"

"We probably will," Bones replied, "but I'm damn sick of the same stuff. Either of you guys see where they put the Speakers' Safe Spaces? I have a feeling we'll find something a cut above dog food there." He rifled through Smythe's furry green army coat, pulling out a compass and map. "I fucking knew it. The map covers the whole damn lake up to Reno and Truckee. But in Smythe's paws, it may as well have been a bed for kitty litter."

Quinceton walked a few paces beyond the edge of the Holiday Inn Express and gazed west, but darkness had consumed everything. "You remember when we first got here, that boiling parking lot? I saw them take the Speakers somewhere way behind the Raley's. I'm down to look, but let's check our barracks first. Who knows—could be supplies."

Sure enough, the lobby and kitchen of the Holiday Inn Express were totally barren, but the electricity still worked, even if the water had been shut off. Bones opened the refrigerator standing at one height and deflated at the results.

"Well, at least they aren't hiding the ketchup," he said. "You think we should bother checking the rooms?"

Quinceton looked from Bones—who might have been hungry, yet stood steadfastly unruffled—to Sarah, who hadn't gotten comfortable since the first round went through the last penal battalion volunteer. But Quinceton had been beside her all the while and saw something more urgent bothering her now. Something that had nothing to do with the empty fridge.

"I don't think there's any point looking around here," Sarah answered. "They don't even have enough drinking water to refill the whole battalion." Her larger suspicion passed to the men immediately.

From the time Quinceton signed up for soldier duty and spent only a weekend learning to shoot from long range, he had been surprised at the brevity and sloppiness of JSS government military preparation. He'd matured from untrained civilian to protective cover for over a hundred infantry in only a few days, all of which had apparently deserted or presently lay dead on the battlefield except for Bones. The Knower's speech in the Raley's had felt all too familiar, but Captain Redgrave laid out the whole battle plan in barely ten minutes. The coordination of unfamiliar divers, infantry, and snipers had happened at the very last minute—the night before the attack—and, given the catastrophic outcome, had seemed pretty haphazard to Quinceton, even before witnessing the hollowed-out Holiday Inn Express kitchen. But Sarah's concern now hinted at something intentional. Something wicked.

"Those bastards," Bones spat. "Those absolute swine."

Sarah tried on a poker face of forced serenity, but it wasn't at all convincing. "I'm not convinced we know anything for sure. But either of you see them clearing the building today, this afternoon?" The men shook their heads. "Yeah, me neither. And Quinceton and I were out here early."

"So if we assume the kitchen wasn't packed up today, can we agree they just never planned to feed us again?" Bones's voice rose as he paced around the kitchen, staring at the floor. "And in that scenario, can we agree they didn't think we'd be coming back here? And if that's true … God help us." Bones stopped moving and looked back at the fridge. "Is there any way or any explanation for this which doesn't mean we got sent out here today on a mission they didn't think we'd survive? Was this a screwup, or a suicide mission?"

"Maybe they had other food and supplies somewhere else," Sarah said hopefully. "Or maybe they were worried about how the infantry would react to the border violence poster and wanted to hide food as insurance, to keep soldiers in line." There was no conceivable way Quinceton was going to comment on the poster violence among New California company, but it had begged some pesky questions.

Quinceton wanted to believe that Sarah could be right—that the JSS government wouldn't just willingly sacrifice so many people. He wanted to believe that in spite of fools like Smythe and devils like Redgrave, there was righteousness behind their devotion to Anti-Racism. That those who died did so to combat the cisheteropatriarchy. To combat evil, even outside New California.

"Well, you remember our orders. We were supposed to take the casinos across the border and hold them. So, maybe they just packed up the food to restock us on the front lines. And there was always a chance we'd find stuff in Nevada."

Quinceton didn't see much agreement in his comrades, but he clung to his upbringing and his country. The JSS government wasn't perfect; it was still developing into the force of liberation it sought to be, but at least it had rid New California of American attachments.

Once further speculation seemed aimless, the trio trudged west from the Holiday Inn Express, the street lit by the smoldering Raley's, in search of wherever the Elect Safe Spaces had been situated. Quinceton couldn't wait to discover what Elect living spaces looked like, especially the Speakers'. He figured that the other two were occupied with the same thoughts, though none said it. No one spoke at all as they navigated through the darkness.

Quinceton smelled some kind of electrical smoke churning from the Raley's. It irritated his eyes, but he was almost glad for the small fires. They illuminated a backdrop of well-kept cabins looming ahead, and the light helped to avoid stepping on more limbs or bodies in the street. The charred sandbags in front of the Raley's had survived better than anything else, and nothing moved now except the prancing flames.

An old Pizza Hut chain restaurant rotted across the street to the north, but just beyond it lay the Lakeland Village Resort at Heavenly, an elegant collection of beachfront buildings that showed every sign of recent occupation, with paths worn into thinning grass and the rainbow baby flag still hanging from a few cabins.

"Which one is their hotel?" Quinceton asked, immediately feeling foolish. Neither of his companions could suppress a look of amused surprise.

"So you've never seen any real Safe Spaces," Sarah mused, voice falling at the last word so as not to confuse the statement with a question. "They're all for the Elect. Mostly Speakers and a few high IS scores that do the grunt work, hoping to get promoted." A brief pause. "I did some food prep for Elect parties last summer and saw some of the Pacific Heights Safe Spaces."

Quinceton had so many questions. He had always wanted to know how the Elect lived, as his mother had been implicated in a Racist scandal before they were invited to live in a Safe Space. It also dawned on Quinceton that his companions had had more exposure to the Elect than him, and so he quickly tempered his curiosity with the shame of exposing his naïveté.

"Let's grab what we can and put some distance between us and this place," Quinceton said with newfound conviction. "I don't trust it around here. We can't let up until we get far enough to set up a camp they can't see from the border."

They scrambled across the broken shards of the Raley's to the row of cottages nearest the highway. These were a number of seemingly identical condos stacked next to each other, and Quinceton chose the closest one so he could open the door and enter first. He expected something gold, some fancy decorating equivalent to a Knower's Kafkani headdress, and didn't want the other two to see his reaction, but even without discovering any jewels or velvet or ketchup, Quinceton was impressed with the well-lit, polished feel of the building. There were curtains on each window that all matched, and though the furniture seemed to come from different places, none of it was worn through with holes and exposed stuffing. A high-sloping log cabin roof drew eyes to the living room fireplace as the vibrant center of a happy house. Even more luxuriously, everything was so … clean.

"I agree with Quinceton. Let's keep moving," Bones said as he fingered a JSS government flag that sat folded on the couch. "But I'd bet you my last credit we won't find a tent around here." It wasn't a big statement. With only a fraction of their former population, housing was about the only thing the JSS government owned in ample supply, even if upkeep and access to potable water had become cause for regular grumbling.

"Feel this fabric," Bones continued, not looking at either of them. "Have you ever touched anything like this? It feels light enough to carry, but strong enough to give us some wind cover." Sarah walked over and pawed at the flag, finding an edge she could isolate into a single fold. If it were the size of the ones hanging outside, it would be pretty huge, well over a dozen feet in every direction.

"It's not just cotton," Sarah said. "They must've made it carefully to be waterproof. They must've planned to hang these for a long time."

"So then maybe it wasn't all a big suicide-discovery mission," Quinceton said thoughtfully. He wandered into the kitchen and opened cupboards and the refrigerator with no luck in the way of food, but he did find a rust-free pocket knife that folded in on itself to conceal the blade. With no owner around, Quinceton felt empowered to claim it, just like any food they could scrounge up. His stomach pleaded with him for nourishment, as he'd already eaten the protein packet that came with his battle gear. The tent covering sounded all fine and good, but it was of distant secondary importance to his grumbling stomach.

"How are you guys not starving?" Quinceton asked with genuine surprise. "It's all I can think about."

"Maybe I've just trained my stomach not to ask for anything it won't get," Bones replied. "But we do need food. Once we get far from South Lake, we might find some animals we can eat." Looking at Bones under the functioning light bulbs of the wide log cabin made him appear even slimmer, almost sickly. Quinceton felt proud of the nickname he'd bestowed on the guy, but he didn't want to wind up with those kind of narrow shoulders or he'd never get another Natalie.

"I think we're in the wrong house," Sarah said. "I think this is a house for the Elect just to live in. Maybe they eat here, too, but they wouldn't cook their own meals, so the food has to be stored somewhere else. Has to be nearby." As she spoke, Bones unfolded the flag, rolled it like a cigarette, and fastened it atop his backpack.

Finding the cafeteria house in the middle of the complex turned out to be faster than Quinceton had feared, as it was the only one that wasn't in a row of similar architecture. Once inside, the trio made straight for the kitchen.

"Sons of whores," Bones said under his breath as he opened the first of four refrigerators. "Those greedy swine."

The fridge was loaded with translucent boxes with labels like "Onions," "Thyme," and "Steak." Quinceton hadn't heard about most of the ingredients in there, but there was enough of it to arouse his tongue like a hot womxn might do for the rest of his existence. Bones reached deep inside the cool box to pull out a platter wrapped in thin plastic and placed it on a special counter in the center of the kitchen. Quinceton rejoiced to see different colors of cheese and different cuts of meat on it.

"Eat!" Bones said in a voice of sheer ecstasy. Quinceton tore through the plastic, wrapped a piece of cheese in meat, bit down, and almost collapsed, all motor functions climaxing at once.

"Wait, wait! They have different bread and crackers, too!" Sarah called as she opened cupboards, but Quinceton's pace never slowed, even with Bones reaching in beside him.

In this moment of total satisfaction, there could be no other consideration in the world. Sarah cut a few slices of bread on which to place her cheese and meat, but Quinceton didn't bother, so eager was he to taste all different combinations before his stomach tapped out. They ate in total rapture, polishing the platter off in minutes.

"I never thought I'd get to eat charcuterie," Sarah sighed contentedly, now sitting on the steel counter.

"I haven't heard that word in ages," Bones replied. His face was hard to read. He looked full but not quite happy, almost melancholy. "I haven't eaten like this in ages ... definitely since before California split from the Federals in the Rupture."

Sarah quivered at the controversial remark. No one ever said something positive about the old world, even indirectly. It would draw attention immediately from those one wanted to avoid. "Slow down, Bones," she said in a comforting tone. "That's dangerous talk, even if they aren't around right now. You don't want to get in the habit of saying something like that, or one day they'll hear and think you're an Anti-Anti-Racist." She might have continued with the warning, but Bones cut her off.

"There *are no* Anti-Anti-Racists," he growled. He stopped moving and looked at her with a war face of reckless contempt. "Don't ever talk to me about Anti-Anti-Racists."

The previously joyful mood died right then along with Quinceton's hunger. The three barely spoke afterwards as they each filled their packs with nonperishable canned foods that were all too familiar to JSS government laborers and soldiers alike.

As they trudged west out of South Lake, Quinceton almost regretted all those blissful bites of meat and cheese. Life for the privileged citizen was about sacrifice, not luxury, and he missed the ignorance he'd enjoyed before learning the word "charcuterie."

ACT II, CHAPTER TWO

To Gender, To Misgender; To Speak, To Silence

QUINCETON STARED AT THE CAMPFIRE, trying not to move. His whole body ached. The day he'd arrived at South Lake had been long, but not like this. He'd been in near constant motion from the moment he'd met Bones on the battlefield.

The only talk since leaving Tahoe had been about pushing on, going farther, trying to find just the right spot where a fire could burn casually without raising enough smoke to alert the Nevada border. Bones drove them onward with few words. His mood had not improved since Sarah's Anti-Anti-Racist comment, and Sarah didn't challenge him on the grueling march, which Quinceton viewed as a form of silent contrition.

At least the camp was fairly close to a creek and had some wind cover. The moment they arrived they set to laying out the large flag in a triangle shape against a steep mountain, arranged with the bottom side to sleep on and the side with the JSS government rainbow baby logo facing anyone who might stumble upon the camp from below. Even if the makeshift tent functioned more as a wind tunnel than a barricade, it was worth it; any wandering Anti-Anti-Anti-Racist patrolpersons would recognize them as allies immediately, and it was essential to have some kind of signal to ward off these trigger-prone AAA agents. They were known to attack at night without warning and sort out the loyalists from deserters once they had everyone bound and bagged. Compared to the AAA, even the reputation of the Americans seemed timid and feckless.

"Any canned peaches left?" Bones asked Sarah. She nodded, handing him her plate. He took a few bites and handed it back. "It was about three years ago, maybe," he began, his eyes fixed on the flames. "In the old world, I had a very advanced education and worked as an engineer—a builder of complicated stuff. That kind of training was still valuable under the JSS government, but they used us differently, mostly on repairing key infrastructure and using equipment to watch people, what we would call 'surveillance.' Working in engineering started us out with good housing and it got even better, with my daughter and I being upgraded from a tiny apartment in the SOMA neighborhood to a huge condo on Van Ness with great views and fancy new everything.

"It was good, for a while. They seemed to appreciate us more as veteran engineers dropped out over time and their replacements were completely useless. We got pretty good food, my daughter got some real schooling in those days. As long as we did their work, we were treated like the Elect without really having to grovel to any Speakers or Knowers." Bones suddenly stood, walked over to their taco tent, and began checking lines and tightening knots.

Quinceton grew eager to hear the rest of the story. "Then what happened?" He'd already guessed at what being sent to the frontlines meant. Perhaps they all had the second they read the *Intellectualism for Idiots* poster.

"Anyway, I worked a lot, had a daughter to look after by myself, and didn't really pay attention to politics," he continued as he picked a new seat farther removed from the fire, his face barely visible. "I saw things change when they'd shuttle us to and from work. I knew gender was becoming something of a big hobby, but I felt protected—safe, almost, as I did a job that fewer and fewer people knew how to do, and I did it well. So one day, this new kid—a total novice who was better at getting offended by math than using it—introduced themselves to the team by saying they were 'persanogender.' That was the first time I'd heard of it."

Sarah murmured something that Quinceton didn't quite catch, but he figured they both knew where this tale was heading.

"The kid said they identified as the sole inhabitant of their own specific gender universe and used I/me/my pronouns. The kid looked just like an average white boy. Average in every way—simple clothes, nothing that suggested a claim to an oppressed existence. So, I thought he was joking, and I laughed in front of all my coworkers." Silence followed. Quinceton had assumed correctly.

"I mean, do you know how hard it is to speak around someone who claims I/me/my as their own pronouns?" Bones said, his voice rising and becoming defensive. "You can't ever refer to your own self without immediate confusion! It's a constant infuriating annoyance which converts technical communication into a slow crawl through a minefield of gender identity. You guys have to realize, I grew up in an age when 'they' and 'their' referred to two or more persons—I saw this as simple retardation of language that couldn't possibly help any society progress. Especially in the realm of engineering, which has math to it, so you'd think they'd want to protect it from certain identitarian excesses. But that's when I learned that the JSS version of 'progressive' has a pretty specific and revolutionary idea of progress. It has no use for the objectivity of something like math." He paused. "But that last bit you already know."

"So they fired you from the good job," Quinceton said. "They do anything else?"

"Well, they did, though they didn't *totally* fire me—they still needed the work. We lost the nice condo and food, of course, but they kept us around the city in a shoebox studio. And I was labeled a suspected Anti-Anti-Racist, obviously. We found surveillance equipment all over the new place, so I was probably being watched the whole time, maybe even when I left the shoebox. Even today, I'm sure that Anti-Anti-Racist label follows me from assignment to assignment—like this one. They promised me a clean record for helping out with demolitions engineering, but then I got a racial reassignment, so I suppose the deal is off. Once you get canceled from the Elect, you can never come back."

Quinceton knew this well enough from his own mother's downfall, as he'd dropped out of school at fifteen to live in government-supported housing. "I feel you, Bones," he sympathized. "People mess up, and sometimes they don't mean it. Sometimes I think you can forgive and just move on. Your daughter okay?"

"Oh, she's fine. Fucking *hates* me, but she grew up in this world and fits right in—doesn't know any different. She'll go to the public cancellations for fun and cheer right along with the crowd at the people in stockades. Like a Roman."

"What's a Roman again?" Quinceton asked. He didn't get the reference, but he'd definitely heard something about it before.

"They're the barbaric Italians who had a huge empire thousands of years ago," Sarah answered. "They conquered other places, enslaved most of the people they found there, and enjoyed watching people kill each other just for fun."

"The people who had to kill each other as entertainment were called gladiators," Bones added. "Gladiators were essentially slaves condemned to death, kinda like the people sent to DIE reeducation today. When I was young, we viewed gladiators killing each other as violence. Back in the Federal world, it was hard for me to see how people could do such things, or watch public humiliation for fun. I honestly don't know if my daughter would see gladiators as being capable of violence against each other if their tongues were cut out and they couldn't speak up for harmful ideas. 'Violence' is a totally different word to this generation, but looking at her, now I understand the Romans. I think my daughter watches forced personal denunciations just like the Romans watched slaves stab each other to death—with gleeful ignorance."

As Quinceton thought on this, he wanted to ask about his mother, to ask if Bones remembered anything specific about the 2020 Project. Now was not the time, but he felt confident that a deposed radical was the right identity to ask.

ACT II, CHAPTER THREE
Naked Truth

QUINCETON WOKE TO THE SOUND of a stream rushing nearby and a stiff neck. He didn't mind sleeping in his clothes, but it was impossible to situate his head in one settled spot. At least he had California weather on his side. There were limits to what whiteness could ruin.

"Breakfast?" Bones asked as Quinceton groggily strolled into camp. Quinceton looked at the pot on the fire, an empty can of baked beans beside it.

"Naw," he said. "I wanna find the creek and go for a rinse."

"Could be chilly. But you won't be alone down there."

Sunshine shone through the California pine in such a way as to illuminate everything alive in the woods, from the moss growing on trees to the squirrels conspiring about their next adventure. Quinceton took a deep breath just to taste it—the city never smelled this way. Maybe he could get used to this and settle somewhere quiet. Dating options being slim out here in the boondocks, he'd need to find the right lady beforehand, of course.

Quinceton removed his boots, stripped down to the buff, and touched a toe to the creek—cold, but not arctic. One toe became one foot, two feet, then up to the knees, the waist, and deeper into the stream until Quinceton pushed off and fully submerged. The current pulled cool water across his body as he held his breath and scrubbed at his torso and scalp with rounded fingernails. He didn't have soap, but that was alright. This stream could cleanse even the Devil's dirty mouth.

The middle seemed to be deepest, somewhere between three and four feet, and Quinceton had to be careful to find the right footing as he waded to the far shore. The current had some real momentum behind it, but Quinceton's core muscles were his best, and he appreciated the resistance. Rising out of the creek, he aimed his penis downstream and started relieving himself.

"Hey, don't mind me!" Sarah shouted as she hustled to the opposite edge a few dozen ripples in front of Quinceton's contribution.

"Whoop—sorry there," Quinceton said as he trudged to the shore and redirected his stream to some weeds. The urine washed through the plants and back to the creek, but Sarah wouldn't see. He hadn't even noticed her; he wasn't really thinking about anything much beyond the splendor of newfound cleanliness, and now he'd just exposed himself to a member of the opposite sex. Whipping it out at an inopportune moment had downed many a JSS government power broker before, and since intent was legally irrelevant, this could be pretty problematic.

Once he finished, he turned back to Sarah. She stood stark naked on the opposite shore, the water at her knees, breasts and firebush totally exposed.

"I really *am* sorry about that," he sighed, trying not to look below her neck. "I just woke up and came down here. Totally my fault."

She gave him a nodding smile. "Nice cock."

Quinceton laughed. "Nice bush," he returned, "and the breasts ain't too bad, either." He didn't actually love the bush or the breasts, but it seemed a polite thing to say.

Sarah took a few steps upstream, closer to him, and waded into the deeper middle. She dove, came up for air, and splashed Quinceton with a judo chop into the water.

"Come closer and I'll tell you a secret," she said. "You know I get paranoid about them listening, and I lied before." Quinceton was curious. If she hadn't mentioned clearing up a lie, he might have wondered about a kiss or something. But at the same time, it was *Sarah*.

"What's up?" he asked when they were a few feet away from each other in the deep middle, both crouching so that only their heads remained afloat.

"You know when I told you I was bi? Or at least identified that way? You remember?"

"Yeah."

"Well, I guess I do *identify* as bi, but the truth is, I'm really a dyke. Total, full-blown bull dyke, without the hooves. I'm just not into dick. No dick. I don't want any dick." She paused, watching Quinceton's expression. "But, obviously, yours is gorgeous."

"Thanks. So what's it like? Actually being a lezzie, even if you don't cop to it?"

"It's hard." Sarah finally looked away. She gazed up at the trees and a ray of light poking through and shining on a boulder in the middle of the creek. A few careful steps later she was sitting on the rock, one leg over the other to shield the snatch but her breasts just as happy and free as before. Her comfort with nudity impressed Quinceton; he'd always felt pretty good about his body, but he still kinda viewed Sarah as a womxn and felt odd prancing around with his cock out. She clearly thought of him as a man and didn't give much of a damn what he thought of her body, which, he had to admit, was a superior form of confidence.

"I had a girlfriend about a year ago named Darcy," Sarah continued. "She was a little older than me, a really brave, unapologetic womxn. The sort of person who has a hard time conforming to other people's standards. Darcy put up with the JSS government, but I wouldn't say she was ever really a fan."

"So what happened? She still your lady?"

"Legally, she identified as a lesbian since forever, and it seemed like she got a lot of scrutiny for it—her workmaster would always ask about who she was dating and whether or not they were trans. She really didn't want a trans womxn, and for a while she sidestepped the real implications of the questioning. But then one day—after some pretty heavy pressure to explain why she never dated trans—my girlfriend said something like, 'I just don't like dick, okay? I'm gay, as in I'm attracted to bodies like my own.' Darcy told me the story that night, and was even joking about wanting bodies similar to but better than her own, and then … *boom.*"

"Good God. They grabbed her?"

"Yeah, they did. They came in the middle of the night, put that hood on, and I haven't seen or heard word one of her since. She's in some DIE Camp somewhere, but I still think I'll see her again. It was only about a year ago. But from the beginning, I've never told them I'm a dyke. I always said 'bi' like everyone else, and then they don't really look at you."

"Did you have to prove it? Like with a trans womxn?"

"No, no, nothing like that. All I had to do was give my workmaster a hand job. He filed the necessary paperwork, so I'm in the clear, at least for now." Quinceton considered her words. It didn't really seem right, not at all, even if it proved Sarah wasn't transphobic.

The sound of splashing came from the camp-side shore. Bones, wearing only underwear, looked at the two of them with curious amusement.

"I didn't know we were skinny-dipping. Am I not cool if I keep these on?"

"You may be a little old for 'cool,' Bones," Quinceton replied. "But you do you. Sarah already seen all of me and if that didn't do it for her, I think you're safe." Quinceton looked back at Sarah as Bones doffed his boxers and waded toward them.

"You wanna know something you already know?" Sarah asked Bones. "I'm a big dyke. I just told Quinceton."

"Yeah, no shit, Sherlock," Bones said before crouching below the surface. He re-emerged and spat a little arc of water downstream. "When she walks, it's all shoulders—couldn't you tell, Quinceton? What, are you going to end the suspense now and tell me you're a Black guy?"

Sarah laughed, but Quinceton didn't get it. "How'd you know she wasn't bi or non-binary or a specially oppressed gender identity or anything else? And who's Sherlock?"

"Oh, oh, I know this one!" Sarah said with great excitement. Bones seemed far more interested in his refreshing dip. "Sherlock is a reference to a detective from European mystery stories. Sherlock something, and he had a doctor for a sidekick. I can't remember if it got whitelisted for celebrating whiteness or criminal justice, but my seeder, he knew the stories well and would tell me before bed."

"Yeap," Bones confirmed between half dives into the deep middle.

"And at Bones's age—no offense—they don't really get offended by straight-up lesbians," Sarah said. "Transphobia laws developed and changed a lot in just the last decade. The elderly tend to keep older ideas about sexuality."

"Damn right," Bones replied. "I really don't care who you bang. But I do appreciate the view—I haven't seen a decent rack since Knowing Leader Mustafah X. Kendaoi ran the show."

"Compliments of the house," Sarah said, and they both laughed.

Quinceton didn't always get every reference, but he liked these people. They were different, and they spoke with such ... calm? Or tolerance? Maybe resilience? He couldn't think of quite the right word for it.

Gazing downstream, Quinceton wondered if there were many people who lived outside the city quarantine zones. He dared to wonder if his lady really was out there waiting for him, and if he could find her without ever going back to the city.

ACT II, CHAPTER FOUR

The Work Done at Work Doing

IT WAS THE LONGEST DAY of walking in Quinceton's life, trudging through tall trees and along ridgelines, beside streams and mountain views, all decided by Bones's compass. "Gotta take this path up and over," he might say, or "We're close to where we should be, a few clicks to the northwest this time." Sarah walked between the men and said very little. Quinceton could easily keep up while gazing at the tall trees and scurrying animals, and he was constantly impressed by his companions, especially Bones, who never seemed to tire in spite of his dotage.

"We head through that way and should find a town," Bones said after what felt like an hour of a steady downhill breather in lighter vegetation. "At least it *used* to be a town. Don't expect charcuterie."

Brown-green foliage soon turned to pavement and abandoned houses as they passed through the first rural neighborhood Quinceton had ever seen up close. They'd slept in old abandoned motel rooms when he did a sunny vacation detail, picking tomatoes in the Central Valley, and he was too young to remember when JSS government citizens had been allowed to live outside official Anti-Racist Safe Space cities. Early in the formation of the JSS government, a smaller metropolis could be used as an Anti-Racist satellite station, but they soon became hotbeds of Anti-Anti-Racist rebellion and the so-called "Rooftop Railroad," a network of interconnected buildings and mountain paths that coordinated to help traitors leave the state. Simple towns without properly fortified borders were subsequently shuttered, and now they were only intermittently patrolled by roving bands of the AAA.

"Just south, through those trees, and we should see something bigger," Bones instructed. "We're close."

Going past one more thicket, they stood in a gaping parking lot with two large buildings at the far side. One was labeled Schnell Elementary School and the other was Placerville Union Elementary. Quinceton shuddered. He could guess where all this was heading.

"Can we keep going?" he asked. "I don't like the look of this—I don't like old Work Doing centers."

"Really?" Sarah asked. "This probably hasn't been used for 'doing the work' in at least a decade, and look at how the dust is all disrupted on the windows—they've been here recently. It could be loaded with supplies." The AAA were known to sleep in buildings when possible, and since they had so many to pick from, they tended to go with something that offered an ample kitchen. Former Work Doing buildings were preferable to hospitals; everyone hated hospitals. No one trusted doctors and the outcomes of identity-adjusted medical training. Once school became about correcting societal power imbalances and all ways to measure knowledge were considered Racist, public faith in hospitals dried up along with the funding to keep things sanitary.

Quinceton doubted they'd find much food worth eating, and he'd resented buildings of Work Doing since way before he dropped out. These places always made him think of the same thing. But he supposed he could silence his reservations for a little longer, following his companions inside the big glass double doors underneath the "Placerville Union Elementary" sign.

"Smells a little like mildew, but these carpets look pretty soft," Bones observed. A very relative statement, considering they'd been sleeping on thin piles of dirt over stone. "Let's find the kitchen."

They didn't make it that far before discovering the source of the sour, rotting smell. Dingy hallways extended from the entranceway in opposite directions with faded footprints etched into the dust. A draft coming from an open classroom drew their attention: A hole had been cut out of the ceiling, with a makeshift fire pit underneath. There was a desk at one end of the room underneath a stained chalkboard and loose chairs piled in a corner. Previous campfires had burned through the carpet such that charred wood and ash sat on exposed gray concrete, surrounded by a circle of scorched rock. Ugly black spots on a light-blue fungus spread around the ceiling with the hole as its bullseye.

"It won't smell so bad once we get the fire going," Bones said. He'd been in a good mood all day and Quinceton wanted to share his optimism, but he probably wouldn't until they ditched this place.

"Let's look for food," Quinceton said to Sarah as the old man threw a couple of loose logs in the middle of the stone circle. "Bones doesn't want our help with his fires." The two of them filed out, leaving Bones to scrounge for kindling.

The sun had set, bringing a chilling darkness that seemed to amplify the sound of thumping soldier boots in the hollow hallway. The rows of one classroom after another pushed them to keep marching for sustenance, but Quinceton wasn't nearly as hungry as he was irritable.

"Maybe it's quicker if we split up," he said. Sarah kept walking and pointed ahead.

"Let's reach that bend there, and if we don't see anything promising … we'll split up then."

The hallway turned into a short atrium lined by offices, not classrooms, and desks separated by low walls in the middle of the space. A rusted hammer and a metal stake of about the same length sat on the cluster of central workspaces.

"Well, no cafeteria here. Time to divide and conquer," Quinceton said quickly.

"What are you talking about?" Sarah answered rhetorically. "Can't you see this is where the leaders of the Work Doing Center hung out? They didn't have caterers in those days. They'd want to be near the food."

"Alright, boss, following you," Quinceton said with derision. He had to admit that her logic made some sense, but he didn't have to admit it out loud. Sarah hurried along, rushing past the cubicles as if now personally responsible for delivering immediate success.

Out of sheer curiosity more than anything else, Quinceton opened the door to the nearest office, labeled "Headmaster," and sneezed. A heavier layer of dust suggested this room hadn't been a favorite for the AAA patrolpersons, and from the looks of it, no one had ventured into the space for many years. The room was about the size of the hole-cut classroom, with a massive wood desk on one side and four faded armchairs surrounding a low table on the other.

Quinceton casually wandered over to the desk and gazed at the dead computational device occupying stage left. He slapped at the side of the screen, knowing nothing would happen, and nothing did. Sitting in the chair sent dust into the air, and Quinceton's eyes watered in preparation for a sneeze that never came. He tried the top drawer in the middle of the desk, amused to find it was locked. Remembering his new tool, Quinceton wedged the pocketknife between the wood and metal latch, breaking it clean off from the desk with ease.

A document on top of a thin stack of papers announced itself with a boldface "CORRECTIVES TO 2020 PROJECT" header, stopping Quinceton's heart. He couldn't breathe, his autonomous body functions halted in an instant. This particular internal document was new to him, but he could guess what it contained with complete confidence. He had lived through it.

"Yo! Where you at, soldier?" Sarah called from somewhere in the atrium. "I found the cafeteria room. It's pretty massive, so I need your help searching the kitchen."

"Right here," Quinceton called, snapping back to reality. The document was only one sheet, text on both the front and back, with directives numbered in bullet points. He folded it twice, tucked it into his backpack, and rose to find Sarah.

The cafeteria wasn't far from the cubicles, and Quinceton didn't listen to a word about the building as Sarah jabbered at him excitedly. He now saw the inevitability of unburdening his psyche with a total confession about his birther. Sarah and Bones would be the first such witnesses to his version of the tale, and if not for them, he feared he would bury the topic somewhere deep. Maybe for life.

Quinceton and Sarah rummaged around the kitchen for anything of value, finding it to be far from a gold mine of smoked meat and fresh cheeses. The room had been used at some point in the last few months, as most surfaces displayed obvious smudges in the layers of dust. After rifling through six empty cabinets, Quinceton found a fat bag of dried brown rice.

"Success!" Sarah cheered.

"It's no charcuterie."

"But it's food. We can eat it."

Disappointingly, it was the only food they found, and Quinceton lugged it back to Bones on his back. Sarah offered to help, but he rejected it. This was his find.

Bones was pulling a long pole through a nearby window and had a sizable fire burning when they returned—and it did indeed mask some of the smell. "Jackpot!" he exclaimed with real delight as soon as he saw Quinceton.

"Well, it's the best we could do," the young man replied.

Getting a fire started was far easier than preparing the rice, which required a pot of boiling water. This meant balancing the pole across the fire, supported by two peripheral chairs shoved into opposite walls, and hanging a pot of water above the flames. Bones had saved three chairs—the least damaged three, from the look of it—and arranged them around the fire. Quinceton unloaded the sack of rice at Bones's feet, sat, and opened his backpack. He wanted to read the document he'd found, but he also wanted them to see him reading it.

No authors claimed credit with a byline underneath "CORRECTIVES TO 2020 PROJECT," which made sense, as those who had claimed credit for the invention of the 2020 Project were now being targeting by this self-same document. The words were brief and direct, with an underlined note at the top followed by numbered initiatives.

The document began with a direct message to instructors. "**Take care not to weaponize academic freedom and academic integrity as tools to impede equity in an academic discipline or inflict curricular trauma on our students, especially historically marginalized students.**" The remainder of the artifact listed the necessary steps to pursue in order to defang the intellectual and academic search for truth that schools had once conducted before they committed to "doing the work with these correctives.

#1: The 2020 Project is hereby deemed Racist in the first degree and could only be written and/or enabled by Anti-Anti-Racist double agents working at the highest levels of the JSS government, including former Knowing Leader Mustafah X. Kendaoi.

#2: All original authors and perpetrators of the 2020 Project are to be detained in a DIE Camp for professional assessment and reeducation of all Anti-Anti-Racist attitudes.

#3: 'Schools' and 'education' will henceforth be known as 'Work Doing Centers/Stations' and 'Work Doing.'

#4: All forms of formal Work Doing assessment and measurement—including tests, written work assignments, counting classroom attendance, and instructor feedback with a numerical or alphabetical grade—are outlawed and will be treated as a direct imposition of whiteness, white supremacy, and Anti-Anti-Racism on young workdoers.

#5: Work Doing Centers will now guarantee equity to each child body who walks through their doors, with no exceptions.

There you have it, Quinceton thought. *An easy fix to an impossible problem.*

"Whatcha got there?" Bones asked as he carefully attached a pot to the pole above the fire. Quinceton couldn't tell if this was genuine curiosity or if he already knew.

"I found something about the old 2020 Project, and how to fix it in the aftermath. Must be many years old."

"I was pretty young then, but I remember it going from the standard thing to basically the most Racist concept we'd ever known, and the shift happened essentially overnight, or maybe one weekend," Sarah added.

"But no one could ask about it. It was something about grades being Racist because after that, no more grades."

"Yeah, it's a little more than that, but you got the concept," Quinceton answered. "I hate to say it, but my birther was involved. At the time, the 2020 Project was all about centering society around the rebellious emotions of 2020 in an effort to unite around equity. They really did have the same equity goals as the Work Doing that replaced it."

"In your birther's defense—assuming she identifies as a womxn—this was a pretty popular idea for decades," Bones said with unexpected consolation. "Either of you ever heard of the SAT?" Having received blank stares, he continued, "The SAT was a great, long test they gave high school kids way back in the Federal days, and your score really mattered. Your teachers' grades mattered, too, but the SAT was the same for every kid in the country. And because different groups fared so differently, it was said to be culturally biased."

"So it was all dominated by whiteness?" Quinceton asked.

"Well, yes and no. They said the SAT highlighted classic values of whiteness—like deductive reasoning, delayed gratification, and the rules of formal English—which were being best displayed by Asian Americans at the time. *That*, I can't explain. But I do get why they invented the 2020 Project. It was supposed to be a corrective to the cultural bias that plagued schools and supposedly made equal outcomes impossible in the old format, but it still kept grades and tests and that stuff. But then we went in another, almost entirely opposite direction with the Work Doing initiative—a corrective to the corrective."

"So what happened to the 2020 Project people?" Quinceton could see that Sarah's question came from total engagement. She was sitting forward on her chair, staring at Bones in rapt attention. The young man wasn't the only one curious about the past.

"Well, if the SAT was culturally biased in one direction, it could be just as easily culturally biased in the opposite direction. That was their logic, in any case. I remember the old former Knowing Leader—Kendaoi, right?— giving a big speech on it in Union Square. He promised to bring equity to education, which is what they called Work Doing in those days. That was basically how he became our first Knowing Leader—he promised to have all the answers, enforce equity everywhere and for everyone. You know, the whole 'reversing the targets of Racism is the only way to end Racism' thing.

"After the Intersectional Equity Laws went through, we all figured they would aim at schooling next. And they did, lead by Kendaoi. The promise was to change the focus of education into something which would prioritize BIPOC knowledge, therefore reversing educational outcomes. The hope was to elevate BIPOC knowledge above whiteness so as to promote the knowledge and lived experience of the historically marginalized to the top of every class."

"What do you mean 'cultural bias'?" Quinceton asked. "And how do you culturally bias a test so that you change which races do well or not?" The pot simmered over the flames but earned no attention.

"So to say that the SAT was culturally biased toward whiteness meant that the questions it asked were mostly ideas and concepts that primarily applied to, and promoted, white supremacy by way of emphasizing white knowledge. This claim survived decades of Asians doing better than whites on the SAT, but it didn't survive the 2020 Project. In retrospect, it might be easy to blame people who thought like your birther, although that's not really fair. When the 2020 Project was first announced, it had total support from the Elect. No one doubted it, or at least no one spoke up with their doubts. And then it brought down each and every person who created it."

"I remember that," Quinceton said. He folded his arms, bending his head down. "My birther was picked up at an emergency meeting to discuss the correctives to the 2020 Project, but they never even gave her a chance. Charged her with Racism, just like everyone else who added to that thing, and I never saw her again. Busloads of the Elect were carted off to DIE, and all I got was a notice in the mail that she'd been found guilty of this and that."

"I'm sorry, Quinceton," Sarah replied. "That's just awful. I hope you get to see her again … I hope they start letting people come back after they go to DIE."

"But why did the 2020 Project fail to bring equity?" Quinceton pressed on, pushing hope aside in search of truth, or at least a rumor that had to be hushed. "How did they label it 'Racist' if they had the same goals as the Work Doing initiative?"

Bones rotated abruptly, failing to hide a smile from Quinceton. "I'm sorry, but you had to actually read the shit they rolled out with the 2020 Project. I mean, there's no way I can do it justice now. Have you ever heard the term 'Ebonics'? You guys know all about 'lived experience,' and how promoting certain lived experiences is what 'doing the work' is all about, but do you remember anything about how they combined it with Saint Floyd?"

The other two nodded in response. "We learned all about Saint Floyd," Sarah assured him. "What do you mean?"

"Well, in the past, his death would have been covered in history class, or maybe civics. But the 2020 Project platformed the lived experiences of erased victims like Saint Floyd to the exclusion of basically everything else. And they did so in a form of English known previously as Ebonics, a mostly spoken African American slang that few people actually used. So instead of a test question being something like 'Who killed Saint Floyd?' you'd read 'Who dat homey don off'd free dog Floyd?' My accent is terrible, but you get the idea. The 2020 Project intended to promote Black equity through slang and highlighting things they figured Black people had a cultural advantage already knowing about. BIPOC knowledge supposedly replacing whiteness was supposed to reverse what groups got the good grades. You can probably guess what happened next, if you don't remember."

"Total fucking shit show," Sarah muttered.

"Yeah, this I do remember," Quinceton said. "People were furious. Maybe Black people were the most pissed. My classmates knew my birther was involved, and they just let me have it—'You don't think we can speak English?' or 'What, math and science are too smart for us?' It was constant, even after they buried the 2020 Project." He paused, deep in reverie. "Dad would've been so proud."

"That's what I saw," Bones confirmed. "I didn't know that many Blacks outside work, but I saw the demonstrations. Was Xumwaza even a Speaker before he rode the outrage to Knowing Leader? I can't remember. He had to at least be Elect."

"The whites I knew made no protest against the 2020 Project or the corrective measures," Sarah said. "They basically just went with whatever, without really studying much of it."

"But a lot of the Yellows did," Quinceton remembered. "Those damn Asians just studied it like a new language, a set of historical facts. I think that's really what fucked the whole thing—the Asians still getting the best grades. If they'd gotten the equity they wanted, the 2020 Project might have survived."

"Was Saint Floyd the only reason they labeled it with 2020?" Sarah asked.

"No, definitely not." Bones shook his head side to side in a slow exaggeration as he dumped some rice into the boiling pot. "That was the year when the old Republic really started to crumble. We got our first preview of the kind of 'direct action' that the AAA runs on today as major cities caved to mobs and the takeover of public spaces was orchestrated by autonomous actors. The idea of armed citizens running their own traffic checkpoint—usually demanding some small gesture of solidarity, like the raised fist, in the beginning—was really unthinkable prior to 2020. The country had all different ideas about it at the time, but people everywhere were livid about something or other, and no one really knew what to trust.

"There were riots every day and billions of credits of property was destroyed that summer, and while the ZNN news people of the day called them 'mostly peaceful protests,' their media rivals saw it as Armageddon's arrival. The divisions of 2020 pit neighbor against neighbor on an increasingly identitarian or ideological basis, and that anger has been used ever since to introduce one new decolonization initiative after another."

"Yeah, like the 'Violence' poster of the Knowing Leader Jumping Bull," Sarah added. "The Americans exaggerated to make him uglier, but they got the identitarian warfare part right by turning him into some kind of cannibalistic puppeteer. And they seem to know what goes on inside New California at least as well as we do."

Quinceton thought hard about being a Black student and being told about how Racist the world was, and how much it could consume some BIPOC kids while the privileged ones got to study and think without all that distraction.

"What if expecting and believing in Racism makes people act up?" Quinceton wondered out loud. "The more someone thinks the world isn't fair to them, the more they give up on themselves. Imagine a Black kid in San Francisco, thinking the white supremacist world will never give him a fair shot … so, he has a great excuse to give up, believe his effort won't be worth it, and feel okay about getting outworked by the untargeted groups. The message to victim groups doesn't ever change—Racism against them is promised, forever and ever—and it could cause a Racist reality of different groups acting differently, with different grades and stuff in schooling … and it sure won't end Racism to guarantee different groups act differently. But assuming Racism is your only problem could be used to keep the races as different as possible."

Bones just nodded slowly. It was a ton to absorb, but what felt most true about the story was the constant rage. In every JSS government speech Quinceton had ever heard, there was always an enemy to be feared and/or hunted and destroyed, even if the enemy was not a person but a group or concept. Quinceton considered all the cancellations he'd seen, and how everyone who drew the wrath of the Elect were called Racists even if they'd spent their whole life thinking they were fighting Racism, like his birther.

Whatever faith he had that he would meet her again faded into the harsh reality of the room, the smoke billowing through a diseased hole above, while he waited to spoon rice out of boiling water on the scarred floor of an abandoned Work Doing Station. He wasn't quite sure what he thought of it all and couldn't know that any of Bones's words were true, but he nonetheless resolved to welcome all new information, believe no public proclamation without silent scrutiny, and burrow deeper into all the hows and whys of his world.

ACT II, CHAPTER FIVE

Refugees, Deserters, Exiles

BREAKFAST WAS THE SAME RICE, albeit much cooler this time, as Bones pitched a southern route to keep some elevation.

"We're beyond the biggest mountains. If we head west, we could reach the Central Valley by this evening, and that means we're more likely to get raided by the AAA as we sleep. They should let us go, but who knows with the AAA. I think we go south instead, keeping high enough to make them work if they want to find us. It'll also be much cooler than the scorching valley."

"Second that," Quinceton said. He'd already spent enough sweat in those fields and had no love for 115-degree heat.

They packed up with practiced speed and cut south across Placerville. The sight of rusting cars, broken storefront windows, and collapsed roofs made Quinceton feel like an alien explorer of lost American humanity. Here, weeds rose through cracked pavement with newborn innocence; sidewalks crumbled all over San Francisco but little grew in the cracks, as any gap in SF concrete was tainted with refuse, urine, and rodent grime. There was no apparent reason why the town Quinceton presently admired should be such an unhappy place, but maybe it was just an illusion created by the previous dominance of whiteness. Even so, Quinceton could imagine working in one of these capitalist product storage buildings or eating in one of these cafeterias, and maybe even kinda liking it.

After a few hours of uphill trekking, they reached a narrow rocky creek that led to a decent-sized pond—a perfect scene to enjoy with lunch. A collection of branches, mud, stones, and leaves barricaded the water before it spilled into another stream that kept rolling west, toward the valley and the city beyond.

"Interesting," Bones said as he walked around, inspecting the barricade.

Quinceton admired the details of the scene without comment. The pond looked deep enough to swim in, but he didn't really feel like getting wet before embarking on another hike. Instead, he passed some stored rice to Sarah and took enough bites to satiate himself, nothing more. Eventually Bones joined in, too, and they sat in silence, enjoying the sunshine beaming down on water clear enough to see a few fish darting back and forth.

"Back in a minute," Quinceton said, grabbing some toilet paper and army-issued gel sanitizer without the slightest effort to obscure his intentions with other gear. He wandered downhill past the makeshift barricade, looking for a solid log on flat ground he could sit on. The stream reached a fork, with one current running naturally and the other obstructed by a makeshift metal valve stuck in the dirt with a handle attached at the top to regulate it.

In comparison to the free-flowing stream, what passed through this water gate was barely a trickle. He followed the trickle as it wound around to far more level ground with a large clearing in the distance and quickly found a fallen tree to support his weight. As Quinceton sat, leaned forward, and proceeded to defecate, he took a deep breath and smelled California pine. This wasn't his favorite part of roughing it in the woods, but it sure beat the outhouses and overflowing porta-potties he'd seen all too much of in his young life. Looking down at the dirt made this almost feel clean.

"Hi." A soft voice not far from his scalp. "Who are you?"

It was a child, a little girl maybe ten years old with jet-black hair wearing an oversized pink T-shirt, shoes that appeared to be knitted, and a blank stare of casual regard. He had seen her race before, but not in some time—

perhaps years, as purebloods of her hue were so closely associated with the JSS government withdrawal that those who remained survived on a low profile, discouraging all forms of attention as a precursor to DIE. She had tan off-white skin somewhat lighter than a Mexican laborer, with different eyes and a big forehead. *One of the Yellows.*

"Ummm," Quinceton mumbled, buying time. He leaned even farther forward to mask his lowered pants. "Are either of your parents around? Can you tell them I'm lost?"

"My parents aren't here, but my grandfather is close. I can tell him you're here." The girl stood straight as a Speaker yet wore a shirt that looked to be sewn from thick dyed thread, which was probably what she wore on her feet too. She spoke with a calm that suggested she had nothing to fear, that she wasn't even aware that fear was something powerful people imposed and maintained. Unfamiliar Yellow words poured from her in a controlled shout as she spun in the opposite direction.

"Yeah, thanks," Quinceton said, rushing to wipe and pull his pants up as soon as she turned her back. Whoever the little girl called out for had to be close by; he didn't have much time.

He was still wiping his hands with sanitizer gel when an ancient Oriental man approached with a gait that looked spry enough to fit the legs of a teenager. He carried a crossbow that looked to be homemade, as the loaded arrow had clearly been cut and carved out of forest wood, and a small brown metal box impaled by random wires of assorted colors. The little girl stood at his side with the same nonchalant expression she'd worn when she burst in on Quinceton's dump.

"Who are you?" he asked with an accent Quinceton didn't recognize but could easily understand. "Deserters? JSS? You aren't one of the AAA."

"I'm Quinceton, and I'm one of the survivors from the Battle of South Lake. Did you hear any explosions a couple days ago?" The ancient man ignored the question and aimed the bow directly at Quinceton's forehead.

"Don't move. Where are the others? What do you want?"

"We just wandered here trying to get back to the valley without running into the AAA—we don't know what they've heard about the battle and we don't want to trigger them. We just want to be safe, to have good food to eat and a good place to sleep, you know—we just want to live, man."

"Show me the others," the geezer said as he pointed back up toward the pond with the crossbow. "You just go poo?"

"I did."

"Clean up your feces. Use dirt to cover, leaves also. Then show me the others."

Quinceton climbed over the log to the dirty side, kicked some dirt onto his mess, then gathered some leaves and dropped them on top of it all.

"Yeah, sorry about this," Quinceton said. "I didn't know anyone was around here." The old man's shoulders eased—though there wasn't much there even at his most intimidating—and lowered his crossbow slightly.

"It's okay, Mai, he's not one of the AAA." The little girl looked just as nonplussed as she had before and followed closely behind her grandfather as Quinceton, arms raised, guided them back to the pond.

"Sarah, Bones!" Quinceton called out while still a good dozen yards shy of his companions. "Don't shoot, just stay calm. I met some people, but we can work this out."

Sarah emerged with her rifle aimed at the Yellow man. "Drop the bow," she demanded, "and we can talk." Quinceton couldn't see the old man. He listened to his own breathing as he waited.

"Holy *shit,* is that a radio??" Bones cried out, emerging on the scene like a puppy, panting and oblivious. His rifle hung loosely on his back; he didn't seem to care about the threat of force on either side as he stared at the small metal box in the older man's hands. Bones removed his firearm and laid it on the ground at his feet, where it slowly tumbled down the hill toward the Yellows and Quinceton. "Sarah, drop your gun. This man is my hero."

Bones raised his hands and approached the Orientals with a wide smile as they stood motionless, watching him, likely judging him for their own protection.

"Pick up the rifle," he said to the ancient man. "But you won't need it with us. It's okay. I was one of you, and still would be if I were as brave. I've been a Liberati since the beginning."

The harsh stoicism of the old man's face broke into an open-mouthed expression of startled ecstasy—*Could this really be happening?* it seemed to say. His right hand opened to drop the crossbow as it extended toward Bones.

"John nine twenty-five," he said.

"One thing I do know: I was blind, but now I see," Bones replied. He opened his arms wide. "John eight, thirty-two."

"The truth will set you free." The ancient man abandoned the handshake to embrace Bones with a bear hug, like he was welcoming a long-lost son back from the dead.

ACT II, CHAPTER SIX

The Cabin on the Mountain

AS QUINCETON WATCHED BONES INTERROGATE his fellow Liberati about
the mountainside setup, the young man wondered whether he'd ever had a
friend with whom he was so damn simpatico. The way these guys interacted
impressed him with their immediate intimacy; the two men went from a
hug to a sort of student and tour guide relationship, with Bones following
his host around the pond. No one seemed to mind the tense standoff that
had interrupted Quinceton's otherwise satisfying dump. The child followed
loosely behind her kin but seemed preoccupied by the different-shaped
stones on the ground, pocketing at least two that Quinceton witnessed.

Sarah's gun hung limp at her side. She still looked dumbfounded, totally ignored by the rest of them, as the rifle now seemed as dangerous as a
daffodil. She could shove it straight up her ass for all anyone gave a damn.

"I figured Bones for an Anti-Anti-Racist Liberati from the jump," she
said to Quinceton. "But I had no idea he was a Christian. You pick up on
that?"

"I didn't see it before, and I'm not sure what he really believes, but using Bible words makes sense to identify each other," Quinceton answered.
"And I didn't know the Anti-Anti-Racists had a name for themselves; I've
never heard that word 'Liberati' before. You know what that's all about?
The Liberati thing?"

"I think it came from the old word 'liberal,' as in, like, 'liberal values,' combined with 'Illuminati,' a secret organization that started to protect freedom of thought in Old Europe. Liberals used to dominate in California, especially cities like SF. Stuff like 'everyone gets to speak,' and so you could mention ideas without having to be prescreened for past victimhood, and you didn't have to submit to someone with better Standpoint position. So the Anti-Anti-Racists—before they went into hiding or stopped having the ability to make arguments against the JSS government—they tried to adopt the name Liberati to remind the Elect of where they came from. And what they'd disgraced."

"This all goes so deep," Quinceton marveled. It thrilled him, actually, realizing how many layers there were to society, and how differently everyone thought once you got outside a place where everyone had to pretend to think the same way. Dad understood all this from the beginning. "But I wanna find out more—if they get into it again, you gotta get me, or tell me everything later. And I'll do the same for you."

"Deal."

Quinceton and Sarah climbed back up to the pond but didn't speak, not wanting to interrupt.

"Yeah, you know, I figured there had to be people around," Bones said in his most comfortable tone, "because this dam was too tight to be done by nature, but not quite so good as to implicate beavers. I'm Phil, by the way, but they call me Bones."

"Yes, my granddaughter, Mai, helped me, but it needs attention. The current carries most everything downstream eventually. And I'm Tinh, with an *H*, but Mai calls me *ong noi*, 'grandfather' in Vietnamese." Everything was said with smiles.

"Well, it's a pretty good spot, this pond. D'you come up here to use that radio? Ever get any reception? And how do you power it?"

"Once you have the quartz crystal and copper coils, you can pick up radio waves, but using the quartz to find the right frequency is very difficult. It is my project, my next big project, to contact the outside. We have rechargeable batteries, but to charge them is very difficult. We use hydro power, but it is slower now. Not as much water as a few years ago. Come here, I will show you." The old Oriental turned to the young girl, said something in another language, and pointed downhill. Bones asked something about magnetic field rotation as Mai followed, Sarah and Quinceton not far behind.

"Any idea what they're talking about?" Sarah asked her fellow sniper.

"I don't know how they're doing it, but the super-old guy, Tinh, he's up to some illegal shit and Bones can't get enough. Have you ever heard of anyone contacting the outside? I've seen people get sent off to DIE just for building a little raft, not even a boat." They reached the downstream fork and Quinceton relaxed to see Tinh trek the free-flowing side, away from the slow trickle and log he'd used for private business.

"No, never seen any device that could reach outsiders," Sarah confirmed. "But I do know one guy who joined the AAA, and he was always talking about technology they were developing to make a radio impossible in California, and how much DIE someone would get if they ever pulled it off." Quinceton groaned with some volume. JSS government technology usually guarded against tech from the past in order to stop something in the present, rather than creating a new and better thing for the future.

The downhill current eventually reached a modest one-story house, where it passed through a giant spinning wheel propelled by water. The building sat against thick tree cover but shone with a pride Quinceton hadn't seen in ages. The building seemed to have been repainted in the last few seasons, with shutters all hanging in their proper place, and a sign on the front door read "WELCOME, FRIEND." A rainbow collage of flowers adorned the front around a black metal door, with ivy rising from the ground to cradle the cottage.

"We get electricity from here," the Yellow man said to Bones, sweeping a hand across the water wheel. "The wheel spins the rotor of a generator inside. I had to build some of it myself, but I brought many pieces with me from the city. I had more help in those days ... but Mai is good help. She has grown up here."

"It's a different way to live, but I can dig it," Bones replied. "Your house is very good-looking. Are you part of a larger community? Are Mai's parents inside?"

"No," said the old Oriental, glancing quickly at Mai, then at the ground, then back to Bones. "Come inside and we will talk. Your friends, too." He turned back to his granddaughter, who watched the interaction with polite concern. "Mai, go pick some food for dinner. The tomatoes should be ripe, and check the asparagus."

"Yes, ong noi," the little girl said before grabbing a plastic basket near the flowers and scampering back up the hill.

"Come inside," the Yellow man instructed, opening the door to his cabin and ushering his three companions inside. Quinceton walked through the entryway and was promptly plunged into a scene of picturesque rustic serenity: a rectangular wood table with rounded edges in the middle of the room with a fireplace behind it, a kitchen to the left with a hand pump attached to the spout on the sink faucet, and four bunk beds dodging windows to the right. A door next to the kitchen probably led to another room or two, while a pair of rocking chairs adorned the scene on either side of the fireplace. One sat empty while the other was filled with a bundle of blankets. Suddenly, it spoke.

"*Baizuo?*" said the blankets. Quinceton knew this word from his youth—it meant something like "white Elect" in Chinese, but it didn't take long for the term to spread beyond just the Yellows. It had been used widely by angry residents of New California to describe JSS government Elect and ZNN mouthpieces the speaker didn't like, usually for some new plan that centered Anti-Racism even further in the dialogue of decolonization. When he heard it again now, Quinceton thought about the shaved-headed womxn in the hot dog line that Smythe had sent off to DIE.

The young sniper looked closer and saw a pair of eyes emerge from the coils of fabric, connected to a face and head. The person underneath all that cotton ignored him as she stared back and forth from Sarah to Bones with skin that appeared to be prehistoric. She was easily the oldest human Quinceton had ever seen—she had to be at least one hundred and ten.

Their host responded in rapid Asian speech, not one word decipherable, but the message was apparently something like *It's chill*. Then, turning to the whites, he said, "I apologize for my son's wife's grandmother. She grew up in China, then moved to the California Bay Area, where she grew to fear the *baizuo*. White people still frighten her sometimes. I'm sorry."

Bones raised his open palms, stepped forward, and sat in the other rocking chair, facing hers. "It's alright," he said slowly, as though he spoke to a baby. "I'm a Liberati, like your son. We are not baizuo; we are the opposite of baizuo. We will not hurt you. In fact, if there's any way we can help out around here … anything we can do, we'd be happy to do."

The ossified old womxn gave a snort, something that sounded like a targeted *harrumph*, at Bones. "Trust a snake before American president," she announced with conviction. "Trust American president before Communist dictator. But never trust the *baizuo*." With that, she closed her eyes and leaned her head back into a quilt cocoon, point clearly made. It had to be a good eighty degrees inside, but back underneath the blankets she went.

"It's her favorite expression," Tinh said, slightly flustered but likely comforted by Quinceton's immediate laughter.

"Awesome," Quinceton assured him. "I wouldn't trust these crackers, either, if I didn't have to. But they sure ain't baizuo."

"Yeah, it's all good," Sarah added, advancing slowly on the bunk beds.

"Yes, you will sleep there as long as you like," Tinh offered. "I have a bedroom in back, and Mai has her own room, too, but these beds are very good beds. They have not been used in a long time."

"You part of the Rooftop Railroad, then?" Quinceton asked, taking a gray metal chair at the wood table. He felt a bit surprised he was comfortable enough to proffer a query that, in the wrong circumstance, was punishable by immediate humane dispatchment.

"It was Mai's parents, my son and his wife. They were Anti-Anti-Racist Liberati, too, and helped many people leave through the mountains. There was a time, just after the Intersectional Equity Law, when there were so many people here, we started to dig tunnels through the mountain on both sides of the cabin." The old guy shuffled to the kitchen, pumped some water into an electric boiler hot pot, and plugged it into something which had to connect to the stream-generated power source. "We will have tea and I will tell you. Sit, sit."

The three soldiers removed their packs and placed them along with their rifles on the bunk beds, then immediately obliged their host and relocated to the table. It was unclear if the prehistoric womxn heard the suggestion, as the blankets didn't stir.

"What's the plan here, guys?" Sarah said at standard volume, loud enough for the tea maker to hear it all. "They seem as nice as can be, but this is off-the-grid living. You think we put them in danger being here?"

"They're already Liberati," Bones reminded her, "so what more trouble can they be in if they get caught? What, you think the AAA goons will forget the public humiliation and just give them an endless DIE lecture until they croak?"

"I'd prefer gallows," Tinh called from the kitchen.

Quinceton noticed something different about Bones, who was the only one to hear Tinh's words as a joke. It had started from the moment he'd met another Liberati at the pond, and it was striking how easily his barriers of suspicion came down to speak freely to this new, yet old political acquaintance. This trust contrasted sharply from that first night, when Bones had snapped at Sarah for using the term "Anti-Anti-Racist." Even in his best moods, Bones had never really relaxed as he did now, sitting back in his chair with a soft grin.

"No matter what, we can always head back and no one will ask any questions once we get there." Quinceton looked directly at Bones. "And you can do whatever you want, live wherever you need to, and we'll just say you fled east or died in the woods on the way."

"My death would be good for the equity numbers, too," Bones agreed and, turning back to Sarah, added, "so I don't have a plan, but I want to help them out for a little bit, at least. Probably some heavier lifting when it comes to midsummer farming we can do."

"Digging to direct irrigation flow was the hardest work, and pulling a disc to turn over the fields happens mostly in spring," Tinh replied, arriving at the table with a silver kettle, a small wooden box, and four porcelain coffee cups with white bags of superfine mesh in each. He filled them with crumbled dry green leaves from the box—perhaps his special supply—and poured steaming water on top to complete the arcane recipe. "But we can use you. And you can stay here as long as you want—all of you. No problem."

"Fancy," Quinceton said as he took a careful sip. "And thank you, sir."

"Welcome. Been so long since I was called 'sir.' You're welcome. Now, your names?"

"I'm Quinceton, and she's Sarah. You met Bones. I came up with his nickname, but you can use it whenever you want."

"We're all introduced, all familiar now," Bones said, leaning into the table but not reaching for his tea. "So, Tinh, please tell us your story: what you did back in the old world, why you came here, and … what happened to your son and Mai's mother. And you gotta tell me about that radio, though I can't imagine you're getting much from it yet. When you're ready."

"My story probably starts a lot like yours. I worked a good job, as an engineer in tech, before the Great Rupture. When the Great Rupture happened and California officially broke off from the United States, I did not know what to expect, but most of my family lived in the Bay Area, all of us many different ages, and so we didn't leave when we all could. We watched them pick apart advanced education for Anti-Racism even before the Rupture—that's when my family started to notice politics. We stayed even when the JSS government got rid of the rest of real education, because we could teach our kids at home, and we would be very valuable in a world where no one knew how to divide numbers or write words. But when they passed the Intersectional Equity Law, that was it. It was like socialism, only based in identity, so maybe even worse. We had to leave then. We didn't think it would be so violent so quickly, but we could see some of the things Dr. Pithawalla warned about."

Quinceton had never imagined he would hear such straightforward heresy. Compared to Tinh, Bones was basically a professional virtue-signaling Elect who'd just de-cockified and replaced their genitals with a rhino horn to invent a new gender for career advancement.

"But why here?" Bones asked. "If you're going to skip town, why not go all the way across the border?"

"That was what we intended to do, even though we did not know what to expect. My last job for the JSS government was to help disconnect all communication with the outside world, mainly detaching from the internet—"

"The biggest and easiest way to communicate back in the day," Bones interrupted to explain to Sarah and Quinceton. "You could send messages or talk to people in different states instantly, and with video." It still sounded impossible to Quinceton, but he'd heard these claims before. "Sorry, Tinh, please continue. What'd they do with the internet?"

"The hardest part was to cut the intercontinental Ethernet cables under the ocean, but I didn't have to do that—swimmers did. Cutting the ones between states was easier, but we also had to destroy radio towers, so I got to drive around California and visit many mountain peaks. Gas was valuable then, but not as rare as it became. I also remembered that separating people from communicating was a way of forcing government policy by separating people, preventing them from organizing around other beliefs. I was born during the Vietnam War, and it reminded me of the split between North and South, dividing many families and forcing people to join whatever side controlled their land. We didn't have a choice, just like after the Great Rupture. So, I expected to be a refugee again, this time escaping California, and I used the drives around California to figure out ways to leave. We were more prepared when they passed the Intersectional Socialism law."

"Smart," Bones said. "I was stuck in place with a young daughter. But then why'd you all wind up here? Why not go all the way to Arizona or Nevada?"

"Had to be all those warnings, right?" Quinceton offered. He vividly remembered a huge ZNN news campaign decorating streetlights and statues of Knowers all over the city. "You guys see those signs everywhere, something like 'Traitors to California will be sent to DIE, deserters will be shot at the border'? It was the pictures that did it for me. Photos of people with big backpacks getting shot by Americans as soon as they left, bodies piled up like we saw in South Lake." Tinh couldn't have known about the recent battle, but he understood anyway.

"Of course, if those pictures were real, who took them? And how'd they ever get back to us?" Sarah had a point. "Maybe some of what they said was true about the Americans, but some of it seemed so fake. Staged, even."

"Who knows," Bones said, not really as a question.

"Not us," Tinh replied, "and we decided to leave anyway. We didn't know what we'd find in America, but we had to leave, so we did. Same as in California, only this time there was no boat, so much easier. There was a plan to go through the mountains, but when we found this place, well, we stopped one night and I've lived here with Mai and her great-grandmother ever since."

"Mai's parents kept going to Nevada?" Sarah asked.

"No. They stayed here, too, but took many risks. When we found this place, it was mostly empty, but clean, and had the beds already. It was a gift from God, but my son—he and his wife—wanted to help other California refugees." Tinh paused and took a careful sip of his steaming drink.

"After we explored the area, my son snuck back to the East Bay, to my sister's family, and told them about this house, how to get here, and how close we are to the Nevada border. My son gave directions how to get here, using landmarks like nearby towns but no map—he is very smart. The new California JSS government elites, the Elect—increasingly stupid compared to the American version of Elect—they did not expect to have so many people leave, and at first they did not want to stop it, because when so many people leave, they leave everything behind, and most of the Elect got new houses and condos. At least it was finally a solution to the California housing crisis, and without the economy to support illegal drugs, no houseless addict problem, either. The AAA were still called 'Antifa' in those days, but there were not so many of them that the ruling Anti-Racists had to give them something to make them feel important. That was the best time to leave, but we stayed here to help many others as a part of the Rooftop Railroad."

Each sentence Tinh spoke provoked questions in Quinceton's mind that the experienced man only hurtled past with more and more revelations. *Why would the JSS government want or promote stupidity, or why should their elites lack intelligence?* Quinceton didn't get that. He had seen the AAA rise in stature, beginning as a fringe group of impatient former Anti-Racists who remained tacitly supportive of the JSS government's equity goals but promoted a more aggressive timeline and methods. They first gained a place in government through vigilante direct action campaigns, then by stocking the ranks of Community Safety patrolpersons and staffing the DIE Camps. If the ruling Anti-Racist Elect were afraid of anything in California—other than the rise of white supremacy, however real it was—it had to be the AAA thugs, as they spoke the same uncompromising language, but with a fiercer, scowling tone.

"Wait, wait," Quinceton interjected, "why would the JSS government want their top people, their Elect, to be dumb? How does that help achieve anything?"

Sarah looked as interested in the answer as Quinceton was, but the question broke the stony expressions on the faces of the other two men. Bones, battling back a deep chuckle, took the first stab at an explanation.

"Well, I'm not sure they actually have to *be* dumb; they just have to act that way. They have to swallow ideas which are so obviously doomed to immanent failure, and do so with gratitude and enthusiasm. The Elect, under the JSS government, did not become elite the way the Old Americans did—either by making a lot of money doing something valuable, or by marrying or being born from someone who did. These Elect are there to support and execute on the Speakers' and the Knowers' wants, whatever they are, and whatever next initiative they're centering in the equity crusade.

"So, if you're Elect and your race is terrible—white, Asian, Parsee, whatever—then in order to stay on top, you have to work extra hard to restrict other bad races from rising and making the power structure *in-*

equitable." He looked directly at Tinh. "I should know. I was Elect for a while, working in surveillance tech and keeping my mouth shut until I got confused and was cancelled anyway."

"I understand," Tinh offered as consolation. "Yes, I agree. I don't think all Elect actually have to be stupid. But they do have to stay silent when bad ideas are first proposed, and stay supportive when they start failing." Quinceton remembered the violence poster hanging from Harvey's, and how much of that image really applied in some way to their world.

"Like the Intersectional Socialism law," Bones added. "The more it failed, the more the Elect had to voice their support. Whether their identity group benefitted or not, they *all* sat atop a JSS government system that dispensed power based more on loyalty to dogma than anything else. Your skills, or your trade, as we might call it back in the day, didn't matter so much, because the Intersectional Equity laws eliminated a free market to sell your work at a fair price. A price determined by demand, like with the Federals."

"But didn't that lead to massive inequality?" Sarah asked. "You're talking about American capitalism, yeah? We were taught that American capitalism caused more Racism and inequity than any other system ever invented." A beat of silence passed. Quinceton smelled his tea and drank. It was slightly bitter—fresh, though, with a subtle hint of pine, pine needles, or maybe mint, like the special toothpaste they got from workmasters for good deeds.

"Yes and no," Bones finally answered. "It's more complicated than I can probably do justice to right now. You gotta know America invented their special brand of Black-white Racism to justify slavery, which ran in direct contradiction of many founding principles in their constitution. Slavery was all over the world when America was invented—every race had been enslaved at one point or another in history—but the African slave market had been set up for the Arab world well before the founding of the United States, and so Africans were the cheapest slaves to use for labor in the New World.

"It was a long, bloody sin the country never recovered from. The founding principles later led to the end of slavery over the Civil War, and then it took a hundred years for Blacks to achieve anything close to equal rights in America with MLK and other self-sacrificing Americans. But a few decades later, when all seemed to head in the right direction—when Blacks existed in every industry and downright dominated many, and after we had a Black president—things broke down again. Over identity, again, just with a different logic, a different goal, and a different set of winners and losers."

"Yes," Tinh said. "I agree. We had many good years in America before it all fell apart."

Quinceton could hardly believe his luck, but he wasn't entirely surprised that the opportunity he'd waited for since childhood finally emerged with these two Liberati.

"MLK!" he exclaimed with a passion that pushed against the table between them. "I know of the American king! My dad told me about him. My dad was probably a Liberati, too, and he loved the American king."

"Me too," Bones said with a bemused smile. "He wasn't a king like some all-powerful ruler, but his name was Dr. Martin Luther King, and he was a Christian preacher while he became famous for demanding, and ultimately achieving, legal equality between races."

"But he was cancelled?" Sarah said, her voice rising into a query.

"Well, he was a Christian, for starters," Tinh began. "But he also said people should be judged for who they are, what they do, not what they look like." This rang familiar to Quinceton, echoing something from long ago, but it was just about the purest verbalization of colorblind Racism in today's world.

Bones nodded along, reminding Quinceton of his father when he spoke. "You know, when we believed that, when we were still on the MLK page of judging others by the 'content of their character,' as it was, America functioned ... well, not perfectly, but better than ever before. Better and better, and with more opportunity for the individual than they could find anywhere else. And once the individual became just one representative of a larger group that politicians could politicize, it all came crashing down with too much animosity to bother with another unifying revolution."

"So that's how it happened?" Quinceton asked. "People from different states hated each other so much, they didn't want to be 'United States' anymore?"

"Again, that's a yes and no, but basically ... kind of," Bones continued. "It had more to do with the two big political parties and the rise of competing identitarian movements—the evolution of racial grievances into the total takeover of the identitarian grifter class. That's who made 'equity' the top, and usually only, goal of governments like the JSS, replacing pesky things like progress, efficiency, and basic human flourishing."

"Identitarian—I know that word," Quinceton whispered, mostly to himself. "If America was doing so well, how did the identitarians take power? 'Grifters,' you called them? Like con artists?"

"I like this talk, but the sun will go down soon," Tinh said in his serene voice of total authority. "Mai might need some help in the garden, and her great-grandmother needs to be ... cleaned before dinner." Quinceton suspected he was referring to a diaper of some kind. He had barely noticed her shrouded presence since they'd first entered. "Please give me some time alone in the house and come back with food for dinner."

"You got it," Quinceton answered, swiftly rising, barely able to contain his elation. He couldn't wait to eat so he could keep probing back into the past. It was as if he'd never before spent a day in a Work Doing Center, never spent a day being educated—their words explained so many things he'd constantly wondered about, worried about, and wanted to know. His spirit surged with a strange sort of pride that healed a buried wound, raising the real possibility that his father was no cowardly traitor, but a principled individual their jangled society couldn't bend.

ACT II, CHAPTER SEVEN

Garden Daydream

"I THINK SHE WENT UP this way," Quinceton called to Sarah and Bones as they exited the house, his quick pace halting to wait up for their slow asses. "Mai went up here, to the left, I think … you can see where footsteps are worn into the grass."

"Hold your horses, man," Bones grumbled, working out the kinks in his stiff old legs by lunging forward with a hamstring stretch in each stride.

"You can go on ahead," Sarah assured Quinceton. "I'll make sure he makes it up there alive, with or without a wheelchair."

Quinceton arrived on the agriculture scene to find a gated wildlife fence about his height protecting a long rectangular field with different colors and shapes sprouting from the Earth. On the fringe of the garden, Mai knelt in the dirt beside a little mound of harvested vegetables, wearing a hat of woven branches decorated with flowers. She seemed to be comparing different carrots.

"Hello," she said in the same cheerful voice Quinceton had heard the first time around, when it was she who pulled the surprise appearance.

"What's that hat you've got on?"

"This is my crown. I'm the princess of this forest. All the food and animals are free to grow and live here, but I'm the princess."

Quinceton nodded in sincere agreement. "I can see that. You are the princess. Can I join you?"

"If you want to," Mai said, thinking it over. "Ong noi is the king, but you could be a knight."

"I want to be a knight. What do I have to do?"

"Well, you already have armor on," she answered, referring to his JSS government soldier shirt. "But you need something to wear on your head."

Quinceton looked around his feet and found two straight sticks of roughly the same length, just over six inches. He tucked one above each ear. "How's this?"

She gave the twigs a solid once-over. "It's okay. But it would be better with flowers or leaves, too."

"You're right," Quinceton said. "Let me know if you find anything better." As Sarah and Bones approached, he pointed to his twigs. "I was just knighted by the princess of the forest here. I don't know if there's much room left in the kingdom for you, but you can ask."

Bones gave the little girl a wide grin and asked, "Is there a prince around here? I am, after all, known as a perfect gentlemen."

Mai shot him a stern, searching look, then shook her head. "No. Sorry, you don't look like a prince. But maybe you could be a wizard."

Bones's face fell into histrionic dismay as he clutched at his heart. "Oh, *ouch*. I could grow a pretty good beard, but it's been a while since I could do my best magic." He pointed at Sarah, who loomed in the background. "What about her? I don't think she's queen material. Maybe another princess?"

"No, I don't think so," Mai concluded after a brief pause, probably judging Sarah's gait. "I think she's a knight, like Quinceton. You can help protect the forest together, and you can use the wizard's magic, too."

"Deal," Sarah said. "But first, we need to help your granddad make dinner. Looks like you already picked carrots, tomatoes, and radish. Can you show me what else you grow here?"

Mai rose and waved Sarah to a farther edge of the field. Different produce had been carefully separated, labeled, and planted in rows on a rare flat section of the sloped mountain. As he took it in, Quinceton was reminded of his time in the Central Valley, only this time shade surrounded the most valuable dirt from which plants arose. He noticed that the borders of the field were not contained so much by the curvature of the hill but by the sunlight now pouring in from the west.

"Hey, you wanna check out the irrigation system they set up?" Bones asked him. "Maybe it can use some rebar, and I wanna see how Tinh controls the flow."

Quinceton shook him off. "Do your thing, I'm going to cut down on this shade. You can see how it's blocking off some sunlight from the edges."

Giving a quick nod, Bones wandered up the mountain, following the trickle that led to the larger stream, as Quinceton pulled out his pocket knife and began cutting lower branches that crept into the cultivated garden soil. The field had some real size to it, but he didn't know what it was in acres, which was how they measured everything in the Central Valley.

It quickly became obvious that the easiest branches to clip were the least intrusive, and he'd have to really get into the middle tier to do real damage. He found a couple trees with enough sturdy lower branches to access the thicker middle ones and was lucky to have a serrated edge on his knife, which cut through wood far more easily. From the perch of one tree, he noticed a particularly intrusive branch already invading the precious dirt from the far side, near Sarah and Mai.

"Yo!" he called from cover, some dozen feet above the ground. "Wanna help me clear some shade? I'm coming down."

Mai wanted to be the monkey who got to climb, but neither of the young knights felt good about it; the princess probably wouldn't fall, but wielding that knife was a different risk. Quinceton was taller than Sarah, but thinner, too, and her shoulders were seriously impressive for a womxn. She put two hands together and boosted Quinceton high enough to grab ahold of a stout limb.

"Watch out below!" Quinceton called as loose branches fell, followed by one larger bough and then another. Mai danced in the floating pine below, singing to herself as she did so. She seemed so happy with so little.

When he looked back up for more branches to cull, there was the same big blue-eyed bug he'd seen from the ski chair tower just before the Battle of South Lake kicked off. The massive insect suspended itself in the air with wings beating so rapidly they were practically invisible, just as before. And just as before, the thing appeared to look directly at Quinceton. *Do bugs have personalities?* he wondered.

"Yo," the sniper said to the fist-sized fly. "There something I can help you out with?"

"What?" Sarah called from below.

"The bug, I mean. It was looking right at me. Just like the one at South Lake. You know what kinda bug that is?"

"I didn't see it. What'd it look like?"

"Never mind," Quinceton said. He'd probably see it again, and when he did, he'd make sure someone else saw it too. "That's all for this tree, but I'm seeing two others we could do."

Mai picked up different twigs as Quinceton carefully climbed back down. The next two trees were much of the same, with even easier boosts to get started, while Mai lingered over the fallen brush, picking at it for some hidden treasure.

"This is one impressive place," Bones announced, casually strolling back into the picture with Quinceton halfway up the final tree. "Sorry I missed the clipping. Tinh's dams are really impressive, though. Could use a little touching up, but the trench they dug to redirect flow here is pretty deep, and looks mostly human-made."

"You can compliment him back at the house," Sarah said with deadpan bluntness. "Mai and I gathered our dinner in a basket. You can carry it back for us." The little girl appeared with a handful of pine twigs, and left the basket for Bones to worry about as Quinceton hoisted himself down from the last tree.

"Kneel, good knight," the forest princess commanded. Quinceton stifled a smirk, dropped to one knee, and bowed his head. Mai added a larger twig behind Quinceton's head to the two already pinned by his ears, fastening the whole thing together with a long piece of peeled bark. Quinceton felt the strips of wood surrounding his cranium and imagined three pillars of pine rising out of his head like the forest bordering this garden. It wasn't comfortable, but he didn't mind; Mai could barely contain her glee, and it had probably been quite some time since she'd last had someone under eighty to play with.

"Now you have a helmet. A knight of the forest needs a forest helmet, and now you are protected!"

"Does Sarah get one too?" Quinceton asked, his head nodding in the other knight's direction. "I think you could fit a lot of twigs in that messy hedge of hair she's got."

"Yes, she gets one, too. A good princess always takes care of her knights."

Sarah, following suit, dropped to one knee and accepted the royal treatment with a bowed head. As Quinceton looked at Mai, he knew damn well he'd never met such a pure soul in his whole life. He couldn't imagine a kid from the city having such a vivid imagination—let alone living with the freedom to use it.

He was struck by a great desire to tell her something useful. He wanted to warn her about the city, to shield her from a world that viewed her race as 'white supremacy-adjacent' with the attending subordinations, but there weren't the words for all that.

"Thank you, good princess," he said as she finished the final touches on Sarah's helmet. "A good princess takes care of her knights, and a good knight doesn't forget their princess."

ACT II, CHAPTER EIGHT

Politics at Dinner

THE SCENE LOOKED MUCH THE same as they'd left it when the four dinner-pickers returned from the field: Tinh at the sink, washing something, and a big pile of laundry in a rocking chair representing great-grandmother. No one stirred when they barged in.

"It was a wild success!" Bones announced to the whole room. "You have a great thing going on up there. How did you install that heavy metal irrigation wall?"

"Came with the house," Tinh replied. "Land was mostly flat already. Bring me the food."

Mai looked restless as Sarah and Bones rushed to help out in the kitchen. "Can I show you my room?" she asked Quinceton, who quickly accepted.

"Nice bedroom," he said approvingly, more polite than honest. Light crept in through one small window, but most came from the attached hallway. He checked around for a switch and finally found one between the hall door and closet. Flipping it ignited a small bulb in the middle of the room, illuminating a single bed, a few picture books on a bedside table, and a floor strewn with finds from outside. She'd built different figures mostly from sticks, leaves, and bark while using tree tops thick with brush to depict landmarks in nature scenes. Smooth stones and patches of moss adorned the floor with color and texture far different from the dark wood of the cabin.

"This is me, the princess," she said, noting one particular figure with a leaf wrapped around its head. She picked up another one with a stone at the top of a stick wrapped in bark. "I sometimes use this as the prince, but he can be a knight now."

"Thank you," Quinceton replied, looking distractedly around the dim room. Mai seemed to want to alleviate his boredom.

"Oh, this is a secret, but I can tell you." She carefully stepped over the sticks and stones to open the closet door. A wooden hatch with a big handle lay on the floor below a rack of different sized garments. Quinceton stepped forward for a closer look.

"Did you and your grandfather build that?"

"Not all of it. We started it when more people were here, but they weren't here long enough to finish the tunnel." Mai sidled past Quinceton into the closet and pulled at the trapdoor, opening it with some effort. Though the covering had to be a square with at least two-foot sides, the hole below was much smaller. It cut through the wood floor beyond some tight insulation foam and right into the dirt below. Mai climbed in, showing Quinceton the depth as all but her head was submerged in the hole.

"Seems to be perfect width for Vietnamese," Quinceton said, thinking more of Tinh than the little girl before him.

"Yes, I can fit, and ong noi can also. I dug the dirt, and he would cut thin logs to support the tunnel below. We finished over a year ago, and now sometimes I go down here to get away. It's like a dungeon—a dungeon in the bottom of the castle. But he doesn't go in here anymore."

"Does the tunnel come out another side?"

"Yes, we finished it. The other end comes out farther down the mountain. Not on the stream side, the other side."

"Makes sense." Quinceton considered the people who had lived here before Mai. How many people could they actually feed with that one field, and for how long? It was so much smaller than what he'd seen across the Central Valley. And who had had the idea to start building a tunnel? Mai seemed to ache for hobbies, her imagination blooming to entertain herself as much as anything, but the people who'd started this secret tunnel had to be planning for something pretty threatening. And since they weren't around when Mai arrived with her family to an empty cottage, all their work and planning evidently hadn't kept them here. Or maybe they escaped.

There was a knock on the door as Sarah appeared with one wonderful word: "Dinnertime."

Someone had set up a short desk-chair combo under the rim of the larger dining room table, and Quinceton sat beside it just before Mai naturally assumed the seat. He and Mai covered the fireplace side of the table, with great-grandmother behind them, Tinh across the table by the front door, and Bones and Sarah at either short end. Tinh scooped their dinner from a large bowl with two big spoons, distributing the assorted vegetable combo onto five plates—if great-grandmother ate, or had any other bodily function, it was not visible to her guests. The top of Mai's head barely reached the table though the desk fit her well.

"Please join hands," Tinh requested, and Quinceton reached out for Mai to his left and Bones to his right as their host delivered what Quinceton's father would have called a "grace." Perhaps one could call it a "toast" or an "offering," but Quinceton had always liked the way Dad said it, the sound of the word.

"Lord, we see and thank you for the many gifts you've given us," Tinh continued. "We are grateful for food on our plates, friends in our home, and love in our hearts."

A brief pause.

"Amen," he said in unison with Bones and Sarah. Quinceton wished he'd joined in, too. He would make sure to remember the word for next time.

They began by complimenting Tinh on the meal, especially his lemony salad dressing, but he brushed off the pleasantries and reminisced about all the best meals he'd had. There was something called "fah" in Vietnam, a few choice crab dishes in the Bay, and a piece of beef he had traded for and "shaken" for his family. Sarah listened quietly, as did Quinceton and

Mai, but Bones interjected with more present longing than fond memory.

"I remember that," he said. "I remember when you could get all different kinds of food from all over the world. I remember when people would compete to have the best restaurants. Of all the things I've lost, I probably miss food the most often. At least two or three times a day."

"Well, why can't ..." Quinceton began, a question begging to burst from his lips but too large to direct into anything specific. "Why can't we all have charcuterie in California?" Noticing the dubious expressions around him, he added, "Not every day, I mean, but sometimes."

"Remember Advi Pithawalla?" Tinh replied. "Same reason."

"Because we lost the will to contribute, to achieve, to strive and succeed," Bones added. "Because there is no market for excellence, there is nothing to trade excellence for, or at least nothing worth trading it for that is worth the risk of standing out."

Tinh nodded. "Yes. Imagine you were the best cook in California—how would that help you and your family?"

"Exactly," Bones interrupted. "You could cook for Elect banquets, you could even rise to be *Knowing Leader* Kendaoi's personal cook, but that means exposure. Other Elect will taste your cooking soon, they'll get jealous, and then it's only a matter of time before your skill becomes a living, breathing example of *inequity*. No special skill can survive before it makes someone feel inferior to you, which means unequal ... which means your final reward is *DIE*." Some sacred words were said with such venom that Quinceton winced at the open defiance.

"It's true," Sarah agreed, "I don't know how many times my family warned me not to stand out, not to do anything that could lead to personal credit. Unless you did it in secret, your expertise would expose whatever privilege you'd been born with, and then that—rather than your talent—would become the ultimate conclusion about your life. Off to DIE. The charcuterie we ate was probably churned out of some big system with many people so no one would be marked for accommodation." She hesitated, looking at Bones. "And Kendaoi is a goner, remember? It's Knowing Leader Xumwaza Q. Jumping Bull now."

Tinh raised a hand to stifle further explanation.

"Please," he said, "I am too old to worry about current California politicians. I do not care. If the new leader leads the JSS government, I already know all I want to know; please don't tell me any more."

"Well, *I* want to know more about the old Federal California," Quinceton piped up. His itch for this moment had only gained momentum after their cup of tea, and the old men seemed to enjoy the past more than anything in the present. "Why couldn't we keep the good things about the old world—like the food, like the push to be the best—while also fighting for Social Justice?"

"C'mon, kid, time to wake up," Bones snorted as Tinh filled his fork with veggies. "We haven't been fighting for anything resembling any kind of justice in well over a generation. We had the world in our hands, we had the best of everything and the best of everyone coming here to join this 'Immigrant All-Star Team,' but we couldn't escape our past. We couldn't defeat the historical grievance grifters, not even the first wave, so now we're up to our neck in their successor's bullshit. You know the grifters better than you know your own balls. They deconstructed the old world to rule over the rubble around you, to the exclusion of everyone and everything else. No idea is too extreme so long as it has the right winners and losers." When Bones was in a good mood, he didn't try to hide anything or make it sound any better than it really was. Quinceton loved this about him.

Tinh nodded right along. "Yes, the race and gender people. I thought they were harmless for many years, because they couldn't make any two of their ideas fit. I thought they were just silly at first, too lazy to succeed in a place as free as the Federal world, but it happened like it does anywhere. First, just a few extremists push bad ideas in the right environment; second, the ideas find an audience with some part of the sad population who wants to believe they now hold the key to making a perfect world; third, people of action take over, making wild dreams reality with violence, intimidation, fear."

"I don't think it's really about 'smart' and 'stupid,'" Bones countered.

"The good are divided, separate, and stand alone against what looks like the scorn of the whole society, too frightened to fight back and seemingly be the only one to take the heat. I was one of them. Remember, it wasn't about the threat of total DIE Camp reeducation until the JSS government took over everything—at first it was just about getting into good schools … keeping your job. When it was my chance to speak, when I could have actually done something, I chickened out and stayed silent.

"But I think most people knew then what was going on, and they virtually all do today, which is why they're so happy to be part of the pious pile-on: It's your best—and maybe only—protection. Only in recent years was a lack of intelligence useful for Speakers and such—easier to control, easier to turn into true believers. But those ruling on top of the trash heap aren't fools. They're just skilled at playing each other at a foolish game."

"Okay, I agree," Tinh confirmed. "The competition is to out-victim your neighbor; then you can claim power over their speech and ideas. They must ignore this contradiction first, then every other. It seems stupid to believe it is about anything other than power. But I agree it is not an easy game to win power over other Elect and become Knowing Leader."

Bones nodded right along. "Seeing the contradiction and not being able to argue against it is a big part of the point." He used his fingers to show these words were someone else's quote. "'Powerless victims' occupying every position of power while claiming to 'speak truth to power' on the condition that they increasingly emphasize victimhood, both collective and their own. Imagine how different it would be if they actually produced their own form of objective, useful knowledge? Their own E equals MC squared?"

Suddenly Mai laughed, reminding the table of her presence. "How do we get an E and an MC? Is that new food, or new people?"

Bones had to smile, even if he didn't have the words to reach Mai. "No, those are just ideas, Mai. All you need to know is, you're lucky to be here. The whole outside world of the JSS government is one big nonfunctioning power play no one is allowed to notice, or if they do, they have to be scared into silence. That's the overnight Accountability Circles, the public self-cancellations, and the DIE Camps no one seems to return from. It really is good if you have no idea what I'm talking about. And yet, the problems in San Francisco all evolved from something true, something real, good, and necessary, even."

"You mean the Civil Rights Movement?" Sarah asked. "Wasn't that, like, one hundred years ago, though?"

"Exactly," Bones kept going. "Finally, after so much painful struggle in the 1960s, the Federals gave equal protection to different groups, and further power to enforce equal treatment." He winked at Quinceton. "A lot of that was thanks to your man, the 'American King.' After slavery, segregation, and then fighting wars together, the Federals finally admitted that groups like Blacks were owed every right and opportunity, same as everyone else. I don't think that was the high point of Federal history—it came decades later, when most of the country came to view American racial and social diversity as a strength and selling point."

"It seems like a different world," Quinceton said.

"It was," Tinh replied. "But then we started making different standards for different groups ... thinking that lower standards were somehow a blessing. It took a few generations. We didn't hate each other at the end of the twentieth century; we all cried together when a big terrorist attack hit New York, and only crazy people talked about breaking up the Federal system. People with different politics still watched many of the same movies, and sports, and had friends who didn't always agree with them." He paused. "Did you get enough to eat, Mai?"

She just nodded, allowing the conversation to continue. Quinceton couldn't imagine what she was taking from all this, but she had to have any number of curiosities about the big world out there.

"What changed, Tinh?" Quinceton asked. He was glad to have Mai and Sarah there too; he didn't like being the only one who knew nothing, and they seemed to listen as intently as he did. The whole story felt like a myth, a forbidden myth, which made it sound true.

"Technology, debt, and group identity politics," Tinh replied. "It made everyone lose faith in the system."

"Yeah, you said it." Tinh gave them the skeleton, but Bones added the meat. "Our technology advanced too rapidly for the Federals to understand its effects. New communication inventions inflamed differences of identity and amplified the most extreme opinions, cutting out all the sober voices in the middle. Politicians responded by being more extreme, aiming for radical-base voters, often targeting specific identity groups rather than aiming for the good of the country."

"But if those identity groups really were ignored previously, politically powerless for centuries, why wasn't their explicit representation a good thing?" Sarah asked.

"Because one identity-driven person motivates another to think along the same lines, and then you've got two artificial groups warring against each other when they should share some loyalty to the same country, the same ideas." Bones recited the words as if they were from a memorized speech. "Near-exclusive focus on identity politics doesn't make the world more open, feel more inclusive, but just the opposite: It convinced each citizen that government, society, and damn near all institutions were really constructed for the benefit of someone else—*That group over there that has what you want.* So then everything from the two-parent family to education to criminal justice to democracy—well, it all went out the window here after New California went independent. Those institutions, one and all, were forever stained with the assumption of white supremacy, as inherited from the American system."

"In all that craziness, wouldn't someone get really popular by talking common sense?" Quinceton asked. It felt like a naïve question, but he had to ask anyway.

"In all that craziness, with only two parties, they only got crazier," Tinh added. "They did not try to compromise, but blamed more and more on the other party. To demonize the opposition as an enemy to be defeated, and never to look weak by compromising."

"That's right," Bones said. "And as we grew to regard other groups of Americans as the real enemy to hate and overcome, the Federals racked up an enormous debt to other nations—there just wasn't enough loyalty to the future of the country for people to vote for anything but their own here and now. Soon, the states started viewing the Federals as a sinking ship. Even before the Great Rupture in 2039, California talked a lot about secession. Our economy was massive, our tech and movies and produce brought in cash from everywhere, so what did we need the Federals for? In the end, all it cost California was some national parks, a lot of coastline, some scorching desert, and Los Angeles—now an open septic tank in a dust storm, but at the time it was the entertainment capital of the world, with awesome Mexican food and beautiful women everywhere."

That last bit made the most sense to Quinceton. He could live in most toilets if there were beautiful women everywhere. He also remembered Dad cursing "gutless" Hollywood while watching the all-female remake of the *Saving Private Ryan* movie—those "politicized attacks on reality" (in Dad's words) had supposedly hastened the indifference toward the long-lost industry for many years before Quinceton was born. But the idea of California as a rich place—rich like the Federals were when they built all the skyscrapers—just wasn't something he could picture. However, luxury was the price of equity, as he'd been taught in his Work Doing Center.

"You didn't mention the culture wars," Tinh added. "The takeover of institutions."

Bones nodded. "That's right. Most schools and big business, media, entertainment, and sports became controlled by one super-powerful group of desperate elites trapped by enormous schooling debts, all pushing the same equity message—one that made the Great Rupture acceptable, whereas before it was unthinkable. Because that super-party owned and controlled California, many people blamed Californians and thought they could save the Federals by removing California's influence and big voting population. When the lesser party lost its way, becoming almost totally irrelevant to mainstream culture and particularly in California, the major party could not hold back anymore and developed 'equity' as their unique brand of Racism, expecting it would guarantee future election victories. Please pass the salad."

158

"Yes, that's true." Tinh kept smiling as he reached for the food bowl. "And then they wanted to save the American states by putting all the crazy people in a new, separate California country."

Bones had blathered so much, he now hustled to fill his plate and eat as he spoke. "The JSS government and all the other Social Justice groups came from one party, which was popular on the wealthy coasts and generally despised everywhere else. They had done some good things in different decades, but in the end it was only one idea that tore the whole thing apart in the 2020s: the idea that all difference between groups is the result of Racism or some other discrimination ... that all the problems in any given group are the fault and sole responsibility of outside forces."

He chewed for a moment, then resumed the thought. "That was the logic behind all our equity laws, and no matter how glaring the contradictions, it became the gospel no one was allowed to question. Social Justice blah blah blah and the threat of being called a Racist or an Anti-Anti-Racist was the distraction that then drowned out every other concern."

"The contradictions are not a distraction, they are the whole point!" Tinh argued, putting his fork down. Quinceton was intrigued to finally see the man animated. "Every immigrant group was treated with discrimination when they got to Federal America, then outworked the original groups; Colonial Americans lived off old privilege and got outworked. Different groups of white people made very different money doing very different work, like different groups of every race. But once you go silent about something you know is not true, your enemies have already won. Each contradiction you ignore gives power to the liars to force more and more nonsense. And then nothing makes sense anymore ... but by then, you can't say anything."

"Hey, I'm with you, man," Bones said with a chuckle. Everyone liked seeing Tinh's immigrant pride. Looking between the younger adults, Bones added, "You guys have to remember that in the beginning, these bad ideas were just mocked. I don't know anyone who thought they would take over—I certainly didn't. But one day, you go from joking about how hard it is to fire an edgy heterosexual gender non-binary person without getting sued, and the next minute we have freaking 'persanogender' ruining lives and careers."

"You spend decades in the struggle for 'women's rights' and then suddenly you can't say 'woman' anymore, because gender is a social construct and there's no such thing as a woman," Sarah embellished. "And then you have to respell it 'womxn' because of psychological independence, even if the concept doesn't exist anymore."

Bones kept nodding slowly. "Hundreds of years spent learning to treat people as individuals, to see a person for who they are rather than whatever their identity is, and then suddenly identity is all that matters, and the only cure to past bigotry is more bigotry in the present … as a corrective measure. Just bizarre."

"They go from 'gay rights' to pressuring gay people to sleep with the opposite sex," Sarah carried on. "And you have to sleep with the guy you're not attracted to just to show that gender is whatever they say it is, which defeats the whole idea of 'gay' in the first place!"

"Madness," Bones concurred. The table watched him chew. Quinceton had finished his salad, gathering up every little scrap of lettuce he could find, but felt pretty full. Bones downed another bite, his plate looking equally empty. There was a pause before Tinh rose, his plate in one hand as he reached for Sarah's.

"No!" she cried, startling Quinceton with the sudden volume. "Let me—let *us* do the dishes. Really, seriously, it's the least we can do for the meal." Bones and Quinceton rose in unison, overriding Tinh's protests with their insistence.

"Okay, okay," he relented. "You can do the dishes. Just scrub and then place them on the drying rack. I will get you towels, but there is no shower, so you will have to use the stream."

"We're used to it," Bones assured him.

"Love it," Quinceton added. "Probably my favorite part of waking up."

Tinh disappeared down the hallway to the left of the fireplace, the side opposite Mai's room. Mai carried her glass to the kitchen, wanting to help, but with Sarah clearing, Bones washing, and Quinceton drying, there wasn't much left to do for a fourth person.

Tinh quickly re-emerged and placed blue towels on three of the four bunk beds. Noticing their JSS government rifles, he asked, "Do any of you know how to hunt?"

"I've been out there a time or two," Bones replied from the kitchen. "But I wouldn't say I'm an expert."

"I'm not a bad shot," Quinceton offered.

After a moment of thought, Tinh shook his head. "No, we cannot use a rifle. It is too loud. But my crossbow is accurate, and it can kill a deer in one shot if you hit the vitals. I do not like to hunt for deer meat because we can only store it in the stream for a few days before it is no good. But with you here, I think we won't waste so much if you stay a few days. If we hunt, we should leave tomorrow morning, early."

The three soldiers looked at each other and confirmed the outing in unanimous agreement. Quinceton wasn't even thinking of the stories he might hear, but solely the natural environment around him. "Equity" mandates were for the JSS government stooges; these people just wanted to live in peace. If Quinceton had a womxn like Natalie out here, he might've been able to make it work for life. They could recruit more people, anyone who saw what they saw, and build more houses, grow more food, and never fight again.

Mai cheered and ran around the dining room table, her hands raised. She covered far more ground here than during her celebration under the falling branches at the garden, but it was the same exploding elation. *Everyone needs a friend or two*, Quinceton thought with a smile.

"Mai, I'm sorry, but hunting is not safe for you," Tinh said. "You can help us prepare the food if we find a deer, but it is not safe." Quinceton didn't think deer were so dangerous, but he knew he had much to learn about the wilderness.

"Yes, ong noi," Mai answered, only slightly deflated. "I will help you cook." She shot the soldiers a wide smile and opened her arms wide. "I hope you stay here *forever!*"

She wanted a hug, but the best Quinceton could offer was a fist bump.

The purity of her excitement intimidated him somehow. Maybe he was a bit jealous of it, too.

Mai looked at his clenched hand quizzically, withdrew her arms, and bowed forward slowly, touching her forehead to Quinceton's knuckles.

"That works, too," he said. "Goodnight, Mai."

She faced the other adults in turn and bowed again to each of them, not forgetting her great-grandmother.

"Have a good night," she said softly. "I'm so glad you're finally here." The eyes of each JSS government soldier slowly turned to Tinh as she scampered off to bed.

"Yes, well, I promised Mai that more people would come after her parents didn't return," the grandfather explained. "She has been waiting, and she's been lonely. But you're here now. And we're all glad you are." His expression beamed like the midday sun with all the calm of a full moon, and with a nod, he made off for his room beyond the fireplace.

Quinceton wandered to his backpack by the bunk beds and fished out his toothbrush. Sarah already had the same idea and he trailed her outside, quickly closing the door behind them to keep the bugs out. He sat next to the stream, filled his brush with paste, and dipped it in the rushing water. After a few swirls around his gums, he sat. Sarah lay on her side nearby, gazing up at the stars as she brushed. A minute or two later, she spat and looked at him with a face of total serenity. Quinceton had never seen such a look before, not on her or Bones or anyone else he knew—except, maybe, on Tinh.

"Fuckin' A," Quinceton said between his brush and foamy spit. He bent down with cupped hands and sipped from the stream using his palms.

"I know, right? I don't know how it happened. Call it what you want, but we got lucky as hell finding these people." Quinceton didn't have to agree with her out loud. They both knew it damn well.

"You know, I keep thinking," Quinceton replied, "if these people can do it, why can't others? Who knows—maybe there's a whole lot of people up in the mountains or tucked somewhere quiet that would want to join up, make life easier for us all."

"I thought about that, too, but you remember what Tinh said about Mai's parents and all? It's pretty risky. But you might be right. There are probably all kinds of people living off-the-grid however they can."

Bones tumbled out of the front door and lay spread-eagle on the grass, just looking up. No matter what Bones and Sarah might add to Quinceton's life, not even they could replace the one thing he missed most about San Francisco. A few people in a log cabin could be a family, but never a whole community. Sooner or later that yearning would bring Quinceton out of hiding, and probably with Sarah. Bones might stay here permanently, but eventually Quinceton would return, and if he could find the right lady to join him, next time he'd make a home of it here. Life was always a struggle in some way, but the struggles out at this cabin didn't make him feel so isolated. Over there you lived crowded against other people but always alone, and perpetually under the glare of some indiscernible force of judgement.

Quinceton gargled and spat again, this time feeling fully rinsed.

"Everything is a risk. No matter how you play it, there's always some way to step out of line and get carted off to DIE," he said with conviction. "I don't know what I'm going to do, but now that I've seen this place I don't know how I'd forget it. There are other ways to live."

"*This* is the way to live," Bones cut in, still stargazing. "To hell with the Anti-Racists and the Americans. To hell with their fight. I don't care enough to pretend anymore, not again. When you guys go back, I'll have a letter for you to drop off for my daughter, but I don't want you saying I'm still alive. I died somewhere on the way from a wound I got. She won't want to read what I've got to say, but she might if you tell her I'm dead. I'm not a good father, but maybe a mediocre one, and once you deliver that letter I think I can be at peace with it all … the effort I made, the failed attempt to raise a person with similar values. Do that for me, and you'll both be in my good book for life."

"You got it." Sarah dunked her face into the stream, shaking it around in the cleansing chill.

"That's easy, man," Quinceton added. "And if she looks anything like you, I can promise I'll still be single after the drop-off."

"You got no chance, even on your worst day—not nearly *victim* enough. But give me a little warning before you go, will you? Pretty sure I'm going to try and be useful so I can stick."

"I could do a week here, easy," Sarah said, standing up. "Ready for sleep?" she asked Quinceton. He nodded, and they left Bones lying there looking up at the heavens.

A moment later they reached the bunk beds, surrounded by their weapons and backpacks. Sarah collected all the rifles and deposited them on one top bunk and climbed up to the other before Quinceton could protest.

"I hope you didn't take top bunk because of my IS score. You know I owe you bed choice after the night in the motel."

"You do, and I took it," she replied. "I'm happy up here, and the guns are safe on the other side. Besides, you never know what can wake you up on the bottom bunk." He watched a JSS government soldier shirt and pants fall to the ground.

"Alright, good," Quinceton said, stripping himself and climbing onto the bottom bunk. "G'night, Sarah."

"G'night, friend," she answered.

With the bed cradling him with firm flexibility, Quinceton listened to great-grandmother's heavy breathing and nodded off to sleep.

ACT II, CHAPTER NINE

The Hunt

THERE WAS SOME KIND OF tugging at Quinceton's shoulders, and before he realized he was awake, he saw a huge pair of eyes burning a hole through his head.

"Holy—!" he cried, pushing deeper into the pillow. The picture quickly clarified itself as Mai laughed and grabbed hold of his exposed bicep.

"Get up!" she shouted amid shrieks of delight. "The sun is out and it's a beautiful day!" Tinh stood in the kitchen, hands moving vigorously.

"I'm awake," Quinceton promised, "I'm awake, I'm getting up." He rubbed his eyes and sat up in bed. "Give me a little space to breathe here, and put my pants on."

"Hurry!" Mai demanded as though ushering him into a spaceship scheduled for launch in thirty seconds. "Breakfast is almost ready!" But despite her insistence, she dutifully turned around and took a few paces forward, giving him just enough privacy to dress and put his boots back on. Sarah had the same idea, her top already fixed around her torso, but Bones hadn't stirred, snoring with the conviction of one thousand kings.

Quinceton stood and gave him the eyes-up-close Mai method as Bones fought to retain slumber. It was Quinceton who emerged victorious, and with near-total submission.

"I'm up, geez, I'm *up*," Bones groaned. His haggard expression suggested he'd spent a little too long with the stars. "Give me a minute here, and pass me my pants."

Tinh had food on the table by the time Quinceton ambled over. It looked much like the previous evening's salad, but with a dressing of a different color. Noticing Quinceton's slackened energy, Tinh said, "Don't worry. Tonight there will be meat. Now that you've come, we will eat meat again like regular Americans—like free people." It was bold talk from the humble man.

After breakfast, Tinh recovered his crossbow from its Mai-proof hiding place in an upper kitchen cabinet. He requested the soldiers leave their rifles behind, but they protested vehemently. Not on account of the deer, they argued, but the possibility of human contact.

"Okay," Tinh finally relented. "But the guns are too loud, not for deer—only for people. My crossbow, *only*, for the deer." This compromise was accepted immediately.

The four adults filed out of the cabin without much protest from Mai as her grandfather took over as guide. He wore the only backpack, and Quinceton took it on faith that whatever they'd need was in there. Tinh marched them straight up to the pond but commanded them to hold back. "And don't step on any tracks." The soldiers watched him scan the dirt around the pond.

"What exactly are we looking for?" Quinceton asked. "I mean, what do the tracks look like?"

"Looks like a small hoofprint," Bones answered. "Ain't that right?"

"Yes, two long ovals pointed toward each other at the top, two smaller dots underneath. The whole print is smaller than a fist." Tinh didn't look up. "But what really matters is when it was here last." Quinceton had no idea how Tinh could tell the timing of a track, but he wanted Bones to ask that one. He didn't know shit about hunting, but Bones didn't, either, and only one of them was really honest about it.

"Yes," Bones agreed with a few steps toward the pond. "We want fresh tracks, fresh tracks only." He looked at the ground but didn't move, suggesting he didn't know fresh deer tracks from a pile of stale bear shit.

From across the pond, the other side from where they'd arrived, Tinh spoke up. "This looks good. Come here." His pupils quickly approached, halting a good dozen feet away so as not to disturb the clues. "Anything dry and hard will be old but this looks wetter, probably from last night. And it heads due south, away from the stream."

"That's good," Bones added.

"Yes, it is. Stay behind me and hope this deer didn't double back into the stream, or we will lose the track."

Within an hour they entered a shorter forest, something that had to have been cleared out by a fire a decade or two earlier. Quinceton could see much farther in this thinner brush, especially to his right, a downhill slope that led west to the valley and the rest of California.

As if to help Bones save face on potential failed guesswork, Tinh related some basic knowledge as he led them through the low forest. Deer were a nocturnal animal, and also quick and jumpy, so it was best to find one snoozing, probably around midday. The ground also appeared to be littered with many other tracks—larger tracks, too, as Tinh reasoned that this animal kingdom hadn't gotten much interruption from humanity lately. Quinceton also learned that they were chasing a blacktail deer, much smaller than a mule deer, which would still give them more than enough meat and be far lighter to carry. Tinh would occasionally veer off in a new direction or put up a hand to halt his party, indicating the deer had run in some circle they could inadvertently step on. Bones eventually stopped trying to impress his elder with hunting knowledge but followed closely behind Tinh, acting like the anointed number two in the platoon.

Eventually, after a good few hours, Tinh stopped short with a flat palm to the group connected to an elbow that jerked to the side in two rapid movements. Sarah and Quinceton were already crouching when Bones attempted to copy the arm signal for their sake. Tinh held a finger to his lips, and everyone waited for him to speak as they tried to stifle their heavy breathing.

"I see it," Tinh whispered, pointing. "Bedded down, about ten feet from that tall California pine there. Maybe fifty yards from here to there.

My bow will be much more accurate at half this distance, and better even closer." He paused. "I'm old—sometimes my hand will shake. Who will take the shot?"

"I could do it," Quinceton offered. "Never shot a bow, but I've got some practice with the rifle."

Bones scoffed with incredulity. "C'mon, man, I was out there shooting while you were sucking titties."

"I still like sucking titties," Sarah quipped.

"Yeah, me too," Quinceton added. "I think Tinh, too, probably would also appreciate the right titty. What, you retired from romance, old man?" Tinh grinned peacefully, letting them sort this out among themselves.

"I mean, your birther—never mind the titties. I'm a good shot, and you both know I can commando crawl like a legit pro," Bones said, applying for the job a second time. Quinceton remembered his long creep around the South Lake battlefield, and how he'd avoided all detection from the fixed guns.

"Alright, Bones," he relented. "You got this."

Tinh handed over the crossbow. "Don't try for a headshot," the real hunter advised. "Shoot for the heart so if you miss, you'll hit something anyway." Bones likely would have nodded if he weren't already on his belly.

The remaining trio watched Bones slither toward the deer, who Quinceton now viewed through his scope. The old soldier sure was slow as a constipated JSS government-issued bowel movement, but quiet, and careful to take cover behind any brush or tree trunk. Déjà vu pinched at the back of Quinceton's mind as Bones found the right stump and took aim.

Quinceton never saw an arrow in flight, but he did see one planted in the deer's front shoulder as it jerked to its feet. Bones was standing, shouting about another arrow.

"No!" Tinh shouted back. "No, sit, no—DON'T MOVE!" The deer took off as fast as it could go as Bones sheepishly turned to his companions, his inexperience finally laid bare for all to see. Shame spread across his face as Tinh motioned the younger soldiers to follow.

"We will wait," Tinh said to Bones as soon as he no longer had to shout. "Just wait."

"But you did well," Sarah assured her crestfallen colleague.

"Yeah, good crawling, and you hit the deer," Quinceton agreed. "We'll find her."

The worry in Bones's wrinkles lightened. "Yeah—sorry, guys. Got excited. And you know *I* don't know what I'm doing."

"Never chase the deer," Tinh explained as Bones returned the bow. "Not after you hit the deer. She will leave a blood trail, and we don't want to scare her into making us walk farther."

"So what do we do now?" Sarah asked.

"We wait. We find a place to sit. In the shade, like under the big pine."

The sun cut enough holes through the tree to make Quinceton sweat and thirst for a swim in the pond. They passed Tinh's canteen between them, but the water tasted about as hot as it'd been when the stream had been boiled out of it. The energy of the chase waned into a daze of summer heat and conflicting tempos. It reminded Quinceton of the constant "wait for the last moment, then hurry" philosophy that pervaded every action in his JSS government boot camp.

After what felt like at least an hour, Tinh spoke. "Okay, it's been thirty minutes. Let's follow the blood trail, but slowly, and *no* talking. Tap me if you want to stop and say something. If it's alive, the deer will be nervous."

Quinceton followed a few paces behind Tinh with Bones bringing up the rear, and getting moving again lifted all their spirits. The deer had cut north back toward their cabin, which Quinceton appreciated, as he imagined the carcass would be a heavy haul. Perhaps it was the slant of the familiar mountain, the low tree cover, or the placement of the sun, but he felt increasingly secure about his sense of direction and wondered how hard it would be to guide them back to camp, or at least to the right stream, which he could follow home. The deer's blood trail was much easier to track than the hoofprints, as a few crimson drops stood out against the light-brown dirt every few feet or so.

Suddenly, Tinh halted and turned to the novices. "Be careful," he said softly. He pointed to different sections of the ground on either side of the blood trail. "I see some large tracks—not too fresh, but many tracks. There are many animals around who want a wounded deer."

"Nature thrives when civilization recedes," Bones chimed in. He hadn't finished the deer, but at least his confidence was coming back.

Tinh crept onward, following the trail slightly up the mountain, but still veering north in Quinceton's estimation.

The droplets of blood now came closer together, and Quinceton knew what to expect the next time Tinh stopped the group. From a crouch, Quinceton put the rifle scope to his eye and saw the deer lying on its side not fifty yards away, the arrow still lodged in its flesh. Its head twitched, still alive, accompanied by the sound of braying every now and again, and Quinceton considered the deer's plight for the first time.

"Give me the crossbow," he asked Tinh. "It's suffering, you can see it. I'll end it."

No one objected as Quinceton traded his rifle for Tinh's bow. Only one arrow could be loaded at once, but the young soldier didn't think he'd need another to finish the job.

Quinceton crept closer, attempting to mimic Bones's moves. Crawling hadn't been covered at the boot camp, and Quinceton didn't like his eyes so close to the ground. Disturbed dust and ash rose to obscure the target but he would not relent, not under the current spotlight. A bush not far from the fallen animal became the ultimate destination, and when Quinceton reached it, he wiped his eyes, aimed for the deer's exposed neck, and exhaled.

The arrow went straight into the deer's hide, the point breaking clean through. If the deer took a final breath, Quinceton had missed it. But it stirred no more.

Quinceton stood and hovered over the carcass, staring into its eyes, as his companions congratulated him on the shot. The animal's life was over, and its last moments had been a gruesome combination of terror and agony. A swift exit for anyone was a privilege of the past in the present world, but that didn't exonerate any individual executioner.

"Never killed anything before?" Sarah asked, noticing Quinceton's comedown.

"Yeah, never. Well, bugs and a snake years ago, but never anything so big and alive."

"We won't waste anything. The deer died for us, and we'll respect the sacrifice."

"Yes," Tinh said, reaching into his backpack. "We will use everything we can. Now, skin the deer and take off the head."

"Take ... off ... the head?" Quinceton repeated, reality setting back in to make a mockery of his pacifist idealism. "I think that's a job for skilled hunters—like Bones here."

Tinh removed a massive knife, something longer than his forearm and sheathed in leather, and handed it to Bones, who eagerly squatted over the blank eyes of the recently departed. He then handed his canteen to Quinceton, who carried it a few paces to sit on a fat half-burnt stump in the shade.

"You good?" Sarah asked, joining him on the other side of the long-dead tree base. He couldn't see her face, so he craned his neck to keep his voice down.

"Yeah, I think so. New thing for me, I like meat—I'm going to eat this deer tonight, I just wish it could've been quicker, you know? Like a painless one-shot kill."

"Most don't get so lucky, but I hear you." Sarah kept her voice down too. When it came to reading unspoken feelings, she was a pro.

"And we saw so much death in Tahoe, so it shouldn't be a big deal. But these past few days ... I don't know. It seems different now. The whole program we went along with, and all the killing, and all the fear, social pressure ... it's not for me. Seeing that deer's eyes made me think about the AAA patrolpersons and how they always mask their own faces. To hide their whiteness from the higher IS scores they get to arrest, or for extra intimidation, I think. So we don't see what's really happening and have to trust our imagination, which is shaped by the Elect."

"I think you're right." Sarah paused, reached for the canteen, and gulped down one big swig. "But I'm not Bones, and you aren't, either. One way or another, we're going to need some more people our age—I don't know, maybe a community or something. If we're going to stay, I mean." Quinceton nodded. This was the thorn that kept puncturing his desire to never return to the world of intersectional grievance and historical revenge.

"We can't stay," he sighed. "Not forever. I know."

Sarah passed the canteen back to Quinceton and they sat in a contemplative daze, listening to the occasional hack of blade against bone.

Tinh soon approached with a bloody bedsheet slung over his shoulder. "We have the meat divided four ways to carry." He handed the bag to Quinceton, who accepted it with the promise to himself that he would indeed swim in the pond as soon as it became possible.

"Hey, anyone mind if I try leading us back?" Quinceton asked his posse.

It was an easy sell, particularly to Tinh. "Yes, you lead, and next time Sarah or Bones will lead. I want you all to learn where we are so you can always return."

"A compass could help," Bones added. "But these low trees let you see up the mountain, at least, and that helps, too." Bones was miles behind Quinceton in the scouting department, despite his familiarity with the commando crawl.

The prized meat now separated into four different loads with the hide held by Tinh, they left only the head and legs, the stench of slaughter spreading as far as the wind would carry it. For a while, Bones followed closely behind Quinceton and talked about harvesting the animal—"Can't let the guts touch the good meat" and "Supposedly the tenderloins are the best part, but we got solid backstraps, too" and so forth—but the developing scout paid little attention. Quinceton noted that his own eyes were always raised and scoping the landscape and terrain, while Bones talked with his face pressed to the ground as though avoiding human feces on a walk through San Francisco. Eventually Bones lagged into the space between Quinceton and the others.

The low brush grew higher for a spell before crumpling in a heap of scorched earth, trees cowed by past flame and exposed boulders overlooking the whole scene. Quinceton remembered traversing the top of this fertile wasteland while Tinh had tracked, and perhaps the relatively recent fire had cut deeper at a lower elevation. Or maybe it was a smaller, newer outburst. Either way, he knew he could steer the party home. Perhaps it was this confidence, or this concentration, that quickened Quinceton's pace as the rest of the group strolled along in his wake.

If it weren't for the eyes Quinceton probably would have missed it, but even against the afternoon glare of a California summer, those green eyes shone like jade bullets against a dusty brown desert. They didn't move, and Quinceton didn't either. Surveying the scene from an elevated rock not even a hundred feet ahead, the cougar finally raised its head as the conversation somewhere behind Quinceton died mid-sentence. On sheer instinct, Quinceton dropped the bag of deer meat, crouched behind it, and aimed his crossbow at the cougar. He hadn't replaced the arrow since the last kill shot, however, and the crossbow was little more than a wooden club without one.

The cougar ambled down and around from its perch, emerald eyes trained on Quinceton the whole time. If there had been time for thought, the young soldier would have dumped the deer meat on the ground and run for dear life, but mortal fear is its own enemy, and paralysis glued Quinceton to the spot.

The cougar descended to Quinceton's plane, paused for a slow pan of the surroundings, and blasted into an oncoming sprint. In a few strides the predator was upon the new hunter, bearing down on the exposed meat, when a cacophony of bangs uncorked from the periphery.

By the time Quinceton regained his senses, the cougar lay in tatters, its hide torn apart by a storm of propelled lead. Sarah and Bones seemed as dumbfounded as their fellow soldier, but not Tinh, whose conspicuous anxiety was emphasized by the smoking rifle in his hands.

"That was too loud," he said, approaching the fallen animal with the gun still raised. "It is dead, but that was too loud. We need to hurry now and find the stream away from the house." Bones offered Quinceton a hand, lifting the shaken young solider to his feet.

"I would have done the same thing," Bones said. "That fucking cross-bow needs more goddamn arrows, am I right?" Quinceton could only snicker, mostly forced.

When thinking became crucial, he had shielded himself behind a meaty target with an ammunition-free weapon. He probably deserved to lose a limb, but he'd been saved by the actions of a man committed to a silence that listed such noticeable gunfire as treason to his own code of survival.

Quinceton could not have known how different the mountain lion threat would feel compared to the bullets whizzing through South Lake, nor how he'd act in response to it. The difference here was the speed and the sur-prise: Quinceton had been expecting the noise in Tahoe. It also seemed to be exclusively focused on other people. If there were lessons to learn from the cougar's demise, the first was to always be prepared—always carry a loaded weapon if you needed one at all. The second lesson had to be some-thing about thinking under pressure. The harder it is to use your brain, the more important such a challenge became.

The group moved more quickly now, all seeming to know how to head north and the necessity of finding the stream away from the house, even if none but Tinh understood the full plan. A guide was unnecessary; some-how they knew where to keep the view of the mountain crest as they hiked, each totally confident that Tinh would intervene if they lost the way back.

They reached a stream not long after, unrecognizable to Quinceton's eye, but clearly *the* stream from the way Tinh immediately removed his socks and shoes.

"Do like me," he told the others. "Tie your laces together and put them over your neck." In response to questioning stares, he added, "This is to hide our tracks."

With the deer hanging from his shoulders, shoes slung around his neck, and pants rolled up to the knees, Quinceton felt the cool stream chill his weary calves as he climbed the mountain second in line behind Tinh. If the elder statesmen were overcome by the head-on current, then Quinceton would catch him, slightly returning the favor which had necessitated such extreme caution. The current had some muscle to it, and even the young

JSS government soldier had to lean far forward to account for the opposing momentum.

They hadn't gone even a dozen yards before Tinh tossed his bundle of meat onto the other shore from which they'd arrived.

"I'm too old," he explained. "We can stop here and put our shoes back on. No animal will track our smell through the stream, but we won't really be safe from humans until the next time it rains." They all knew that such precipitation was rare to come by in a California summer, but with such companions, Quinceton could hardly worry.

The hike up the mountain battled a steeper slope than they'd tackled before. Quinceton offered to carry Tinh's sack and regretted it as soon as the offer was rejected. Advanced as the Vietnamese man's age was, it had not dimmed his drive to work at least as hard as everyone else.

"You're back!" Mai called before Quinceton had even seen the house. "Let's go explore. What do you want to see?" Quinceton looked at Sarah, seeing the same weariness he'd likely worn ever since slinging a quarter of the deer over his back.

"Sarah and I want to see the pond," he answered. "I want to see your favorite swimming spot, and I want to jump in as soon as you're ready." Mai cheered as Bones and Tinh gathered stones for a fire pit.

For now, Quinceton would swim like an Elect kid in his own pond-pool, and tonight he would dine on fresh meat like the kings and politicians and capitalists of yesteryear. Not all of life was intra-demographic strife, fear, and toil—that was just society. Go far enough for long enough, and the land would still be there to reward you with beauty and freedom. Maybe even a family.

Throw a larger community into the mix, and life could be even better than alright.

ACT II, CHAPTER TEN

The Feast

"IT'S CALLED VENISON—THE DEER MEAT," Bones said as he placed a loaded silver dish in the middle of the table. He spoke to no one in particular in a voice that seemed to mimic Tinh's humble authority. "We cooked it perfectly. Mixed up a salad, too, but no one needs to worry about getting in their greens … tonight, we got the goods."

The group congregated around the dining room table, with great-grandmother still planted in her rocking chair and Mai eating at her low desk-table beside Quinceton. Perhaps it was a sign of communal habit forming, but they all took the same seats they'd had the previous day: Tinh sat beside the front door with Quinceton and Mai facing him and Bones facing Sarah at the short ends of the long rectangular table. When Tinh asked if "someone would like to say a few words," they reached for each other's hands with a practiced obedience.

"I do," Quinceton said. "I remember Dad—I think you'd like him—would do this. He'd call it a 'grace.' Lemme give it a shot." Mai squeezed his knuckles from down below.

"God Lord, thank you … for giving us … this deer, on the table, which we're going to eat. Thank you for giving us this mountain, and the pond, this land, to explore, and live on. Thank you for showing me the cougar, and saving me, and showing me something about thinking—thinking under pressure. But most of all, thank you for giving us each other." This time Quinceton remembered the line, and they all said "Amen" in unison.

"So, what's on the agenda for tonight—sex and religion?" Bones asked. Quinceton cut off a piece of meat, dunked it in whatever juice surrounded it, and ate. A wonderful earthy taste bloomed on his tongue, sort of like the smells he discovered walking through the forest. With food like this, sex, religion, the downfall of his family or society—he would have been fine with any topic.

"Speaking only for myself, and no doubt you, too, Bones, I've got nothing on the sex front," Sarah said.

"Well, religion then," Bones concluded. "Quinceton, you had a little face time with God when that cougar came for you? I assume the social grievance sermons of the JSS government Speakers didn't flash before your eyes."

"I'm not sure." Quinceton wanted to give a pithy answer, but the moment had happened too quickly, adrenaline pumping though his veins faster than his brain could process one action after another. "I didn't think much—if I had, I probably would have done a little more than crouch and wait. If God was there and helping me out, I didn't see him."

"That's how it works," Tinh said. "God is everywhere. Even where there is evil, God is there. Many religions believe that, not just Christians. There is a larger plan you must have faith in, and that faith comes from somewhere you can't explain. The JSS government demands faith, too, in something they can't explain or justify, but they are not God. Most evil is okay to the JSS government, but in God's world, Christians believe it is a means to teach us and make us better people. Evil is a constant for good to rise against and prove itself."

"Jews kinda think that, too," Sarah offered. "As far as I know. Didn't spend much time hearing from a rabbi growing up." Quinceton assumed that was a Jewish priest. He'd heard from his father about a Christian priest who fled California, and in the story the priest had helped others escape as well. The ethical tinge to this memory had entirely reversed itself in the last week.

"What about the Parsees?" Quinceton asked. "I know all about Advi Pithawalla and how he took trillions of credits from California before he left. But is that the only reason the Parsees are so hated by the JSS government people?"

"I mean, basically," Bones replied. "I know it had nothing to do with whatever Zoroastrian religious beliefs the Parsees have. But the Intersectional Equity law, when applied to a tiny population with a single super-duper rich guy, is immediately exposed for what it is: collective punishment of a group for the success of the members of that group. So, literally, the only way for a group to earn government favor is for their masses to fail spectacularly, work as little as possible, and contribute nothing to society—then everyone else in your group will be perceived as oppressed and get subsidies rather than a fat Parsee tax bill. Oppression is the only allowable explanation. This is only one of the twisted incentives of identitarian Marxism, and then it's only a matter of time before people realize it … the carrots, Mai?"

"Yes, please," she said. Bones handed them to Quinceton and kept talking. When Quinceton continued the carrot relay to Mai, she giggled. The impromptu reaction suggested that the forest princess may not have been following all the finer points of the conversation, but she clearly enjoyed the dinner table companionship all the same.

"So, the Parsees," Bones carried on, "with Pithawalla paying the tab, they opted out. And ever since, the JSS tax collectors have been figuring out new ways to trap poor fools into providing a meager living for the other manipulated masses. As long as people view oppression and privilege strictly through the lens of identity, that's what they'll fight about, and ignore how wildly unfair the rest of everything is. That explains the closed borders and constant fearmongering, though I still can't tell you exactly why we were actually at South Lake, other than to hide the 'Violence' banner from everyone else. Anyway, it takes a lot of fatty food to keep a Knower in their weight class, so they get victimy about lookism and whatever outrage comes next, and someone has to bring home the bacon."

Quinceton liked these long rants, especially when they reassured him of something he already suspected. The more he heard about the machinations of the JSS government, the more he saw their rhetoric and theatrics as an open diversion, but he didn't quite see the point of it all, or how anyone from the outside could fix it.

"Have you ever been to a Fire Temple?" Tinh asked Bones. He'd cut his venison into very small square pieces, which he ate slowly. "My son taught me how to recognize other Liberati with the Bible verse, but I was never political in the city. I've never been to a Fire Temple, if they really do exist."

He had only ever heard Dad use that phrase before, and just speaking the words had drawn ample tongue-lashing from Quinceton's birther. At any other time in his life, Quinceton would have worried that the topic they now discussed was grounds for an immediate invitation to DIE.

"You know …" Bones said, leaning in to divulge this prized secret, "I do know one. A Fire Temple, an actual freaking Fire Temple, in San Francisco. Right there on Fillmore in Pacific Heights, too, right under those smug Elect noses. I only went there once years ago, invited by a cousin who was later dispatched ever so humanely, and I didn't get through the initial screening, but I remember it."

"What screening?" Sarah asked. She pointed to the carrots, and Mai passed them her way.

"Well, they can't just welcome you right in and start badmouthing everyone in power immediately. You have to get through some vetting process where they cling to their cover story while eyeing you suspiciously. But I knew, and *they knew I knew*, that it was a maw-flipping Fire Temple." Bones eyed Mai, likely trying to edit some of his language for her sake.

"Otherwise, I wouldn't be so encouraged to speak honestly about the state," he went on. "The JSS government can't survive criticism. You know that, which is why we got rid of metrics to measure anything. I guess I didn't go far enough bashing the JSS government, so I got sent off. But they were friendly about it, as though they wanted me to come back a second time just to prove more loyalty."

"That makes sense," Tinh said. "They have to be careful."

"You know why the Anti-Anti-Racists called their meeting place a Fire Temple?" Bones asked Quinceton. "Even before they started calling themselves Liberati, I mean."

"Nope. Why's that?"

"It's because that's what the Parsees called their house of worship. A Fire Temple is like their church. Copying the name is also why some people think the Liberati are still in contact with Advi Pithawalla somehow, maybe even close enough to him to get some white market supplies. I've never seen anything like it, but that's the rumor."

"Something about all this still doesn't make sense to me," Quinceton admitted after a large herby swallow. "I guess I still don't get why the Federals would do this, or why California left during the Great Rupture. It seems they had so much—so much land and food and everything else. Why would those people choose a world like this?"

"Do you know about socialism, and what Bones means when he talks about California's identitarian Marxism?" Tinh asked.

"No. Or at least, not really."

"Socialism—a loose form of Communism—is what took over Vietnam after the war, and it's what's taken over California now. The people are supposed to own everything collectively, all the businesses and the credits, which means the government steps in to assign work and pay people about the same to do very different things. As a result, the people lose ambition, because they can't decide their own future. It never works out like it is promised in the beginning."

"You've seen how it turned out for the JSS government," Bones interjected. "You haven't seen unchecked capitalism at work, though, and that isn't perfect, either."

"About one hundred years ago, ideas like Communism and socialism started to get very popular in unsettled countries like Vietnam," Tinh continued. "People traded freedom for the hope of a better life. The idea behind a super-powerful government was to make everyone equal; they claimed the poor will rise up against the rich and make things the same for everyone, but it never works that way. Instead, many hard workers move somewhere else, somewhere better, and everyone leftover becomes poor, except the people who introduced the communal government—they take ownership of everything. The populations change but every one of those governments has a special Elect, just like ours."

"So that's part of the why," Quinceton said. "But there's got to be more. I just don't get why here, why now?"

Bones chimed in with specifics. "In the past, socialism was never popular in America. Many think that's because there was enough opportunity for people to decide their own lives and work without giving all that responsibility to the government. In every society, the rich have a tendency to exploit the poor for more profit, and the poor know it and resent the rich for it. That's one reason you need a large, happy middle class. There was once a strong middle class to keep the peace between the rich and poor. But California lost the middle class long ago."

"That's true," Tinh agreed. "I never thought about it then, but you're right. In Old California, the state was attractive to rich and smart people from all over. But then they made things too expensive in the cities, which made things worse for everyone who wasn't rich."

"Why?" Sarah asked. "I don't get the economics."

"It's complicated," Bones sighed. "But basically, like in San Francisco, the Elect took over everything, priced the middle class out of housing virtually overnight. The cities bring in more money from outside, even from other countries, but the quality of life continued to decline everywhere except in the wealthy, often gated communities. Before the JSS government, we were coming close to a feudal society, where the rich landowning kings and lords give the poor peasants just enough to survive, largely through big-government taxation. It was billionaires flying around in private planes to virtue signal about hurting the environment while houselessness, drug abuse, and government dependence consumed more and more of the citizenry. Big money for some, government handouts for everyone else."

"But why did the rich professionals, the managers ... why did they let things get so bad?" Quinceton asked. It seemed like the million-credit question.

"The managerial class of high-paid employees have it so good, they just want to keep their share of things the same," Bones explained. "So they mouth any and all luxury beliefs to stay in lockstep with the status quo—that's how we got 'DEFUND THE POLICE' and 'equitable law enforcement outcomes.' They start with a pressure campaign just to say 'Black Lives Matter'—which everyone agrees with—and then turn around the next minute to tell you that thinking Black lives matter means we have to get rid of police, prisons, school, and standards. The Anti-Racists just shrank the difference between the rhetoric and the reality."

"Those are 'luxury beliefs,' right?" Sarah clarified. "Bad ideas mouthed by powerful people because just saying the stuff draws rewards from the culture around you, even if the ideas are ultimately doomed for the powerless. My father would talk about ideas like that. Ideas which benefit a rich person to say, like 'DEFUND POLICE,' but in reality just make life worse for the poor—everyone else who actually relies on the system."

Tinh was nodding now too. "Correct."

"Yeah, that's right." Bones smiled and set his fork down. "'Luxury beliefs' sound great when you say them to people they'll never affect, but their failure turns the poor against each other, keeps them needy for government intervention while the managerial class virtue signals from above about mangling American education and law enforcement to stop Anti-Black Racism. Hopelessness was bound to happen, bound to claim millions of voters, and then a politician just needs the right scapegoat to assert power. With such extreme and humiliating in-your-face inequality, we were ripe for the taking."

"But why did the JSS government have to be socialist?" Sarah asked. "That part seems fishy. Couldn't they have fought for Social Justice-ness or whatever without everyone being subjects to a tyrannical government?"

"No!" Tinh said immediately, dropping his fork and shaking his head with surprising energy. "Once the JSS made their whole government against fighting white stuff and American history, they had no choice. In order to destroy any loyalty to the old country, the Anti-Racists did two things: make all American values and history evil, and then insist on their own explanation for all that was unfair in America. Anything else could not be said. In truth, the more obvious the contradictions, the more important it is that you can't speak about them."

"From what I was told, that first part started happening long before the JSS government," she replied. "Especially in California. People were very, very ready to label the Federals a 'Racist cisheteropatriarchy' hellhole. Then you can throw all their ideas and values right out the window, even the things that worked."

"Especially the things that worked," Tinh agreed.

"Like the free market rewarding ambition, talent, and hard work," Bones added, jumping off Tinh's lead once more. "Ambition and hard work are good traits, but they are impossible to manage equally. And 'equal everything for everybody' was the promise. It was the solution to everything that was wrong with capitalism, by basically being the opposite."

"So then under socialism," Quinceton concluded for the table, "everyone is equal ... but that's bullshit. No one is equal to the Anti-Racists. That's the whole point of having different IS scores and dividing people."

"Ah, you're catching on now," Bones said. "We are all treated differently according to the popularity of our identities, on the promise that our systemic identitarianism will make us all equal in the end, but it's a scam fundamentally based in self-serving theories and grift. Only fear keeps it going, but hey, that fear was large enough to shut my trap tight."

"Socialism combined with the religion of the JSS government," Quinceton muttered. He was gazing into the table, thinking too hard to eat. "Hopefully a house built on bullshit isn't going to hold very long. All these lies crisscrossing each other can't survive forever."

"A thousand contradictions," Tinh agreed. Night had fallen outside, and the forest calmed to a rare stillness. "Because we were becoming a country that really tried to treat everyone the same, the identitarians were going to lose their jobs. They had to deny all progress and attack Federal America as 'systemically Racist' because there wasn't enough individual Racism to sell. The supply of Racism wasn't enough to meet the demand for it."

"Damn straight," Bones said, chewing happily. "By some measurements, with, like, ninety-five percent national approval of interracial marriage, America looked like the least Racist multicultural country in world history. And then we elected a multiracial Black guy to be president, and what's even worse for the racemongers is that he earned it through smarts, work, and ambition rewarded like they should be—transferred from a shitty layabout college to a good one, starred in grad school and took off from there … sorry, Mai, a *crappy* school. I didn't mean to swear."

"That's okay," she said, flapping her legs around restlessly underneath the table.

"At the same time," Bones continued, "we're selling a million college degrees in social grievance for a fortune of debt each, and those useless scholars had to pay off tuition somehow. The answer, to pay off diploma debt for an officially official degree in Racism Detection, was to ignore all data which might show social progress, ignore all data about how different standards for different groups hurts everyone, and push this vague, permanent ghost of 'systemic Racism.' Even at the outset, this ghost was invisible and banned by the Federals' law, but was still said to be totally pervasive, everywhere at all times and absolutely permanent. Every attack on the ghost distracts society from every other problem, but only mentioning the ghost helps the social standing of any individual virtue signaling the popular virtues with their attack."

"Those were the early Anti-Racists," Tinh agreed. "I think most knew they were tricking vulnerable people."

"But some were true believers!" Bones shot back. "That's how they took control of the Social Justice narratives from other groups in the original coalition, like the environmentalists. The Anti-Racists made *everything* about *their thing,* and were quick to accuse anyone of evil for divided attention. No passion for any other idea would be forgiven as identitarian politics subsumed every passion for any other concern. Some Anti-Racists really thought they were curing society of a Racist disease by destroying society. Instead, they pushed out God to make room for their own Devil."

"I think the first Knowing Leader, Kendaoi, was a true believer,"

Quinceton said. "Maybe you'd call him a 'first-wave grifter,' but I don't think Kendaoi thought of himself as a con man. Otherwise, why would he push the 2020 Project? Wouldn't he have to believe he was actually correcting for discrimination in order to promote such a risky solution?"

"Yeah, makes sense," Bones added. "But the JSS government and their Speakers and Knowers and ZNN news turned grifters into religious leaders because no one else was allowed a voice. That's why all the other religions had to go—they already had a God, so there was no need to worship some obese identitarian in a tall gold hat.

"Let's be real here: The second-wave grifters know exactly what they're doing, who they need to attack, and who they need to keep divided. They cannot allow open discussion of their ideas or make any falsifiable claims, or acknowledge any statistic to measure anything tangible, as their power doesn't come from the consent of the people. Identitarian entitlement to power arises from the narrative, which now rules people through fear of being socially ostracized, of being that person without friends, family, a job, and a home. And what separated the second-wave identitarian grifters from their misguided predecessors was just one belief put into practice. One idea, manipulated through law and enforced by violence, destroyed the bonds tying Federal states together, and now everything within the dominion of the JSS government."

Tinh nodded. "I think I know. You mean about winning through failure?"

"Exactly," Bones continued. "If the public silently accepts that all differences between groups equals discrimination, and their leaders make equity the signature goal of society, then those leaders have every incentive to—"

A window cracked somewhere behind Bones, glass falling to the floor. Quinceton stared at the broken pane as two more exploded. An arm, covered in a black sleeve, waved somewhere beyond the window.

"What the ..." Bones said, touching a hand to his cheek and seeing his own blood. More dark shapes moved outside. Tinh rose, brandishing his fork like a sword, and immediately wilted, a red stain spreading down from his shoulder.

That's when Mai screamed, tearing Quinceton's mind back from frozen shock. He reacted on instinct, tackling the tiny girl out of her chair with one arm and supporting their weight on the other.

"Crawl," he whispered urgently. "To your room—the tunnel. Hurry. Don't turn around." It was her eyes that disturbed him the most. He'd remember those eyes better than any other image from this mountain—filling with tears but not spilling down, eyes that had hardened from innocence to hatred in a flash, and yet somehow looked … ready.

She flipped onto her hands and scurried past the fireplace toward her bedroom. Quinceton followed for a few arm lengths but rotated, watching Sarah rush toward Tinh's slumped body and fall forward, gunfire appearing to catch her from behind.

Bones stood and raised two bloody hands. "We surrender!" he shouted with blood-soaked words. "Stop shooting! We surrender!"

"Keep going," Quinceton said to Mai, reaching her at the doorway to her bedroom. He held out his pocketknife. "Take this, hide in the forest tonight, and when the sun rises, follow it over the mountains."

She wiped her eyes and took the knife. She nodded, squeezing her face tight, trying to halt the flow that now ran down her neck.

"You're very brave," she said. Quinceton closed the door behind her, praying she would escape without notice. He thought, *Lord save this child and it won't matter what happens to the rest of us.* And then he cried, hands and knees facing Mai's bedroom, cried with a fury and lifelong torment he'd never been able to admit.

"Stop moving!" called a commanding voice from outside. "Raise your arms and stay right where you are. We're coming in." Quinceton raised his arms, shuffling carefully out of the hallway and reaching the fireplace of the main living room as the front door fell open. It was unlocked, but they still used a log battering ram.

A few figures entered covered in black clothing with black pads on their knees, chests, and elbows and hoods—not helmets—over their faces. These were the Anti-Anti-Anti-Racist patrolpersons, the notorious AAA agents, come to claim their Liberati bounties at last.

Tinh raised one hand, holding his wound with the other, as Sarah labored to kneel, her outstretched hands shielding a murderous expression that would not relent.

"Easy," Bones garbled, now standing, arms over his head but bleeding through his teeth. A bullet seemed to have entered his open mouth and left through one cheek. "We're soldiers for the JSS government, survivors of the battle for South Lake. We can show you our flag, our papers. I'm not even a white guy—I'm half Mexican."

The tallest figure directed the butt of their silenced machine gun into Bones's stomach, crumpling the wounded man into a heap on the floor.

"One whitey is as white as another," they said. "And you might be anything, but the chinks sure aren't fighting age. And yet here you are, with them. JSS soldiers associating with Anti-Anti-Racists." They turned to the other hooded vigilantes. "Search the house."

One quickly seized upon Quinceton and demanded to know why he'd moved so far from the table.

"Because ... I'm a coward," he answered. "I'm not supposed to be here. When the shooting started, I thought to leave, get out through a window in the bedroom." Tinh, breathing heavily, put his wet hand over his heart and tilted his neck in the slightest of bows. It was a look of infinite gratitude. Tinh knew who he really was and what he'd done; it barely mattered what the AAA did to them now.

Quinceton's inquisitor pushed past him to inspect Mai's bedroom, and Quinceton's spirit lifted to see the same person re-emerge and head straight for the other hallway, where Tinh slept. "It's clear," he announced to the tallest figure, presumably their commanding officer. "And there is a low window in each bedroom."

"Okay," the leader said. "We'll find out who is what back at camp, but you're coming with us. And first, the chink." He pointed at the person nearest Tinh, then at the dying man. They all knew what was coming, but only Tinh seemed to accept it.

"Not a ... chink," he said in a pained whisper. "I'm a ... slope ... or ... gook ..." The nearest vigilante brought his rifle butt down from above, buckling the ageless man, and they kept bludgeoning his skull until it caved into a jagged, lumpy pile of bone shards and red-pink brain matter.

Quinceton couldn't look away. Tinh had seen this coming but would not stir. Once Mai had fled, his resistance died with her. But his spirit still endured somewhere, even now.

"Never waste a bullet," Tinh's killer said.

The commanding vigilante saluted the murderer. "If you can get up and walk, you can come with us," they announced to the room. "Or we can leave you here. But we won't waste another bullet."

The three surviving soldiers struggled to their feet. There would be time to mourn later, to cry and curse about all the horror in the world. But for now they needed to survive, to keep surviving.

Quinceton, the last one out, took a final glance at the cottage. At the kitchen, the fireplace, and the table, seeing all the shared meals, warmth, and love it had held only minutes ago.

"Baizuo," a voice said from the covers on the rocking chair.

ACT II, CHAPTER ELEVEN
Enter DIE

THEY MARCHED THROUGH THE NIGHT mostly in silence, save for some pointed conjecture between the Anti-Anti-Anti-Racist agents about who should receive the most commendation for their retrieval. The conversation probably wasn't intended to humiliate the captured for bringing such attention to the mountain cabin that directly led to the death of a good man, and it was this casualty that consumed Quinceton's mind when he wasn't thinking about Mai. Tinh had always seen this coming—not in the moment he'd welcomed the three wayward JSS government soldiers into his home, but long before. He'd *always* known how it would end.

"When we get back, I want it in the report that I heard their shots first," one of the AAA agents said as they paused for a breather on the flat still land of the Central Valley. The leader, now identifiable as the one holding the compass, nodded.

"You'll get your cut," they said. "I can't promise the best, but beef of some kind, to be sure. And Ezeetus, you won't be forgotten either. Fucking bloodhound tracker. We obviously had something judging by that cougar corpse, but I doubted you at the stream. When you saw the blood trail again on the other side ... well, it'll be noted."

"Thank you, Lieutenant Timetaker," one of them said.

"I also want it noted by the three of you that the apprehension went perfectly," the boss, Timetaker, continued. "Waiting for nightfall was the right move, as I said. When you're running your own campaign, remember that—don't rush it once you find the water source. That's ninety percent of the game. Follow the water, and the rest is easy." Quinceton's spirit rose. If they'd waited up the mountain for darkness, they really might have over-looked Mai. She certainly wasn't much of a vocal presence and, hidden by the high table, may not have even been visible from their vantage point.

"That's right, LT, no doubt," the tracker said. "When we manage our own teams, we'll know who got us there. No one better. Hell, you should be our next Chairperson." Timetaker's spine stiffened at the remark. A vigilante can cover their face, but the body never lies.

"Yeah, well, I wouldn't hold out much hope for it," the top dog said. "Those feckless fools in San Francisco always pick some clown for Chairperson. Like the last guy. Honestly, if he didn't give us free reign on patrols, I'd think he was just a plant from the Anti-Racists to watch us, keep tabs on us—keep us on their leash and under control."

"Well, they should pick you," the suck-up scout said. "And they have to decide soon. How long has it been since we had an official Chairperson? All spring, at least. Maybe even six months? We can't stay in limbo like this forever."

"We'll see," Timetaker said with another glance at his compass. "Who knows? But we gotta get moving. There's another ten or so miles to go, and I want that morning bonus."

Whatever the "morning bonus" was, Quinceton didn't want it, and he didn't want his captors to get it either. The moon had come and gone, leaving only the predawn darkness behind, and it wouldn't last, just like the body. Eventually Quinceton would follow Tinh, and if there was any lesson to be learned from the longtime holdout, it was to approach both life and death with the same calm. To do, and ultimately be undone, with the same inner peace.

They stood, marching on, for hours more, heading past a peeking sun and into early morning with the glare threatening to tax everyone's exhaustion with its own burning attention. As the rising heat began to shadow over their silhouettes, far from its peak height, they reached a crumbling road, and soon a gray chain-link fence appeared in the distance. Long before there was another building, there was simply the barbed-wire-topped iron of the perimeter, a few dozen feet high, rising out of a surrounding moat of broken glass. When they got close enough to see their road arrive at an entrance gate guarded by many pairs of shrouded eyeballs, a sign forged from metal became legible.

The top line read: "STOCKTON DIVERSITY, EQUITY & INCLUSION CAMP." Below, in a sort of glamorous cursive font of bent wire, another sign read: "FREEDOM IS WORK."

"I never would have believed it," Sarah's voice cracked from behind Quinceton. "Never again—never again, even here."

"Quiet yourself," Timetaker said with menace. "You'll be sorted out soon."

Quinceton didn't like the way Timetaker spoke to Sarah, but he liked the way the other AAA goons looked at her even less. The Anti-Anti-Anti-Racists had been originally formed by the Elect to do the unenviable task of replacing traditional American law enforcement with a humane, restorative, and rehabilitation-focused program that could simultaneously bolster food supplies across the state. But the early AAA recruits were mostly social outcasts, the most vile and hideous of all honkeys, with radical politics and a willingness to stand out by doing what others wouldn't, frequently punctuated by Fetal Alcohol Syndrome skulls and other hallmarks of white trash lineage.

Many of them had also been involuntary celibate "incels" before they were officially AAA, and that's why Quinceton watched them so closely around Sarah—you couldn't trust a sexless man around a womxn, *any* womxn. Sexless men had to be either liars or dangerously repressed, and either should be avoided. At least Timetaker was a new breed of AAA agent, and as he seemed both capable and not all that inbred, he had perhaps chosen law enforcement as a career path among some other options.

In another few paces, they reached the entrance as the boss relayed details of the capture—three possible deserters, claiming to be survivors from the Battle of South Lake, caught boarding with an aged Oriental Anti-Anti-Racist in an unsanctioned mountain compound. As Timetaker finished the explanation, he took off his gloves and showed a light-skinned right hand to the entrance guard, palm forward. Then the other AAA rangers did the same and the guard matched their gesture, showing his right-hand palm to the boss and Quinceton standing nearby. Some sort of burned tattoo of a black skull had been scorched onto each palm. Fittingly, the entrance guard and all of the other AAA rangers had pretty light skin.

"Your direct action campaign appears to be a success," the guard said to the boss. "A good haul ... and didn't you get a couple last week, too? Continue to processing." They waved to some other black-clad AAA guards who pulled at barricades blocking the gate and heaved it open.

The fence stretched farther in either direction than Quinceton could squint, and he couldn't see where the road ended, just that it pushed through field after field of farmland. Various people with big empty sacks slung over their shoulders picked at the stalks of different plants, wearing tattered shirts and pants with holes at the knees instead of the AAA's trademark black block armor. None looked up as Quinceton and the others passed by in silence.

A massive multistory mansion appeared in the distance and they soon walked along a gravel street lined by tall oaks and green grass, watered by sprinklers that rose out of the ground. The manicured lawn and ample shade, clearly approved by the top of the government bureaucracy, suggested a cheerfulness in the DIE Camp that Quinceton hadn't seen coming. What did he really know about the Anti-Anti-Anti-Racists? After all, weren't they a nomadic institution composed of dogmatic individuals the ruling JSS Anti-Racists couldn't control? So who knew *anything* firm about what really happened here? This posse of AAA rangers were bloodthirsty killers, but they had no way of knowing about the loyalties of Quinceton and the other Battle of South Lake survivors. If there was any hope for New California under the current government, it would have to come from the AAA, savage though their tactics happened to be.

The road lead to a cul-de-sac abutting a mansion with huge columns adorning the front against a flowing staircase that curved its way up to the second floor from both the left and right wings. A handful of black-tuxedo-clad BIPOCs lined the ground with grim smiles, hands at their sides, and the same rigid posture holding their shoulders upright. A light-skinned gender-bending-presenting person sat in a big armchair in a bathing suit watching the new arrivals with an eerily familiar face. Everything besides this looming figure of prestige in a red bikini seemed very formal—fancy, even, but stiff, and forced.

"Bring forward our new guests!" the sitting person called to Quinceton's exhausted gang. Reaching the foot of the stairs enabled a closer inspection, revealing the sight of Redgrave—maniacal former Captain of the army at South Lake—certainly here to do much more than quash Quinceton's faint hope for an easy exit from DIE. His tortured bikini stretched in all directions as he motioned them forward from the armchair.

A ripple of hesitation circulated through the familiar AAA rangers as three turned to their leader for guidance. Quinceton understood at once that they'd left under different circumstances than they now found themselves in, and they were all about to meet a new figure in the AAA hierarchy. There was no way of knowing how long the rangers had been combing the land for Liberati—or Anti-Anti-Racists, as the Anti-Anti-Anti-Racists would call them—but it must have been only a few days since Redgrave's disastrous stewardship of the Battle of South Lake had led to this apparent career advancement.

"Well, then," Timetaker began, pocketing his compass. "Let's meet the new brains." At these words, Quinceton felt the shove of a rifle in his back as the rangers pushed their captives up the stairs to greet Redgrave—the nemesis of many fallen JSS government soldiers, and now perhaps Quinceton's only savior.

He had one leg slung over the other, sipping from a glass of floating ice cubes and lemon, with so many shards of citrus concentrated in the drink that it had lost translucence. An elder Black man in a loose tuxedo fanned Redgrave with a big flat circle of intertwined green reeds connected to a wooden pole. Once the roving posse reached the top of the staircase, the rangers felled their captives with rifle butts to the back of their knees.

"Welcome to Stockton, New California," Redgrave said to the captives, who shuddered in the no-man's-land between the rangers and their new despot. As he scanned the new prisoners, Redgrave's eyes seemed to linger on Quinceton, looking him up and down.

"Stockton, New California: not the home you want, maybe not a home you can survive, but the only home you'll ever need. Now, you're here because you've got a lot to learn, but don't worry, I promise you the time to learn it." His eyes peered up at the rangers. "And allow me to introduce myself to these esteemed agents of Social Justice. I was born John Charles, but for now I'll serve as Anti-Anti-Anti-Racist Chairperson Redgrave: he/him pronouns. Here to lead all criminal justice reeducation establishments throughout California, through our humble outpost here in lovely Stockton."

Figures moved behind Quinceton, and he turned to see the AAA rangers all standing with a naked palm extended toward Redgrave. The dark skull brands varied in clarity—they must have been administered at very different times—but it was unmistakably the same.

A look of concern flashed across Redgrave's face as he holstered his drink on a side table and reset his massive bulk on the cushions, squirming without satisfaction.

"Your commitment is noted—my de-whitening ceremony is this evening. You will all receive the morning bonus on three detainees. And perhaps after enjoying some of your bounty, you will attend my initiation on the Great Lawn. Now, which one of you is Lieutenant Timetaker?"

"I am, sir," the ranger boss answered. "We are ready to conduct interrogation as soon as you assign status."

Redgrave—former Captain, current Chairperson—winced again at the shrouded suggestion, as though it were a reminder of something he'd forgotten. These had to be his first days, explaining why the de-whitening initiation had yet to commence. Once again his eyes fell on Quinceton.

"Of course. That one, the fit Black one, he looks like a real Blue Flame Special: 'Young, dumb, and fulla come.' He may be cut out for the house—

you do the questioning and report back. The other two, I wouldn't hold out much hope for; you can do whatever you want with those. The old one needs a bandage for the mouth or he won't last two meals. We're short in the fields now anyway, and San Francisco is calling for help, too."

"Yes, sir," Timetaker said, grabbing Quinceton's arm and yanking him to his feet. There was no way of knowing Timetaker's officially legal gender, but from the power in his hands, he had to have been born male.

"Ezeetus, deal with these two," Timetaker commanded with a nod. "Take them to the viewing barn."

And then Quinceton trudged along again, down the curving staircase, past the side of the mansion, and into the backyard, where he saw rows of tin-roof cabins lined up on either side of an open, freshly cut lawn with a wooden humane dispatchment platform separating the domiciles about one hundred yards out from the mansion. The pocked tin roof and gaps between cabin panels didn't seem to fit with the perfectly manicured grass, nor the precise carpentry of the execution contraption. The stage rose from the ground with sanded edges, stairs of the same height, and a trapdoor/noose combo dead center. Quinceton's carpenter father would have happily signed off on the quality of the work.

"Over there," the Lieutenant said, pointing behind the cabins to some hole in the Earth that Quinceton couldn't quite make out. Timetaker didn't touch Quinceton this time, and his tone veered from the intentionally intimidating commands the hostages had received up to this point into a form of simple guidance. As if transforming into a tour guide, he explained, "The mansion is here, the prisoners are here, and the next thing is over this way," all ho-hum and business as usual.

The shape of the hole mutated into a low wall guarding a set of stairs that cut directly into the ground. At the top of the steps, Quinceton turned back to the mansion only to see the view obscured by the rickety huts between them.

Timetaker descended first, keeping an eye on Quinceton but trusting that the captive would not run. "Down here," he said about halfway to a big black metal door at the base of the stairs. "A few questions and you'll get water, then you can sleep." It was the right bribe; Quinceton followed dutifully. He noticed streaks of blood on the gray concrete walls surrounding the steps but tried to keep his pace.

Timetaker pulled open the heavy door and Quinceton followed him into the bunker. Another AAA guard in identical all-black garb sat at a simple wooden table, their feet up, reading from a leaflet. They straightened up when they saw Timetaker.

"Rooms five and thirteen are open, sir," they said.

Timetaker nodded. "We do not yet know the true nature of this individual," the Lieutenant responded. "I need to piss. Restraints, but no screws."

It was at the word *screws* that made Quinceton finally understand where he was, who the AAA were, and how he might escape. As Timetaker disappeared and the guard led Quinceton down the hall toward a room labeled *V*, they passed an open door with an obese Black womxn pacing in front of a room of seated whites.

"… got another thing coming, if you think that. Really, now it's time to listen, or you wouldn't be needing to be sitting here right now. So if you think it's going to be easy *doing the work* here in Stockton, you've really got another thing coming. Seriously, who *the fuck* thinks I'm going to privilege White Tears up in this bunker? Do any of you *seriously* think I'm going to be privileging White Tears up in this piece?"

Quinceton looked closer and saw the whites were all strapped into their seats, foreheads tied back to keep the audience facing forward, eyelids fastened open with tape. Silently, the captive audience seemed to agree that the days of privileging White Tears were over.

The young sniper clasped his hands together and thought about the child he had known until mere hours ago. *She will survive,* he told himself. *She knows those woods, she's smart, and she's a survivor. She will survive somehow.*

He closed his eyes, letting the guard guide him forward, and prayed never to see Mai again.

ACT II, CHAPTER TWELVE

Identitarian Interrogation

THE ROOM WAS BARE SAVE for the table and two very different chairs, one of which had Quinceton attached by the wrists. It could have been worse: this chair had a high back and a horrid metal helmet-looking contraption which hung loosely behind his neck. The guard hadn't bothered with it—a good sign. Quinceton had caught an eyeful of its reeducation utility being displayed on some whites coming in, and he didn't need another demonstration. Minutes passed in dim silence, a weak overhead bulb illuminating little more than the stark concrete walls.

The door cranked open, and a figure stepped through with two large plastic cups of water. They placed one in front of Quinceton and sat on the opposing stool. With a careful tug, the familiar lieutenant of the AAA took off his mask and sipped away. Quinceton took this as his go-ahead and downed half his portion. It did little to quench his parched throat.

"We can take them off when we eat or drink," Timetaker said. This would defeat the widely assumed purpose of such a mask—preserving anonymity—but Quinceton's attention was focused on the shocking visage of the lieutenant. His voice didn't fit his face. On the mountain and the way back, there had been no hint of compassion or sympathy from this ranger boss man, but here he sat, almost justifying his actions ethically to a restrained prisoner. He was tall and built even in a hood, but Quinceton really hadn't expected handsome, with a jawbone that could define a generation.

In the beginning, when the AAA were becoming an organization you could identify with a three-letter acronym, their numbers were propped up by Elect rejects who had the right patter laudably memorized. But they were rejects nonetheless: faces you wouldn't want to see speaking to a crowd, skeletons you couldn't use to lift a spade, much less plow a field, and ambitious curiosity you could satiate by planting it in an isolated prison compound. Whatever Timetaker was, he wasn't any of these things, and as he watched Quinceton, the taste of an emerging power struggle seemed to rise out of the dank floor. It smelled like sweat, dirt, and lemonade.

"It's cool, comrade," Quinceton said, guessing at the right lingo but nailing the tone. "You don't need to mask up with me. I really have no idea what's going on, anyway. I was at South Lake, wound up at the mountain cabin place on the search back, and now I'm here. But I'm not a bad guy you have to worry about."

"Well, that's why we're here," Timetaker replied, shifting on the stool but loosening his tight, focused expression. "And we'll find out who is what. Now, I'm going to ask you some questions, and the most important thing isn't that you tell me the answer you *think* I want to hear, but just the truth. Pretend I already know every answer I'm asking for, and everything that comes next is a simple test of your ability to confirm what I already know. Can you do that? You understand what I'm saying?"

"Yes, sir. I won't lie. I've got no reason to do that."

"Okay. Great. Let's start with your name."

"I'm Quinceton Rift. Tactical sniper for the army of the JSS government."

"Where did you grow up? Who were your birthing parents?"

"I grew up in the Sunset District of San Francisco. My parents are Horace and Marcy Rift. They are gone now. I haven't seen either in years."

"What happened to them? Were they traitors to the state?"

"Truth is—I don't really know. I for sure don't know what happened to my seeder—he didn't like something about Work Doing Centers and left when I was a kid—but I think my birther went to a DIE Camp. At least that's what they told me. She was a part of the 2020 Project."

"Good!" Timetaker interjected with more passion than Quinceton thought him capable of. "You listened to me. Most people don't, you understand. Most people try to smart their way out of here. Finish that water and you can have mine."

Quinceton downed his remaining cup in two gulps. Timetaker's was in front of him when his eyes returned to the table.

"Thank you," Quinceton said. "I'm very thirsty and we've been up all night, so I hope I can give you what you want. For both our sakes."

"Yeah, I hear you. You won't be here any longer than I need. Now, to the best of your knowledge, what is your Intersectional IS score?"

"In the latest version, I think it was down to something like seven or six and a half."

"And where did those points come from?"

"Being Black, mostly, maybe entirely. For a little while I got a boost from being raised outside a nuclear family, but I think they changed that into a privilege, or maybe I got too old for it to matter. I don't follow politics that much, but I don't think I have any other victim status to submit. No religion or gender or body positivity or anything."

"Okay. Good. We can work with this. And were both of your parents Black? As in formerly African American? Descended from Africa and brought to America, as slaves, in chains?"

Quinceton hadn't expected this question. It wasn't something he had ever really considered, seeing as the three of them all *looked* Black and there was no cause to think otherwise.

"Well, yeah, I think so. They were Black, I'm Black. My seeder grew up in New Orleans—American South—and my birther was from a bigger city. Atlanta, I think. But I don't know how many slaves I came from. Just Black … I'm a Black guy."

"It's better to say you don't know than to know and lie. So, this question is important: Do you have any ancestors who immigrated to America

199

in the 1900s or later? Any Nigerian or Jamaican or Haitian blood in you? Especially Nigerian."

"No, I don't think so. My parents never said anything like that, and my skin isn't that dark. Well, you can see. I'm, like you said, a 'formerly African American' Black guy."

"That's good. Good to know who you are. And as a Black man, how do you feel about Social Justice? The Anti-Racist JSS government? How do you feel about fighting for the JSS government at South Lake Tahoe?"

This was the question Quinceton had anticipated long before the iron gates of Stockton, and he was less concerned with his words than his delivery. Most people sitting in this chair probably used the same words.

"Well, as a Black man, of course I know the value of Social Justice. That's what separates us from America: We are correcting the wrongs of the past. The JSS government does things I don't always understand, but— as a Black man—they give us Social Justice, and that's always worth it. So, like in South Lake, as a Black man, I don't maybe understand all the details, but I'm there to do my part." Reminders of identity were usually a safe habit, but Quinceton warned himself not to overdo it or it might make the lies stand out. He wished he had a better identity to list than "as a Black man," but it was the best stuff he had.

"And the Violence at South Lake Tahoe, the Violence hanging off the wall of the Nevada casino facing the border … did you see it? Did you force or allow yourself to read the poster?"

Timetaker sat quietly, his hands underneath the table, just staring at Quinceton. The whole ordeal, beginning at the cabin and continuing in this room, seemed to hinge on this single question. Quinceton wanted to know the grading but dare not ask.

"Yes," Quinceton admitted after some thought. "I remember being there at my sniper's perch, looking out at the whole scene, and thinking I should know the Violence that each other soldier had to deal with during the assault."

"And what did you see? What did the Nevada Violence tell you or say about the world of Social Justice we're creating?"

"I saw them making Knowing Leader Mumwaza out to be really ugly—pretty much what you might expect. They made Mumwaza seem even more ... body positive than the Knowing Leader might be in real life. It was an attack on all of us, really—just some basic American cisheteropatriarchy Violence to keep Anti-Racists penned in the only place where they're safe."

"Okay ..." Timetaker spoke slowly, eyes still stabbing at Quinceton's poker face. The pause dragged on as Quinceton sipped from Timetaker's gifted water cup with stiff formality, but the next questions seemed to confirm that the captive had avoided a previous trap.

"You spent a number of days and nights with the other survivors from South Lake," Timetaker said. "You must have gotten familiar with them." This wasn't a question, but it felt like coming to the climax of the interrogation.

"Yeah, comrade, we talked sometimes." Quinceton didn't know where to go with this—better redirect, he decided. "If you have a map, I can try to sketch our path out of Tahoe and to the cabin. We stopped in Placer—"

"That won't be necessary," Timetaker cut in. "The truth is, I want to help you, Quinceton. There is real potential in you. But we found you eating at a confirmed Anti-Anti-Racist compound. It's already in the report. And there must be some explanation, someone responsible. You understand."

"Oh I see." Quinceton understood all too well. "We were hungry, stopped at a pond to eat. It was a pond not too far from the mountain cabin, and the old man just found us and offered to help us out—feed us, give us a bed to sleep in. We didn't get into the politics of it. All those days hiking and scavenging ... I didn't think to argue with a little comfort."

Timetaker smiled softly, then leaned in with a look of sudden malevolence.

"Tell me, if you had to decide: Who was the most Anti-Anti Racist individual in the mountain compound?"

"Oh, the old Vietnamese man, definitely." A good answer. Dead men feel no pain.

"Is that how you found out he was a gook? Spouting some Racist Yellow bullshit?"

"Well, I don't know about all that," Quinceton responded, hesitant to totally smear the old man, even here. "He was just old, talked about coming from Vietnam and helping out the JSS government by cutting off the internet thing. But the way he talked, you could kinda tell he wasn't really loyal to New California. That's probably why he went hermit."

"No doubt. But your compatriots, the other survivors—did they mention anything that could be perceived as Anti-Anti-Racist? Think hard now, Quinceton. And remember, they will be asked the same about you."

"You know, in those few days we talked a little about our soldiering, but I'm not really into talking politics with people." Quinceton opened his arms to indicate the room, if not the whole camp. "People hear rumors about this place, and to be honest, they fear it. I think most people get in the habit of keeping their politics to themselves, but I have to admit I did tell them my birther was an Anti-Anti-Racist convicted over the 2020 Project. It was years ago, but maybe you've met her—Marcy Rift?"

"And the other two, how did they respond to your story about your birther?" Timetaker patently ignored the question Quinceton had pondered for close to a decade. "What did they think about the 2020 Project?"

"I don't think they said much of anything about it. We were eating at the time, in Placerville, and that was probably our longest day. The Jew girl remembered something about ending grades when she was in school, and the old soldier said his daughter really liked the replacement Work Doing Centers. If you want more, you'd have to ask them."

"We'll be sure to." Timetaker exhaled audibly. "Finish your water. I'm going to approve you for the house—trust me, that's me doing you a massive solid. And some free advice on the side: make friends around here. People from the house can get ahead ... no, really. In time, maybe they'll trust you again, or maybe even let you be an official ranger for the AAA."

"Well yeah, you just tell me where to go and how to get it done. I'm a good shot. You send me back, and no doubt I can help out the JSS government army."

"We'll see," Timetaker mused, rising to crank the heavy metal door open and calling for the lackey guard.

"You're one lucky son of a bitch," the lackey told Quinceton as they emerged from the underground staircase on the walk back to the mansion. That the lackey guided Quinceton with words, and not shoves, gave the distinct impression that the new prisoner had climbed a significant rung on the DIE Camp depth chart. "Not one in fifty people get to be houseguests—almost all become DIE reeducation patients in the fields. The lieutenant sees something in you, that's why." It wasn't menacing—it was congratulations.

"Yeah, I have no idea what's going on," Quinceton replied honestly as they passed by a row of shacks. The carpentry would have offended Dad more than the camp itself: No two boards lined up, and the wind whistled through cracks in both walls and ceiling. "So what's the deal with the house?"

"It's where you want to be, comrade," the guard said. "Believe that. You'd rather be in the house than the sheds—you'd take the sheds over the viewing barn, though—and you'd rather do a year of housework than a week in those fields." Quinceton had no trouble believing it. Sarah and Bones had gotten sent to the viewing barn, but it sounded like it could be temporary, and when they got to the sheds maybe they could all work on an escape.

As the guard walked him up the rear stairs to the mansion, Quinceton's view stretched across the horizon to an ocean of sunlight. The stairs arrived at a pleasant patio fit with a long table and bar. In the corner, tucked behind a jagged Corinthian column, was a door labeled "Servants' Quarters." The underground bunker guard handed the bewildered prisoner off to another stationed outside the Servants' Quarters with instructions to "get [Quinceton] some sleep." Nothing could have sounded sweeter.

Up another staircase, the new guard opened a light wood door to a simple room with a bed on either side. A person of indistinguishable everything lay on one, with the other bed's sheets tucked tight in a frozen promise to privilege—the good kind. The kind you could enjoy.

"This is your new roommate," the guard said to the lounger. "He's going to pass out, but wake him for dinner. We've got a de-whitening tonight."

His new roommate said something about something, but Quinceton didn't hear it. Sweet slumber instantly consumed his fears for the most necessary of respites.

ACT II, CHAPTER THIRTEEN

Houseguests

"HEY THERE ... IT'S TIME. It's time to get up." A rough, unrelenting voice eased Quinceton into the tragic news. He'd been dreaming of something warm, nourishing, happy, but it was already beyond recognition.

"Just a little more ... was up all night," he said without opening his eyes.

"You gotta wake up now." Quinceton felt a pinch at his shoulder and surrendered. He sat up, staring at his roommate for the first time. The person wasn't white, clearly wasn't cisgender, and currently eyed him with suspicion.

"I'm Quinceton—Black, cis man, blandbrain, he/him, full body privilege."

The person half chuckled and stood, crossing the small room in two gaping strides to face Quinceton from their own bed. "Once you make it to the house, you can't really get any further on your Intersectional IS Score. I'm Juniper—non-white mixed race trans womxn she/her with all other privilege." She caught Quinceton's astonishment, almost expecting it. "Yeah, trans people can go to DIE, too."

"Sorry, I just ... you know, I don't get the rules here. Your IS Score must be double most Elect. Can I ask ... how did you get here?"

"I miscommunicated. It's a mistake, and I've been in treatment ever since. They know my story, though, and I'll make it out of the house eventually. But it's pretty easy in here. You'll get used to it."

Quinceton's good fortune at landing such a cushy "house" gig seemed awfully relative given that he'd been happily frolicking on an open mountain just the day before. He shuddered to think where Bones and Sarah had been stuck, what with their inferior, practically worthless race, gender, and body-neutral identities.

"What do we do in the house? And where do the others go?"

"We serve the Anti-Anti-Anti-Racists. This is their headquarters, obviously, but there are other DIE Camps to the north and south. We make sure everyone has everything they need to promote Social Justice. And everyone else works the fields to help feed us, them, the JSS government's Anti-Racists, and even workers all over the state. Everyone relies on us, and for you and me, that means keeping the AAA happy."

"Okay," Quinceton said, careful to remember where he was and who he might be speaking to. "I can see how some good people can make mistakes, and they come here to learn from them. But then what happens? After you do your time here, I mean."

Juniper's eyes tightened into a look of suspicious confusion, which in turn perplexed Quinceton. Even though prisons and jails had been abolished along with official "policepersons" years back in a successful effort to eliminate all inequitable categories of crime, it seemed obvious that "houseguests" like Quinceton and Juniper were not allowed to leave, and that this lack of mobility might be generally unpleasant to most.

"It's not about 'doing time' or whatever happens to you next," Juniper scolded. "We've come here to grow and become better contributors to Social Justice. Roles may change, but if you just want to leave, you won't learn whatever lessons you need to learn."

"Oh, you're totally right," Quinceton said with not a moment's hesitation. "I was up all night marching here, answered some questions, and woke up five seconds ago. I'm just trying to figure out how I can improve my allyship in the cause. Please, Juniper, I hope you'll show me how to act right and learn from my mistakes."

Her face brightened once again. All was well, and now having confirmed that they played for the same team, Juniper hastily agreed to mentor her new roommate.

"We, guests of the house, have free-roaming privileges," she explained as they exited their room and strolled down the hallway. "But you can't abuse them or you'll lose them."

There had to be at least a dozen rooms on either side of a baby-blue hallway, painted all white save for shiny bronze numbers that all seemed to hang from the same height. Quinceton could hear commotion somewhere but saw no one.

A stairwell met them at the end of the hall, and they climbed a floor into a scene that reminded Quinceton of a wall he might see at San Francisco's MOMA art gallery. Intricate portraits of American horror, from the slavery of Africans to the genocide of the Indigenous, covered every inch of wall space. One such image of a slave market auction halted Quinceton's pace, gasping at seeping whip wounds crisscrossing the back of one doomed soul.

"I know, right?" Juniper confirmed cheerfully. "Any reminder helps." She pointed to the top half of a mural on a far wall. "And I helped with that one of Saint Floyd when he'd hand out presents to orphan BIPOC children at the beginning of the winter season."

It was unmistakably St. Floyd, the painting split by a bright line separating the picture of generosity above with St. Floyd's suffocating murder by a white policeperson below. The powerful juxtaposition matched the appearance of the ornate mansion beside windswept shacks.

"Is this hall for the AAA rangers?" Quinceton asked.

"Oh, no, they mostly live in quieter houses spread around the compound. You know, to keep some eyes everywhere and keep guards close to their stations. This hall is for VIP guests—that stands for 'Very Important Person.'"

"Like Knowing Leader Xumwaza Q. Jumping Bull? VIPs like the Speakers and Knowers?" Quinceton knew the Knowing Leader had to live in a nice San Francisco Safe Space, but it was possible Jumping Bull kept a penthouse suite everywhere it was useful.

"Not exactly." Juniper wore the same blank stare that had first appeared when Quinceton asked about life after the DIE Camp. It was a flat-lipped expression that could just pass for a smile at the upturned corners of the mouth, but there was no happiness to it. And whatever explanation Quinceton actually wanted to hear was never really accessible.

There were only three rooms in this hallway for three big suites, and though they all faced outwards for a VIP view, the doors were an intimidating presence with metal frames and no keylocks or doorknobs. Interior windows opposite the VIP rooms revealed a gathering party on the rear patio. A line of tuxedo-clad persons of color served drinks and took orders from hoodless off-duty AAA agents at long tables as a larger crowd of lesser "rehabilitation patients" (rather than selected houseguests, like Quinceton) gathered on the grass below. Their clothes were something of a tattered, faded rainbow, as they lacked any cohesive uniform, but they all carried the same fieldwork stains on their clothes.

"It hasn't started yet, but we need to hurry," Juniper continued. "This is the quickest way to show you. See the people in tuxedo uniforms? See what they're doing—how they never stop moving? Those are the houseguests, like us, and doing some version of that work is the privilege you've been granted."

"I see," Quinceton said.

They retreated to the same staircase they'd used before, descending four or five flights this time into a boiling basement filled with the commotion of catering. Sarah had prepared Quinceton for this with her tales of attending to San Francisco's Elect, and since everyone had something to do, no one really paid him much attention.

"This is Margarite, the head houseguest," Juniper said, introducing Quinceton to a flustered middle-aged womxn around thirty of Mexican hue and the ample heft of body positivity. "She will set you up."

"June, they need help behind the bar—change and get over there." She turned to Quinceton and spoke with the same impatience. "Follow me."

"I know you're the new guy," Margarite continued as they weaved through streams of hurried houseguests. "No time for intros, and no time to tailor a tux, although"—she took a longer look at Quinceton's upper body without slowing her pace—"you're just about the perfect size. Six feet and skinny is easy. Just don't drink from the bar. No alcohol for houseguests."

They arrived in a large laundry room with a very old Black man folding white fabric. He didn't look up as they entered, nor did he look up when Margarite instructed him to outfit Quinceton for a "bar-back" role. The head houseguest was back in the mix before a quiet "Yes, ma'am" fell from the elderly man's lips. He gazed at Quinceton for a split second, then shuffled to the opposite corner of the room where a line of hangers emerged from a deep enclave.

"About six feet, one seventy, one seventy-five?" he asked.

"That should fit."

The man hit a button and a motorized machine propelled the hangers along their track. He stopped on a tuxedo with a green bow tie and handed it to Quinceton. "Put this on. The green means you work the bar, so once you have it on, they will expect you behind the bar."

Quinceton nodded and undressed as the old man returned to his folding. "What should I do with my clothes?"

The old man pointed to a stack of tickets beside the laundry door. "Fill out one of these with your room number, and I'll wash them and get them back to you. Your soldier gear might get used again, and it's a good reminder to them that you served in some way before you got here."

"Thank you, sir."

The old man stopped what he was doing. "I'm no 'sir.' Just like I'm no friend, no enemy." He watched Quinceton struggle with his knot. "You need help with that bow tie?"

"Yes, please. Yes I do."

The old man ambled over. His fingers fluttered around Quinceton's neck with amazing speed, and in seconds, the green guest assignment had been secured.

"You're young. You have a lot to see, but time to do it," the old man said as he returned to his folding table. "Anything might happen to you. But remember this: be careful about your friends, be careful about your enemies ... might be safer to make none of either. Good luck out there, son."

ACT II, CHAPTER FOURTEEN
De-Whitening

FROM HIS PERCH BEHIND THE bar, Quinceton had a fairly good view of the patio crowd, the accumulating rehabilitation patients on the grass below, and his own dumb luck. Juniper was responsible for knowing things, whereas he just had to follow simple directions. It wasn't hard to mix a shot from a plastic container of vodka with a shot of orange juice while saying nothing and listening to everything.

"Act servile," he'd been told by the head bartender upon arriving with the requisite bow tie. "That means you obey, you do as you're told, and you don't speak unless absolutely necessary. Usually a nod will do. 'Servile' means we're the background, here to support the work of the AAA agents by attending to their needs."

Most of it was instinctive, except Quinceton needed to work on his emotionally blank face. He couldn't just *not* listen to conversations that interested him, which was fine, so long as he looked pleasantly indifferent. It was Redgrave, that maniacal magician of Social Justice politics, who seemed to delight in tearing at other AAA agents' composure.

"It's barely a promotion," former Captain Redgrave's naked face snorted to another agent while hanging his cleavage over the bar. "If those cocks want me working DIE, they just made one hell of an Anti-Anti-Anti-Racist to deal with later. Those cocks told me to handle South Lake, and

I'd be set. And I handled South Lake, all right, but now here I am, sweating balls in Stockton." Redgrave was never the right temperature. Whenever he said "cocks," he meant the JSS government Anti-Racist decision-makers, which was simultaneously amusing, thought-provoking, and proof of incredible power; and whenever he said "balls," it was usually a reference to hardship, particularly his own.

"So you feel more Anti-Anti-Anti-Racist than Anti-Racist these days?" Redgrave's companion asked. They still wore their hood over their eyes and scalp.

"Sure, why not?" Redgrave gave his tumbler a long pull before setting it back in front of Quinceton. "Hit me again, hot stuff." Quinceton hurried in with equal parts "gin" and "tonic," plus a lime wedge hanging from the glass.

"Do you have any big plans for the AAA?" the companion asked carefully.

This is probably the question they've been heading toward all night, Quinceton thought.

"Once I get a lay of the land … we'll see." Redgrave appeared to consider the question for the first time. What with him running the show and all, one might think he'd had a strategic plan to pitch somewhat *before* landing the top job, but then one would be mistaken. Or perhaps getting the job hadn't required a new strategy for the AAA, and it was strategy that would free Redgrave from Stockton, just like Quinceton.

"And, honestly, fuck that name. 'The AAA'—it sounds like a car company. It's about time we stop naming ourselves in opposition to whatever came before. People will think we're out of ideas except bitching about the past. I want suggestions. A new name."

The companion offered no alternatives before Quinceton was swept to the rear of the bar to splinter more ice. Trays of food, hoisted by a line of red-bow-tied waiters, floated in from the mansion as the AAA agents took this as a cue to seat themselves. There were racks of meat still attached to the bone, fried chicken wings, and mashed potatoes with butter puddling in the center. Quinceton eyed the amount of food, the number of AAA agents, and calculated a high probability that leftovers would come his way.

Chairperson Redgrave chose the head of the largest table—back to the mansion, facing the rehabilitation patients down on the great lawn—but his demeanor changed over the course of the meal as he gradually went silent, save for bossing around some houseguest staff. Before the tables were cleared, a gang of hooded AAA agents carried two arm-length poles stuck in some kind of metal box to the edge of the patio where all could see. The crowd hushed as Redgrave rose to assume his position in the ceremony.

"We, the Anti-Anti-Anti-Racists of the Stockton Diversity, Inclusion, and Equity camp, are privileged to receive and anoint John Charles Redgrave as our new acting Chairperson," one agent intoned. They kept their hood on, even as most others doffed their own to eat, drink, and whisper. "In accordance with our original bylaws, no legal member of the Caucasian race is eligible for membership in the Anti-Anti-Anti-Racist coalition. We will therefore commence with the de-whitening." The agent removed the poles from their cage, exposing the same red-hot shape attached to the end of each one. Redgrave stood stiff, like a JSS soldier at attention.

"Do you renounce all that is white or whiteness, including your ancestral history, all forms of self-reliance, and the nuclear family?"

"I do."

"Do you declare that rational thinking, logical reasoning, and the scientific method are Racist forms of knowledge acquisition, and that lived experience is the authentic source of truth?"

"I do."

The officiant extended the hot tips of the poles to Redgrave, the menacing shape at the end of each sizzling stake growing closer to his skin.

"Accept the purification with the center of your palms," the officiant said, and without a moment's hesitation Redgrave pressed the center of his hands against the searing rods. The smell of roasting human flesh wafted past Quinceton's nose. It was a familiar smell, and he, like Redgrave, never flinched. Perhaps they thought of the same rolling firestorms in South Lake.

"Do you pledge to hold all Racists accountable for their actions in this life and throughout history? To avenge the eternal savagery perpetrated against BIPOC bodies? And to never waver in the war for Justice, be it social, racial, and/or historic?"

"I do." Redgrave stared straight ahead as the AAA skull seared itself into his flat hands.

"Enough—you are cleansed of whiteness! Behold, our Anti-Anti-Anti-Racist leader!" Redgrave let go and held his arms straight up, displaying his new skull burns for all to witness. The crowd clapped as he rotated briefly to show the captive patients on the grass below.

At the edge of the huddled masses, cowering with exhaustion, Quinceton saw the unmistakable JSS government camouflage shirts he'd so recently worn below his body armor. Battered, bruised, and bleeding from their eye sockets, Sarah and Bones watched the spectacle with indifference. Their escape from whiteness would not be so easy.

ACT II, CHAPTER FIFTEEN

VIP Reservations

IN SPITE OF HIS PRIVILEGES and freedom to roam, Quinceton couldn't locate either of his friends in his first week at the mansion. The highest hurdle was the impossibility of gathering information on their whereabouts without revealing that he cared about such a thing, and beyond that, the AAA kept him busy. There was always something to learn by shadowing someone who'd done it before, and when he finally got the chance to sleep, he did not question it.

Quinceton also didn't need another lecture from his roommate. Juniper didn't leave shit around the room and made her bed each morning, which removed any cause for further communication. Convinced as she was that her status as a "guest" was only temporary—"It was a mistake to begin with. I would never question the methods of Social Justice!"—she spoke pure orthodoxy, and couldn't be trusted with even the most mundane queries. It went without saying that she would report Quinceton for even asking about his former fellow JSS government soldiers, and as such, the offense for which she'd been sent to DIE remained a mystery.

It was on Quinceton's third day as guest staff that he first got to deliver meals to the VIP hallway, and it was this hall of well-kept Very Important Persons that finally held the promise of further insight. The VIP celebrities fascinated him. Unlike Redgrave, whom he delivered to with increasing frequency, the duty-free guests spoke to him like a person—one human be-ing to another, without regard to DIE Camp status, Intersectional IS Score, previous JSS government record, or any other form of socially constructed consideration.

There were only three suites on the VIP floor, and suites they were: luscious two-bedroom condos beginning with a private living room that Quinceton could see through the bars behind the hallway doors. Guests and even AAA agents were banned from entering the VIP suites, just as the VIPs were prevented from exiting. This reality appeared permanent, as the secu-rity gates lacked a keyhole, giving every appearance of having been welded shut. Quinceton would pass VIP food through a thin slit around waist level and usually collected the previous tray without further interaction.

An elder dark-skinned Muslim man lived in VIP#1. Quinceton knew this from his first delivery, as the man prayed facing the same direction around the time lunch usually arrived. He was probably in his mid-forties, Arab of some kind and, compounded by genuine Muslim faith, would have had a pretty decent Intersectional IS score back in San Francisco.

The womxn-appearing person in VIP#2 crushed "her" neighbor on in-tersectional points, though, what with African American heritage and some kind of impressive gender identity, all while confined to a wheelchair at an age just above Quinceton's. Everything about this person suggested an identitarian prodigy who would spend the next half century defining and redefining race and gender norms as a Speaker or Knower for the benefit of all. That Quinceton now found her rolling around the top floor of the AAA mansion requesting white market books to read had to be a stunning fall from grace that few could ever comprehend. Quinceton's mother would have been able to relate, but to Quinceton, this person just begged ques-tions that would never be answered. Perhaps asking too often was what had landed her here.

But it was the man in VIP#3 that held actual promise; he verbally thanked Quinceton each and every time he came around. He was an In-digenous individual so old, he might have been around for the cowboys' systemic genocide of the American West, and he wore a beaded headdress whenever Quinceton saw him through the bars, the flashy dyed feathers extending vertically from the base. Just from the look of this fancy garb, Quinceton decided he was some kind of wise leader.

"You're welcome," Quinceton said to the man in his second week. "Anything else I can get for you?"

The man watched Quinceton for a beat, holding his tray without a flicker of emotion.

"Not unless you're serving strong drink," he answered. "And they told me when I got here that I'd had my last 'firewater,' they called it. So now I have everything I can have, but you ..." He paused, looking deeper into Quinceton's face. "You are new here, and still so young."

"I'm eighteen," Quinceton said, almost defensively. "I've worked in the fields before, fought in the JSS government army, and explored all over California. So I might not be as young as you think." He glanced down the hallway just to be safe. He heard and saw no one else.

"When I was eighteen, I knew how to hunt, how to roam. I was not so unlike you. I knew everything then, too. And how much good did it do me? Now I'm here, and so are you."

"Well, I survived the Battle of South Lake with two other soldiers, but on our way back we stopped at a mountain cabin. It turned out to be an Anti-Anti-Racist outpost, so now I'm here to cleanse myself so I can rejoin society."

"Oh, is that what you want? To rejoin them, and continue the fight for ... what you're fighting for?"

"To be honest, I still don't know how it works around here," Quinceton responded. He'd learned that ignorance was his greatest asset, perhaps his only inquisitive mechanism, and his most valuable claim. It encouraged some people to assume whatever they wanted to think about him and speak without extra suspicion.

"You know enough to see the truth," the old man said. "Thank you for the meal." He turned away, and it wasn't until the following day that Quinceton was able to continue the conversation. When he had his chance, he couldn't resist some incalculable risk.

"You're welcome," Quinceton said quickly after being thanked. "And I thought about what you said, and it makes me very curious. I've learned that I'm lucky to be a houseguest, rather than a field patient, and that some houseguests become AAA and others can go other places, even back to the city. Is that true?"

"As far as I know," the old man replied. "I have been in this room for years, and I've seen many, many different people come to my door. So some move on, but as to where, I cannot be sure." There was a kindness to his words, but even more crucial, there was truth.

"I survived a battle with two other soldiers," Quinceton reminded the VIP. "And we all came here together but were separated, and now they are field patients. Do you know what will happen to them?"

"I know that most new slaves are watched closely. They need to build trust before they are housed in the regular shacks you see on the lawn. When they make it out of the interrogation bunker, they will work during the day and are sent to sleep in a big animal barn to the west. You're probably going to find some older prisoners there, too—ones who couldn't graduate for any reason. The big red barn is a place the slavers can watch the prisoners interact with each other. The strongest test of loyalty comes when one believes they are safe."

From another person's mouth this could have sounded like a warning, but the message contained too much information to put Quinceton in more danger than its source. The old man could already tell that Quinceton cared about his former companions.

"Do you think your friend would be willing to lay with one of the AAA? That's one way I've seen people come out of the big red barn."

"Definitely, definitely not," Quinceton said, shaking his head. "Which barn is it?"

"It's right there," he said, pointing through his window. "The tall red barn with the steep roof that parts in the middle." There were a few buildings on the horizon, most of which had to be food storage and packaging, but Quinceton could easily see the one he meant.

"You know ..." Quinceton trailed off. "I really—thank you. If there's anything I can get for you, do for you, just let me know."

The old man simply nodded. "You come across an extra bottle of whiskey, you stick it through the gate any time—day, night, dawn, whatever. They won't let us drink nothing, but they don't punish us, neither, so anything'll be safe with me. I'd watch the last of the world burn for one damn bottle of whiskey."

"One more question: Why are you here?" Quinceton couldn't resist. He had to know. "You do something Racist against the state?"

"No. I'm here because I'm too dangerous to let roam free." The old man saw this answer fail to blunt Quinceton's curiosity. "I'm Ohlone," he offered.

Quinceton had heard the name so many times before but still felt he missed whatever implication was made. "The San Francisco tribe? I've heard ten million land acknowledgements for you guys. They kicked you out of San Francisco?"

"Yes. The Americans did, over one hundred and fifty years ago. I was living on the edge of California, way up in the North State, when these new JSS government people found me."

"To get you back in San Francisco?" Quinceton could imagine the old man being paraded around a Union Square art installation in even more garb, casting white guilt in all directions—an effective reminder of the forgotten beneficiaries of Social Justice.

"Nope. When they came to our reservation, promising to give us the things they valued, they told us they would fix all our racial problems and—what was their word?—'liberate' the oppressed something-men or something-women. I can't recall all the right words now, or who was living among us at the time. There was this one pamphlet I remember: '*What part of your tribal ancestry qualifies you for intersectional Indigenous victimization benefits, and in what ways are you prepared to verbalize your historic oppression?*' Unreal. It didn't make any sense, not then, and not telling it to you now. It was like aliens coming down from space and telling you that they know you better than you know yourself, and it's Racist not to see yourself like all of the outsider race experts do."

"So the Anti-Racist JSS government people helped you out, did they? Very helpful, understanding, tolerant, good listeners?"

"Not exactly. They gave me a lot of papers to fill out and demanded I go through some racial request department to keep our land on the opposite side of California. I didn't understand what they meant, but I spoke out for my people anyway. I didn't fill out the forms—I didn't understand the many different categories of victim qualifications, their different share of resources, and that whole reward system. I asked only for that which my father and my ancestors before him have wanted: to be left alone. To live as we always have, but separate from the busy city world—only in peace. To rely on our own customs, food supplies, and people: to realize a community for ourselves. And for that, for not understanding the victimhood of we last remaining Ohlone, they didn't want me speaking up anymore and reserved this room for me. From the American reservation to exclusive reservations for the best suite in New California: VIP cage number three."

The VIPS did have the nicer rooms, but suddenly Quinceton felt certain the "houseguests" had the better deal.

ACT II, CHAPTER SIXTEEN

Redgrave's Approval

THE FIRST TIME QUINCETON VENTURED into Redgrave's main office, he wasn't thinking much about local politics. He carried a tray containing a meat-filled omelet and hot coffee, mostly focused on making the delivery without spilling anything.

Chairperson John Charles Redgrave had wasted no time decorating the place, assuming the interior décor had been his choice, which seemed a safe assumption. The walls were covered with framed images of wartime genocide, slavery, rape, and burning buildings amidst rainbow Black Bipolar Disabled Trans Lives Matter flags and an old black-and-red Antifa banner. By calling themselves "Anti-Fascist" and asserting American values of individual liberty and self-determination as the fascist threat, these "Anti-Fascist" Antifa were crucial in persuading impressionable young people that American democracy and laws were the contemporary presence of evil/white supremacy.

Quinceton lingered on the Antifa logo as he waited in the entryway with the full tray. He wondered how much the early American Antifa "direct action" campaigns to disrupt society and demand displays of conformity were inspiration for California's modern AAA.

"Set it down here, on the desk," Redgrave commanded. He rarely spoke casually—everything came as a command from the belly, with force.

"Yes, sir," Quinceton responded, dutifully setting the tray down where instructed. Redgrave watched him in silence, just as he had when Quinceton first arrived.

"You're one of the soldiers from South Lake," he said. "Have a chair and sit. We never got to meet, but as you know, I was there, too. What did you see?"

"It seemed to be well planned," Quinceton answered, a bald-faced lie, as he assumed one of two chairs facing the mahogany desk. "And I remember the speech you gave the night before, in the Holiday Inn Express. I think the soldiers really wanted to win for you, but we didn't plan on those fixed guns. They seemed invincible. And no matter how many waves of people we sent in, we just couldn't seem to dig in, knock any of them out, and push forward."

"It was that detestable Smythe," Redgrave cut in with surprising scorn, recalling the Command Sergeant Major who had actually revered the former Captain far more than anyone else had. "That worthless pussy. This is who they give me, so what can they expect? I mean, can you imagine Smythe being respected, listened to, or in charge of anything else? That's way too many of the early Anti-Anti-Anti-Racist recruits, to be honest."

Quinceton didn't know what to say, so he stayed silent. Redgrave could criticize anyone he damn well pleased in this room, but Quinceton would be a fool to guess about who he could badmouth, much less when or why.

Redgrave seemed to want to explain the outcome of the Battle of South Lake as a disaster without coming right out and literally admitting as much. "I get sent a useless pussy like Smythe because there's nothing anyone else can do with xir. You get that, right? Take one look at the guy and you know xir was some totally unfuckable loser every day of *his* life before he became a *xir* they could promote to an operation like the attack on the Nevada casinos. Freaks, outcasts, and the perpetually unable to get laid are really who built the ground floor of what you're currently enjoying around you. But all people need a guiding light. The people need a vision … enter a visionary. So either that's why they wanted me here, or that's why they should've never let me take over."

"I can see that," Quinceton agreed. "And you were born to lead."

Redgrave nodded. "Anyway, in spite of how little human capital we had to work with, we didn't anticipate such cowardice in Tahoe, and so many soldiers abandoning the cause for Social Justice. You were a sniper. Where was your perch?"

"I lucked out with the southernmost spot, up at the top of one of those chairlift poles. We were at the base of Mount Heavenly, southwest of the action, but elevated so I could see the water landing and everything. Truth is, we never even took incoming from the fixed guns. Maybe just too far away, or too far outside the scope of their view."

Redgrave liked this answer. He clapped and actually circled around the desk to slap Quinceton on the back and sit down next to him. Placing one leg over the other, both hairy things barely hidden by a miniskirt, he leaned in and showed off some unusually pearly whites.

"No doubt you did get lucky," he said, grinning. "You watched a lot of your fellow infantry get caught up in an old-fashioned pincer movement— caught between the enemy and your own people shooting at you! Doomed on both sides, the sorry bastards." Redgrave neglected to mention that he was the one doing a lot of the dooming. "And lucky you were named a houseguest after being discovered in an Anti-Anti-Racist compound! But here you are. Do you know how lucky you are, Quinceton?"

"Yes, yes I do, sir. I haven't seen the other two soldiers I came with, so I know not everybody is as lucky."

"I'm familiar with their cases. They have much loyalty to prove to the state before they may be redirected. Did you sense their traitorous sensibilities on your return journey?"

"Not at all," Quinceton said, almost too quickly. Super-polite vocab made him nervous. "We didn't speak that much, though. Most people don't talk about politics in the open."

"I believe you. The cocks in San Francisco don't really tell me what they're thinking, either. I just reported back after Tahoe, and then got promised this place. No explanation. No one telling me where all this leads, although it won't lead to Knowing Leader for me, that's for sure.

Not everyone gets lucky. Not everyone finds favor with the right people."

Quinceton listened intently, maintaining eye contact. He nodded. He didn't want to risk interrupting Redgrave when he started divulging actual information.

"But real champions, real champions of righteousness—they persevere. They get done what needs to get done. And they thrive. Everyone you see around you in the mansion is learning to work toward a more equitable future, with or without the JSS government." Quinceton stifled a gasp as Redgrave continued. "The future of New California is the AAA, although named something else. We're working on it. It all comes down to the *I* in DIE. Tell me, young man, do you know why they call it a Diversity, Equity, and Inclusion Camp? They changed the letters around in the DIE acronym, but the words are the same, even if the meaning is different."

There was a pause as Quinceton felt the gnawing sensation that he was supposed to answer a question. "No. I don't actually know why they call it Diversity, Equity, and Inclusion, but I think that title comes from decades ago."

"Well, the diversity bit, you can see with your own two eyes, right?" Redgrave asked.

Quinceton had stumbled upon the right topic, as it allowed the big guy to make the speech he clearly wanted to make. "Yeah, totally. You got every race under the sun to worry about in New California."

"We do, but is that really what diversity means? Like when you see people in Union Square, crying and apologizing for some offense against diversity, what have they really done to apologize for? In the most general sense."

"They stepped out somehow … said something they shouldn't have." Quinceton was searching for an answer, and using Redgrave's face to judge its accuracy. "They committed actions that went against the JSS government's 'diversity' way of thinking?"

"Exactly!" Redgrave looked genuinely pleased with Quinceton's on-the-spot progress and returned to his padded office chair. "When the JSS government uses the word, 'diversity' is both a way of thinking and the protected class you always need to center. Sure, many races are paraded in front of your face and referred to as 'diversity,' but when you're apologizing in Union Square before a decade in Stockton, it's because you forgot that there is an orthodox Anti-Racist code that is supposed to promote specific groups known as 'diversity,' and you offended the diversity group. They will never define the groups so they can always manipulate them, but the word 'diversity' is a cover for that code; it is itself a code to remind the New California citizen that actual diversity of thought is forbidden."

"Okay," Quinceton replied, still trying to play the part. "I see that every guest and patient in Stockton got sent here because they broke the social rules."

"Pretty much," Redgrave said, nodding slowly. He watched Quinceton with unusual concentration for a person in power. "And how about the 'equity' you've seen in action all over the state? Do you know what 'equity' means and how it's used to maintain the social order?"

"I think so. I think it's there to prevent any group from getting too far ahead of any other group, so they can all stay equal."

"That's the claim, certainly." Redgrave leaned back in his seat, which reclined without toppling over. The thing must have been specially outfitted by engineers to pull off a trick like that. "How does equity impact daily life? Like in San Francisco. What did you see the people working toward, striving for, or using to justify their ambitions?"

"Not much," Quinceton said with accidental bluntness. "The people don't do anything like that—that I saw, at least. It's hard to stand out, as it can be dangerous or 'inequitable' to be really good at something when other people aren't, but at least most all the people have most all they need. Most of the time."

"Life is a series of trade-offs, isn't it?" At least it didn't sound like another question Quinceton had to struggle through.

"Yes it is," the sniper agreed.

"Which brings us to inclusion. You've seen Anti-Racist inclusion, like in South Lake Tahoe. Who gets to be 'included' when it comes to attacking the Americans across the Nevada border? Or who gets to be 'included' when it comes to choosing Elect, future Elect, and even the next all-know-ing Leader? Who, really, is included, then, in New California? What does inclusion really mean here, after all?"

"I don't know, sir." Quinceton wasn't lying; he really didn't. This helped his confused, vulnerable, but open-minded posture.

"Well, you saw the De-Whitening ceremony last night?" The question came suddenly, surprising the young sniper in context.

"Yes ... I did."

"Perhaps the Anti-Racists in San Francisco will appreciate our efforts to assist their 'inclusion' efforts. Perhaps. Now that we have revealed a means of racial forgiveness, the future will benefit from the contributions of more minds. Diversity, Equity, and Inclusion: the words won't change, even as the concepts do every single day, forever and ever."

"Like violence," Quinceton added. "I think there was a time when getting shot at in South Lake would be considered more violent than the poster we were there to defeat."

"That's ... exactly right," Redgrave answered very slowly, watch-ing Quinceton. It was a strategy by the young sniper to admit to seeing the Violence poster without taking an illegal or dangerous stance on it, but Quinceton worried he'd gone too far with his confessions of truthful opinion. When the Chairperson spoke again, it was in a lower tone and volume.

"The word 'violence' has gone through some of the most profound transformations, no doubt. Physical assault and death doesn't worry the Elect so much, as long as it happens in the Tenderloin of San Francisco or the highway in front of the Nevada casinos. These days, 'violence' as in 'ideas that weren't sanctioned by the JSS government' has become the only thing that the Elect, and the Knowers especially, fear most. In time—if you don't already know—you'll see what they are for yourself, and why."

Silence took hold of the office for a moment before they heard some shouting from the lawn outside—someone being ordered by someone else to do something. It was a typical sound, but one that registered on Red-grave's face as a reminder to interrupt the deepening heresy.

"So finally we come to you, Quinceton. How would you like to be welcomed into the AAA?"

Beyond the tightrope he walked daily in the halls of his new home, Quinceton understood at once that this heightened attention from the local boss man was both a new threat and an opportunity. He hadn't forgotten what the wise old laundryman told him, and he'd probably have figured out such caution on his own anyway.

"I'm seeing what the AAA does, and I respect it. You guys keep the peace and teach transgressors what's what. But I was born in the city, and I'm still a city guy—that's why I never thought we'd be at the mountain cabin for more than a hot minute. So I could work for the AAA, but I would want to be back in the city. I miss the freedom to walk around, explore, and be with all kinds of different people, like in the city."

"That, I get," Redgrave concurred. He was nodding, probably deep in thought about his younger days. "Well, I want you to know that I hear good things about you. Hustle and obedience will get you where you want to go. And with such loyalty, trust is earned. You have my permission to walk the grounds near the mansion, even outside, so long as you don't stray into the fields or get near the outer fence, obviously. Take time off and skip the evening Historical Reminder video when you want. But you wear your mansion guest uniform, and I don't think anyone will bother you, but if they do, you tell 'em I said it was okay."

Yet again, Quinceton couldn't believe his dumb luck—his friends were locked in a barn, while he could leave the mansion for a midnight jaunt around campus. He'd been given a gift, a privilege the likes of which few damned souls would ever receive, and he wouldn't waste it.

"I don't know what to say, but *thank you,* sir. This means a ton to me. And I'll work hard for you. Whatever it is, I'm your man."

"I know." Redgrave smiled. "Just keep doing your best, and I'll open doors for you. Trust is earned, never given, but the more trust you earn, the more freedoms I will uncover."

ACT II, CHAPTER SEVENTEEN

Midnight Stroll

IF QUINCETON HAD LEARNED ANYTHING from July of 2048, it was the value of caution. Every decision demanded thought since every action invited risk. Knowing this, he couldn't rush a visit to the red new patient cattle barn.

The first night after receiving Redgrave's permission to roam, he wandered conspicuously around the mansion. Quinceton wouldn't miss anything useful from this evening's Historical Reminder video: it was another Hollywood bowel movement with a bunch of white capitalists ignoring the problems of the BIPOC people in the film. The underlying message was supposed to make Quinceton angry, but what bothered him even more was the incessant bitching about the free world without the slightest agency given to any of the non-whites. Just like the reeducational viewings of any other night, the message of the film was about how much it sucked to be trapped in the free world while more powerful people ignored your problems and worried about their own. One could only imagine what an involuntary Stockton audience thought of the predicament.

On this first test of boundaries, Quinceton got a few questions from AAA agents, but none pressed him further when he'd said it was greenlit by Redgrave. The whole plan was to gradually enlarge his radius around the mansion such that no one would care when he roamed to distances as far as the red cattle barn.

A few nights later, he stargazed for a good hour in the direction of some AAA houses, on the opposite side of the mansion from the barn. The idea came to fruition when a clan of AAA agents happened by, saying something like, "Just because we have to play this identity game doesn't mean we have to lose it," and halted the conversation as soon as they noticed Quinceton lying on the grass. One of them was Lieutenant Timetaker, and it was his newfound friendliness which set the tone.

"How's the view?" he asked Quinceton. "See any shooting stars tonight?"

"Nope, not yet. But I'll keep looking."

"So they just let you guys roam around at night?" another agent asked. "You must be popular in the mansion."

"I do as I'm told," Quinceton replied.

"Redgrave give you the go-ahead?" Timetaker asked with some curiosity. "The last Chairperson wasn't so easy, but it sure doesn't bother me."

"Yeah, he did. He doesn't seem to mind if you get your work done."

Timetaker nodded. "Redgrave come up with a new name yet? I hear Anti-Anti-Anti-Racist is on the way out and the new Chairperson won't feel settled until he's rebranded it. Here a week, and already a new name. Probably'll change something else, too. Gotta make your mark early."

"I heard we might get a new name, too, but he hasn't said anything about what it'll be."

"Well, enjoy yourself, Quinceton. I have a feeling you'll be popular here." It was impossible to forget that throwaway line about not losing the "identity game." If Timetaker distrusted Redgrave—and that was a good guess—then the friction could be good for Quinceton, so long as he didn't get caught in between …

Notes for another time.

"Yeah, will do, Lieutenant. And g'night to each of you."

A week later, Quinceton felt ready. Enough AAA agents recognized him by now, and those July nights in the Central Valley offered warm enough evening weather to bolster a possible excuse. The only other avenue Quinceton considered for additional cover was strolling around with a companion, but with no one of similar privilege to trust, this idea was quickly discarded.

It was a quiet night in either direction as Quinceton scanned for threats. The red barn loomed in the distance, with some high-strung central light visible even from beside the mansion. It clearly illuminated the front of the barn but seemed to dim the sight of everywhere else. As Quinceton approached, he noticed a hush that surprised him. He'd seen many dozens, if not hundreds, of patients on the lawn at Redgrave's introduction, but when they spread across the property for field work their numbers were impossible to calculate. Worse still, there was no knowing how many were kept in underground interrogation chambers at any one time.

It would be foolish to be seen approaching directly, so Quinceton took a wide loop around the target before cutting straight to his western destination from the south. The red barn, which he'd assumed to be a squarish box, turned out to be a rectangle with an astonishing depth of hundreds of yards. A big padlocked gate at the front entrance was the only element of the exterior that light couldn't penetrate, as cracks between the wall panels were so large that Quinceton need not squint to view the scene inside. Even without an explicit rule forbidding contact between patients and guests, Quinceton knew he might end up living in the barn if his connection to Bones and Sarah was confirmed.

The south side of the barn felt safely obscure. The bright-red front, where light poured over the harsh front gate from above, was easy to avoid from a southern approach. Against each side panel, rows and rows of rickety bunk beds were stacked against the inside, and they continued in identical fashion as Quinceton paced the far edges of the perimeter. The bottom mattress lay on the floor while the upper bunk hovered on thin metal slats roughly five feet off the ground. Quinceton scanned the heads atop each stacked set of pillows and heard stifled murmuring as he passed—an unavoidable risk. He saw mostly black hair, some brownish-blond, but even brownish-red would not suffice. There was only one color that mattered, and it was bright as fire.

As he reached the end of the south wall, he finally saw her—Sarah, hair of flame and soul of fury, a heap on the floor mattress. Quinceton thought about sticking a finger through the wall to alert her but decided against it.

"Sarah Goldstein," he said in a clear whisper, lowering his mouth in a hovering crouch. "Sarah, I'm here ... your friend."

Remaining on her side, she turned her head ever so slightly. Her gunshot wound seeped through a thin bandage. Her face had not healed from the initial interrogation, and stained cotton across her back told a story from decades and centuries past. As soon as she saw Quinceton she looked away, as if stung by the sight of him.

"You stupid fool," she hissed. "You can't be here. Cameras everywhere in here." The top bunk body stirred. It was Bones. He pushed closer to the wall and rotated onto his stomach but would not look in Quinceton's direction.

"There's nothing you can do for us," Bones murmured. "They have us now."

Quinceton hid as best he could behind a wall plank, but a good camera would catch some part of his mouth, and that would be enough. *Fuck it,* he thought and stood to address Bones, whose back was clean. "Look, guys, I'm doing well in the mansion. Even Redgrave is starting to like me. Maybe you do whatever they say, and then you get to be houseguests, and maybe then we can get the hell out of here."

"You don't get it," Bones said. "There are camps like this all over the state, and slaves never leave. They can't afford to let us leave. Not your mother or father or Sarah's girl are in Stockton, and probably never were— there's nothing to gain."

"Quinceton, you need to go," Sarah repeated, body held stiff as stone. "All you can do is endanger yourself. And if they stick you in here, you won't help us, and you'll never get out."

"I don't know ..." Quinceton knew they were right but didn't want to just give up. Besides Sarah and Bones and escaping, he didn't have much else to hope for.

"One thing, though," Bones added. "If you do ever get released and somehow wind up in the city, find my daughter, Jessica Bondurant. She worked a low-level job in communications at ZNN last I knew, so she's probably living in Elect-adjacent workers quarters on the coast near downtown, in some place elevated from the worst flooding. If you find her, tell her that I still love her. And if she asks—she won't, but if she does—tell her how I turned out."

"That's easy," Quinceton said. "I swear I will."

"Down here," Sarah said, quieter than Bones. "You gotta promise me something hard. Something you won't want to promise, but you gotta."

Quinceton knelt once again. "Tell me," he said. "I'll do it."

Sarah paused for a moment, and then looked him in the eyes. It was a face of torment and sorrow, a near-suicidal display of human degradation and loss to the point of nothingness: physical bondage breaking the belief in the possibility of psychological freedom.

"We're slaves in here, Quinceton, and there is no life for a slave. But you can still have a life. And anything you have to do to escape, you do it, and don't think twice. Might be you have to give us up, tell them we're Racists, whatever you have to do—it's over for us anyway. No matter what, you get the fuck out, yeah?"

Quinceton recoiled at the request. He had thought it would be something like *"Pick this up for me from the mansion."* He'd have preferred the theft.

"I won't betray you guys, but if I see a way to get out, I will," he agreed. "They don't suspect me of anything, not yet, so I may not even be asked again."

"They will," Sarah said, turning away, struggling to level the tones of her voice. "They really will. Go now, friend."

Quinceton couldn't move. "Okay, Sarah." He didn't know what else to say.

Bones, with his trademark timing, broke the silence from above. "We really got out there . . . did some living, though, didn't we?" Quinceton saw undimmed pride on Bones's face that he wanted to remember forever. "Not in my whole life could I ever breathe like that, that free, like with you guys, as though we owed nothing to nobody and could just … exist for our own sake and reasons."

"Me neither," Quinceton said. "It was the time of my whole godforsaken life. You're the only real people I ever knew."

"It was worth it," Sarah said from below. "No matter what, it was worth every minute of this." She didn't crane her neck to look at him, so she couldn't have seen Quinceton nod, return to the mansion, and pray to the best God available before bed. Pray for those who persevered through life in the big red cattle barn.

ACT II, CHAPTER EIGHTEEN

Forgiveness

A FEW DAYS LATER, SARAH was dead. It had to be Sarah. Quinceton heard the announcement at breakfast, at the same time as everyone else. With the houseguests eating eggs on the patio and the field patients filing through the oatmeal line on the grass below, Redgrave took position between them, leaning casually on the railing as he called his charges to attention.

"I have some unfortunate news many of you already know: Last night, a few hours before dawn, a rehabilitation patient attempted escape from the red cattle barn. They were apprehended well before the gate, summarily dealt with, and disposed." His eyes fell on Quinceton, three tables away and perched close to the mansion double doors. "Expect an investigation and any coconspirators to be exposed and punished," he seemed to warn Quinceton from across the patio.

Redgrave turned his back to address the lawn exclusively. "If you divulge any information related to the planning, execution, or knowledge of this attempted escape, you will be instantly forgiven for having such knowledge and will be rewarded for its confession."

Quinceton barely ate, and when he was summoned to Redgrave's office afterwards, he figured to be lying for his life. He'd been caught on the camera, or someone inside the red barn had tattled on his visit, or he'd been witnessed by someone else somehow—one way or another, his cover was blown.

"Come in, sit," Redgrave said when Quinceton approached, double mahogany doors wide open. Quinceton entered and obeyed, facing Redgrave from across a table strewn with colorful designs and various fonts.

"I've settled on a name, and we're close to a full rebrand," Redgrave explained, noticing Quinceton's gaze. "But that's not why you're here. Tell me why you're here, Quinceton."

"Well, I'll admit it, I go for a walk just about every night, and a few nights ago I went to the patients' barn," he said, shaking his head and doing his best to look remorseful. He hoped this face differed from the one he usually practiced, which aimed for the camouflage of dedicated servility. "So I assume one, or maybe both, of the old JSS government soldiers I was with, I assume they had to be the ones to try to escape. I had no idea, and I'm so, so sorr—"

"Balls!" Redgrave interrupted. "I like you, Quinceton. You've always been straight with me, but understand this is a very dangerous moment for you. And right when the cocks in San Francisco want us to help cover their dedicated labor shortage! I was going to tell you about those cocks and what they want—you were actually someone I was considering. But never without trust. So why test my trust by consorting with suspected Anti-Anti-Racist rehabilitation patients? Why did you go to the barn?"

Quinceton nodded slowly. He exhaled, took a deep breath, and saw in Redgrave's face a person who craved loyalty so deeply, he didn't want to believe he'd been betrayed. In fact, with the possible exception of smarmy Command Sergeant Major Smythe, Quinceton couldn't think of anyone who truly respected Redgrave, making the mystery of his promotions all the more compelling. In any case, Quinceton couldn't risk the appearance of divided loyalty and figured it was suicide to ask what had actually happened to his friends.

"It was because of my parents, Horace and Marcy Rift. When I first got here, Timetaker asked me about them, and I've been reminded ever since whenever I see that barn. I know at least my birther was sent to a DIE Camp, and as my seeder was an Anti-Anti-Racist, I figured he might be here too. They aren't so old to be guaranteed deceased—probably in their fifties now. And if they were houseguests, I'd have seen them."

"Okay. You say you were looking for your birther and seeder. Then why did you contact your traitorous former companions?"

"Well, I don't know anyone else." Quinceton shrugged. "I didn't think ... I don't know any other way to find out. I asked Timetaker on my first morning but he didn't hear me, or in any case, he didn't tell me."

"Balls! Why you would ever think to get a real answer from Timetaker, that conniving ... you should have asked me, Quinceton," Redgrave boomed with enunciated disapproval in all directions. "Didn't I give you roaming privileges? Haven't I told you I'd help you out if you do your part? Well, up 'til last night, you were doing your part, and I could've told you they aren't here and never were. Then we could've avoided this whole mess. There's a cost to all this, you understand."

"And I want to pay it, Mr. Chairperson, sir. I should have trusted you."

"Well, if you did like you say, I see no reason to rehabilitate you." Sinister understanding flashed across his face. "You'll just have to prove it."

Quinceton waited.

"On one hand, we have you talking to a Jewess the night before her attempted escape," he continued. "And on the other, we have video evidence that you weren't there long, didn't or couldn't pass anything through the wall, and, according to a nearby witness, were essentially told to piss off by the Jewess."

Quinceton wished he could disconnect his face from his brain. It really had been Sarah—a warrior to the end. Quinceton wanted to think she'd gone out on her own terms, that her refusal to bluff and prevaricate were a testament to her strength, but all he could imagine was her cold body lying in an unmarked pit at the forgotten corner of a Stockton work farm.

"If you hadn't 'fessed up about your visit, well, young man, your young ass would be in that big red barn tout suite 'til it wasn't so young. But you did. So, your opportunity here continues. There is just one little detail left to cross off, and then we can move on from this entire ordeal."

"Absolutely, Mr. Chairperson. And thank you—truly, thank you for this chance."

"Our witness told a different story about the Jewess's co-conspirator, the other man with whom you arrived. We are told he is fond of you. Is this true?"

"I mean, sure," Quinceton said uneasily. "More than the Jew girl, at least. He was the one who told me my parents weren't in the barn, and that was about it. But I think it's just because his daughter hates him and he's got no one left."

"Very good," Redgrave said with a smile. "Then it's decided. Tonight you will prove your loyalty, and then we'll put all this ugliness behind us, and maybe I'll make you a mole in the city after all. Just after one little detail, and you'll have a *tabula rasa*—a blank slate. Learn to forgive, I always say, and tonight you will be forgiven."

ACT II, CHAPTER NINETEEN

Forgotten Fruit

QUINCETON STOOD ON THE EXECUTION stage in a pressed tuxedo, listening to Redgrave's proclamations and trying not to think about the trapdoor lever within easy reach of his left hand. He would not look at Bones; he'd caught a peek at the old man's face, bruised and beaten to a red-streaked purple, and never wanted another. Every pair of eyes watched him now—agents on the patio, guests serving and pouring, patients on the lawn. They all watched him over the meandering volume of Redgrave's drone, and if they saw Quinceton's true mind, he might swing next. It helped that the preamble to this spectacle of collective punishment was a topic no one in attendance gave a damn for, least of all Quinceton.

"... careful consideration of past social movements, potential allies in foreign locales, and commitment to the eradication of tolerance in the execution of Social Justice, we've concluded that Anti-Anti-Anti-Racism will be better served with a new acronym and logo to represent our irreplaceable role in California. The Anti-Racists running the JSS government from the city have made 'equity' their primary focus, and while we naturally support this initiative in addition to the necessities of diversity and inclusion, we refuse to wait, negotiate, or excuse that which threatens Social Justice in our state. After all, justice delayed is justice denied, and for centuries the forces of whiteness have oppressed and enslaved the BI-

POC and de-whitened."

Quinceton looked up, hearing definite murmurs of something, before remembering himself. The patients were not, in fact, looking at him; their bowed heads suggested the only safety available, and he'd be a fool not to heed the silent advice.

"So it is justice—only justice—that we represent, which is our charge, and only swift and equal retribution for injustice—past, present, and future—is what separates us from the spineless cocks in San Francisco who are too clean to do their own dirty work." Redgrave halted, glanced quickly around the surrounding faces, and seemed to reconsider the aim of this point. "Not all people in SF are cocks, of course, but you know they couldn't talk high and mighty about abolishing prisons and law enforcement if they didn't have our patrolpersons backing them up. We are the muscle that allows the body of government to enforce their equity mandates, the bulging bicep that controls the peace between competing social groups—the people of action who convert Racist human waste into food for all. And one day, we'll get the credit for it."

Quinceton thought back to Redgrave's first public address, back in the courtyard of the Holiday Inn Express. In spite of his many faults and irrepressible opportunism, the guy had some oratory talent, and he could weave sentences together that gave the appearance of respectability to an identitarian slave state run for the stated purpose of imposing identitarian sameness. Despite coming from a dogshit race bereft of any claim to victimhood, Redgrave had learned the jargon, de-cockified early to side-step any association with inherited racial privilege, and played the system with the finesse of a top-hatted capitalist eliminating overtime pay. It made some sense that the Anti-Racists wouldn't want to share the same backyard with someone so conscious of and attracted to the greater identity-infused power game. So, they stuck him here: a Stockton grave from whence few return.

"That's why, henceforth and forevermore, we—the managers and laborers and executioners of JSS government policy—will be known as the JJJ: Justice, Justice, and more Justice still." Redgrave paused for applause or reaction of some kind, and when none came, he continued in the same breath. "True justice is present justice, it is eternal justice, it is unflinching justice. Justice today, justice tomorrow—justice for*ever.* That is Social Justice!" He shouted the last line such that the crowd could not ignore the hint and they relented, clapping hastily.

"*Now,*" Redgrave clamored unnecessarily over the low din of the compliant audience. "That brings us to here, now, and the privileged colonizer before you." Quinceton figured they were supposed to look at Bones, but few did; many, maybe most, looked at him instead. Their faces were a memory from some distant place where ordinary people shared the same struggle regardless of skin color, gender status, or legally recognized sexuality.

Redgrave circled behind Bones to place his large hands on both of the condemned's shoulders. Bones stood center stage on the square trapdoor panel with his hands tied behind his back but gave no sign of discomfort, nor any desire to be anywhere else. His resignation felt familiar to Quinceton, but not so recognizable as the eternal plight of the masses.

"Here, we have a citizen of the JSS government who broke his oath to live by the tenets of Diversity, Equity, and Inclusion," Redgrave continued. "He did knowingly and admittedly aid the escape of another patient in rehabilitation. He did also consort with a houseguest of good standing. In order to grant forgiveness for the associated individual with a previously unblemished record, he will carry out this humane dispatchment to cleanse past transgressions."

Redgrave affixed the noose around Bones's throat, tightening the looped end in three swift pulls. The crowd hushed. All turned to Quinceton, who finally looked at his friend, but Bones refused the gaze. Quinceton heard the sound of wind rushing through veteran patient shacks and smelled freshly trimmed grass.

"Death is the price of life," Bones suddenly announced to the captive audience. Time for an Accountability Statement wasn't generally included in the Stockton execution script, but the doomed didn't much care for JSS or now "JJJ" tradition.

Bones turned to meet Quinceton's stare, and in this look, the old man didn't appear so old. He didn't seem to have any age at all, really, nor was there any hint of fear. His eyes were as young as they'd ever been. They were the same lonely eyes he'd met in Tahoe, the same ones that seemed to have found their forever place before coming here. This, here, was not a life. Quinceton couldn't see any other way to grant mercy to the truly destitute, and because he was not such a person himself, he would live on. He had become a man without being aware of the transformation, and now he was too old for false hope. No more excuses—no room for idealism.

"And when the bill for life comes due, pay it willingly," Bones said to Quinceton.

Then the one with the ticket to exoneration pulled the trapdoor lever, and his last friend fell with a polite snap.

Quinceton might have preferred the nothingness, at least in this moment of familial abandonment, but he still had a whole life to live.

ACT II, CHAPTER TWENTY

Loose Ends

QUINCETON STARED AT THE CEILING; sleep would not come so easily to-night. Bones had been either buried or cremated, but at least he was with Sarah, he told himself. On nights like this, Quinceton wished he was alone with his forbidden thoughts. In spite of sharing a room with Juniper, they rarely spoke, a common condition Quinceton assumed to be built on mutual distrust.

"I saw you onstage this morning," Juniper said with unusual understanding. "The man—the Anti-Anti-Racist transgressor—was he your friend?"

"No, he was just some guy I got stuck with after the Battle of South Lake." Quinceton twisted in the dark to get a better look at Juniper's expression, but no clarity came. Any conversation at all surprised him, but not nearly so much as the possible emergence of Juniper's softer side. It had been hidden so well, it was fair to wonder if it had been totally purged in childhood, and true believers, as a rule, cannot be swayed by reason.

"It just seemed like he cared about you," Juniper answered. "I don't know what it was, not exactly, but at the end there, the way he spoke … it seemed like he almost *wanted* to die. And wanted to forgive you for pulling the switch, even before you did."

"Yeah—I don't know what to tell you. But I kinda saw that, too. He'd had enough of it, of *this,* I suppose, and definitely looked ready." Even in the dark, Quinceton could see his roommate nodding. "I'm not sure why they kept him in the red microscope barn, but I get why they figured him for an Anti-Anti-Racist ultimately. The other girl with us, the one who tried to escape, now *she* definitely was an Anti-Anti-Racist because of the attempt, but even her, no, I couldn't tell she was such a rebel before we got here. We just kept to ourselves, mostly."

"So you just got picked up for being with them? That was your mistake?"

"Well, yeah. That, and we'd stopped at some mountain cabin where this old man lived. He turned out to be Anti-Anti-Racist, so I can see why they suspected all of us."

"Well, they make a mistake with me. I was never disloyal; they should never have put me here." The comment made Quinceton sit up, and Juniper must have noticed. "No, seriously. I said something I shouldn't have, but it was simply in support of the trans community. I never meant to marginalize anyone."

"What did you say?" It was the first honest moment Quinceton had ever experienced in this room. And he really was curious about the answer.

"Oh, it was nothing, really. I'm a fully transitioned womxn, and I was just talking about how that might be different than someone who is curious, or experimenting, or who may have trans feelings without wanting a physical transformation. And—I know this is wrong—but I wondered aloud if preadolescence is the right time to make a permanent body decision."

"So you questioned someone's trans identity claims and the age of surgical transitioning," Quinceton deadpanned. "At least they didn't shoot you on the spot."

"I didn't mean to challenge anyone's gender identity!" Juniper still felt the need to defend herself, which gave Quinceton some confidence that he had the person properly hoodwinked about his true mind. "I just said that there may be a difference between a trans womxn who long ago committed to their innate identity and a trans womxn who presents as male in every way, but declared themselves trans five minutes ago and got promoted two minutes later. I mean, right?"

She needed some reassurance, and Quinceton wasn't too callous to deny it to her. "Well, sure, I suppose. I don't really know about the trans mindset, but I guess there's some difference. De-cockification is at least real commitment, and no one can say otherwise. Not sure kids can understand what they're getting into before they have an adult body."

"Exactly. And post-capitalism hormone therapy, just getting the right drugs and simplifying complicated surgeries—you really have no idea."

"I don't," Quinceton agreed. "I fully admit it."

"So you agree, then, that I can still be loyal and useful to the movement? That I just saw some harmless difference between the transitioned and those who have yet to fully realize their identity? I'm really not transphobic. You see that, right?" The more Quinceton realized this wasn't about Bones's humane dispatchment but Juniper's backstory, the more comfortable he felt.

"Yeah, I see that," Quinceton replied in the low light. "You're just speaking your truth, revealed through your own lived experience as a trans womxn."

"Exactly!" Now Juniper sat on the edge of her bed. Where all this was going would soon be clear. "And I can still be useful to the movement. I hope you see that, too."

"Yes. Yes, I do." There was a brief pause.

"So will you put in a word for me with Redgrave?"

"Ummm ... what?" Quinceton wondered aloud. "Why the hell would he care what I say?"

"Oh, come *on*. Everyone knows you're Redgrave's boy. He even asked me about you after dinner one night early on. I couldn't tell him very much, but he wanted to know anything about you, anything at all. All I could say is you were committed to proving yourself. But really, Quinceton, now I could use the favor returned."

"Might be because we both survived the Battle of South Lake together, and I have his back defending how it went down that day. But okay, alright, if he asks, what do you want me to say?"

"Just what I told you here." Juniper's shoulders eased, and she lay down on her side. "Just tell him I'm a trans individual, committed to the cause, and I can be trusted with whatever they need me to do outside the mansion. I'm theirs. If they'll only use me a little more, outside the Stockton compound, you know, I could do even more Social Justice than I'm doing here, now."

"You got it, Juniper. And you're still working behind the bar, right? Know what you can do for me?"

"Ugh, lord. What's your poison?"

"Whiskey." Quinceton cracked a smile in the dark. "A whole bottle of it. And Redgrave will think you're a trans angel sent from God to be a battering ram for equity mandates and diversity inclusion."

ACT II, CHAPTER TWENTY-ONE

Emancipation

WHEN IT WAS ALL OVER with Redgrave, well after midnight, Quinceton fled to his room for the bottle Juniper had fetched for him. *Only one thing left to do in this ornate prison.* Afterwards, Quinceton would sleep, wake at dawn, and shuttle off to San Francisco in an automobile with the rest of Redgrave's moles. He had earned it—so much so that he resolved to forget the how and why as quickly as possible, even though such relief would never happen. Juniper was asleep when Quinceton stole away with the brownish liquor, wrapping it carefully in a towel first.

Quinceton held the bottle against his chest as he knocked on VIP#3. There was no answer, but he heard ruffling around the condo inside and waited dutifully.

The ancient American Indian opened the door with sleep in his eyes and a curious smile on his face. Darkness announced what time it was, and that meant Quinceton wasn't here on official mansion business. This had to be something better.

"Good evening," the old man said, watching Quinceton's expression.

"Yeah—you know, a while back you mentioned … well, I brought whiskey for you."

The man fell to his knees with instant neglect of all lower-body motor function but raised his hands to accept the gift in a prostrate position, as though accepting a divine gift from the heavens. Quinceton had never felt so generous in all his life, and it embarrassed him. "He who makes a beast of himself gets rid of the pain of being a man," the guy effused from the floor, unscrewing the top with frenetic haste.

"Please ... stand up," Quinceton answered. "It's no big deal."

The Native didn't answer for a time, the bottle vertical and fully upside down as he quaffed in ravenous rapture. He breathed heavily after a few open-throated gulps but didn't stand, so Quinceton sat on the floor too.

"No," the old man finally said. "In here, this is everything. To go numb for just a few passing seconds ..." He didn't finish the sentence, but Quinceton understood. And when he passed the bottle back, Quinceton tried to copy the old man, retching at first contact.

"It's all yours," he said, returning the whiskey with a shove. "I don't know how you can stomach that shit."

"It's a long way from rye," the old man replied. "But it helps you forget. And when all reason is treason, what feeling, memory, or passion is better than none at all?" The young man didn't know what rye was, but he could safely assume it was a superior capitalist drink.

"Revenge," Quinceton answered immediately. "Everything else can be used against you. But not revenge. Truly committing to truth means vengeance, and vengeance alone—then all of the rest of it won't matter. *You*, just one person, don't matter. But follow any goal hard enough, and you'll have a reason for living. That's numbing, too, kinda, but with a purpose."

The man nodded. "I felt that way, once, and got too old. But you be careful, son. Imagine the whole world may be out to get you. And you will be in my prayers." He paused for another sip. "In fact, you were in my meditation even before this, and now definitely in my prayers, too, and you've given me more to pray on. So Godspeed, young man. Remember, all love is liability in this world, so pick your friends and family with open eyes. Be careful out there."

It was genuine advice, but only a tardy reminder on this, Quinceton's final night in Stockton. He had learned to distrust all positions of power in the JSS government world long ago, and a few hours prior, he'd gotten confirmation seared into his soul.

In the early evening, after the sun had set and with Juniper likely rifling through the basement liquor storage, Quinceton was summoned to "meet Redgrave in the bunker." He'd been waiting for the call since Bones and the gallows, and walking past them to the staircase underground reminded him of his initial interrogation. Next should be Quinceton's exit interview, and the realization of loyalty he'd earned the lethal way. He'd committed to be the perfect mole, and the perfect mole had to be set free.

An agent of the now-rebranded JJJ led Quinceton down three different hallways to a much larger metal door than he remembered seeing before. Inside, four hooded JJJ stood around a male whose hands were tied behind their back. Across an empty table sat Redgrave, one leg hanging casually from the knee of the other. When Quinceton fully entered the room, he noticed that the bound suspect was Timetaker. The room smelled like a male-identifying locker room: sweaty armpits, fists, and testicles. *All according to plan.*

"You boys are early," Redgrave said in a cheerful voice, as though meeting a friend for lunch. "We haven't finished with Timetaker. You know him, don't you, Quinceton?"

"I sure do. His team found us in the mountains. He conducted my interrogation, and I've seen him around the estate a few times since."

"And what do you think of the man? Do you believe in his commitment to Diversity, Equity, and Inclusion?" Timetaker's face told Quinceton what to say—after a few rounds of beatings, they'd carved "U.S.A." across his forehead.

"I don't trust him," Quinceton responded without the slightest equivocation. "I don't know about his commitment to anything—I don't know him that well—but I don't trust him."

"Smart boy. And what should be done with him?"

Quinceton paused to think on this one. "Well, I don't know what you know, so I'd say whatever you decide is what should be done with him."

"And if I say he swings?"

"I'll be there to pull the lever." Timetaker finally looked at Quinceton. There was some surprise in his expression, but more rage than anything else, and not necessarily directed at the houseguest. Timetaker didn't speak. What could he have said?

"Splendid!" Redgrave clapped his hands in delight. "Guards, take the prisoner to the gallows and string him up like a puppet. Quinceton and I have more important things to discuss."

Quinceton didn't watch them remove Timetaker, but he heard it. There was commotion, some more blows sliding across bloodied skin, but Quinceton would not flinch. Redgrave's eyes were always on him, and he was so close.

"Sit," Redgrave said in a calm voice when echoes of the struggle faded down the hallway. Quinceton obeyed.

"I have some great news for you, Quinceton: I think you're almost ready to return to San Francisco. They need bodyguards and extra security personnel for the SOMA MOMA Momalla Gala for Love this year—something about expanding the audience for the unveiling of a new Anti-Racism solution. And I can hardly think of a better, more rehabilitated person than you, my dear boy." The Museum of Modern Art (MOMA) in the SOMA neighborhood was the officially sanctioned Social Justice gallery of art stuff in San Francisco, and they always hosted the annual New Year's Eve event.

"Thank you, sir," Quinceton answered.

"And in exchange for my permission, can you guess what I'd like from you, when you're living in the city and working for the top of the JSS government?"

"Report back to you?"

"Oh, I'm not sure I'd say it that way, not now," Redgrave said with narrowed eyes. "And Knowing Leader Mumwaza Q. Jumping Bull no doubt has everything fully under control. I just want to help make sure that the top of the Elect are who they should be—that everything is on the level, especially with the Gala coming up. They've got to be more worried than ever to ask us for help, or maybe just severely understaffed. I'm a leader in my own right—you understand—and it's my duty to the state to keep my eyes open for Anti-Anti-Racists anywhere I can, even where I'm not. You understand, don't you, Quinceton?"

"Of course, sir. You're just doing all you can do for DIE."

"Precisely. Precisely right, Quinceton. And do you know what quality you possess that is most important? The one quality I can't live without?"

"Trust?" Quinceton guessed confidently. "I think my roommate, Juniper, is very trustworthy, and could also be a great help to you in your cause." No matter what and to whom, Quinceton felt good about keeping his word.

"Close enough. And she's not my type, at all. I was thinking 'loyalty,' but 'trust' is at least a close cousin." Redgrave rose, circled the table, and leaned against it, hovering just above Quinceton. "You aren't the only one who needs to prove yourself loyal. Do you know anything about where I came from? Who I came from?"

"No, sir."

"One thousand years of the smart guy breeding the hot girl, one thousand years of sailing around the world to conquer it, and one thousand years of accumulated privileges which are the enemy of all our current state stands for. You see, my dear boy, in a certain way of thinking, I should be the outcast. And in spite of millennia of oppression, they were not prepared for a John Charles Redgrave. It can be reduced to a simple question of will and willpower, and I'm here to show you the triumph of such things. I am the spear that pierces the impenetrable armor. And it's all because I proved myself beyond question or reproach."

Without warning, Redgrave stood and lowered his pants, exposing a hideous oval venis carved and planted above a perfectly normal set of hairy balls. This was not an attempt to transition into a womxn, but a self-inflicted rejection of the cisheteropatriarchy that no true believer could possibly discredit, especially not an Elect who claimed any sort of added gender IS points without a form of body mutilation.

"Started it myself, before they even had the name 'venis' in common circulation, because I knew the price of certain ambitions from the beginning. And since I wanted it done right, I found an old doctor facing cancellation to complete the look—the kind of cisgender white man they let operate before the medical schools were really set up for diversity. Sometimes backing the right horse is worth some sacrifice in confronting the cis-hetero gender binary."

Quinceton couldn't even be offended by the positive mention of a white man, so intently was he staring at the venis before him in horror. Nothing about this felt like anything to do with combating the cisheteropatriarchy.

"But I couldn't have them taking all my manhood," Redgrave added. "Lest I lose all ambition for Social Justice. And so now, we arrive at your test of loyalty … and I really don't care what you call it. You don't have to like it. I don't care if you eat it or suck it. But I sure didn't take it out to be inspected for more Intersectional IS points, and you don't look much like a government IS score counter."

Quinceton looked at the concavity and shuddered. There was no telling what had healed, what hadn't, and what never would.

"Do you really want to genital-shame me? Do you, Quinceton?"

A pause of silent mourning.

"So, what'll it be: sacrifice now, or Stockton, forever?"

INTERLUDE

IT WAS SAID THAT JUST before the close of the nineteenth century, a young African American man ventured north from Dallas, Texas, with the intention to resettle in Chicago, Illinois. While traversing Choctaw Nation in Southeastern Oklahoma, and in significant need of lodging, the man was accommodated for an evening by an Indigenous family. During the course of this night—and according to oral, then written history—the man made the acquaintance of a young Choctaw womxn, and nine months later, an ancestor was born that would constitute the backbone of Knowing Leader Mumwaza Q. Jumping Bull's indomitable biology a century and a half later.

In addition to his racial qualifications, tomes of prose were published annually on the status of Knowing Leader Jumping Bull's gender identity, which could not be represented by the mere words or artistic designs of humanity, but could best be understood as "the embodiment of a slave freed from bondage, born again as both servant and conqueror to a world of hatred, bigotry, and binary thinking." Though Mumwaza's pronouns were forbidden speech for the first few years of Mumwaza's political career, the Knowing Leader eventually instructed society to adopt INRI/INRIs when speaking about the knowing-est possessor of lived experience in the history of Anti-Racism and added the following directive: "The INRI/INRIs pronouns of current Knowing Leader Mumwaza Q. Jumping Bull should henceforth be pronounced in a muffled whisper as 'in-rye,' and are never to be said with the full-throated sound of total conviction by even other Knowers, as any verbal messaging is a poor substitute for that which could only be understood by those with the greatest and truest possible lived experience."

As he sat alone in the spacious waiting room of the Knowing Leader's Secure Space, located in the Flood Mansion atop the Broadway ridge in Pacific Heights, Quinceton closed the government history pamphlet and resolved to never even attempt Jumping Bull's pronouns, should he actually be assigned somewhere near the Knowing Leader—it was just too dangerous. The employment opportunity suddenly made perfect sense, due to some sort of labor shortage in San Francisco arising from dubious, unexplained complications. There were more than enough people in the city to provide a hand servant for every Elect, but he, Quinceton, was here because they specifically required those who'd been DIE-rehabilitated.

And so be it. He'd returned with a number of mandated objectives, but really only one purpose. So if society wouldn't up and free itself, well, maybe that was why God made one Quinceton Rift: an avenging angel around whom the whole world could incinerate.

ACT III

The SOMA MOMA Momalla Gala for Love Massacre

ACT III, CHAPTER ONE

The Secure Space

"QUINCETON RIFT," THE SERVANT SAID to the near-empty waiting room. "They are expecting you." After six weeks in the tumbleweeds of Stockton, Quinceton was accustomed to seeing servants in the standard pressed tuxedo, but this one wore the typical JSS government uniform of loose jeans and a black-on-white pin-striped T-shirt. There was no expression on the male-presenting person's face, and Quinceton was long past the point of anticipating teamwork.

A set of double doors gave way to a short walk to another set of double doors, and then Quinceton found himself standing in an impossibly bright room filled with glistening sunlight. There were columns inside the room, similar to the ones standing tall on the patio of the Stockton mansion. A blinding glare shone through windows covering the entire rear wall, against which a few dozen Knowers lounged on ambulatory quarantine stations under blankets with a velvety gleam. The Kafkani hats and limited numbers implied these were the top of the lot: Level Two Knowers and their sole superior, Knowing Leader Mumwaza Q. Jumping Bull, in all INRIs glory.

Before Quinceton could fully appreciate the detailed embroidery of Jumping Bull's robes or the fine gold rims on INRIs ambulatory quarantine station (known in the previous year as merely a "wheelchair"), he was dumbstruck by the perfect Aryan composition of the Knowing Leader's face. One of the primary subjects in any Work Doing Center is the study of different white ethnic evils and their specific Racism, and Jumping Bull looked exactly like a champion from a Central European doctrine of genocide, right down to the finely cropped blond hair and bright-blue eyes. Slim the male-born person down a couple hundred pounds and you could almost imagine his face on a Nazi poster advertising the beauty and strength of biological whiteness. It was lucky, no doubt, that the Knowing Leader was protected by the contemporary Colorism Accords, which prevented the questioning of a superior racial identity based purely on the presentation and appearance of skin color.

The Knowers were talking about the JJJs but still referring to them as the AAAs, in open defiance of the law enforcement group's recent rebranding. This had to be true—Quinceton had heard the term "de-whitening" as he walked in, and it couldn't have come from anywhere else.

Knowing Leader Mumwaza Q. Jumping Bull raised a hand, and all other conjecture ceased immediately.

"Comrades," INRI said in a loud, forcefully informative voice. "Allow me to introduce Quinceton Rift. Quinceton has been sent to us from the Stockton labor camp and comes with the highest possible recommendation from our former colleague, AAA Chairperson John Charles Redgrave."

The room reacted to the name in a way Quinceton couldn't discern, but one that Jumping Bull paused to appreciate. It sounded like excited chatter in a direction the young sniper couldn't place, but it indicated they knew all about the Stockton Chairperson.

"Yes, indeed—*that* Redgrave. Quinceton was formerly a soldier at South Lake Tahoe, and after having been discovered post-battle under dubious circumstances, young Mr. Rift here has labored tirelessly to reeducate himself and recommit to the tenets of Social Justice. Isn't that right, Mr. Rift?"

"Yes, Knowing Leader," Quinceton said obediently. "I've learned a lifetime in my time away, and I hope you put my commitment to the test." Murmurs of support splashed around the room.

"That's what I like to hear. And during your time in Stockton, did you get a good look at Chairperson Redgrave?"

Quinceton shuddered before speaking again. "Yes, Knowing Leader, I did. I was a houseguest in my time there, and I served him almost exclusively during my last weeks."

"Splendid. Just splendid, Mr. Rift. And what was your opinion of the new Chairperson? Did Redgrave seem to enjoy his new position?"

Quinceton had not expected to think much during this interview. He'd figured he would recite the proper boilerplate, get a foot in the door somewhere inside the Knower's landscape, and take it from there. Internecine struggles between the JSS government and the AAA/JJJ law enforcement apparatus had huge potential to fix New California by way of weakening both dominant ideologies in competition with each other, but probably not fast enough for Quinceton's timeline.

"Redgrave isn't someone really to talk openly about how happy or grateful he is," Quinceton responded with as much truth as he could afford. He'd like nothing more than to bury Redgrave, but not himself along with the vile bastard. "He seems ambitious, no doubt. I remember him talking about how he'd done a good job at Tahoe, and not getting enough credit for it or something."

Silence flooded the room as Quinceton noticed faces turning to their Knowing Leader for whatever confirmation or opinion would be considered Anti-Racist. But clarity would continue to be a luxury Quinceton lived without.

"Is that how the Battle of South Lake appeared to you? A success worthy of promotion?"

"I can't say so exactly, Knowing Leader. But I didn't quite see it that way. The divers seemed committed, but got trapped on the Nevada side and seemed to get gunned down to a pulp. And the main infantry that was supposed to be attacking the main gate from the highway, they just collapsed under Command Sergeant Major Smythe's 'leadership,' such as it was."

"Smythe was always Redgrave's favorite lapdog," Knowing Leader

Mumwaza finally offered, the closest Quinceton would get to an explana-tion. "Or, technically, his favorite pussy."

The room burst into exaggerated laughter. Everyone had to have made this joke about Smythe at least forty times already. Quinceton smiled, try-ing to mimic the Level Two Knowers, but he really couldn't laugh at the standard jokes anymore. He nodded at Mumwaza and waited.

"And when you were around Redgrave, what did you think of his iden-tity? Did you get a sense of his whiteness, his gender presentation, his mental complexities?"

"I don't know about his potential alternate ways of knowing, but he could easily be bipolar or something. And I might still see him as a white man, even after the de-whitening ceremony." Quinceton paused as the all-powerful gazed on him with interest. "And yes, I don't know what his gen-der identity is technically, but he sure acts like a man and goes by he/him."

Mumwaza liked the answer, smiling and saying something about Red-grave's "decided exterior" to the others. There was an element of Mum-waza's divided but serene attention that calmed Quinceton after his time in the manor. Mumwaza seemed to hear Quinceton when INRI listened—in-stead of just waiting for a word or two to indicate the orthodox answer—and did so without the same implied threat one would expect from a JSS government official. INRIs focus wafted aimlessly between the people in the room, also very unlike Redgrave.

"Knowing Leader," a lesser Knower began, "have we learned all there is to know about de-whitening?" The speaker was a dark, svelte male-presenting person around Quinceton's height, close to twice his weight, but probably not a full three hundred pounds.

"I think we could learn more," Mumwaza assented with a soft nod. "Mr. Rift, if you please?"

"Certainly, Knowing Leader. I saw Redgrave's ceremony, and a few others in my time there. I can tell you anything I know."

"If I may," the previous Knower piped up, "during the so-called 'de-whitening' ceremony, the individual to be de-whitened grasps a heated skull rod to scar themselves. But there must be words, too. What is said?"

Mumwaza looked from the Knower to Quinceton, clearly approving the question.

"Well, I didn't know it, but I guess white people couldn't get certain powers among Anti-Anti-Anti-Racist agents before, in their original by-laws—maybe that was the JSS government protection against future white supremacy, or whatever's happening now. So during the ceremony, they denounce whiteness and so forth—the white supremacist scientific method and all that—so that afterward, the white guy can join the AAA like any-one else."

"So they want to change the rules," Mumwaza said, finally serious. "They want it to be as possible to transition your race as it is your gender—or even easier!" The room exploded in shouts of exaggerated offense. "As though our groupings of identity are totally arbitrary and can be changed at any time!"

The room's groaning gave way to sycophantic agreement. It was im-possible to tell when Mumwaza Q. Jumping Bull was performing, what separated performance from authenticity, and if INRI were still capable of a distinction between the two.

"Participate like *anyone else*—as though the white face will assume all historical understanding from the BIPOC!" one nearby Knower tossed in with enunciated incredulity.

"As though transitioning race and gender are the same thing!" another older Knower attempted to repeat from over Quinceton's right shoulder. The room immediately fell silent as all eyes turned to Mumwaza, and Mumwaza turned to the speaker.

"Does one … ever truly … *transition* their gender?" INRI said slowly, the room now stiff with tension. Double doors behind Quinceton opened, and two Kevlar-clad bodyguards positioned themselves on either side of the entryway.

"Mr. Rift," Mumwaza said without a look in his direction. "I'll be see-ing you again. For now, dismissed."

Quinceton turned and filed out of the Secure Space. He didn't listen to the offending Knower's walk-back of the forbidden simile or expect to see them again, nor did he give a hot damn about the recklessly verbal politician's fate. They were all doomed anyhow.

Quinceton Rift, teen soldier-slave-survivor, had returned to San Francisco a man.

ACT III, CHAPTER TWO

Smiling, Starving

THERE WERE TWO CHALLENGES THAT awaited Quinceton's quest to infiltrate the ranks of the Anti-Racist government in the same way he'd slipped through the Stockton Anti-Anti-Anti-Racists: one, there were a hell of a lot more Elect to worry about in San Francisco, and two, Knowing Leader Mumwaza Q. Jumping Bull acted exclusively heterosexual, even if INRIs power freed INRI from ever having to admit it.

These bureaucratic hurdles were evident in every staffing decision made inside the hallowed marble of the Flood Mansion, where Level Two Knowers each handpicked their own retinue of "relievers." It was a new word, but it made perfect sense in the context of the unendurable hardship said to be felt in every interaction by the neo-knowing, gender-ratified BIPOC who reached this second-highest rung of society. The relievers, like the Stockton houseguests, capitulated to every request, whether it was helping the Knower transition from their "ambulatory quarantine station" (wheelchair) into bed each night, carry heavy forkfuls of food from plate to mouth, or satiating the essential needs of the flesh.

The mystery of why the San Francisco Anti-Racists would draw humans from the Anti-Anti-Anti-Racist labor camps—thereby risking possibly divided loyalty between the dueling New California power poles—was also explained in Quinceton's first days there. Civilians who hadn't been to DIE were like Quinceton himself before South Lake—they just didn't get it and were prone to getting confused about something, which then led directly to DIE reeducation. Those who'd already DIE'd never needed to be reminded, and were often said to be "reborn" when receiving praise for the requisite drudgery. These perfections of servility kept their heads down, spoke only when spoken to, had no opinions worth listening to, and operated more as ephemeral ghosts floating between unenvious tasks than living spirits.

Quinceton refused to let them haunt his thoughts. In the difference between uninitiated civilian labor and those "relievers" who'd been reborn after DIE, Quinceton saw that true slaves were not born, but crafted by society. The camp taught certain lessons to the soul that could be learned no other way while also openly displaying every fear a skeptic might have about how resources were divided among members of historically mis-aligned groups, what groups were politically relevant in such economic decisions, and which people should decide such things at the top. Nothing taught you about reality quite like surviving Diversity, Equity & Inclusion Camp in Stockton, New California.

There was a power structure that one needed to understand and accept without acknowledging that such an authoritarian thing existed for the evident reasons, and if you could do this without blinking, each and every day, you were grade A, top choice slave meat. In the Flood Mansion's perverse brand of excellence, this meant serving the best food to the most gilded wheelchairs in the company of the quietest, most passive servants.

Quinceton showed up each day and assented to whatever the Flood Mansion labor master assigned, usually to chauffeur a Knower or Speaker to a different corner of the city, where they would relay the freshly updated battle plan in the war against Racism over alcohol, meat, and dairy products. With a youthful combination of speed and strength, Quinceton made an excellent chauffer as he carried different Elects' rickshaws back and forth to meetings across San Francisco's many landscapes. These quiet conferences began in a familiar fashion, with concerned back-and-forth about the destabilizing de-whitening ceremony brewing up in DIE Camps all over the state, and ended in assurances that Knowing Leader Mumwaza had a corrective to be unveiled at the upcoming New Year's Eve SOMA Momalla Gala for Love.

Questions from incredulous Speakers or lesser Knowers told Quinceton all he'd needed to know about the implicit threat of de-whitening to those for whom identity was a sufficient claim to victimhood, and therefore power. "How does it work?" and "What races are eligible to de-whiten?" quickly turned into practical considerations of political survival. As frightening as the possibility of de-racialized whites were, the truly dangerous reality was that such a practice had originated even before Redgrave's seizure of Stockton; it couldn't be contained with just him. It had been released out in the open now, and what with the upper ranks of the AAA—or JJJ—being almost entirely made up of white people, one could see why the elimination of racial limitations would grow popular outside the control of San Francisco Secure Spaces.

Quinceton had just returned to the Flood Mansion from the latest visit to a Knower's Secure Space in nearby Laurel Heights and was waiting for another assignment in the reliever's basement lounge when about a dozen emaciated women dressed in tightly tailored clothing entered. The last of them, bringing up the rear in line position only, was Natalie.

The past few weeks had not apparently aged her as they had Quinceton, but her spirit seemed to have been dulled, along with her appetite. When she closed the lounge door behind herself, she assumed a seat without looking around or meeting Quinceton's stare. Like the other girls, her tank top and pants seemed to have been sewn especially for the wearer, as they actually accentuated the remaining curves of her Latina figure instead of hiding it among the layers of extra fabric suggested for inclusive sizing laws. Any garment that wasn't made to accommodate the largest sufferers of lookism had to be especially approved by a powerful member of the Elect, but that wasn't too hard to find in the Flood Mansion these days.

Every few minutes a workmaster would return, call out a name or two, and some of the smiling, starving women would file toward the door. Quinceton, keeping his back to Natalie, zigged and zagged across the room in her general direction, careful to disguise his intentions from any watchful eyes. He snuck a peek at Natalie as a new name was called at about ten feet away, using a refill from a water station as an alibi. Most of the original women she'd arrived with had already been called—he'd have to hurry. She still wasn't looking up; she had her hands on both her knees, staring at the floor beneath her feet. Using her distraction to be obvious, Quinceton turned in her direction and made an overt scan of her section, presumably for an empty seat. She didn't see any of this, and he assumed a seat next to her without her noticing.

"Hi, Natalie," he said without looking at her. It reminded him of his last conversation with Sarah, but he couldn't be sure about Natalie's level of caution. He'd have to play it careful. Her head spasmed vertically, but only for a moment of lost motor control, and then she settled herself quickly. Quinceton saw her peripherally glance at his face, but she wouldn't risk full-on eye contact.

"I heard you all died in Tahoe," she whispered. "I'm not sure I believed it, but I didn't think I'd see you back here, either. What happened to you?"

"Just met the world we live in … too much to explain. But I work here now, in the Flood, as a bodyguard-chauffeur." He saw a few other potential Momalla Gala dates watching them from across the aisle and remembered himself. "And it's good to see you doing well, after all these years—what's it been, five, maybe, since we were at Work Doing together?" he said loudly enough for others to hear, finally turning in her direction.

She was just as attractive as he'd remembered, and in her face he saw comprehension of his public deflection, which suggested she might one day understand him. In this spark of hope, he saw validation of all his time away from San Francisco, the torture he'd survived, and the worldview he'd earned as a result. Natalie was so much more beautiful than before.

"Yeah, it's been forever," she answered, playing to the crowd. "And it's a surprise to see you here, now, but no doubt they picked a good one." She paused and looked around for threats. "I'm close to being a Knower's escort—*reliever*, sorry—to the Momalla, and have already been through a bunch of interviews. So I'm sure we'll have another chance to catch up."

"I'd like that," Quinceton said, undaunted by Natalie's auditioning to be sexual property. They would never claim her mind, just as they hadn't gotten to his.

"I would, too." They paused again, just staring into each other's eyes, likely imagining what the other had been through, and who they were now as a result.

"Natalie Gutierrez," a scratchy voice called from a far doorway.

She rose, risked a moment of truth by touching a hand to Quinceton's cheek with one final look, and followed the voice to whichever Knower had called.

ACT III, CHAPTER THREE

In Search of Fire

QUINCETON HAD NOT REALIZED IT when he was first applying for work in the Flood Mansion, but as a Knower's bodyguard who saw plenty of JSS government business conversations, handled requests from different Speakers to meet with different Knowers, and just generally had some stature in society, he was occasionally regarded with Elect status simply by working in proximity to so much power. The perks were real.

With a room in a decent new building from the 2020s along Van Ness Avenue, in addition to Elect cafeteria and social event access all over the city, Quinceton also knew some San Francisco scuttlebutt: Something big was coming from the Knowers to adapt the whole paradigm of Social Justice against the unpredictable and contemporary threat of de-whitening. Everyone knew that de-whitening was an offense against everything their Anti-Racist society stood for—even if they didn't yet know why in Speaker-approved terminology—but they had no clue how the Knowers would respond.

It seemed to Quinceton that the only choice they had was to somehow consecrate the importance of race, reaffirming why it couldn't be changed or why a white person couldn't just "de-whiten" themselves, and then cast this specified elevation of racial caste as a new eternal tenet of Social Justice and the rest of the buzzwords.

Was this any more intellectually insulting than the rest of the bullshit they'd already swallowed? And if so, why did anyone care that another layer of propaganda might get heaped on top of what they'd already been dealt? Quinceton well understood that each Elect's real concern was over how the new changes would impact their settled, legally earned identity, but none would say it, or even take a guess at what solution might emerge from their Knowing Leader. And so, meeting these different faces of the same frightened Elect fit the standard social malaise of his younger days. He didn't even have the patience to want to sleep with any of them; it was too repetitive, plus, all the constant lying exhausted him.

It was little more than killing time that brought Quinceton to the Marina on his first post-work stroll around San Francisco on a windy day in mid-October. The views of the Golden Gate Bridge and Alcatraz Island were worth the walk down the hill to the top of the city. Even though the neighborhood was primarily comprised of ZNN Speakers that the Knowers could easily afford to dump onto a soft landfill atop a restless earthquake zone, Quinceton didn't feel even slightly anxious. Perhaps he was partially inspired by his peaceful stargazing patrols around the Stockton mansion, but another memory motivated the first deviation from Quinceton's basic revenge scheme.

On Chestnut Street, the bustling commercial center of the old Marina where mostly rich American whites shopped and toasted each other's abundant success, a fading turquoise awning shadowed the street from one story above. Unilluminated cursive signage announced the last name of the decaying business—Presidio—and though it had long gone dark, the rotting carcass of this movie theater beckoned to Quinceton with the possibility of finding friends in a terrified town. He tried the door—locked. But it gave him an idea.

For the next week, Quinceton visited a new neighborhood of the city each night on his excursions. He'd walk in one direction for hours sometimes, maybe all the way to the cold beach at the west end of the city, where he'd find a landmark to investigate. Most of these landmarks meant nothing to him—just fading relics from the high point of an age that was so impossible to replicate by its replacements that the whole effort had been dubbed white supremacist evil.

Concrete rectangle foundations like the Sutro Baths at Lands End told so little of the story, it didn't even make Quinceton curious. Things were built—at some previous time, for some unexplained reason—and then one day, around the time Quinceton was born, the JSS government came into power, and seemingly overnight, such things were no longer feasible. All that mattered was that something better was possible, and that possibility was retarded in its cradle by a competition among actors in which almost nothing tangible could ever be openly valued again. Everything Quinceton saw everywhere he looked was just another sentence in the same tired tale, and since he knew how it must end, he paid attention only to a few specific details.

The hidden and amazing benefit of these evening adventures was the abandoned treasures one might find in the most neglected spots. Anything you might be able to trade openly—like toilet paper or diapers or something—had been picked clean years ago, but many who had vacated New California with all deliberate speed left apartments and offices behind containing the greatest find of all: American books.

If you looked closely—and wanted it bad enough for long enough, with real effort behind it—there was actually knowledge to be found in forgotten places all over the city. One especially incendiary collection of pages with its cover torn off held these words inside: "When you want to help people, you tell them the truth. When you want to help yourself, you tell them what they want to hear." Quinceton couldn't stop thinking about the profound simplicity of such an idea. He wanted to write the quote down and stick it next to his bathroom mirror to memorize, but then remembered that such an idea would bring an immediate end to Anti-Racism. So, he left the book in the deserted office desk where he'd found it, but the knowledge he would keep forever.

It was the last day of October when Quinceton finally decided to try the Clay Theater, half a dozen blocks away from the Flood Mansion. The thirty-first of October, known as All Atonement's Eve, was once a bigger holiday than it was now, but Quinceton still saw a few chain gangs roving around. Traditionally, young people of ample privilege fastened themselves together and canvassed Elect neighborhoods to volunteer encouragement, assurances of historical guilt, and an act(s) of servitude the homeowner felt necessary to mollify their last week/month/year/century of endured identitarian animus. Black people had never really been into All Atonement's Eve, and since the other 364 days a year had essentially become the same thing minus the evening chain gang, tonight it was little more than added street traffic that Quinceton might use to hide his incendiary intent.

Unlike most other storefronts on Fillmore—mostly cafeterias and garment-fitting stations that the Elect could access with special stipend credits only they received—the Clay Theater appeared totally abandoned. Like most things in New California, if there were a way to fix the space without expending any effort or energy, it might have been completed by now, but in the current reality it would simply rot into sand and signage.

The vertical "Clay Theater" marquee facing Fillmore Street looked minutes away from collapse, and the glass double doors were similarly locked and inhospitable, but a large hole in the bottom of the right door would have allowed a deer to jump through. Quinceton glanced up and down Fillmore, half expecting to see someone who gave a shit, but he saw no one, and promptly felt silly for assuming such self-importance. Besides, if the Anti-Racists had any saving grace, it was their laziness, and tracking him around town couldn't have happened without suspicion and focus— that pair, totally feasible—but then effort, too, a typical deal-breaker.

The deep-maroon carpet and walls of the theater lobby bloomed with filthy fungus that stank like that of the deserted Work Doing Center Quinceton had visited in Placerville, in another lifetime when he could safely choose what to ignore. A rat scurried across the mess to find disappointment in the same piece of mold it must have checked a thousand times before.

Through the lobby was a large theater, the *only* theater, with a stage and curtain like those you might have found American capitalists gathering before to view films. Well-worn velvet seats surrounded the stage from all angles, but they didn't smell, as whatever leak had doomed the lobby seemed to have dried up before further infection here.

Quinceton walked down the center aisle, scanning the seats for a clue, anything that might back the story he'd heard at Tinh's dinner table. If this was once a Fire Temple for Anti-Anti-Racist Liberati, his father might have come here, and the thought fixed him with purpose and strength.

"You so young," Quinceton heard from somewhere around the stage. The curtain didn't move. "Hell are you doing here, boy?"

At the foot of the curtain, wrapped in a tattered old green sleeping bag, lay a grumpy old Black womxn. A half-filled water bottle and food wrappers circled the floor around her chosen bed space. She scowled, but didn't rise.

"... Well?" she demanded after a beat. Quinceton took a moment to eliminate all possibility that this ratty houseless wretch was his mother, which he deduced on size alone, even from across the theater. His birther had some extra skeleton to her, and even Mai might dominate this lounging body here. But there was no bullshit in the womxn's tone.

Quinceton's pulse calmed as he approached the stage.

"Truth is—I'm not sure. I was in the Battle of South Lake, got sent to DIE afterwards, and now I'm back in the city, bodyguard to Flood Mansion Knowers. Doesn't make a ton of sense to me, either. And what are you—under the curtain—doing here?"

"The hell it looks like," she said, but she appeared to be actively listening to his backstory. "And fuck do I know about your battle in the South Lake?"

Quinceton looked at the stage once more, trying to imagine if this could really be, or once have been, a Fire Temple. And what did he expect to get out of this incursion? How could he prove himself to anyone after all the reeducation he'd endured? The dark-red interior made him want to see fire in the place, a Fire Temple to match the fury he lived on, but all he had was this reality.

"Ma'am, I'm sorry if I bothered you. I really don't know what I was hoping to find here—I guess I just like exploring the old San Francisco. I don't know why. I'm not here to bother you; I respect your privacy."

The last word was the only hint Quinceton would drop before leaving, but the old womxn's face changed as soon as he said it. To speak of privacy was to believe in the concept at all, and this tiny idea would be enough of a clue for the right mind.

"You take care, then," she said from over Quinceton's shoulder as he walked back up the center aisle. "Never forget the real lessons they taught you."

It was a different voice than he'd heard before, one with a hint of comradery. *She is one of them*, Quinceton thought, before correcting himself. *She is one of us.*

ACT III, CHAPTER FOUR

Surrender the BIPOC

SOMETHING IN THE WORLD HAD changed since the day Quinceton visited the Clay Theater. What had been barely perceptible at first, with certain long-held glances dismissed as paranoia, became something of a suspicion when a middle-aged Latina reliever actually gave Quinceton a long nod and an extra dessert muffin from across the counter in the cafeteria line. Then, when he was leaving the Flood one day, he passed another young Black reliever, and when the guy made eye contact, the stranger smiled and held his hand out for a fist bump without calling Quinceton "vic" or "victim," as might normally be expected over shared racial comradery. A total unknown, in broad daylight, seemed to know Quinceton beyond the familiar, or recognize him somehow. Even with a positive association, the situation made the fearless warrior cautious.

If these people knew who he was, he must have actually stumbled into a Fire Temple that night. In this scenario, the old lady in the sleeping bag was some kind of security guard for the Anti-Anti-Racist Liberati—the first line of defense against nefarious agents of the state, and it was her duty to vet any potential recruit for possible admission into whatever secret society they had, or whatever plan they were working on. The other possibility was that this was all some giant setup. In that case, Quinceton's end would be about the same he figured it'd be if he failed; it didn't fright-

273

en him so much as it threatened his chance at inciting revolution.

There was also Natalie to consider. As she passed round after round of Knower inspections against better smiles on far less attractive faces, her spirit deteriorated. Quinceton would have suggested they meet outside the Flood—they were old friends according to their cover story, after all—but she just didn't have spirit enough to carry on much conversation inside the Reliever Lounge. The force of her willpower seemed to drain by the day, and when Quinceton remembered the most depressing times in his own life, he recalled being similarly bored by everything.

Preparations for the grand reveal at the SOMA MOMA Momalla Gala for Love continued behind closed doors, on which Quinceton eavesdropped only intermittently while standing at this post or that. The Knowers liked to have security stationed at various intervals, protecting the Flood Mansion, and rarely took the risk of voicing an opinion in the presence of the Knowing Leader, but they did talk and worry openly about the right enemies of Social Justice when surrounded by lesser IS identity scores. Knowers' closed-door statements did not follow the virtue-signaling patterns of the Speakers' public addresses, and though they delivered daily talking points to the top Speakers running ZNN public information dispersal about this or that identity that needed to be highlighted or condemned, the words they used in demanding these edicts were not orthodox JJJ equity speak. The Knowers' general ease when Mumwaza wasn't in the room made the atmosphere noticeably more comfortable for everyone, as unlike the Stockton AAA/JJJ agents, those at the top of San Francisco must have been there long enough to foster some sense of security and stability in the understanding that their blind support for Mumwaza was essential to maintaining the entire power structure.

One afternoon in early November, Quinceton was called from a perch at the door into the Knowing Leader's Secure Space. There were only a few other Knowers lying around, all elite Level Two wall meat handpicked from the dozens of supplicants Quinceton had witnessed on his first day.

"We're collecting lived experience as part of outreach efforts for the final Anti-Racist initiative, and you're Black," Knowing Leader Mumwaza began. "And we'd love to know how we can do an even better job of guaranteeing equity to all, especially your African American community, without, of course, asking anyone to alter their historically derived attitude or to correspond to the Racist standards of white supremacy. We've already unraveled cultural loyalty to the two-parent household and eliminated all Racist academic standards while introducing race-based judgements of all illegal actions to guarantee equity in all endeavors at the outset—we've come so far. I know this always seemed impossible. But is there anything else Anti-Racism can do to model society even closer to the necessities of the African American experience? Tell us Quinceton, tell us truly: How can we do even better?"

It occurred to Quinceton that not everything behind Anti-Racist JSS government policy was Racism disguised as a virtue signal to supposedly end Racism. Some of it may, in fact, have been interweaving racial discriminations for the sake of preserving racial distinctions and the power their identitarian politicians received as a result. Quinceton liked that the Knowing Leader thought so little of Blacks (such as himself) that INRI could be forthright about the childlike treatment with which Quinceton's "community" was to be privileged. The proof was there for all to see: With the right strategy at the right time, this reversal of cause and effect could be openly realized. Then, it would be a shining gold opportunity. Still, there was no predicting if the great masses of patsies in New California—weak, shamed, and afraid—could awaken to the right alarm.

"I'm not sure, Knowing Leader." Quinceton paused, looked down, and scratched his chin. He hoped it looked sincere. "Maybe I don't understand the question. What's the problem—exactly—in my African American community?" The room stopped moving. Quinceton forgot the rules and must've said something stupid.

"Well … were you not instructed in a Work Doing Center about the horrors of slavery, Jim Crow, and redlining that have systemically denied access to BIPOC individuals such as yourself for centuries?" the Knowing Leader recited. "Is it *fair* that the descendants of slavery lack the resources today that were stolen from their ancestors in yesteryear? Of course not.

And is it *fair* that society should be run by the descendants of slave own-ers, for the benefit of slave owners, to the obvious destruction of every other human's *humanity?* Is it *equitable?*

"Surely, Quinceton, *surely* you would agree that the problem for Af-rican Americans and all other BIPOC is that until the Justice of Social Soldiers government here in New California, no one truly centered mar-ginalized voices or took on the full burden of decolonization to liberate equity for all. Absolutely no one's even tried—not like we have, and not for Black BIPOCs especially like you. Do you not see how much you've risen since slavery?"

If INRI felt irritated, INRI hid it well, and whenever a word called for emphasis, INRI gave a little face flick to a new member of the captive audience. Evidently, speeches like this seemed a perk more than a nuisance to the Knowing Leader. The young soldier well understood how to build trust by ceding all moral authority, and he figured he'd assist the portly politician to bathe in his own sty by piling on more slop.

"No one has done more to reverse the Racism of the past, that's for sure. And you've done so well putting historically disadvantaged com-munities into the same boat—makes me understand why you can't just treat different races like each other. No one ever told me the whole plan, or when we go from equity to equality, but y'know, I can see it working, and I love what you've done with the place." He raised his eyebrows as he rotated his skull to indicate the ornate room overlooking the bay and felt the Knowers settle deeper into their cushions.

"We know 'equality' will be achieved once we've provided equity and eradicated all systemic Racism against BIPOCs, of course," Mumwaza said with a snigger to his associates. "A 'transition to equality' will hardly be necessary once equity is realized. And no doubt you realize that full equity is the first step to achieving full racial equality, of course. Which is why we ask for your two cents getting us there—in order to make BIPOCs full members of a Racist society, we must guarantee the essential vitality of their voices and lived experience, right?"

Quinceton nodded, scanning the room. They'd all heard this circular reasoning a thousand times before without a word of protest, it seemed. So had he. Back to INRIs lecture: "For example, would it help if no one could challenge anything you said, due to BIPOC lived experience and such? Especially white people, I mean—what would you like white people not to be able to challenge you on, to call you out about?"

"I don't know. Maybe I'm the wrong Black guy to ask, because I didn't grow up with white friends, and don't know any whites now." Quinceton wanted to change the subject before Mumwaza might see him connect the two ideas. "But none really confront me much anyway."

"Precisely!" Mumwaza piped up with enthusiasm. "No doubt you had your reasons for choosing the company you did, and interracial relationships are no match for the millennia of slavery that separates you. So, could an interracial communication amendment help rectify the distance between you? The distance that their ancestors invented and enforced through the whip?"

"Yes," Quinceton agreed, trying to meet Mumwaza wherever he was heading. An "interracial communication amendment" sounded exactly like all the other usual bullshit. "I'll never forget about the slavery, Jim Crow, or redlining. Nothing in the future will change the past."

"Then you, especially, may appreciate our plans for the next Anti-Racism corrective. It's helping young BIPOCs achieve equity. That's what all this is for. You understand, don't you, Quinceton?"

He did understand, finally, and all too well. The JSS government function truly laid itself bare for anyone to see, if they only thought to look. Why government efforts to "end Racism" actually increased and cemented skin-color categories of racial hierarchy was no longer a mystery, if it ever was, yet there was reassurance in the belief that if *he* saw the systemic con game this clearly, he could not be alone.

ACT III, CHAPTER FIVE

Mr. Rift

QUINCETON HAD TO BIDE HIS time before revisiting the Clay Theater. It was necessary to throw anyone off his scent should his cover be blown, and he wanted to win over the sleeping-bag womxn with some kind of offering that would prove his intentions. Then, with her speaking freely to another trusted Anti-Anti-Racist Liberati, he would finally figure out the rational response to this next iteration of JSS government-induced racial alienation.

But first, he had to spread out his walks around town to neighborhoods and buildings as different from the Clay as possible, particularly ones without a hint of Liberati suspicion. He figured neighborhoods that were mostly occupied were safer to visit, as were scenic walks around the Embarcadero Coast. Quinceton liked when ocean water overflowed onto the street there. It washed away the stink for a little while, but eventually the salt-grime would always return.

Yet it was while returning to his apartment that the Anti-Anti-Racists in San Francisco finally contacted him.

Quinceton had to be at the Flood earlier that day to schlep a rickshaw to the cold beaches on the western side of town, and he was just too tired to roam after work. So as he stumbled south down the gaping six lanes of Van Ness Avenue, he wasn't really thinking much about his surroundings, and he certainly didn't expect to hear a voice he recognized.

"Quinceton—what *the hell* is this *bullshit*?"

Immediately, the young man couldn't help but smile just as big as he had when he was a boy.

Quinceton's father had lost weight, but he'd added a dyed-blue goatee to his face below hot-pink hair while sporting faded rainbow sweats and cheap painted-gold Speaker-style sandals. In spite of the getup, he stood straight, shoulders back—still an undiminished individual, even now.

"S'just camouflage," his old seeder said, passing two fingers across his visage and placing his other hand on Quinceton's shoulder. "Now, lemme look at you." The son wanted to hug his father but copied his posture instead, adjusting to the surprise of looking him in the eye at even height.

"Grew up a man," he continued. "Couldn't happen any other way. I didn't like leaving you, though. You sore at me for leaving?"

"No, Dad," Quinceton said. "You taught me what I needed to figure out myself. And some things, you just gotta see with your own eyes."

"I'd've stepped in if I knew you were getting sent off to South Lake, but didn't hear it in time. Not safe here—walk with me another block, then I'm out." Quinceton nodded, strolling slowly in the direction of his apartment. "Tomorrow morning, be at the ocean side of Marina Green, five a.m. Wear something to run in. When I come up beside you, don't act surprised, and don't slow down."

"Yes, Dad." Quinceton couldn't imagine all his father might know about the JSS government-issued mess, but he trusted his views. Finally, he might learn whatever secrets of the universe Sarah, Tinh, and Bones had lacked the time to unearth.

"It hurts to see you now, after these years, and not be able to sit down, listen to your life," Dad said. "It's the world we got, and the world we got to change. Maybe they taught you how to kill, but you've still got to have some better world to fight for."

"I'm ready. I'm ready for anything." There was a pause as they reached the next street corner.

"Then maybe you'll forgive me for ditching you way back when. Hardest thing I've ever done, but I couldn't see no other way. And you can't really blame your mother Marcy too much, either—you didn't see all the pressure they put on women to raise kids alone, break us up, break up the *nuclear family* for the sake of reducing male role models and leadership, *matriarchically* independent child-parent relationships ending the *patriarchy* … and you gotta know—I missed you the whole time. The whole damn time, I was thinking about you, and I've thought about this moment every day since I crawled out your bedroom window."

"I remember," Quinceton said. "And I missed you, too. I didn't know I'd see you again, but I always thought I would anyway."

The elder Mr. Rift, so frequently a bottomless box of opinions and filial entertainment, went silent as he stared at his son. They held a look, maybe both thinking the same thing, neither saying it.

"Quinceton Rift," Dad said with pride. "Like a badass Winston Smith, the soft-rhyme inspiration for your name, even if your mother never knew. I had a feeling you'd grow up and learn the truth about everything. I just didn't know what you'd do with it."

"Winston Smith?" Quinceton asked.

"A very important book character, the classic everyman, trapped in a world of lies and fear and isolation." The young man made a note to read about Winston Smith … when the world would let him. There was a brief silence in which Quinceton imagined them both seeing the same world, facing up to the same challenge, together, with the same determination.

"I missed you, Quinceton. Really did." Then Dad turned off toward the old Fillmore neighborhood, leaving Quinceton to nibble at his dinner in silence, lie in bed for longer than he could sleep, and be up at dawn before his alarm had anything to say.

ACT III, CHAPTER SIX

To Run, Fight, and Never Sleep Again

QUINCETON COULDN'T UNDERSTAND WHY THEY called it the Marina Green, considering this brown rectangle of dirt at the top of the San Francisco peninsula showed no sign of life. Still, it was a landmark of sorts, and when a ball with some air in it could be procured, this was as good a place as any to kick it around in the afternoon. Never at daybreak, however, and as the day began, Quinceton couldn't see a soul, not even his seeder. But he was early.

Turning west on a stretch of concrete between dirt rectangle and coast, Quinceton ran toward the Golden Gate. Not everything had completely crumbled in San Francisco, and what had could be rebuilt. Quinceton turned left to remain at the edge of the rectangle, following it south briefly, then east again, toward Alcatraz Island. Just as he was about to turn north once more, he saw a tall hooded shape running in his direction and slowed his pace considerably.

Dad caught up with Quinceton after another left turn to the west.

"Keep running," Dad said in a pretty level voice. "Don't need to go fast, but stay in motion. Makes us much harder to track, if they even cared that much. Right now, all the different racialists are obsessed with each other. So you know what that means."

"Yeah, I do," Quinceton replied. "Now is the time."

"True. Smart boy all grown up into a smart man. Also means their distraction takes their focus off us, and whatever we got going on." The elder Mr. Rift was always an activist, never long on emotional explanation, but there was a good decade missing from their relationship Quinceton couldn't think past yet.

"Yeah, but slow down, Dad, and just talk to me about *you* for a second," Quinceton asked without reducing speed, like a pro. "I got why you left, but no contact, all these years—really, Dad? The hell is that? I mean, where the hell were you?" When he was a boy, he wouldn't have dreamed of speaking to Dad like that, but on this morning he'd earned it.

"I—a'course I *wanted* to, so many times," Dad stuttered, actually falling behind a step before hustling back into position. "But you gotta understand, during those early JSS government purges, it wasn't like this. They had to teach everyone the rules of what they had to do and couldn't say or think without ever being honest about anything—without ever saying, literally, what they're really doing—and that kinda top-down intimidation takes time to set up. And when the Anti-Racist JSS government didn't have to worry about a power grab from its Anti-Anti-Anti-Racist law enforcement thugs, they'd worry about an average Joe, like I was, because there were so many average Joes they had to scare into silence. The damn con artists—almost hard to believe they got away with it for so long. It didn't have to be me and you, but it was always going to have to be someone stepping up."

"What were you doing, though? Like, where were you all these years?"

"When I left you and your mom, I caught on with a Harriet in the Rooftop Railroad. Want to find where the real racial diversity is in the JSS California? It's on the trails of the Rooftop, people of every group on Earth filing out to Nevada or East Oregon as fast as their feet carry them. Anyway, you heard of a Harriet?"

"Nope."

"Named after an American badass, the Harriets in California helped

282

get people out. And when they got me to the border with a dozen other people, I got cold feet. I didn't know if I'd ever get to come back, *how* I would ever get back even if I wanted to, but I just couldn't leave. So instead, I became a Harriet myself—mostly for a far north route past the Central Valley, and up past a big-ass mountain called Shasta. They got some pretty plantations up there, but not much else, and once you got people out of the Bay, the job relaxed. It was good for the soul. It was the beginning of my fight. But just the last year or two, I heard the AAA Anti-Anti-Anti-Racists were building strength, and that's when I came back to SF. Maybe—hopefully—for good."

"But what changed? The Anti-Racists still control the government, and the Anti-Anti-Anti-Racists running the plantations do whatever they want. What's different?" They got to the end of the Marina Green and kept heading west along the waterfront, keeping the same pace.

"The Anti-Racist government bars most people from power, keeping their number of true believers limited to whomever they can personally bribe, radicalize, or intimidate into silence, while the AAA thugs made the effort to include the excluded. Remember, when the Great Rupture happened, there was time for reasonable people to leave Old California. At the same time, only radicals were moving in, but a ton of whites and Mexicans in the center of the state just missed the message. They'd made a life out of ignoring San Francisco anyway, so they weren't moving a muscle during the legal window. You gotta figure this was inevitable: The numbers of the AAA kept growing relative to the Anti-Racists running the government and tacitly supporting it like the Elect, and now the AAA outsiders are ready to challenge for power. This is a moment years and decades in the making."

"Just a power struggle between the government and law enforcement—that's all you want? What you've been waiting on?"

"Bet your ass. That's all we need. In recent years, we had a Harriet cross deep into Eastern Oregon with a message that supposedly got to Pithawalla. Advi Pithawalla, the trillionaire Zoroastrian who figured this all out first and bailed early. Remember him?"

"Yeah, I do. It's Pithawalla and his people that made them name it a 'Fire Temple,' right? Like named after their church." Quinceton saw a few random bodies in various directions moving around with intention, but they weren't nearly close enough to hear anything, and they were neither obese enough to be politicians nor chiseled enough to be their servants.

"That's right. And good thing you found the Clay Theater one. When I heard the description, I didn't know it was you, but I felt it was somewhere deep down. Maybe I did know, somehow."

"That old womxn in the sleeping bag, in the Clay—she's one of you. I fuckin' knew it!" Quinceton was all too pleased that the very first part of the plan he'd thought up all on his own had actually worked—so much so that'd he'd forgotten himself and cursed out loud in front of his seeder for what had to be the first time in his life. He watched Dad flinch, not fully turning to make it obvious, but seeing him clearly in the periphery.

"Alright, son," the elder Rift said slowly. Back in the day he hadn't tolerated cursing, not at all. "You're a man now, and a man can pick his words how he wants, but don't go messing your mind up with pride. Know how much brains it took to make it this far, to come back to this battlefield on your own and find me. You got nothing to prove. If, any time, you want to cut and run for Nevada, you do it and don't look back. Not for me, not for nothing."

"Yeah, Dad, I've also given that speech before, and I'm seeing this thing through." Quinceton saw something flash across his father's face he hadn't seen in a while, but it gave him the same feeling as when he'd seen it as a boy. It was the same face Dad had when he'd do something smart, or when he'd use an advanced vocab word correctly in a sentence.

There was a moment of hesitation, and Quinceton didn't want to be invited to run like a coward for a second time. "So, what's the plan?" he asked. "I'm working my way inside the Flood Mansion, and so far, they've got no reason to distrust me."

"Alright, well, don't put yourself in danger, but there is a way to help. And remember now, *do not* go so far out on a limb that the JSS government takes notice, or has any reason to come after you. There is no return to a DIE Camp—no second chance once you're already canceled and re-leased. But anything you can do to assist the Anti-Anti-Anti-Racist law enforcement in and around the SOMA MOMA Momalla Gala—you do it. Redgrave, especially. Help him."

"No way," Quinceton reacted, stopping in his tracks. "I'll help that motherfucker meet the Devil in hell if I help him do anything at all!" *And fuck this stupid running for show bullshit and whoever gives a damn about us.*

"Come on, Quinceton, keep up," Dad urged, stopping his progress but jogging in place.

"To hell with Redgrave." It was not a question. Everyone has bound-aries, everyone has pride, and the universe owed Quinceton a debt he'd collect in time.

"You know him? The new top AAA boss from the big camp in Stock-ton?"

"He's not *that* new. But yeah, I know him, and before all this is over I'll be the one to end him, too." Quinceton could see understanding flash across his father's face that wasn't entirely paternal, but nonetheless full of something good. Like respect—respect one had for an equal. It was all he needed to get running again.

"Let's move," Quinceton said, picking up the pace, followed closely by Dad. "What's the plan anyway?"

"I told you," he answered, trying to be helpful, but he really wasn't. "You gotta secretly, silently, back the AAAs around Redgrave and what-ever they have planned."

"Okay, sure, but what's their plan?"

"How should I know? You know how hard it is to get information in and out of a DIE Camp? You'd be better off trying to find a womxn at the ass end of northeast tumbleweed."

"I'm not planning to visit the American state of Maine any time soon," Quinceton replied, thinking it might impress Dad that his son understood the reference to the reclusive northeast forest where men had so little cul-ture to worry about they didn't even mind not having women. "But I don't know what I'm supposed to do here, either."

"No one does, not exactly. There's also the new JSS government initiative they're unloading at the Momalla Gala—I'm not sure they've even settled on what it is yet, but those details don't matter either." Dad almost laughed in spite of the gravity of their aims. "Even if we don't know this new policy, let's be real: *We know this new policy.* It's some new insane bullshit to keep BIPOCs as dependent on the system as slaves for their king—you know, the whole 'fighting Racism with new Racism' thing. What difference would the details make?"

"Well not to us, but from the perspective of Redgrave and his damn goons, it could matter a lot," Quinceton thought out loud. "Could help us predict how they'll act, or respond, or what I gotta do to balance these bastards out."

"So you'll take the job? Even not knowing what it is?"

"Yeah, Dad. In this world, some time it can be no one else but you, and running from it does no good anyway. I won't run. But you can tell whoever you need to that when the job is done, Redgrave is mine. That's my cut of our Social Justice—delivering it to Redgrave."

Dad nodded along before a striking Golden Gate background. "Once it's over, you can have your Social Justice on Redgrave. Won't bother no one. Just don't ask anyone to reveal their true motives and intentions before the full meltdown. We'll have some Anti-Anti-Racist Liberati hiding in cover, willing to help when they can, and plenty of Elect ready to flip— we just gotta break the spell, the fear of personal retribution."

All they needed was a match to ignite the inevitable inferno that would burn the whole thing down. And Quinceton had always kinda felt like being a spark.

ACT III, CHAPTER SEVEN

Officially Official Officiality

QUINCETON HAD EXPECTED MORE OF a crowd at the decrepit Department of Official Officials on Fell Street, but he didn't mind the neglect. They hadn't even bothered to take down the "Department of Motor Vehicles" signage the Americans erected long ago, when there had been Americans here and motor vehicles in the parking lot. Consequently, the conspicuous yellow lines denoting parking spaces made no sense on this asphalt. Each reminder of overarching incompetence felt comforting if you could ignore the consequences—and anger.

There were rows and rows of booths tucked into the low-ceilinged interior, but only one was occupied, with a few hundred workers waiting in a row. As Quinceton took his place at the back, he listened for clues as to the specific stated purpose of this facility. "The Department of Official Officials" was vague, even in a world with ever-evolving meanings of words. Perhaps that was the point of the title: to remind you that individual resistance is pointless in the face of unrelenting bureaucracy. Quinceton figured this was another shoddy attempt to control ideas and their dispersal, but one based in overt admission by those who would become suspects after reporting their concern.

"... if you know that for sure, then at least it's an answer," the guy at the front of the line told the heavyset womxn behind the counter. Though

287

his agitation could be heard across the room, she appeared nonplused as she continued to file and stretch her brightly colored nails.

"I just want to know for sure," the guy kept pleading. "You understand, right?"

"We don't have no information," the womxn said with a head that officially never stopped shaking from left to right without making eye contact. "Your sister's work detail was either extended, or she's been canceled and is rehabilitating indefinitely. ZNN should have the updated list of Racists posted at the usual places around the first week of the month, as usual."

The man could have tried getting on his knees and begging, but even that would have been no match for the womxn's icy boredom and incredible powers of deflection. Whatever conclusion he wanted would go roughly as unsatisfied as the next five hundred or so attempts at learning anything. Evidently, what the Department of Official Officials did was essentially frustrate and confuse you while making absolutely no effort to be helpful, all with an attitude of exasperation by the put-on of your mere presence. Surrender was inescapable under these circumstances. It took hours, but the last to fail to accomplish or discover anything—a young girl immediately in front of Quinceton—simply wanted a written definition of "Racism" she could use "for her knowledge," and to strengthen her commitment to Anti-Racism. She looked as if she meant it, too, yet she still got nowhere—or, to be specific, she was told that the definition of "Racism" is "all around you, and if you can't see it, then you have bigger problems than a dictionary can solve."

When Quinceton spoke, however, the stony glare across the counter turned to warm conviviality, and the womxn actually turned her attention away from her cuticles.

"I'm researching a possible Anti-Anti-Racist dissenter," he said. "This the right place to find her?"

"Yes it is!" the womxn exclaimed with volume. Suddenly her desk was full of folders, paper everywhere, thick black ink marking each page. She frantically shuffled and found a fresh sheet, which she flattened carefully, then poised over with an ink pen.

"I'm writing you an Official speech clearance form," she said with a face pressed to her scribbling. "You just take it to the end of the hall there, turn right, and you'll see a booth with a magnifying glass picture on it—that's the OMC, Office of Misinformation Control. Take this permission slip. That's where you want to go." Typically, the Official Officials banished you to a closed storefront halfway across the city if they were somehow obligated to redirect you on another goose chase, but the OMC was special, real, and extremely locally located.

Quinceton marched the length of the building, feeling the workers' microscope eyes. He wanted to turn on a heel and scream reassurance, to tell them this would all be over soon and that *he*, Quinceton Rift, would be their deliverer. Pride, no longer foreign and now perhaps a foe, would have to be managed. The Knowers had plenty of pride too.

The OMC section of the building offered three different cubicles in a row, all attended by cheerful staff. One of them, a thin light-skinned man, watched Quinceton approach from behind a wooden desk marked with the magnifying glass graffiti sign. Whereas the womxn out front reeked of worker and would always be so, this man's stern expression and fitting shirt could be none but Elect.

"Please sit down," the Official said in a monotone. "You've reached the Office of Misinformation Control. I can help you discover anything you seek about your neighbors, coworkers, friends, and family."

It wasn't so terrifying these days, but in the beginning—before people came to expect and plan for cancelations in their daily life—the Office of Misinformation Control sent more people to DIE than the tax man, or the Grim Reaper. This started back when books were still being printed, but after the popular culture critique titled *The Circular Firing Squad of "Social Justice" Credentialism: Idea Laundering in DEI Academia* pushed too much paper, it was the OMC that tracked down its author and proponents, then banned all future publications on standard Anti-Racism repression logic. Even in theory, an "office of misinformation control" would exist to whitelist and outlaw certain information that was then, by literal definition, *illegal,* leading Quinceton to conclude that the OMC was perhaps the only honestly named institution in New California after one substituted the word "communication" for "misinformation."

The young soldier sat, and waited.

"Tell me everything, from the beginning, with as much detail as you can remember," the Official said. He gestured with a hand flick to indicate the squirming line across the building and added, "It doesn't matter. Take all the time you need." There was no notepad in sight, so Quinceton assumed his words were being recorded.

"I'd like to conduct a worker inquiry into the child of a known Anti-Anti-Racist. I work as a bodyguard at the Flood. I believe I'm in good standing there, but I knew the child's father, and wanted to vet the child, too."

"Elect aspiring," the man said, approving of Quinceton's current labor assignment. "What is your name? And who is the child?"

"I'm Quinceton Rift, and her name is Jessica Bondurant. Now listen— I don't know her, and her father claimed she hated him and was truly Anti-Racist. I was the one to confer humane dispatchment to her seeder, and I'm here to be thorough, just so this suspicion never comes back on me. So I need to investigate the child for myself, just in case. You understand."

"Certainly," the Official said, "and your request is perfectly in line with the new initiative to reduce Community Safety personnel, and the scope of duties they are entrusted to enforce." The man heaped a huge binder onto his spotless desk. "She's currently in full compliance, so your inquiry will be noted here but requires no further promotion up the law enforcement ladder. However, you are naturally encouraged to conduct your own investigation. I'll write her address down for you, and if you find anything—anything at all—report back at once for personal exoneration and potential reward."

And just like that, Quinceton knew where to find Bones's daughter. Once the rest was prepared, he would.

ACT III, CHAPTER EIGHT

Mano a INRI

IT WAS HARD NOT TO think about Redgrave when Quinceton got the call to visit Knowing Leader Mumwaza Q. Jumping Bull's Secure Space for a "conversation between just our voices" at the end of November. Quinceton knew, for example, that Jumping Bull was a heterosexual—INRI would never sacrifice the IS points by admitting it, but that didn't mean it wasn't true—and being a straight guy guaranteed that INRIs interest in alone time with the young soldier couldn't be the same as Redgrave's. But still, any personal attention might never have the same innocence again for Quinceton, especially from a person of significant Social Justice status.

The Secure Space still offered cushions all around the perimeter, but there was now a chair in the direct center of the room, facing Jumping Bull's elevated throne. INRI pointed to the seat and said, "Want something?" Quinceton appreciated the brevity; he liked a Knowing Leader who barely had time for him.

"No thank you, Knowing Leader."

"You know why I remember you, Quinceton? You're not like most of the others. Do you know that about yourself?"

The young soldier leaned forward to the front of his chair. "I'm sorry, Knowing Leader—I really can't say for sure. Was there—?"

"Nothing to apologize for," Jumping Bull said, open palms forward.

"Relax, young man. You were honest about your confusion and your past. We always prefer it that way, so we can create a learning moment—it's when people don't know where to go with their confusion that leads to Racism."

"I know you're fighting Racism, though," Quinceton confirmed. "I don't understand all the details, but I know you're making the world safe for all us BIPOCs." Though he didn't really think of himself as a BIPOC—and knew damn well that at least Mumwaza's skin was pale as paper—the inclusive reference was meant to comfort any insecurity the Knowing Leader suffered over INRIs Irish-white skin.

"Of course. You can see the larger goal even if the specifics elude you. But it all comes down to the workers, the average people. Do you know that's where we get our power from?"

"I do." Quinceton recalled a slogan INRI used in early speeches during former Knowing Leader Kendaoi's downfall: "You're *people-powered.*"

"Excellent!" INRI said with a genuine smile. "That's exactly right! And do you therefore understand the implied covenant we must keep with our people?"

Quinceton couldn't quite recall the meaning of the word "covenant," but he could guess by its use here. "In order to be people-powered, you need to fight against Racism, on behalf of the people?"

"Not far from the truth," INRI replied. "In order to maintain the trust and faith of the people, we must be able to demonstrate how we are winning the larger war against systemic Racism. No system can survive long-term without the will of the masses, and those masses must view the government's authority as legitimate. What belief do you think finally separated Old California from the rest of the Racist United States? So now, for the New California JSS government, what do you think legitimates our power? What do you think the people demand of us in order to sustain their consent to be governed?"

Quinceton didn't see a whole lot of consent when he looked around San Francisco, and he sure didn't see legitimacy, either. But there was power—that was for sure. He just couldn't say out loud how it was enabled, and who had enabled it to flourish this far.

"The people demand you fight Racism," the soldier ventured, searching for the soft answer. "You've given equity to the people, and they demand you maintain it."

"Well ..." The Knowing Leader paused. "Thank you for asserting our society as 'equitable.' Certainly, that is the ultimate, eternal goal. But think, Quinceton: Have we actually reached full equity? And what would that mean if we had?"

The sinister, intentional nature of it all had yet to dawn on Quinceton until this moment, but somehow he'd known it all along.

"Of course we haven't actually achieved full equity," Quinceton backtracked. "That would be impossible—that would be as impossible as changing history books." The Knowing Leader's nod kept Quinceton talking. "So you, as the Knowing Leader, must always keep society moving toward more and more equity, while knowing this is an impossible goal?"

"Exactly! Now you see the conundrum—the paradox, if you will. Our success at ending inequity may make the masses of workers think they can have equity without us, or in some other way. And slavery-Jim Crow-redlining didn't just extend the Racism of the past into today; it created an unequal playing field which the early Anti-Racists only made worse." Quinceton couldn't hide his genuine surprise as Mumwaza rushed to an explanation with unusual haste. "Yes—unfortunate, but true. With the best possible intentions, of course, the early Anti-Racists were so dedicated to not 'blaming the victim' that they over-shielded BIPOCs from all forms of adversity, including some that turned out to be essential. Meanwhile, the non-BIPOCs were privileged by the new system built around ending white fragility, as it seems the equity mechanisms of Anti-Racism unintentionally developed a certain resilience among whites and Yellows and other privileged groups; it only sharpened some psyches and work ethics, and often the more self-reliant were prone to reject the JSS government.

"The farther the privileged got from San Francisco, the more they thought independently. At the same time, we hadn't expected the difficulty of getting oppressed and historically marginalized peoples to sweat for society once they understood the full weight of the centuries that were against them. A new fragility began to emerge in our BIPOCs as we indirectly trained our enemies to work through identitarian concerns, and eventually they viewed *themselves*—the mostly white people, mind you—as the *victims* of Anti-Racism, rather than its historical and present beneficiaries.

"So, you see our predicament. There is a natural unrest among the workers as different levels of lifting between identity groups are not only required to overturn our Racist history, but now to actually feed ourselves and guarantee that the state functions without revolt. That's why we have to watch people in the AAA or JJJ-whatever groups all over New California. This Redgrave—I had thought he would be satisfied with an estate, but now I fear the worst."

"He's not going to be happy with being a DIE Camp Chairperson," Quinceton said with unusual conviction, especially for an un-Knowing voice in this room. He'd forgotten to heed his father's request to back the AAA/JJJ at the explicit mention of Redgrave, and Mumwaza had made him feel important enough to speak off the top of his brain. "You can take my word for it. I know that guy well enough to know he's not satisfied with Stockton."

"So what, then, might he want? Now, or after something specific, or later?" For the first time that Quinceton had witnessed, the Knowing Leader appeared to regard another power pole in the universe, and INRI clearly wasn't comfortable with the thought.

"I can't say so for sure, Knowing Leader." A pause created a moment to consider his father's request. "He feels underappreciated, probably, somehow. Maybe what he wants from all this is some ... attention? Some credit?"

"I hope that's all," Jumping Bull said. "Here, Quinceton, let me show you something." The great statue attempted to dismount from INRIs mantel, and the athletic young man rushed to assist. Quinceton failed to anticipate the weight of Jumping Bull's full momentum and apologized for allowing INRIs ample heft to dislodge itself from underneath reams of fabric. The Knowing Leader graciously accepted the apology and pointed to a patio door.

"Open that one," INRI said between heavy panting. "And walk through." Quinceton did as instructed, and the Knowing Leader quickly assumed the single chair on the patio. "It's all about the *I* in DIE—that's the thing about these DIE Camps which concerns me," the Knowing Leader said upon catching INRIs breath. "Now, tell me, Quinceton, tell me truly: What do you see when you look out at your city?"

With the Golden Gate Bridge to the left and Alcatraz Island to the right and the bay itself shining throughout, it was a special piece of land. It wasn't hard to imagine the Ohlone here a thousand years ago, thinking they'd reached a little heaven on Earth at the end of this peninsula. But when Quinceton looked out at the people, he saw mostly single, scattered characters all milling around in aimless supplication to each other's judgement. Even the couples and groups held a muted silence he could easily imagine from atop the Broadway ridge of Pacific Heights. Maybe they all knew, or assumed, they were being watched. Because they were.

"I see a beautiful place full of vibrant people," Quinceton replied. "What am I looking for?"

"Sure you do, but do you see the 'inclusion' at work?"

"I do," Quinceton lied. "But maybe I've lived with inclusion for so long, I don't know what anything else would look like."

Jumping Bull smiled; INRI liked the answer. "Absolutely right. A privilege from being born in the era you were born into. But this peace you see around you, this harmony—it's all built on the same thing: inclusion. And once people who feel excluded have a place to go and meet each other … well, you can imagine our concerns. And that's why we must pay such close attention to Redgrave and his new JJJ group, this 'de-whitening' and all that. They may betray the very foundations of our society. Do you remember our New California motto?"

"I sure do: *'Certainty is supremacy; confusion is compassion,'* right?" Quinceton answered in his most emotionally supportive tone. "Redgrave and them sure seem to be building a dangerous kind of confidence, then, huh?"

"It's possible. For sure, it's possible. Tell me about the true meaning of our motto, Quinceton. No wrong answers. I want to know what you really think."

"I think it's a reminder of humility to everyone. Like, being 'certain' invalidates the lived experience of our JSS government Elect who have really thought it through, who understand history and how to make it work to the benefit of a diverse society. But being 'certain' of unapproved knowledge is how Racism spreads. And admitting you're 'confused' or you're at least not sure of some ideas, well, that centers and empowers our Knowers to spread the right kind of knowledge about Racism and defeat all the misinformation by mere workers who are 'certain' in their disagreements but actually very wrong and Racist."

"You understand, my young friend. You really get it. Perhaps there could be a Knowing future for you. So you see why Redgrave and this growing AAA/JJJ form of 'certainty' is so dangerous to the Standpoint Mandate, the very foundations of Anti-Racist philosophy?"

"I sure do. So many violent people of privilege out there, especially whites, and Redgrave could be a magnet for them. Racial forgiveness is a dangerous concept, and we must be especially careful in giving the power to grant it."

"Precisely." The Knowing Leader looked out at INRIs bay, satisfied. "We'll do big things before the year is out. You and me both."

Quinceton nodded right along. Finally, they agreed.

ACT III, CHAPTER NINE

The Apple and the Tree

THE BUILDING WAS NEW ENOUGH to make Quinceton wonder if Jessica Bondurant had upgraded her life since her seeder was demoted from the Elect. These new digs, on the South Beach side of SOMA, were much more quiet and bulkier than the big opaque collection of condos on Van Ness where she'd lived with Bones.

It was early evening, just after work, when Quinceton Rift arrived on Jessica Bondurant's doorstep, hitting the buzzer and finding it operable. In moments, she appeared at the door and, before introducing her name, blared her Intersectional value: "Full-body privilege pansexual blandbrain half-Mexicanx feminine-leaning Latinx non-binary they/them."

Using both 'Mexicanx' and 'Latinx'—two words progressive whites had appropriated and forced onto Spanish-speaking peoples—assured Quinceton he'd met the offspring from which Bones had become so alienated. She'd clearly stated "half-Mexicanx," meaning either Bones was telling the truth and had managed to mate with another half-Mexican, or someone somewhere along the way had figured out a way to up the import of their lily-white ass.

In another life, in another time, Quinceton might have thought about flirting with the girl, even if she was a few years older, just because he recognized her type so well. She wore the trademark light-skinned scowl

297

of her generation, a look that demanded you explain yourself in advance of apolitical action, and when she cast those glaring eyes at Quinceton, he got a familiar premonition of inevitable misunderstanding. Somehow, even before he opened his mouth, he could confidently guess at every facet and impulse of Jessica's worldview.

"I'm Quinceton Rift," he announced. "Just a Black he/him reliever at the Flood Mansion—full-mobility blandbrain, like yourself. You don't know me, but I knew your seeder." She didn't flinch, as he'd expected her to.

"And?" she asked, shifting all her weight to one foot. "You want a cookie? 'Cause you met my seeder—so cringe. And you're looking at me like it matters."

The indignity of the person in front of him startled the man who'd been sharpened by battle, servitude, and most other forms of assault. The womxn's frigidity was meant to intimidate, but mostly Quinceton felt the urge to argue with her. And that wasn't the business that brought him to this doorstep.

"I've come to tell you your seeder was found to be an Anti-Anti-Racist and perished in a Stockton DIE Camp," Quinceton sped to the point. She looked ready to close the door in his face if he didn't. "I knew him. I knew him to be an Anti-Anti-Racist, and I'm here to conduct an official citizen inquiry into your loyalties as a result." As her power shriveled around her spine, he added, "And I could use a chair."

"Right—come inside, and sit at my table. Please." Her ferocity wilted into something Quinceton could work with, but he found no pleasure in these identity power politics. He entered and took a seat, but did so as he promised not to stay long. The room was pretty simple. There was a framed picture on each wall that didn't resemble anything Quinceton could recognize; they looked like the god of paint had simply drunk too much and vomited on a canvas before passing out.

"Ask me anything you want," she offered, still aggressive, but on defense now. "I've been in communications at ZNN forever; everyone knows how Anti-Racist I am. Look, I'm no bleeder, and never have been."

"What the heck is a bleeder?" Quinceton asked with genuine surprise.

He'd been away from the city for too long to know all the contemporary lingo.

"You know, a cisgender womxn. A bleeder, get it?"

Quinceton couldn't stifle an awkward chuckle. "Of course," he said. "Not the most attractive image, but makes perfect sense." She said nothing and waited, forcing him to act out his role as inquisitor here.

"Look, I know you're in communications at ZNN," he added to reassure her ego with a reminder of her special Elect societal status. "So I'm sure you're kept to the highest standards of Anti-Racism with God knows how many people around you at all times to keep tabs. But you also gotta understand, I knew your seeder. And he really did love you. One can't be too careful."

Quinceton hated that in order to keep his word to Bones, he'd delivered the message through a lens of suspicion rather than paternal affection. But there was no other way, and at least it would explain his own commitment to the effort—a spy, rather than a friend.

"That's impossible," Jessica said, shaking her head violently and without emotional hesitation. "Racists can't love. And they're way too cringe to matter, anyway. Everyone knows that."

Quinceton watched her hesitate for a beat—was it the memory of one of her father's jokes? Of their last interaction? Whatever it was, it was a flash of truth from a top sheep in the herd, and as soon as she realized the pain on her face for a lost father, she corrected it.

"I suppose." Quinceton expected to feel as he usually did when keeping his word, but instead there was a hint of shame in his voice. If there was a way to avoid the hypocrisy of the Anti-Racist JSS government, it was to do what you said you'd do and mean the things you said, but sometimes that also meant lying like this, somehow.

Quinceton paused, feeling the need to justify himself before the glare of suspicion reversed. "And when was your last contact with your seeder? Just for my own peace of mind. I already know from the Office of Misinformation Control that you're in good standing at ZNN and have no problems with your record."

"Years ago, before I began in communications. And I can understand why you'd reach out this one time, just on suspicion of an Anti-Anti-Racist's spawn, but now you need to remember whose table you're sitting at. We at ZNN do the work of decolonization on a daily basis, holding our sources to the highest possible standard of lived experience, and by centering the right marginalized BIPOC voices we are irreplaceable to the acceptance of the larger message of Diversity, Inclusion, and Equity. And don't forget who decides." Quinceton's eyes drifted up to hers before he could stop himself. "Oh, it's not me who decides the Racists from the Anti-Racists!" Jessica assured her present company. "But we are the first to know so we can be the ones to tell everyone else."

Quinceton knew a true believer when he met one, and he was glad for the reminder. *Only one thing left to do.*

"Well, I'm satisfied. So, if you care, would you like to know what happened to your seeder?"

"What happens to them all, eventually, I'm sure. Don't waste any more of your time telling me." Her face meant it, too.

Quinceton nodded, stood, and made his way home in the dark and lonely night.

ACT III, CHAPTER TEN

Everyone Got a Plan

IT WAS A NIGHT IN the third week of December, a particularly cold one, when Quinceton received the first knock on his apartment door. No one had ever come to visit him in his borderline-Elect building; he didn't have any friends or any family that could acknowledge him, and all assignments from his workmaster happened in person, at the last minute, based on whatever logistical emergency demanded the greatest urgency. Meanwhile, the book he'd brought home to read may not have had anything too illegal in it—it was just about a farm of animals talking like whites and becoming like them, too—but even so, it was safer to tuck it under his bed. For all Quinceton knew, the animals could be accused of bigotry against each other.

He listened again. The knock could have been any sort of the standard banging his building hummed with at all hours meant for sleep. But it happened again, and with a few more pounds.

Quinceton answered the door and half gasped at the sight of Juniper, his old roommate from Stockton, standing in the doorframe and clad in a dapper all-black suit and red shirt you might see in a picture from the American Hollywood days. The suit wasn't shiny around the lapels like a houseguest's tuxedo would be, there was no white anywhere, and it appeared to have been tailored by hand. Since Juniper never had the balls to escape, she'd clearly moved up in the world.

"Quinceton!" she said like they'd always been tight. "Long time since I've seen you! How have you been?"

He didn't try to match her enthusiasm, but he knew to play along. "Juniper—I'll be damned. Good to see you and Redgrave are getting along just fine. I take it those fancy clothes have something to do with you being in town, eh?"

The welcoming smile faded slightly, but didn't disappear. "It's a new look for JJJ diplomats," she explained. "You're right, I've been promoted, working alongside our Chairperson, but these clothes are simply meant to express the inclusion and togetherness of all colors combined in total pitch-blackness. And we all bleed red, right? After a convincing reminder, equity is ours to achieve, too."

"Achieve what, exactly?"

"The racial and social integration of all people into one collective, equitable unit, of course. Isn't that what this has always been for?"

"I dunno … sounds to me like you gotta be careful to avoid colorblindness," Quinceton said, a little too bluntly, before adding, "But I'm sure you've got that under control, too. Why don't you come in and sit down?"

One chair had been provided for domicile comfort by the JSS government, and Quinceton indicated it while he assumed a seat on his bed. He waited to hear more. Juniper looked around the room, probably hoping for a picture or something to distract from her task, which was still unfamiliar to her. But there was nothing to see that wasn't standard-issue.

"So, what's up?" Quinceton finally asked. He almost felt sorry for her, even if it was he who was to be examined under the microscope.

"Okay," Juniper said with official officiality, settling her hands on her knees and looking directly at Quinceton for the first time. It was the whole effort of it all that lent Juniper some sympathy. It was just as nonsensical that she would be here, pitching whatever it was that she had to pitch, as it was for Quinceton to assist her in helping the AAA/JJJ law enforcement slice deeper into humanity's flanks. But the blur of incoherent worldviews warring with each other made the young soldier want to help any individual who actually came into focus.

"So, first of all, it's great to see you again, Quinceton. Whatever you said to Redgrave for me ... well, it worked, and I've been getting trained as a foreign diplomat."

"A what? For the AAA—or the JJJ—you guys have diplomats now?"

"So that's something I wanted to tell you," Juniper said with newfound confidence, leaning forward. "The JJJ law enforcement groups have now collectively grown large enough to be platformed in San Francisco, and as the population of New California cis-hetero males and the de-whitened emerge as two groups of demonstrable disadvantage with overrepresentation in DIE Camps, they, too, become worthy of mention. It's time the JJJ gets political, and helps design future Anti-Racism and pro-gender efforts rather than simply enforcing edicts from above."

"If you can sell cisgender heterosexual mostly white men to the Anti-Racist government ..." Quinceton actually laughed. "I mean, best of luck. Just don't ask me to judge a damn thing. I never know what's going on, and that's all I got to say about that."

"Oh, you have nothing to fear," Juniper said in her most reassuring tone. "Cis-hetero Black males are suffering, too. Don't worry. It's just another means toward equity and inclusion." This, unfortunately, happened to be Quinceton's exact concern.

"Okay," the young spy replied slowly, buying time to calculate reality at lightning speed. So the 'de-whitened' mostly whites in rural parts of New California had finally organized. The great fear of the Knowing Leader was coming true in real time, suspected but still unbeknownst to INRI. It was almost too perfect to be true. Nothing ever happened like this; nothing actually worked out in New California, ever. That something threatened to succeed now was enough to make any thinking person suspicious.

"So what are you telling me, Juniper? After South Lake, and Stockton, I learned to keep my head down as I learn about Racism from the world. I don't want to fight any more wars."

"Of course not, and no one would ever ask you to." Juniper didn't have the diplomatic chops to backtrack effectively. "But I just wanted to explain what we're doing here. You'll see our presence at the SOMA

MOMA Momalla Gala for Love, for sure. And to let you know, in case times change or get hard somehow, we'll have your back."

"You have my back? How so, and in case what happens?"

"The future is uncertain," she said with newfound formality, rising from her chair. "But at least you know me, and you know Redgrave, so you have friends to reach out for just in case. Just in case something happens you didn't expect, or other people you trust let you down, or, who knows, the whole world turns upside down."

"I guess it's happened before, hasn't it?"

Juniper smiled as she reached for the door. She didn't get the reference to South Lake, but it didn't matter anyway. Quinceton had been primed for future assistance, almost certainly scheduled for the spectacle of the Soma Momalla Gala. The information relay that had brought Juniper to Quinceton was complete.

After waiting forty-seven hours, Quinceton visited the Clay Theater once more, careful to step through the front door hole with nary another person in sight. He walked straight through the smelly lobby and right to the stage.

"State your business," the sleeping-bag womxn said as if waking from a long nap. "I don't have all night."

"Of course," he said, then thought frantically about how to phrase his question/statement/request. The womxn appeared to live, eat, and sleep on the same six-by-three stretch of stage in the abandoned theater, but she wasn't one to be bullshat.

"I think you know what's going on in New California better than I do," he began. "I don't quite know who you are, but I think it anyway. And I was recently contacted by an Anti-Anti-Anti-Racist diplomat—or I guess they're called the JJJ now—but in any case, they also have dip-lomats they're sending to the Soma Momalla Gala. I don't know what they're doing, so I don't really know what I'm telling you, but something is in the works."

"Where do you spend your off-work evenings?"

Quinceton wasn't sure if she'd heard what he'd said. "Different places.

I like to roam around at night."

"Pick a place," she commanded.

"Okay." Quinceton considered the visibility of various potential meeting spots. "Okay, I like to spend my evenings in Union Square. Never know what you'll see, from a ZNN report, to personal cancelations, to the Perp Walk. Usually a crowd of some kind. But at night, I like to sit on the middle steps—you know, the ones facing the Macy's apartments, around nine o'clock."

The womxn put her head back down and faced the opposite direction. Their discourse concluded, Quinceton returned to the street, hustled back to his place, and resolved to be at Union Square at 9:00 p.m. every night until contacted.

ACT III, CHAPTER ELEVEN
Natalie's Time

THERE WAS A SEAT NEXT to Natalie in the Flood cafeteria, and Quinceton sniped it before collecting his food. Lunch could wait, but with the SOMA MOMA Momalla Gala coming up the following week, he wouldn't get a better opportunity to contact his crush.

"Hi, friend," he said cheerfully. "How you holding up before the big night?"

Her face responded with a look that made him regret asking. What was draining from her life had continued to bleed out since he'd last seen her. Darkness collected around her eyes, which were always cast downward.

"Surviving," Natalie answered without looking up. Quinceton wondered if she'd recognized the voice, or just didn't care who was speaking. She picked at a puddle of mashed potatoes on her plate, pulling out a spoon with plenty of food on it before putting it back without taking a bite.

"Well, that's good to hear." Quinceton understood her demeanor provided an extremely limited window in which to earn her attention. He just didn't know how to reach a person so emotionally distant from his world. "So, Natalie, any plans for the Momalla? I'll be on a security detail for sure, but they didn't assign anything specific yet. Since I'll have to see it this year, I hope you tell me they figured out how to make you the star of the show."

Natalie forced a smile without looking up. "Thanks, Quinceton," she said. "I think Mumwaza's going to pick me as one of INRIs dates."

"Well … a Knowing Leader probably likes 'em pretty, right?" he said, trying to hide his concern with flattery. He really wasn't surprised; he'd pick Natalie, too, if he had the right to build his own roster. But it still felt like bad news, especially with the way she said it.

"At least INRI doesn't like touching me," she answered, head still down. "At least not yet—thank the Lord Jesus. But I do know what INRI likes. INRI likes some pretty, and others just … pathetic and humiliated."

"What do … you mean … exactly?" Quinceton asked carefully, trying not to allow too much emotion into his words. He wanted Natalie to trust him in a way she might never have trusted anyone else.

"I mean … INRI has a thing." She caught Quinceton's glance, and somehow now it was her comforting him. "He doesn't touch me, hurt me, or anything like that, but he likes to be touched, and he likes to watch."

"What does INRI make you do?" His voice wavered, but Quinceton thought he'd delivered the line with a level tone.

"Mostly just orders me around. Makes me clean and stuff—not naked, but wearing some kinda cheap costume lingerie, like all black with floppy white lace stuff around the collar. And INRI calls me names. That's the kink: sitting back, getting a massage from a blonde white girl—always a white girl, super blonde, and never the same one—as INRI talks to me and tells me to do simple cleaning around the Secure Space. INRI talks and talks, and at some point INRI orders me out, and then I think they have sex. But never with me, Quinceton."

It wasn't as bad as it could've been, he told himself, but Quinceton wasn't thinking about the worst-case scenario. He pictured Jumping Bull lying on INRIs fat ass, being doted on by women who in no other circumstance would be forced to put up with such a cow. Quinceton had heard this could happen in places like Old Hollywood, but surely the outside American world, free or not, would never deign to match something so ugly with someone so pure and beautiful.

"What does INRI say to you? INRI really gets off on it, huh … what the hell does INRI say?" Keeping his volume low took greater effort than he expected, but no one nearby seemed to give a damn for their presidential gossip.

"Well, let me put it this way: It's the only time I wish someone would call me Latinx. The dusting and stuff, the ordering me around … it's all racial, Quinceton." She watched his face as he took in her words, prepared. "I don't get offended, but that's what it's all about for INRI. No one else can use those words, and no one else can tell INRI not to, because Mumwaza controls what is offensive. Calling me a 'dirty beaner' and 'lazy wetback' and a 'little spic whore' as he gets a blonde rubdown. That's INRIs thing. And really, I'd rather be the spic than the blonde girl."

"It's got nothing to do with you, Natalie," Quinceton tried to comfort her without admitting it was he who needed more mental repair. "INRI's the identity-obsessed leader of a race-crazed nation. It's just how he learned to think, and it comes out sexually, too, I guess." The conversation had moved beyond the importance of remembering pronoun puffery.

"I know," Natalie said. "I know it's not me he's talking to. It's his imagination that gets him off somehow, and any Latina or Black girl or Native is just as good as another."

"I'm sure you're right." Quinceton didn't like being the focus of concern. He was trying to help out Natalie, ideally, and not be yet another thing for her to worry about. "I respect what you're sacrificing for, but it won't be like this forever."

"I bet you're right. Jumping Bull is running out of new blonde girls." Quinceton didn't know what to say back, and she went on. "And you know what our options are like in this world."

That, he did. He desperately wanted to explain, to promise and to encourage that all this would be different quite soon, and that it would be soldiers of destiny like he, Quinceton Rift, to deliver the world from the clutches of second-wave slavery profiteers and the insecure slavers they enabled. And yet all he could do, today, was listen and smile along like just another fool.

"You never know what could happen in the future." It was his tone that made her listen. Maybe it was his tone that couldn't hide that which his words attempted to obfuscate from others, and the look he received in reply was better confirmation than anything she could say.

"You never know," she repeated.

"And anyone who knows—who knows anything they shouldn't—can't say it, but that doesn't mean there's nothing to know." As he watched his hint work its way into her comprehension, he couldn't resist a feeling of exultation, of being a potential savior to this one single soul. He wanted to dump his brain on the table in front of her and let her pick and choose what information was useful and sift it from what would get her killed. But instead, all he could do was make these indirect suggestions and hope she heard the deeper truth.

"There's always plenty to know." Color seemed to rush back into Natalie's cheeks. "Maybe you'll teach me a thing or two sometime."

"Maybe even at the SOMA Momalla Gala."

She smiled; she had to know. Or at least Quinceton wanted to believe he'd given her something to hope for.

ACT III, CHAPTER TWELVE

Union Square Redux

8:57 P.M., SITTING ON THE middle steps facing the Macy's apartments, his fourth attempt, two days to the SOMA MOMA Momalla Gala: a soft prodding to the upper back. Quinceton turned to see a Black knee underneath a long bright-pink dashiki. Just as before, the elder Rift was careful to camouflage and knew his audience well.

"Turn and follow me into the crowd," Dad said softly before he walked a few paces toward the Accountability Platform.

The brownish-skinned possibly Latinx male-presenting Speaker on stage recited the crimes of the currently cancelled ("repeated macro-microaggression assaults on persons of greater color"; "failure to report Racist ideas and assumptions") as Quinceton scanned the crowd for problems. There were a few JJJ agents posted at the foot of the platform, the low-level Speaker on stage to consecrate the self-denunciations, and any number of people looking at their fellow citizens with sheepish delight for being on the more populated side of this socially constructed moral repudiation. Nothing unusual, nothing out of the ordinary.

"All looks about right to me," Quinceton said to his father in a voice beneath the debasement blaring from the speakers. "What are we looking for?"

"I don't think many JSS government-spy types are coming to this shit anymore," Dad explained. "When they were still trying to get the Anti-

Racist ideology to take over—you know, in the very beginning—sometimes you'd see a clean-cut white guy with no interest in the stage, just watching the audience. Then they'd report back, and sometimes that's how an official Racism inquiry gets going."

"Why white guys?"

His father coughed with a little laugher mixed in. "I didn't raise no fool. Why d'you think, Quinceton? They aren't going to trust a Black man to brush his teeth in this world, lest he learn how to brush 'em on his own. If he did, putting knowledge and reason behind the potential convincing power of a Black identity—that guy could pose problems later. So, if you got an important job to do, safer to make it a brainwashed white man. Also helps maintain the inequity the government is supposed to be fixing."

"Yeah, I guess," Quinceton said. There was a lot he could add, and plenty he could ask, but not many hours left before game time. "You get my message from the sleeping-bag womxn?"

"If you told her the JJJ and Redgrave and them are planning something for the Momalla and gave her no details, then yeah, I got the message."

"Not many details, I know, but I think you're right about something: that the JJJ is organizing whites and straights and men against Jumping Bull and the rest of the government. I really think so. I think the de-whitening was basically what Jumping Bull fears it to be, so then the JSS government must be aware of the threat somehow."

"Makes sense," Dad said. "Go on. Keep thinking."

"And if the JSS government is aware of the threat, but not doing anything to stop the JJJ agent presence at the Momalla, then they must have something sneaky planned as well."

"They'd have to, but it's not all that sneaky. They loosened identity, ability, and all other standards to recruit for something called 'Peripheral Calm Maintenance.' Hell, the government would arm anyone after you convince the right people. And besides, Mumwaza and them, they've known about de-whitening for a while. They know it's a workaround to the whole hierarchy their power depends on. They're setting up the Momalla as their recourse, too."

"So then … what the fuck, Dad? Like seriously, you're sending me in blind to help an underdog—an underdog who we assume is getting set up. And where're you going to be when it goes down at the gala? How do I know who's Liberati?"

"You aren't blind now, son. *That*, at least, is not true. And you won't be alone, but don't try to ask anyone who they're loyal to. You'd only get a lie back if they're Liberati, so any loyalty you trust, you gotta see it with your own two eyes. Just like always. My new identity is in the mix to get into the gala, but they haven't assigned me yet. Even so, we've got plenty applying for 'Peripheral Calm,' and either way, I'll be somewhere close by. We got word out to Nevada, too, maybe even to Pithawalla himself, and apparently they're ready to move in—not a full-blown invasion, but something to quicken the awakening. But yeah, your ass is in the direct line of fire, and I can't see no two ways about that. So what, you want out?"

Quinceton didn't put much faith in friendly forces coming to save him from a bullet that'd already been fired, or outside forces coming to New California's rescue. If the guns pointed across the South Lake Tahoe were any indication, Old America didn't take too kindly to Californian expats.

"No, I'm not quitting. I'm in, and I'm in 'til the end. But I don't know shit, and I don't like not knowing shit heading into the big dance. How am I even going to know what I've gotta do when the plan is no more specific than 'help the side that's losing'? Not to mention, hey, what if the losing side really does go down, and I go right along with them?"

"That's why, no matter what, you can't throw all your loyalty behind Redgrave and his JJJ thugs. Just like regular life, you always have to maintain your ability to deny, and don't do anything that leaves proof. Don't stick your neck out, you know? Just be ready when it starts. You won't miss it."

"When what starts?" Quinceton had to watch his volume as they cycled out another canceled confessor and replaced them with the next. It was a female-presenting person, so they might get a longer self-denunciation to scheme through.

"So what's supposed to happen is the regular awards show. You know, hand out some special Social Justice accommodations, make speeches we've all heard before—"

"Not this year," Quinceton cut him off. "Jumping Bull has something he's planning. I've heard them all talking about it multiple times, the big-time Knowers, I mean. They're aware of the Anti-Anti-Anti-Racists behind Redgrave and have some initiative cooking up to cut them off at the knees, mostlike."

"My man, my man on the inside. Maybe I'm wrong. What are you hearing?"

"I'm hearing—and I'm seeing—fear that racial classes are being blurred by the prospect of de-whitening. No one has said it exactly, but if you can de-whiten, how come you can't move to Blacken yourself? Maybe then they'd have the whole gender ideology against them, since gender transitions are encouraged, so why not racial ones? They see the problem. Jumping Bull, for sure, he sees the problem."

"Okay ... this is all music to me. This all seems like it puts them in direct opposition to each other. That what you're seeing?"

"Yeah, definitely." Quinceton couldn't decide whether it'd taken a decade or three meetings, but he really liked being treated like a man by his old man. When he was a boy, he'd never known things his father didn't. "But I also see the JSS government drawing in the AAA/JJJ law enforcement, encouraging their presence at the Momalla, so you gotta figure they're prepared for some kinda attack," he added.

They were attempting to set up two sides that were focused on setting each other up, with Quinceton in the well-armed middle of the fight. Dad had to appreciate that.

The womxn on stage wrapped up her soliloquy on "doubting reported Racism" as the elder Mr. Rift turned to look at his son, taking him by the shoulders.

"Bottom line this for me: What do you think Jumping Bull is pushing? Your guess is better than any other we're going to get. You think he's going to try to abolish the Anti-Anti-Anti-Racists bases, disband the DIE Camps, just totally cut Redgrave off at the knees?"

"I'm not even sure he has the power to do that. And they need the food coming from the DIE Camps, right? Jumping Bull's people are mostly held in line by fear; Redgrave's are drawn in by spite, or hate, or anger—whatever you want to call it, I wouldn't necessarily bet on the cowards over the enraged."

"The cowards hold court now, though. The power struggle is all we need for a power vacuum to free the people's minds. Once they don't have to bend their brains to propaganda, and they realize it together, they may find the strength to finally defeat this madness. And we're prepared for the moment, for that one shining moment of true opportunity. When the balance breaks between the Anti-Racists who control government and the Anti-Anti-Anti-Racists who enforce government policy, we will be ready. That's when we free the people."

"Yeah, no big deal, Dad. We'll just go ahead and free the people, then meet after for American cheeseburgers and French fries."

Dad smiled with a shrug. "Ain't nothing French about real fries and a burger," he chuckled. "I'll taste it again someday, and so will you. But true that: In victory, we toast our reclaimed freedom with classic American flavors. That's the payoff for a plan that I realize you know has a couple holes in it."

From Quinceton's vantage point, the plan had no holes at all, mostly because he didn't see a plan in the first place. But at least the goal was clear enough: "free the people." *Just go ahead and free the damn people.* No small ask, and despite the support he'd been promised around the edges, Quinceton neither understood how to incorporate their assistance nor what his own method would be. There really was no plan.

A goal would have to be enough.

ACT III, CHAPTER THIRTEEN

social justice

INITIALLY DESIGNED AS AN AWARDS ceremony to placate the most educated and government-compensated Elect from their own relative speechlessness, the SOMA Momalla Gala quickly became too popular to be limited to the top handful of Speakers and Knowers. It was also a time to unveil the next year's Anti-Racism efforts, which was why the New Year's Eve address by Knowing Leader Mumwaza Q. Jumping Bull would be filmed and played on television machines for audiences in public squares and DIE Camps all over New California. Nobody who was anybody and everybody who wanted to be somebody had to find their way into the biggest, most elaborate party of the year. For Quinceton, it was to be his first and only.

The event location came from the abbreviated "South of Market (Street)" distinction that gave the SOMA neighborhood its name, added to the Museum Of Modern Art acronym of the host building. The original organizers had argued feverishly about the most Anti-Racist way to represent the annual apex of New California, including the possibly white supremacist concept of a "gala," but in the end a compromise was reached through crude combination. The building was repurposed shortly after the Great Rupture as the official JSS Government Center for Arts & Culture, and it had once dictated all legal public messaging and officially accepted historical representations. These San Francisco MOMA headquarters de-

315

termined most resources that were applied to the Work Doing Centers, but had relinquished control of AAA/JJJ Camp reeducation materials a few years back.

The rickshaws lined up for blocks down Third Street for the tenth annual SOMA Momalla Gala, held on New Year's Eve in this year of our Lord 2066. The great avenue had been cleaned meticulously, with nary a scrap of debris nor any squatters in sight. Quinceton, free from chauffeur duty and assigned to extra security—officially titled a "Periphery Calm team member"—weaved through traffic as he scampered to his post a respectable twenty minutes late for his shift, timed precisely to avoid attention.

"Partial pat-downs for relievers and simple Elect, but you can ignore the Speakers and Knowers of all ranks," his workmaster commanded at the great glass doors of the SOMA MOMA. "Whatever happens, the most important thing is that you not offend any Elect with your commitment to security. Definitely, *definitely* don't accuse BIPOC—you know the Racist history there. Just make sure the relievers get all your attention and you'll be fine."

Quinceton took this as confirmation that no one actually cared about security, least of all those tasked with it. In some sense, holding his post tonight felt a little like walking through the Tenderloin at any time of day— just ignore your survival instincts to keep the stress in check. Quinceton figured he might as well just wave everyone through like a matador, hoping that whatever weapons gained entry would be on his side when it came down to it. When the workmaster handed a submachine gun back to a reliever when their associated Knower objected to the search on some sort of Racist profiling, Quinceton knew he'd been given a job it was impossible to screw up so long as he neglected to attempt anything even slightly resembling a thing like "security."

The biggest room in San Francisco's MOMA was the atrium immediately after entry, which extended five floors up to the roof. There was a stage crafted at one end, with seats for whatever Elect had been able to finagle tickets in the middle. Opposite the stage, erected on platforms of ascending rank, were the Speakers' armchairs, and above them the Knowers' thrones. Security that Quinceton recognized from the Flood Mansion ringed the section housing the top brass, fully automatic rifles at the ready. Quinceton hadn't realized how few Speakers and Elect were attending—maybe two dozen of the former and fifty of the latter—but it made sense, as prep for this showdown with Redgrave naturally had to come with some standard pre-purging of potentially disloyal allies. A staircase slicing into the middle rows of the atrium led to a large landing on the second level and gave way to a wide, two-floor lobby on the other side of the building, followed by a series of rear staircases that could be climbed to all floors.

With atrium floor seating—known as the "orchestra"—stretching capacity with especially prestigious Elect, it was time for the Level Three Speakers to make their entrance some hour or so into the event. Their red Kafkani hats rose tall, with flowing gowns trailing behind them, carried by masked relievers. The garment messages were as predictable as any other year, but for contemporary flair, the spelling had evolved. In years past, it was customary to paint some sort of political statement on your gown, a simple testament to your orthodoxy. The messages this year were what you'd expect, only with different phonetical spelling, giving the whole thing a slight amplification of aggression in Quinceton's assessment. He saw "Taxx tha Privlidged" and "Ckill Whyte Soupremacy," "Asssk a Tranz-Womxn" and "Fauk tha Patriarrrchy," and "Dekolonize tha Plattforms" as well as "Eckwitty Fo Awl." Those, he could still read, but some maybe because of their graffiti font—were totally illegible.

The Knowers had selected one of the most comprehensively ambiguous Speakers to be host for the evening, and this individual of indistinguishable ethnicity, gender, and psychological ability (and so forth) hovered around the front doors of the MOMA. This person was trailed by the ZNN news crew for later splicing into a happy video of the festivities and had a microphone connected to the interior audio system, which they shoved in front of some especially fabulous costumed invitees.

"And what're we protesting over here?" the host asked a particularly flamboyant couple of Elect. They wore matching leopard-spotted jackets, perhaps converted directly from fancy curtains, and were overjoyed to be included as members of the political system.

"Inequality," the man of the couple answered immediately. "We're here to bring attention to and heal inequality around the world, and if inequality exists in New California …" The man paused, not expecting to back himself into a corner with a standard-issue justification of gaudy fashion. "You know, we oppose inequality everywhere, wherever it exists."

"You can do better than that," a familiar, but grating, voice invaded from behind Quinceton's back. It was the complete opposite of the host's puffery. "We're going to run that again, and this time I want you to mean it when you tell us what you're protesting—or at least act like it."

It was Jessica Bondurant. Bones might have been surprised to learn his daughter was now some top producer at ZNN, advising both the cameraman, interviewer, and interviewees. Now a big enough deal to edit the Elect's standard virtue signals in public, her youth unburdened her with past concepts of truth. It therefore made sense that someone around Quinceton's age might still believe the latest tenets of Social Justice.

"We're protesting the inequality of beauty," the womxn parried. "We wear these leopard-skin jackets to raise awareness and bring attention to all whose fashion and self-expressive sensibilities are restrained by access to the garments of their choice."

"Better," Jessica said from behind the camera. "But not great. Better think more about what you're here for, and what Social Justice means to you in the future."

The couple nodded and shuffled away, likely relieved that their interrogation had passed. The ambiguous JSS government-appointed and ZNN-approved host took the answer at face value, if they were even listening, and looked for another protest of problematic stuff to platform.

With the top Speakers filing in to the bottom of the Knowers' section, there was a moment to breathe easy. If there was any Knower's privilege Quinceton really wanted, it was the ability to show up wherever, whenever, have everyone waiting around for you, and have the whole tardy arrival considered to actually be a method of practicing Social Justice.

"Seems like a lot of workers came out to cheer this year," Quinceton commented to his workmaster, motioning to the crowds of young people who waved in their government-issued jeans from across Third Street. "But they don't seem too rowdy. You want me on the door all night?"

"They wanted extra guns around the Knowers, like most of security, to be honest. Leaves us a little thin elsewhere, but it's calm here. You the survivor of South Lake, yeah?"

"That's right."

"Regular infantry?"

"Sniper. Pretty decent one, too."

"Check with me after the Knowers come through, but I think they'll want you on the second level." Quinceton had waited a long time for someone to inquire about anything he might already be trained for, and with not a moment to lose, he'd found his huckleberry.

The Level One Knowers arrived before the top dogs, of course, complete with their retinue of water carriers. You got more personality from the Level Three Speakers than Level One Knowers, in Quinceton's estimation, perhaps because some Level Three Speakers no longer aspired to be Knowers, and every Knower had enough proximity to power to want a low profile. A particular Level One Knower actually turned to help their reliever collect the hem of their simple cape. Such humility was unthinkable for most politicians, who typically succumbed to the trappings of historical oppression with narcissistic weakness.

The Level Two Knowers had stepped up their game this year, with a color-coordinated gold-Kafkani-on-green-gown getup that even Quinceton had to admire on pure aesthetics. A Level Two Knower really had two jobs: to explain why no additional Level One Knowers should dilute their power with another rise to Level Two, and to reassure the sole Level Three Knowing Leader that they would forever and eternally be satisfied with the second highest rung in society, usually through unyielding supplication. To this end, fabric coordination was essential; it visually delineated power with the Level One Knowers while demonstrating solidarity with other Level Twos. This gave the impression of unity and contentment to the only audience any of them needed to persuade, Mumwaza Q. Jumping Bull—which could really be said about the whole spectacle of the SOMA MOMA Momalla Gala for Love, in Quinceton's permanently unofficial opinion.

Eyes narrowed in anticipation, the spines of security straightened, and Quinceton restrained the forward surge of bodies as the Knowing Leader rode up in a long stretch limousine-type rickshaw accompanied by four or five girls, but all Quinceton could see was Natalie. She wore a loose white ruffled blouse atop a traditional green, white, and red Mexican huipil skirt. It was hard not to think about why she might be decorated in racialized garb, but she radiated warmth anyway, smiling for the masses with an elbow pinched tightly to Jumping Bull's.

The MOMA host watched Jumping Bull with apprehension, but asserted themselves just as soon as INRI secured solid ground under INRI's feet from a rickshaw dismount that pained all who witnessed the grueling reality of collective responsibility for a single individual's girth.

"Knowing Leader," the host began, bowing their head as they spoke, trailed by the breathless ZNN camera crew. "Your presence graces us at this, our tenth annual SOMA MOMA Momalla Gala for Love. Is there anything special you've got in store for us this evening?"

"Tonight, expect everything. Tonight will be revolutionary. We've coordinated our lived experience with early results and trends of Anti-Racist efforts and have some very exciting conclusions to relay for the final step toward liberation. Tonight, we have the Anti-Racist answers to all remaining issues of managing and preventing tomorrow's inequitable identities."

Quinceton could hear the answer play over the audio speakers for all the early arrivals inside, and he wondered how many believed any of the old applause lines. Jessica Bondurant seemed to accept and believe everything she heard without thinking. The more Quinceton saw her in action, the more he could see why the mental flexibility of true believers like her was so crucial to destroying society. They could do so and insist the flames were an improvement.

Jumping Bull looked like INRI could use a few more Natalies to stabilize the slog through the gaping double-glass doors to the atrium, but the retinue seemed prepared for the physical hurdle, pressing in behind INRI to guide the great heft forward.

Quinceton tried to catch Natalie's eye, but she wouldn't look at him. Her gaze fastened itself so determinedly in the other direction that Quinceton assumed she *had* seen him and just wouldn't acknowledge his presence around Jumping Bull & Co. The young soldier chose to interpret this as a positive signal, one of awareness rather than dismissal.

A horde of security, relievers, and womxn of extremely minimal physical imperfection congealed around Knowing Leader Mumwaza Q. Jumping Bull in the atrium, leaving Quinceton on the outside with his gate workmaster. They could both hear the land acknowledgements starting up, which meant they could expect no more celebrities on Third Street.

"Want me to stick around?" Quinceton asked, his shoulders directed at the atrium for suggestion. His commander considered the situation on the street, then turned to view the commotion inside. Only God knew how long the land acknowledgements would last before the ceremony had been consecrated by every known group of persons of legit color to have been subjugated by the white colonizer.

"No, all looks under control out here," the male-presenting white workmaster said. "Go in there and find the level two master—across the atrium, up the public staircase, right there at the top where it levels out for a two-floor lobby."

"Roger that," Quinceton said. The elevated lobby on level two was okay, but three was better. From level three, you could walk back and forth from a perch at the top of the backside lobby to a perch in the middle of the atrium; you could see the whole awards show down below from over a railing, with easy escape to the rear staircase. This could lead you down to level two, where there was another street exit on the opposite side of the atrium, or upstairs to the fourth and fifth floors. Those upper floors had very limited views of the atrium, as the building coalesced into a shrinking dome at the top that forced snipers to stick their necks out, becoming easy targets more than anything else.

The theme of the evening hadn't occurred to Quinceton before, but now it was obvious: "Love" was stated in huge red letters on a banner above the low-level Speaker currently land acknowledging from the stage. The colors might have to be pinked up a bit, but plenty of swag from the last two Momallas—celebrating "diversity" last year and "unity" the year before—could be effectively reused with minimal active repurposing. Posters and long banners of different-colored hands holding each other, with heart-shaped balloons and red/pink filigree hanging from every pole and protrusion, helped complete the look.

The land acknowledgement was stuck on Hawaii for some reason, or at least that's what the name "King Kamehameha" sounded like, as the big chief was being lauded for killing a white captain's cook for Social Justice at the time. The audience's near total disinterest in the land acknowledgment calmed the young soldier, and he could easily imagine them dropping the practice for something else next year. There seemed very little virtue left to be signaled from King Kamehameha.

And so Quinceton strode across the atrium with more confidence that he should have admitted around such dignitaries. They mostly stood around in intimate circles, ignoring the land acknowledgement blather and congratulating each other with long trains to their dresses carried by masked relievers. A mask would have helped Quinceton now; his face professed feelings his gender, cognitive status, and able body were never supposed to admit, in spite of his race, but thankfully no one looked at him. Only Natalie did. Not more than ten feet away, hostage to flattery aimed at Jumping Bull and looking at Quinceton.

It was when he got about halfway across the slick marble floor that she looked over, and the moment she did, they both froze. It was less dangerous for her, as she was the acquaintance to someone else's conversation and was expected not to speak. But Quinceton was mid-stride when she met his eyes, and the power of her gaze shattered his smooth progress. Mumwaza caught INRIself before falling over, but Mumwaza, the emperor with no clothes, also saw Quinceton stumble, following his eyes to INRIs own beautiful, unfulfilled date. Natalie could hide a lot of feelings, but she was still a grown womxn, and Jumping Bull could ignore a lot of shame, but not INRIs own. Even if the great leader suspected emotional infidelity, INRI couldn't do anything about it for the moment—not with so many eyeballs around to impress.

Righting himself, Quinceton reached the foot of the atrium stairway in a hurry, eager to flee such public surroundings. He had too much to do, and too much to think about, to worry about what his face might do in the meantime. But there was one more witness.

"Quinceton!" Juniper called out in a cheerful voice, bounding over from a clump of bodies near the stage. Her baggy, austere black robes conveyed the opposite statement from her elaborate hairdo, built high in hair-sprayed curls to add another few inches to the top of her dome. But the smile was genuine enough.

"Juniper—I'll be damned. What's your role in all this?"

"Oh, you know about the promotion. I'm here as a Stockton diplomat, here for moral support and emotional guidance for the people. It's all been approved. And where have they got you stationed?"

Quinceton shrugged. "They had me on the door, but probably somewhere else now. Probably upstairs, probably."

"Perfect. Stay ready up there, old friend."

They weren't old friends, but it was better title than some alternatives. Quinceton nodded, then continued up the central atrium staircase to the long, wide lobby above.

There, the second floor workmaster scurried around in a short-staffed panic.

"Where are you stationed?" the brown-skinned womxn asked upon recognizing his Momalla workers getup. Quinceton started to answer before she cut him off. "Just get upstairs. Find the third-floor workmaster—could be on the fourth floor. But I know they'll want you up there. Half the Knowers requested extra relievers, and there's too many on the floor already."

Quinceton was all too happy to oblige, and he had one foot in front of the other before the second-floor workmaster could reconsider staffing. They didn't seem to notice who went where, just that the numbers of public security fit whatever demands were made by the politically protected requester. It was piecemeal security theater meant to establish Anti-Racist bona fides around search profiling (or the lack thereof), but when moments of actual tension arrived, everyone with power wanted their own protectors front and center. Just as at the outbreak of the police/prison abolition movement, those in power said all the right things about mothballing law enforcement for other people in public, yet always retained enough private security for themselves to sleep safe and sound. The hidden upside, which Quinceton was fast learning how to recognize in almost every facet of New California, was that disorganized security theater enabled him to operate on the periphery without garnering too much attention, as was his preference, and with some detachment from the fray his best avenue toward survival.

The practiced sniper climbed the rear staircase to level three, combing through a few high-ceilinged rooms full of desks, chairs, and tables before reaching the railing overlooking the atrium. He saw the Knowers on their platforms to the left, then the Speakers, the Elect in the middle floor audience, and a cluster of empty seats between seated guests and the stage facing them all to the right. Quinceton could surveil everything from here, but there was no one else around—no workmaster. The fourth floor had the almost exact same layout as the third, only without a perch to scope the atrium, and on the fifth Quinceton finally found the upstairs workmaster coordinator.

"They need you on the third floor," the distracted white guy told him. "Take this." A sniper rifle. The same model Quinceton had used in South Lake, loaded and ready for killing.

"Only one clip? What if there's shooting? Where can I get a second?"

"Take these," the fifth-floor workmaster answered, dumping a plastic bag of loaded magazines on the floor between them. "I'm sick of carrying all this heavy bullshit. It's all 7.62 millimeter. Just hand them out to anyone you trust." The ammo fit some long guns—not handguns—which was probably what the workmaster meant by "trust," but Quinceton heard it as he wanted to.

He returned to the rear staircase with purpose and leaped down two flights to reclaim the prime perch overlooking the atrium on level three. If there was anyone worth trusting, they'd have had to reveal themselves by now to get Quinceton's cooperation. Until then, he'd attach the ammo bag to his rear belt loops. If Bones or Sarah were here, or Dad, they'd get some of his ammo, but now it all fell on him to save the world—and Natalie. *To the victor, the spoils.*

When Quinceton peered over the third-floor railing once more, the scene below had solidified. The Knowers sat on their rear platform—Knowing Leader Mumwaza Q. Jumping Bull perched above them all, beside Natalie—then the Speakers sandwiched against the Elect, and as they were all now seated and relatively quiet, one expected the show to begin. But the lights were as bright as ever, and as the land acknowledgment veered into a summary of the mostly peaceful protests that had empowered the roots of the Anti-Racist movement way back in the summer of 2020, the restless audience barely ever glanced at the lowly Speaker who'd been dragged in to do the endless land acknowledging. The crowd kept humming between themselves as they waited for something else, and all present seemed similarly aware of its arrival.

A few tense minutes passed before the first of the black shapes filed into the atrium from some doorway just beyond the foot of the stage, where the old "box office" still stood from when the MOMA had been a museum for rich capitalists. They filled the empty front rows, sitting without turning to look at their superiors. Quinceton eyed the officially official Elect dignitaries, who digested the Anti-Anti-Anti-Racist/JJJ insult with great mental reflux, gazing at each other with baffled expressions.

The important Speakers and Knowers didn't seem bothered so much as amused—entertained by the spectacle of relative outsiders coming into their church without any of the religious garb, and expecting to get their Social Justice by preaching to the converted, or something. Whatever the Anti-Anti-Anti-Racists or JJJ (or whatever they were called now) were planning, the government higher-ups wanted them to try it. And if it happened here, at the MOMA Momalla Gala for Love in old SOMA, everyone would see it.

There was an audible gasp when Chairperson Redgrave strode to a seat in the middle of the front row, but the young sniper couldn't see where exactly it came from—just that it sounded like the entirety of the orchestra in unison. It reminded Quinceton that few in San Francisco had ever had to deal with Redgrave personally, and those interactions all had to have been before his promotion to Anti-Anti-Anti-Racist Chairperson. That Redgrave would show up in a shiny black patent leather suit with a blood-red shirt and ivory-white top hat didn't surprise Quinceton in the least; he'd long assumed that sewing his own outfit would be worth at least a month of focus from Redgrave's lackeys, and no doubt the big Chairperson had designed it himself.

But few in the audience besides Quinceton and the AAA/JJJ retinue had ever been to Stockton, and thus they could not have truly understood the psychological release the law enforcement/food production contingent of society received from de-whitening. To the government Anti-Racists, Redgrave's top hat was an open celebration of capitalism and its Racism, not to mention the white supremacy and other such offenses guaranteed to be associated with it. Quinceton could see in this costume the collision of two irreconcilable worldviews that had been held at bay only through the assumption of inferiority of one toward the other, but without group submission, nothing in New California could function as conceived. Perhaps that explained something else about Redgrave's affronting fashion.

"Enough!" Mumwaza's voice bellowed from across the audience. "Start it up already!" And mid-sentence, as if anticipating the hook at any time, the land acknowledger shut up and disappeared in the waves of curtains ringing the stage.

A few ZNN staff scrambled to arrange a table beside the microphone podium, upon which they fixed a number of wrapped golden scrolls. Quinceton experienced a momentary twitch of expecting something like a musical number, which would have made for an artful segue into the awards portion of the program, but the singing of anthems had been canceled years ago. Once blind auditions were considered Racist, performers were selected for identity, and the race to equity had led directly to the degradation of the auditory art form. Even the JSS government had to admit a lack of talent to showcase, citing "spotlighting constraints," which actually disappointed Quinceton somewhat. His father had always said the music was the last good thing about galas.

A familiar Level Three Speaker of exquisitely unguessable gender, race, and mental status rose from the orchestra to claim their position at center stage. Their Kafkani hat appeared to be unusually tall, and unlike their boss's call to start handing out awards, the Speaker patiently waited for the audience to hush itself and listen.

"Thank you," they said into a stationary microphone when the voices petered out to a whisper. "And welcome to the tenth annual SOMA Momalla Gala!"

The rear audience applauded with concentrating gazes toward the front. Some turned to look at Chairperson Redgrave, but he didn't move, didn't clap. Maybe he felt the eyes on him; if he did, it was probably part of his plan. Everyone was aware of him now, even if it was supposed to be Jumping Bull's show. The Knowing Leader's abrupt call to end the tedium of land acknowledgements had suggested as much to all witnesses in attendance.

"We give thanks and praise to Knowing Leader Mumwaza Q. Jumping Bull for granting us the equity and privilege to host such an event," the dutiful Speaker pronounced, staring directly into the ZNN camera as though people in other places could watch the event as if they were in this room too. The Speaker smiled so serenely in every direction that Quinceton almost believed they were trustworthy.

"In accordance with the founding principles of Anti-Racism upon which our government is founded, we have chosen to make 'Love' the theme of this year's gala, and in so doing, we have extended the first-ever invitation to Justice Justice Justice Chairperson Redgrave and his most esteemed Community Safety patrolpersons from our Diversity, Equity, and Inclusion Camps in the North Mountains and Central Valley."

At this, Redgrave actually turned to salute his superiors with the slightest of nods. His stoic expression contrasted sharply with the Speaker on stage. Redgrave wasn't here to smile, and he sure wasn't here to be placated with niceties, but he'd play the diplomacy game whenever it suited him.

The Speaker onstage hesitated for the crowd to acknowledge Redgrave, and when no applause came with his introduction, the ceremony continued. The first scroll, given for "Anti-Racist Applications in the Field of Cosmetology," went to a thrilled male-born/feminine-leaning Black who delivered a pretty enthusiastic speech. He/she/they/etc. really stood out for appreciation of the Anti-Racist government: here, they received praise for continued commitment to the tenets of Standpoint Theory and asserting the new beautification standards of New California along the lines of confronting oppression and toppling the cisheteropatriarchy. It was said that one day, when equity of skin color was imagined, a beauty product called "makeup" would be reintroduced to all of New California's workers. A pretty common opener, but Quinceton had to concede extra credit for a convincing delivery.

There was a tap on his shoulder, and the young man spun to see his father in standard security garb. The old man held out a hand to prevent Quinceton's rifle from rotating into his grill.

"They re-center the de-centered of colonized centering centration yet?" Dad deadpanned. "I'm terrified that guy won't win for *She Centers His Vagina to Platform Their Penis*. I mean, if you can't take the Social Justice cake for a fundamental masterpiece like *She Centers His Vagina to Platform Their Penis,* then honestly, like what the hell are we even celebrating here?" His tone aged considerably when Quinceton shot him a serious look. "Almost hard to believe it got this far when you're standing right in the middle of it."

Quinceton hadn't been alive for much of the other world, where this display of privileged oppression would have been an absurd parody, but he nodded anyway. He'd have liked some more useful intel right about now, but then again, no one useful knew any more than he did.

"It's tense down there and still going," Quinceton reported. "Basically everyone who came packing got through the door with their guns, no questions asked. The security I was with didn't even try, so long as you walked in with the right people. And the Knowing Leader and the AAA Chairperson, Redgrave—they don't like each other."

"No shit. Can't be two kings in a kingdom. Just make sure when the shooting starts, you're up here and ready to move. I came to confirm we got word out to Pithawalla, and it was all about tonight, and the coup he's been waiting for. So, decent people just gotta hold on to their butts a little longer."

"No way. You're saying Pithawalla and his people are crashing the party? How the hell do they know what's really going on here, or who to trust, who to shoot—what's this mean?"

"It means we aren't here to kill everyone and take over ourselves, and if we get in serious heat, well, we just gotta ditch the party, or maybe dig in and hold out. But who knows—trusting the outside word is a bad bet. Anyway, Pithawalla knows not to trust anyone with JSS government power, and I bet anyone else gets a chance to prove they're alright. I don't know any details, and when we get word out, we don't really get word back, 'cause even our information runners could get intercepted. But we know what Pithawalla and basically all of America's waiting for: to finally set these warring factions against each other for all to see. Watching the madness eat itself in real time is the quickest way people's minds can be freed to think and speak how they want. Then we can start to figure out how to live like similar people, not competing identities fighting for crumbs from the puppeteers who get to judge the value of identities. It's not far off now. But you hear anything else about what's supposed to come next down there? Hear anything about what anyone's planning?"

"They both expect some kinda standoff, I think," Quinceton guessed. "And since they both kinda expect a confrontation, you gotta think they both expect to win it. That's probably why they both wanted the crowd here, to consecrate whatever Social Justice becomes next." Quinceton thought a moment, then added, "Probably about perfect for Pithawalla, actually."

"Okay, that's good. A confrontation is a good thing. Even if people get shot—*especially* if the right people get shot—then the sheep-Elect people all go rudderless together."

Quinceton wasn't so convinced of this part of the "plan," which struck him more as a wish than a circumstance they were likely to introduce intentionally. "So, Dad," Quinceton started, trying to phrase it right, "I'm seeing hundreds of people on the floor down there, probably close to that many weapons, with the AAA/JJJ people in front of the stage, the sheep-Elect in the middle, and the Knowers at the rear platform. At some point, something happens. And then what? Where're you going to be, where's my backup, what, seriously, am I doing here? Seems pretty late in the game. What … is … the plan?" It was hard not to be at least a little pissed, seeing as how no one knew anything about anything, even with all the lives on the line—including his and, by extension, Natalie's.

"The 'plan,' as you call it, well, it's really more of a circumstance," his father explained. "And that circumstance is coming true in front of our eyes in real time. And when it happens, when the two sides finally break and go at each other, we'll jump on it. Feed the flames to torch everything that caused a scene like the godforsaken Momalla Anti-Racism Awards in the first place." Dad saw Quinceton's concern, considered his son's pretty damn justified peril—situated right here for all to see and aim at, if they so chose—and shook his head.

"Look, son, we don't really have a plan, but the good news is, no one else really does either. Part of the problem is that the AAA agents, the JSS security, and the random rebels, well, they were still all raised by the same lazy layabout lunatics. It's been a problem for everyone the last decade or two, increasingly—the modern kids won't *do shit!* Useless, damn near all of them. So we just run with it, dodge the punches as they come, throw our own, and when the real bad boys expose their jugular, one of us will be there with the blade to slit it, even if you and I are finished by then. It's the world I bore you into. In another time and place, we could have lived simply, but in this world we're soldiers until it all comes to ash. You with me?"

"This whole thing is beyond crazy," Quinceton answered. "But yeah, I'm with you, Dad."

"We're close now. Just hang tight." And then his father disappeared again, heading upstairs toward the fourth or fifth floor—that much farther from the street level.

Back on the stage, the practiced Speaker fired off awards for notable actions such as "Most Anti-Racist Expression of Scalp Art" and "Greatest Expression of Gender Identity in Rickshaw Ornamentation," but the Elect weren't paying much attention yet. Many left their seats to mingle with each other on the darker perimeter of the ground floor, where they could comment on the proceedings with each other without being so scrutinized. Quinceton maneuvered to eye Mumwaza Q. Jumping Bull's face and saw an overgrown boy entitled to play God in order to avoid the basic demands of manhood. On some very conscious level, the young sniper couldn't resist the thrill of witnessing the public revelation of the boy-king's mortality, fallibility, and ultimately, mediocrity.

Just like in a poker game, when one side raises, the other has to call. But if both sides are bluffing or think they really do have a better hand, then the stakes rise to the max as the game heads to a showdown after the last bet. No one really knows who's holding the best cards until that decisive moment when there's no more to add to the pot. But perhaps in preparation for the final lay down, additional "Periphery Calm" people (or whatever they were being called) began to collect at the corners of the lower atrium. They stood in pressed workers' white shirts and simple jeans that emphasized the close-combat submachine gun with which they'd each been equipped. A few passed Quinceton in their descent to the ground floor faceoff, but none stopped to hog his prime location.

Golden scrolls were subsequently flung to every corner of the relevant New California social strata for a bevy of oppression-fighting accommodations, with the notable exception of the distinguished dignitaries from outside the city. Whenever the more mobility-restricted Knowers received an accolade they were too heavy to accept without the prolonged hassle of being hauled all the way up to the stage, they sent their favorite Speaker.

No one could question the decisions of the Knowers since the early Standpoint Mandate law made their lived experience the only voices marginalized enough to be relevant. And yet, all this extra lived experience, high IS scores, and all the trappings of New California couldn't distract Quinceton from the stark visual contrast between the casual obesity of those who asserted "their truth" for a living and the lean, focused, flab-free bodies of damn near everyone else. Those who got to decide truth for a living never wound up doing much else and, as a rule, got fatter and dumber over time. Now, perhaps, and finally, their time had come.

Quinceton figured they were heading into the ceremony's finale when scattered relievers and extra security started ushering the Elect back into their orchestra seats—you really couldn't blame Mumwaza for wanting to play to a full house on his home floor. The final award had different names each year, but it always went to the Knowing Leader and segued into a speech about the upcoming year and the Anti-Racist initiatives that would be featured in it. Quinceton had some idea of what to expect in 2067—new regulations to further hoodwink the brainwashed, or new ways to intimidate most to pretend as much—but the real point of Jumping Bull's address wasn't the new identity groups or sexualities or new benefits given to them, but the holding forth of one monarch to their flock. Listening contentedly to things you hated and knew weren't real was truly an act of submission. That's probably why INRI liked it so much.

"And without further ado, the moment you've all been waiting for!" the smiley Speaker onstage announced to the crowd. "The final award of the evening goes to our most tireless ambassador of the historically marginalized, the human most platformed to re-center the erasure of all LGBTQIAA++XW!&, BIPOC, physically unique, neo-knowing, and all other formerly colonized voices. Who could argue that this BIPOC's platform does anything but cancel marginalized systemic erasure of othered queer-centric bodies in doing the tireless work of centering formerly de-centered so-called 'problematic' voices?

"This year's award for 'Champion of the Hegemonically Oppressed' goes to a marginalized BIPOC body with a voice systemically oppressed by the cisheteropatriarchy that centers erasure in order to platform de-colonial othering—nay, whose platform *is* to center!"

This last line of pablum drew some applause from the crowd, which

was likely looking for any decipherable statement it could openly celebrate, and which the presenter paused to appreciate. Quinceton wasn't sure
what meaning was supposed to be gleaned from this particular show of
logorrhea, but he took heart in the knowledge that no one else did either.

"To say this individual rose from oppression to *do the work* is an un-
derstatement. From the blood of slaves and survivors of the American Indigenous genocide, our savior has risen!"

Quinceton couldn't resist casting a glance at the Knowing Leader, even
if it forced him to crane his neck in the opposite direction over the railing.
Upon closer inspection, looking at every facial feature and facet of Jumping Bull's complexion, using his best imagination ... nope, the guy still
looked white as the refrigerated cow's milk served up in Secure Spaces.

The Speaker continued cheerfully, "It's convenient to forget that this
San Francisco land was so recently conquered and colonized by Racist,
transphobic, ableist, and othering voices so hell-bent on denying their
fragility that they endlessly punched down at the forgotten bodies who
now sit before you with pride. To *do the work* of separating that which is
problematic from that which is Anti-Racist, to *do the work* of platforming marginalized voices so that they may rest in power, to *do the work* of
protecting our spaces and bodies and voices from the encroachment of systemic cisheteropatriarchy—as is the historical default—is work that lasts a
lifetime, a century, a millennium, and forever. And so it is with both great
joy and resolute determination in the eternal struggle that I now present the
Tenth Annual SOMA Momalla Gala's award for 'Champion of the Hegemonically Oppressed' to Knowing Leader Mumwaza Q. Jumping Bull!"

And thus the great effort to haul the Knowing Leader onto the stage
began in earnest. First, INRIs body needed to be lifted from the rearmost
throne from which INRI surveilled the proceedings. Like most present,
Quinceton maneuvered to watch this careful dismount, and wondered if
INRI could have been a little more helpful in INRIs own physical transportation.

The Knowing Leader's torso and neck were given ample support as
four or five relievers labored to lift INRI from the base. Somehow, and

impressively without using an intricate system of pulleys and counter-weights, the Knowing Leader's low center of gravity was handed down from INRIs perch and relocated to the gleaming gold ambulatory transpor-tation wheelchair. From there, it took only a fraction of the effort to wheel INRI to the stage and affix the microphone. Luckily, INRI didn't bring any of his dates to the stage, as subsidizing any more of INRIs physical exer-tion would surely have required someone else to power INRIs voice box.

Quinceton eyed Jessica Bondurant, who seemed to direct the ZNN cameraperson. She had the camera pointed at the crowd's applause as Mumwaza labored to the stage and allowed INRI to catch INRIs breath before signaling the recording to resume on the seated Knowing Leader.

"Good evening," the portly leader said like a politician. Quinceton hadn't heard this tone inside the Secure Space—it evidently hadn't been necessary. "And welcome to my distinguished colleagues, friends, and new *invitees*." The last word drew brief eye contact with Redgrave, but the audience could only guess at what face the Chairperson shot back.

"It is with open eyes and an eager heart that we view our own work through an ever-more transparently critical lens and ask ourselves, year af-ter year: How can we do even better? After all the Racism we've defeated, how can we maintain our commitment to Anti-Racism and the decolo-nized society we all want? How do we remember yesterday, so that as we endure the necessary hardships for a better tomorrow, we do not abandon our commitment to truth for an easier path? What truly moors New Cali-fornia to our values, and the doctrine of equity for which we've sacrificed immensely, and whose proceeds may only be passed on to our children, or their children, or children one hundred years in the future?"

The crowd gave some audible approval of the point, but Quinceton wanted to hear what came next. The setup was the same, but this year's payoff might have to account for pressure from the new AAA/JJJ. It might have to produce tangible, falsifiable results that people wanted, and that the Knowing Leader could use to justify the supremacy of INRIs lived experience.

"It is knowledge that moors us to our roots—knowledge, awareness, and commitment to reversing the horrors of history. And that knowledge depends on memory. Our lived experience is nothing without the revelations about the necessity of lived experience, and only our ways of knowing …"

Quinceton's attention trailed off as his focus shifted to the response of the crowd. No doubt everyone in the room had heard every possible version of this speech fifty times before, no matter the final upshot. The AAA/JJJ members up front took the mental break to whisper between themselves. Redgrave leaned down to hear something from a subordinate, but he didn't speak, and he kept his face aimed at the stage. By turning to the back wall of the audience and craning his neck around a big support pole, Quinceton could see Natalie looking right back at him. Maybe she felt a little safer seeing him up there, her own personal sniper watching over the big mess of bodies fighting for social stability on the main floor. Maybe not, but at least she saw him, and as he looked up vertically from Natalie, he noticed one of the themed posters hanging over the super-important back row of Anti-Racists. In rounded bubble letters with tacky hearts fluttering around the border was a single word: LOVE.

Now, when Quinceton looked at Natalie, he didn't know about all that eternal commitment talk or what to call specific feelings and such, but he sure did think about her a lot.

"So in order to ensure that we never forget our commitment to Anti-Racism and the historical roots of our movement, I've decided to designate my birthday, January fifteenth, as twenty-four hours of remembrance, a holiday to recall the gruesome roots of man's inhumanity to non-men, as the official day to anoint as 'The Day that Slavery Never Ended.' From now on, January fifteenth will henceforth be known as 'Janteenth Fifteenth-enteenth.' This, I bequeath to you, now and forevermore."

The words Mumwaza used sounded different from most people's speech, kinda formal and sometimes not, but always said with a way of making you feel like you should be something else—angrier, or more loyal, or even more silent.

"In our unyielding efforts to break the shackles of white supremacist

GEORGE P. DENNY

thinking from our government, language, and education system, we have identified and are working to decolonize the limiting structure of so-called 'English spelling' from our curriculum. For centuries, our BIPOC students have been maligned as perpetual victims of intellectual violence for their inability to conform to the Racist spelling binary that has long invaded our instruction of the written word. Having identified this holdover from the days of white supremacist America, we will eliminate all standards of binary spelling, so that each learner and thinker of the future may transcribe their work in whatever spelling appears most phonetically pleasing to their own racial and gender identity. No longer will any public pronouncements correspond to the old Racist binary; this will be done to enhance communication and allow for seamless transference of ideas across borders of race, gender identity, and language itself."

Alright, Quinceton thought immediately, *what difference does it make anyway? If your ideas are indefensible nonsense on their own, doesn't it only help sell stupidity when no one can read or write? And what if they don't have the lived experience to argue with anything anyway?*

"Additionally, a rising issue threatens the racial distinctions with which we equalize society," Mumwaza continued in a slightly more subdued tone. "As you are aware, it's impossible to properly compensate individuals for the hardships of their ancestors without knowing where they came from, and as we fight the horrors of history, our natural inclination may be toward interracial mixing. Could it be problematic? Certainly! That's where I came from—when a former slave united with an Indigenous target of genocide."

In the context of staring at Mumwaza's white face, the statement came off as more of a reminder of an untouchable identity claim than presentation of convincing evidence. It was one of many, many times when Quinceton wished he could tell what other people were thinking, and if his perceptions were really just his.

"However, the prevalence of miscegenation among the different racial groups of New California will inevitably lead to great complexities of racial privilege and oppression math calculation, and how does one measure

336

the ratio of privileged blood to oppressed? How does one calculate the support one owes to the state if a part of their ethnic makeup owes something, but another part is *owed* something else in equity welfare? You can see the issue, and why it becomes problematic in a world with true commitment to equity. How can we seek to make all groups equal if the members of those groups are constantly changing? What about a person from both a victimized people and also an oppressor group?"

This was a problem that Quinceton had never considered.

"In all our years of Anti-Racism, we've naturally encouraged interconnection, camaraderie, and compassion for that which may be racially or sexually foreign to you. Our efforts have been wildly successful: Look across San Francisco and you can see relationships between someone of any race with someone else of any other race, straight people with lesbians, heterosexual trans men with gay men, and every other combination of everything. What chance do I have myself, even as Knowing Leader, of meeting a Black and Choctaw womxn with whom to raise children of my own racial makeup?"

There was a pretty pathetic forced laugh from the crowd, insofar as volume or believability, at least. Mumwaza paused to let people think about the historical and biological roots of his lived experience power. It was probably very impressive if you believed in all that.

"So I will have to accept that my offspring, no matter their birther, will not suffer from the oppression which has characterized my life. They may have whiter skin than I do, and their gender identity will surely be easier to understand and therefore tolerate, so why should white-passing descendants like I might produce receive the full weight of our counterbalancing the scales of oppression? In truth, they simply should not. Oppressed groups should be limited to only those who truly deserve such counterweights, and in focusing our outreach to only the neediest groups, we can significantly improve the benefits of our government interventions."

If Quinceton didn't know better, he might almost think the Anti-Racists were trying to cut some grift out of the equation, but he'd been wrong too many times before to get confused once again. He expected more of a response from the crowd, some of whom might actually lose some racial IS points from themselves or a family member, but they did not stir. Their uniform stiffness, in fact, said something about the reception of information, as did the increasingly excited murmuring around Redgrave. The Chairperson, however, did not move a single muscle, much like the practiced politicians and Elect in attendance.

"And so it is in the spirit of great personal sacrifice that I now announce a new policy set to platform the needs of only the most historically marginalized. From now on, offspring resulting from an interracial union will be limited to an IS score which is no higher than the lowest of their birthing parents. Offspring resulting from a union involving nontraditional gender identities, all forms of neo-knowing, body privilege, and all other forms of oppression will follow the same rule, and their children will be limited to the IS score held by the more privileged of their parents."

The crowd barely reacted, seeming to take in the revolutionizing of their social order with a surprising level of acceptance, all things considered. "Now, I know you're likely growing tired of fighting Racism and, truth be told, it is painful for me to be here, doing the work of reminding the world once again. Like you, I am deeply uncomfortable having to *do this work*. No one is more exhausted with this struggle than I am, but in order that we prepare for final victory over our history, it is essential that we preserve our most oppressed and marginalized populations—so we know who to help in the future. To support this effort, stay tuned for coordinated special mixers for singles of any gender identity with IS scores of twenty or greater oppression."

The idea of more racial segregation didn't bother Quinceton too much. Beyond that, though, he could scarcely comprehend how excruciating a party solely composed of IS scores over twenty would be—God forbid any name or theme or word fall out of line or else it would become hysterical, or lead to an outright riot, with no end to the self-victimization. *The pronoun introductions alone would take half the night!* Then the attendant accusatory complaining, turning the evening into an oppressor witch hunt before the appetizers could even be bitched about by the uniquely oppressed patrons. Still, it was probably a good idea if the Anti-Racists were worried about cultivating their next generation of overgrown kids to be endlessly promoted based on their victim patter. It also helped limit the future numbers of oppressed people to placate, as anyone breeding with a whitey or similarly worthless group would forfeit their IS score to all descendants.

Is anyone still fooled by this madness, or are they just faking it to stay alive?

Knowing Leader Mumwaza Q. Jumping Bull waited for applause, with some awkward disappointment creeping across INRIs rippling cheeks as the dying echoes of minimal palms being slapped laid bare how little clapping was really going on. There simply wasn't much remaining enthusiasm for new weapons in the war against Racism, even if these three announcements represented some pressure on the New California politicians to produce results, or at least pretend to.

It was actually kind of refreshing to see, in a way that totally validated the Liberati's long-held skepticism. Even though Quinceton hadn't been around to see past Momalla Galas, he was surprised to see an audience of Elect react with such ambivalence to a public pronouncement. Usually, an opportunity to profess loyalty to the state with *any* virtue signal—even one so mundane as exuberant applause—would be seized upon with the zeal of one's entire personal ambition. But in this room, as more eyes darted between heads for a glimpse at the Chairperson seated at the front than the Knowing Leader on stage, yesterday's assumptions appeared to be really old news.

"Tenth annual … wonderful having you all here, the Momalla … to eliminate Racism in 2067 … womxn are womxn …" Mumwaza looked around helplessly for reassurance. Handing over the microphone didn't come naturally to the Knowing Leader, and even though INRI hadn't invited Redgrave to speak, onlookers' expectations could be felt all the way up to where Quinceton stood on the third floor. In a move INRI might soon regret, Mumwaza glanced momentarily at the AAA/JJJ Chairperson and Redgrave rose at once, turning his whole body perpendicular to the audience to exaggerate his upward reach for the mike. The judgement-free blackness of his garb blazed bright beside Mumwaza's desperate, pushy rainbow patterns.

"If I may?" Redgrave asked the Knowing Leader.

Somehow, in spite of INRIs unlimited power, the Knowing Leader really had no choice. INRI thought about including a better last line, evidently couldn't come up with one, and made to give up the voice amplification device. But Redgrave didn't look at him. He didn't move at all, keeping his face to the audience and arm extended. Before Jessica Bondurant or any other ZNN communications producers could swoop in to rectify the situation, Mumwaza Q. Jumping Bull surrendered and deployed to deliver the microphone *himself*, as though he were not an INRI at all, but merely a he/him/his.

Redgrave waited in total stillness. He wouldn't budge, even when the microphone actually reached his hand, except to constrict his fingers, letting the audience listen to the Knowing Leader's overworked lungs as the state's most elite hand-picked retinue carried their prophet from the arena, bloodied and broken, but hardly finished. A boiling, poorly concealed fury filled the Knowing Leader's jowls. He'd forecasted a confrontation, no doubt—he just hadn't expected to compete, least of all in something like showmanship. Working to secure or remain in a position of power came as such a shock to the Knowing Leader that Quinceton almost felt sorry to see the realization dawn that not all reality and outcomes could be avoided forever.

Suddenly, Mumwaza looked right at Quinceton. He/INRI was at the edge of the stage, being wheeled off as fast as the relievers could safely get him/INRI out of the spotlight, but the pointed look reminded the young sniper that he was here to back one side of an impending confrontation. The other side—Redgrave's AAA/JJJ and all them—they had to remember Quinceton and see him as alright, or at least no loyalist to the Anti-Racist government. And then there were Dad and Anti-Anti-Racist Liberati, who had existed almost entirely in Quinceton's imagination up to this point. They were supposed to be a part of the extra "Periphery Calm" detail that'd gotten Quinceton into the Momalla, but it was too risky to identify any of them, and he had to bet they were also biding time in dark corners of the crowd and crouching in cover. So when Knowing Leader Mumwaza Q. Jumping Bull fastened his eyes on Quinceton's, the young sniper felt the weight of yet another person counting on him, yet another complication jeopardizing a coup that had yet to materialize, which Quinceton could then either thwart, support, or flee from. But it probably wouldn't be that simple.

The pause onstage came as a result of a handful of AAA/JJJ agents rushing around to stretch a white screen out in front of a projector. Quinceton hadn't seen where the projector came from, but they planted it on the ground in the middle of the front row, exactly where Redgrave had been seated. The ten-foot square white screen came to life against the back wall of the stage as the projector illuminated the brightly polished seal of New California bearing the now-emblematic rainbow baby, along with the state motto:

CERTAINTY IS SUPREMACY
CONFUSION IS COMPASSION

"Greetings," Redgrave said into the microphone with a grin that clashed mightily with the staid, apprehensive, going-through-the-motions looks on the other bodies to have reached the stage. He waited, taking time to observe specific faces in the crowd—some Elect in the center of the floor, and others seated farther back, where there was more political power.

"I've taped the speech I'd like to make tonight, which I will play over the building music system, but I'll retain this mic to weave in my own wails and murmurings, as is consistent with my gender identity. Please dim the lights."

With this statement hanging in the air, Redgrave did a little ballerina twirl, ending in a curtsy bow. The ZNN camera crew could do nothing but film silently, as even the producer powers of one Jessica Bondurant were no match for the momentum of the coming presentation. Then someone somewhere faded the central atrium beams, leaving the remote upper floors and rear staircase mostly untouched but casting a shadow over the audience that gripped their eyes to the front, to the luminous image on the screen and the person skipping with glee underneath it.

Onstage, Redgrave smiled as he watched the crowd, his back to the screen. A few larger JJJ/AAA collected at the base of the stage below him, but he paid them no attention, and they seemed to operate without further instruction.

"*Let us never forget where we've come from,*" Redgrave's voice echoed overhead from the atrium's audio system. "*From roots of slavery, torture, and genocide, our species has risen.*" The projector churned with a picture of a starving naked man whose hands had been hammered to a wood plank that extended horizontally, then similarly gruesome and violent imagery from humanity's past, much like you'd see in a DIE Camp reeducation session. In fact, it was probable that much of what now played had been lifted directly from the reel they forced on accused Racists.

Quinceton could see one benefit of the pre-taped speech: the words coordinated perfectly with the pictures as they played. It also allowed Redgrave to prance around on full display while turning his attention to anyone in the crowd who needed the glare of his accusatory stares.

The screen flashed to color and lit up with an image of Union Square on the day in 2039 that the Great Rupture between Old California and America was announced. Quinceton actually remembered hearing about this; his birther had mentioned it a lot, and Dad didn't have much to disagree about back then, those conversations being in the 2050s—before he really got political. The person on stage that day, in both Redgrave's video clip and in Quinceton's memory, was the man something-something Kendaoi, who would become the first Knowing Leader of the JSS government. These days, Kendaoi was really only mentioned in connection with the ill-fated 2020 Project—that which would end his time living in the Secure Space as Knowing Leader. But back in Union Square, 2039, the man onstage with his carefully braided dreadlocks and a pressed dashiki really seemed to speak the right language.

"… *the ships of the Middle Passage, brought to this land in bondage, and now in this, the year of our Lord 2039, we hereby proclaim New California as decolonized land for all!"* Somehow, they had synched audio of Kendaoi making the speech all those years ago and played it in time with his delivery. The message hadn't changed all that much in the ensuing decades.

"With the values of diversity, equity, and inclusion, which we extend to populations of all ethnic backgrounds, gender identities, mental status, and physical irregularity, we will create an equal, equitable, diverse, and inclusive utopia the rest of the world could never imagine!" The PA system replayed the echo of these last words as the recording froze on an image of the former Knowing Leader beaming with self-satisfaction.

The still frame shone with enough light that a collection of AAA/JJJ agents at the foot of the stage became clearly visible. Their backs to Redgrave and shoulders touching the next agent beside them, they were an intimidating wall of bodies and unsanctioned will. Quinceton gripped his rifle and looked around for his father or any other potentially friendly members of the "Periphery Calm" team, but saw none.

"The people rejoiced in their newfound freedom, and pledged to forge a new world launched from the lessons of the greedy American Republic." Images from the early years after the Great Rupture played, mainly of human migration to and from California. Quinceton wasn't alive back then, but he remembered hearing about the exodus in his Work Doing Center.

Lest one forget the original Anti-Racist pitch, another clip of original Knowing Leader Kendaoi talking to other Knowers offered a recap: *"Now that we've introduced the Standpoint Mandate—which will address all future disagreements by ordering all speakers of voices and opinions by the legitimacy of their historical power and victimization—the rest of our doctrine will follow naturally. By simply offering ourselves as a unique and equitable alternative to white supremacist systems, New California will voluntarily cleanse itself of American Racism and the progress-crippling moderates who maintain cisheteropatriarchy. In their place, enthusiastic supporters will flock from all corners of the country."*

In some sense this was true, but the pictures eerily corresponded to the rumors Quinceton had heard—where far, *far* more people had left, such that all anyone remembered were long lines of traffic heading for Nevada and the impossibility of getting moving vans back from any other state they had fled to.

"*A new world was minted around the values of diversity, equity, and inclusion.*" The screen flipped from the old Knowing Leader to Mumwaza Q. Jumping Bull, the newest one, without reference to the 2020 Project or anything else that might have sent Kendaoi to a place like Stockton.

"*This world would be people-powered by the lived experience of the marginalized Other: This New California would finally be an America, decolonized.*"

Images of workers taking directions from their workmasters as they served food at a cafeteria or dragged a rake across the sweltering fields of the Central Valley, all smiling, none believable. Onstage, Redgrave appeared not to be listening to his presentation as he sifted through whispers from his darkness-camouflaged posse and pointed at different places in the atrium with a jerk of the skull. There weren't as many AAA/JJJ in the front anymore; they'd spread out some, but down low. Quinceton kept scanning behind him for action on the third floor, but even the Periphery Calm team seemed to have settled in for the speech.

"*The nexus of our world is the belief that we are members of different, competing identity groups who should unite as one whole group on the condition that each of the different identity components will be guaranteed full equity in that larger group.*" The displayed image flashed to a mural in San Francisco's Mission District that had been repurposed to announce the Intersectional Equity law. This natural extension of Standpoint thinking was the game-changer that made it impossible for different races, genders, religions, or able-bodied people to earn unequal income after all groups' total earnings had been pooled and taxed or subsidized to assure fiscal equity.

But in Quinceton's estimation, it also had to be around this time that many ambitious working people left town, privately owned businesses shuttered, and then everything you used and ate came from the JSS government. It all had to happen virtually overnight, even though none of that was in the text of the Intersectional Equity law or publicly predicted so people could have prepared and made their own right decisions.

"The law sought to harmonize all cultural strengths and weaknesses together," as the screen worded it from the loudspeakers, *"with the benefits of such inclusion and diversity being equity for all."*

Then came an early Anti-Racist government marketing poster: a line of beaming workers collecting food on cafeteria trays, smiling so broadly that no one who had ever eaten cafeteria food could mistake their grins for sincerity. Perhaps—and Quinceton was really guessing here—the alienation he felt when seeing these forced poses was part of the point.

"The challenge of combining all oppressed identities under one institution with equity for all, something the United States had never even attempted to achieve, would prove more difficult than originally envisioned." The screen flashed from well-known pictures of Black and trans drug-addicted houseless people in American San Francisco—probably from the decades just preceding the Great Rupture—to a shot of first Knowing Leader Kendaoi addressing the original chamber of Anti-Racist academics, advisors, and accumulated experts of lived experience. This image lingered on the screen as Quinceton's eyes wandered around to the other faces in the Secure Space.

They were virtually all dark-skinned, plenty of womxn, but noticeably few with a modern hairstyle. No Kafkani crowns yet, and none overtly announcing their own personal gender identity. Not many smiles, either, and nothing forced. The faces in this picture, of perhaps the first New California Anti-Racist Council, belonged to serious people with a serious purpose. Quinceton caught himself imagining his birther as one of them.

"How to recognize the historical oppression of one group by asking another to contribute that which they've accumulated through the same oppressive history creates a necessary separation between identities working together for an equitable society," the voice-over carried on amorphously, as if it came from the floor, walls, and roof all at once. In combination with the nervous fringe chatter, it was the sound of God's throat clearing.

"The original framers of New California did not anticipate one par-ticular contradiction: that the effort to equalize all identity groups must begin by identifying those groups, thereby separating and dividing the people it intends to unite under one flag." The pictures flashed quickly now, and they all had the same theme: self-segregated identity groups in New California. A class of young Black and white workdoers sitting on opposite sides of the room, suntanned Latinx's raking side by side in the Central Valley fields, or a line of privileged whites canceling themselves on the familiar Union Square platform.

More eyes than just Quinceton's were searching about for a source of authority, this display being an explicit mention of verboten subject matter. But the question as to who enforced that which was verboten, and with what power, seemed to have occurred to Redgrave in advance of this moment.

"In New California, we all strive to do our share, whatever that con-tribution may be, and have a system to spread the benefits of our labor and resources equitably among all." The old factory shots gave way to some kind of big hotel beneath an open sky that Quinceton didn't recognize. *"Some volunteer to lead those wayward souls who bend to the temptations of bigotry, and outside the capital, those Diversity, Equity, and Inclusion Camps now constitute the primary source of New California agricultural production, packaging, and distribution to feed every hungry mouth that needs feeding."*

We see inside the big hotel and find bunk beds loaded to the ceiling in one room—there had to have been eight or ten people living there. This is one of the DIE Camps, the audience is told, and even though it looks bet-ter than most in Quinceton's educated estimation, the voice-over tells the audience what to see.

"These individuals were relocated to this Modesto Diversity, Equity, and Inclusion reeducation facility after confessing to Crimes Against Per-sons of Greater Victimhood and toil in the fields, day after day, for your forgiveness. They strive to be the Anti-Racist members of New California you so truly want them to be, and after only a few months collecting and

organizing the forgotten workers of our world, I've come to this Tenth Annual SOMA Momalla Gala to platform one more extension of the oppressed Other: the victims of victimhood."

As if the words weren't enough, an accompanying photo of Redgrave with arms around the original field workers, as though he were one of them, flashed on screen, and held. The message to Mumwaza was clear: *Remember that underclass you created to feed everybody? Yeah, well, turns out they aren't all thrilled with their enslavement.*

There was a tug at the bottom of Quinceton's shirt, and he turned to see a dwarfish workmaster from the Periphery Calm team on the verge of a mental breakdown.

"You're here, right?" the tiny person demanded to know. "You *are* here, correct?"

"What do you mean?" Quinceton couldn't resist, in spite of his superior's panic. "Do I exist in this particular time and place, and will that continue to be true?"

"Don't be smart with me! *No one* is where they're supposed to be. *No one* is doing a single thing I told them to do. The ones I put on the floor are all getting nervous, and now no one will stay on the floor, no matter what I say. If you see any come up here, especially from the floor, you give them the third degree, and take their names to tell me for censure later. Can't be public, obviously—this whole mess can't even be touched until they get through the stuff down there, but then *it will be*."

"You got it," Quinceton promised, fairly certain he was talking to the spiritual successor of Command Sergeant Major Smythe, in which case this little lemming was damn sure never walking out of the MOMA. So Quinceton nodded dutifully.

Back onstage, Redgrave was unmasking one after another of his AAA/JJJ henchmen as the voice-over detailed their crimes and duration of continuing sentence at a DIE Camp, which was not Stockton. It never was. Quinceton listened for it and, after hearing a second visitor from the Red Bluff facility, concluded that this was a conscious decision meant to scare the Anti-Racists with the implication of Redgrave's long reach to the entire network of criminal justice reeducation facilities/food production.

It was around this time that Quinceton really began to worry about the scene unfolding two floors below. He thought about Natalie, about why in God's name she had to be on the hip of the walrus everyone seemed to accept with inevitability—*Never true loyalty, ever.* If there was one thing the world had taught him, it was something about listening to people and letting their words and ideas dictate whether he should listen more or agree with them. Guys like Mumwaza, and all the Speakers and Knowers and such—they just demanded obedience without ever justifying or earning it.

That's why, when the Anti-Racists finally needed the pissed-upon, Quinceton was worried about a girl being too close to the leader everyone was supposedly there to celebrate, encourage, and heed for the latest Anti-Racist correctives required for a happy, equitable society. The distracted Elect beneficiaries in the orchestra audience were captive to a new message now, one that none appeared willing or motivated to prevent, like a herd of pigs so accustomed to barn life they hardly noticed the sharpened knives paying for it all. The religious devotion to end "white supremacy" that Quinceton saw in pictures just after the Great Rupture—and remembered in people like his seeder—was present only in appearance, but psychically absent from the room, just at the precise moment when New California's top priest might actually be tested.

"*John Charles Redgrave, Chairperson of the Stockton DIE Camp.*" Someone, somewhere, dimmed all the bulbs that weren't aimed at the stage, bathing the black-robed challenger in the beams of two focused spotlights. "*Forty-six years old. Born in the Eastern state of New York: 2020. Masculine-leaning gender-bending post-op transX he/him individual who immigrated to New California in the year of the Great Rupture and resettlement. Born of pure Anglo-Saxon European colonizer privilege, John Charles Redgrave knowingly and willfully relinquished his 'white supremacy' in July of 2066.*" The agents closed in around Redgrave, a body meeting him at each elbow.

Quinceton didn't see a ton of reasons to want your own "white supremacy," especially if it meant you had to work like a slave, then apologize or thank someone for certifying your racial atonement. But Redgrave knew how to spin the Anti-Racists philosophy for his own agenda.

"We are servants of New California's Justice of Social Soldiers: their food pickers, packers, presenters—their dishwashers. In fields and kitchens and packing factories, we atone for the sins of the father and the grandfather, all in the hope of being invited into the fold of Diversity, Equity, and Inclusion. We strive to uphold the bonds of deconstructed Anti-Racism, the pillar of our world, while so rarely tasting the fruits of our own labor."

Quinceton had himself witnessed Redgrave eating charcuterie and the like, but the momentum was insurmountable. Only the privileged groups were eligible to be watched and canceled for Crimes Against Persons of Greater Victimhood, but everyone in New California knew the sound of a victim narrative. And if they'd paid attention to anything Quinceton had seen, the victim story only ever got used to justify revenge.

"The educated, privileged American managerial class, whose eventual embrace of Anti-Racism gave us the New California which we now celebrate, was handed a fully constructed capitalist system of inequity to perpetuate without a second thought to the BIPOC bodies upon which it was forged in the savagery of slavery. You don't rise to be a managerial standout like Sweatshop Vice President or International Corporation CEO without decades of social training in the right politics, the right ways to distract from inequity with mere virtue signaling to maintain the profits of faceless shareholders. That the elite managerial group, many of whom were white and wealthy beyond comparison in today's San Francisco, did ultimately voice the sacrifices of Diversity, Equity, and Inclusion for all is simply a testament to their risk aversion; they just didn't want to lose their own power in society, so they'd tolerate any system that kept them at the top."

Quinceton couldn't help but wonder: Was Redgrave talking about the Elect, or the Americans who were Elect before they were openly called this specific word?

The screen jumped to a famously gruesome image of police-on-Black Racism. *"Now enter the unicorn, an era-defining symbol of victimhood, like Saint Floyd in 2020: the single individual who reveals truth to power for the benefit of all, at the cost of their own life. The demise of our Patron Saint of Victimhood challenged the assumptions America was built upon, from maintaining all the trappings of white supremacist thinking, like free market economics and Racist rationality, to a push for reform along the necessities of Anti-Racist abolition. Suddenly, the managerial oligarchy was given a new set of virtue signals to mouth in order to keep their big-money salaries."*

Redgrave is really freestyling here, Quinceton thought with surprise. *Managerial class—what the hell is that?* Most of Redgrave's assertions didn't much interest Quinceton—he hadn't been around to remember the hungry young professionals rich people hired to run their businesses—but this part of the preamble seemed to have registered on a bunch of faces in the Elect orchestra. Many of them were making visible appeals to Redgrave, especially the older ones. The obvious bowing and hand-wringing looked like confession.

"The managerial class is accustomed to, and paid handsomely for, maintaining the status quo by not changing anything: peaceful, inoffensive stasis is the goal, for peaceful, inoffensive stasis does not draw attention to any other societal imperfections that may be implicit in every transaction." Quinceton noticed Redgrave's switch to present tense, but wasn't sure who else caught it. *"The managerial class, while best suited to platform Social Justice in their given society, is simultaneously corrupted by having every want at their fingertips: food, housing, status, and the sex that comes with it all. These are the rewards of the managerial Elite. And who among us—who among you or standing up here on stage—who really can resist the trappings of pleasure that ambush and waylay our ascendance to righteousness?"*

It was the most piercing of rhetorical questions—in part because the MOMA was, at present, drowning in displays of those trappings, but also because the whole spectacle had been organized as reassurance and codification of that "righteousness." Did these gowns and awards and platitudes actually convince anyone that Social Justice was a good thing for other people, the people here who didn't get to be considered victims after America had been decolonized?

"Though the previous Justice Justice Justice Chairperson who introduced the de-whitening ceremony was discovered to harbor secret Anti-Anti-Racist sentiments and consequently vanished earlier this year, the tradition they started has endured to liberate hundreds of fully egalitarian individuals who willfully renounce their white supremacy and past American identitarian benefits. So many of the historically privileged deeply yearn to donate their privilege back to the people whom their ancestors oversaw with the slave whip; they want so deeply and truly to be treated as equal peers. Now that we've come so far—and no doubt we can see evidence of progress all around this room—I ask: Have we come far enough to open our tent to include those who so willingly back their oaths with loyalty of action? Or, put another way: How can we deny them, the masses? How can they be forgiven, and why shouldn't they be?"

Pretty smart. Quinceton suddenly remembered a line he'd heard at Stockton—"Just because we have to play this identity game doesn't mean we have to lose it"—and finally saw in their faces the fear the Anti-Racists had built their career on.

"After all," Redgrave continued with his own voice, the recording having expired or stalled, "the meaning and treatment of words change. What constitutes 'White Privilege' or a 'victim' can shift at any minute, as can the presumption that being a 'victim' endows one with preferential treatment from the government forever, or not. What guarantees that the definition of any word will remain constant tomorrow? And how many of you have built your entire life on the guarantee of submission to whatever evolutions and contradictions of these words come next?"

Now this was too much—this *had* to be too much for the Anti-Racists. Tinh's voice sounded in the back of Quinceton's mind: *The contradictions are the point.* Seemingly with every swallowed lie and redefinition there was an opportunity to defect, and when one rejected the choice, their loyalty to the lying Anti-Racist state only grew. The whole trick worked better if no one pointed out its method of survival, but the rewards of the charade

351

applied most fervently to those in this very room. And those who needed that doctrine to have any authority at all had to step out of the shadows and defend it some time—like probably *now*—or it would soon be too late.

Quinceton maneuvered to scope the Knowing Leader, who must've known something the rest of them didn't. INRI smiled serenely, waiting. Not even talking to Natalie or another Knower, pointing out shifting Peripheral Calm team movements to one of INRIs floor lieutenants, or outright panicking—none of this was happening. It seemed everything was still running along according to INRIs plan, too, just like the other ones, scheduling the climax for whenever the two or three different plans all interrupted to eviscerate each other. Up front, even true believers like Jessica Bondurant weren't protesting, because they were individuals now.

Quinceton rolled an ear plug in his left hand, then buried it deep in his left ear. He'd stick one halfway into his right ear, but he needed enough space to hear Redgrave cue him. Looking around the huge, echoing atrium now, all Quinceton could see was a room full of question marks ready to kill, his girl somewhere in the middle of it all, and little to hide behind, except heart-shaped balloons and plastic banners professing stuff like "togetherness" and "unity."

"So it is with forgiveness in mind as we commit and recommit and push forward with our dedication to defeating bigotry," Redgrave bellowed with his own lungs, hands hidden beneath his robes. "Words may change, but hearts do not. We must know for certain who is truly committed to an equitable world in which all peoples of *all* bodies have fully achieved abolition, decolonization, freedom. And in the Anti-Racist society we've already built, would a bigot ever be so foolish as to out themselves? Would they ever be so suicidal as to admit prejudice against a Black body, a womxn's body, or an otherwise abled body—a Masculine-leaning gender-bending post-op transX he/him body? I think not. Which is why we must know who they are—why we must expose them for all to see. Please turn the camera around so that we may see Justice for ourselves."

This was carried out abruptly by an AAA/JJJ agent, their confederates replacing the original cameraperson with a shove and casting Jessica Bondurant adrift, left with no choice but to stand awkwardly in the foreground of the orchestra. These prime Elect suddenly gazed into the glare of their own spotlight, reactions now to be captured and documented forever, as the camera faced the audience like the Stockton Chairperson himself.

A momentary pause, then Redgrave roared, "Look away to confess your bigotry!"

The black robe protecting the audience from Redgrave's nudity flung forward, exposing the Chairperson's hideous venis, spotlight high beams centered on the mangled penis-vagina appendage. Everyone else onstage held guns, two pistols each, pointed directly at the audience.

Before anything else happened, before Quinceton could even think about raising the rifle to his shoulder, he wheeled around to look down at Natalie, gripped by stupefaction, and the huge poster above her, professing "Love," clinging to the third-floor bannister by a single string.

Quinceton listened to panicked murmuring as he crouch-walked to stay low and tore the poster's support with two concentrated fists. As it floated down to the Knower's rear platform, Quinceton saw the pre-pandemonium below, with some weapons drawn by the Peripheral Calm team, some Elect sneaking toward the exits, and others with silent appeals from their seats—prostrate, hands clasped forward, hoping to beg their way to forgiveness from their possibly new next Knowing Leader ... as though this next successor would finally be the omniscient one.

"... waiting for?!" It was Mumwaza, trying to shout over his slumping Elect army. "Can't you recognize Racism? *Do something!*"

Quinceton watched the poster curve through the air before catching an angle and sliding quickly to envelop a dozen people in the rows before Natalie. She saw Quinceton's gaze—she knew what he was trying to do— and he tried to mouth "hide," though she was too far away to see it. He jerked his head to the left, through the atrium and toward the rear staircase, and maybe she caught that—at least she got in with the survivors obscuring themselves with the tarp.

Then the room exploded in sound. It was impossible to tell who got shot and who was caving into a protective ball only to shield their ears, as damn near each and every person in the orchestra and behind it crumpled in agony. Quinceton scrambled to squeeze his right ear plug firmly into place, lessening the audible assault from coma-inducing to a deafening barrage.

The sound did not stop. Noise erupted from the stage, but from everywhere else, too, the acoustics causing the explosions to echo repeatedly up to debilitating decibels.

With his back pressed hard against the railing, Quinceton could feel the menacing reverberations pulsing through the room. He had assumed the noise and imagery of South Lake would have prepared him for more battle, but this was nothing like Tahoe. This bloodshed was so close to his face, he could smell the bile. There was no tower to hide in, no mountains to run for. The Battle of South Lake had carried him here, to a place where he finally understood the larger conflict and his own small part in prolonging it. The war was not about "Social Justice" versus something else; it was about *who* gets to decide what Social Justice is. It always was, and it always would be.

Natalie was down there somewhere, though, and if she weren't, Quinceton could've just said, *To hell with it!* and bounced as soon as he found his father. In the same low crouch, Quinceton waddled to the opposite end of the third-floor balcony to get closer to the stage and maybe, if he were lucky, get some cover from Redgrave's takeover crew. Scattered fire found its way upstairs at times but generally sunk into the walls, far enough from Quinceton's position that he could hope they weren't meant for him. He popped his head up just long enough to see the Love banner crawling across the atrium floor to the rear staircase, limbs churning with clumsy coordination like a crippled centipede.

Next to the seat Natalie had just vacated lay former Knowing Leader Mumwaza Q. Jumping Bull's corpse, unattended and unmourned, a few streams of blood flowing from the chest of INRIs rainbow robes being the last shock to the Knowing Leader. There were a few fallen Periphery Calm guards nearby, but Quinceton couldn't be sure those guys had actually raised their weapons in defense of Mumwaza. More likely, they had just been too close to the target when the throw-down kicked off.

Jessica Bondurant, that truest of True Believers, also lay on her back at the front of the orchestra, pierced by too many bullets to count, eyes still open. Quinceton hadn't seen if she'd resisted in some way when the guns came out, but the position of her body suggested she'd neither run nor charged; she just took the heat and fell without seeing any of it coming. The other Anti-Racist loyalists defending the Anti-Racist government seemed to have all but disbanded, died, or defected to the Anti-Anti-Anti-Racist invaders. Their resistance had expired with Mumwaza's lived experience and Jessica Bondurant's stage direction.

Political questions came from the speed of it all—*Why didn't the former Knowing Leader have enough backing to put up a fight on his own floor?* Just like in South Lake, the promise and display of loyalty was a poor substitute for the real thing. And now what?

There were shouts from down below, and because his ears could nearly register another sound, the drumbeat of gunfire had to be subsiding. He checked the stage and saw AAA/JJJ guards scanning the crowd with guns drawn, but few things, or people, left worth shooting. Redgrave emerged from behind a couple of especially wide agents and actually laughed. He said something to the agents nearby and they did, too—laughing lightheartedly while surveying the massacre, laughing as though the whole game were just that easy, the only surprise being that victory had taken so long.

And Natalie was still down there. The Love banner centipede had stalled behind the central staircase, opposite the stage, and when Quinceton looked closer he saw hands competing to tug the thing in opposing directions. There were just too many frantic people under that flimsy tarp to get any coherent decision made, and it was unfair to expect them to. Quinceton would have to do something about this problem, and the rifle wouldn't help solve it.

Removing his right ear plug would help him glean some fresh intel; he pulled it out and listened. There was less groaning than he expected … no explicit begging—they were all pretty dead for the most part. The blood, like the gun smoke, had nowhere to go, and thus it pooled on the floor as lasting warnings to the others. Whoever had possessed the gall to resist in the atrium was dead, and beyond some collateral damage no one seemed to care about, the coup had been pretty painless. No wonder Redgrave was happy about it. Even though reaching this point was kinda the Liberati plan he'd gotten from his father, it was working so well that surely something else had gone terribly wrong.

Quinceton took a deep breath, stood, and raised the weapon over his shoulders with both arms extended.

"All hail John Charles Redgrave!" he shouted from the third-floor balcony. "All hail he who speaks truth to power! All hail he who speaks power to lies!" Quinceton paused to secure a few more sets of eyes. "All hail he who puts the 'Justice' in Social Justice!" Redgrave grinned up at him, recognized his face from months ago in Stockton, and nodded with a hand clasped to his breast. Quinceton just hoped every one of the AAA/JJJ agents caught it.

The assertion spread quickly on the atrium floor below as surviving members of the orchestra, Periphery Calm team, relievers, workmasters—damn near everybody left down there—all rose in unison to pledge new loyalty. The threat of violence appeared to abate on condition of new allegiance, and with at least the appearance of it secured, Redgrave just beamed and raised his arms high, like it was everything he'd ever wanted all at once. He looked up at Quinceton again, gave him an even wider smile, and saluted him: a general validating a favorite soldier. This was Redgrave's shining moment in the world he'd finally won.

Like a few other limbs from the Love banner centipede, Natalie had been drawn out by Quinceton's announcement and the agreements to follow. She saw Redgrave's salute and cast a gaze of pure astonishment into the young sniper's crosshairs.

"Come join me, friend!" Quinceton shouted to Natalie, opening his arms horizontally, with a smiley face meant for Redgrave but a tone intended to override Natalie's confusion. There were enough loyalty oaths distracting the new bosses up front for Quinceton to momentarily drop the guise. "Seriously, Natalie," he said to the girl, gesturing for her to come up to his floor. "You'll be okay up here with me." One more peek at the stage and she caved, bounding up the central staircase two steps at a time.

Quinceton abandoned his post overlooking the atrium to intercept Natalie on the other side of the building in the cavernous second-floor lobby, which opened to share the same high roof as his third floor. But Quinceton was quickly halted by a group of former Periphery Calm team members blocking the hallway with stacked furniture and filigree.

"What's up with this?" Quinceton demanded. "I've got to get a lady through from the atrium, and she's almost here now."

"Tell her ass to hurry," one sweaty white dude answered. "We can still squeeze her through somewhere, but we're closing those gaps real quick."

"Thanks, man. But why the barricade? And why the hell is the barricade above the exit? You'll be trapped in the upper stories when whatever-the-plan-is fails."

"I'm not sure. I was told after we block this hallway, things slow down, let us organize, maybe negotiate—I don't know. No one tells me if there's a plan, and no one's really in charge. So you do you, man. If she's worth it, go save your lady."

"Word."

Quinceton saw Natalie running through the lobby below toward the staircase. He called her name, pointing to the bramble blocking the hallway. She got the message; by the time she reached the pile of clutter, Quinceton had a path cleared along the outer edge just wide enough for her to squeeze through. Natalie dropped to one knee, but paused.

"You sure I should come to you? Sure you don't want to meet me on this side? That's the roof exit right down there. Goes from the lobby to the street—far from the atrium bodies."

"I'm sure. My father is up there. My dad—he's been preparing for this all his life. So I can't go, but you can, and maybe you should. After it's over, I promise I'll come find you for sure."

"Pshhht," Natalie muttered as she crawled through the barricade. Quinceton offered a hand when she reached his side, and she took it, pulling herself into him faster than he'd anticipated or prepared for psychically.

Holding her now, with the feeling of her body under his arms and the intoxicating scent of it all … Quinceton could almost understand why so many good and honest people before him could betray so many of their values. They didn't do it *for the sake of* cowardice—they were made into cowards. Love did that to good people. Their cowardice came from loving and prioritizing that which was so directly and immediately threatened, and then suddenly traditional "goodness" didn't matter so much anymore. And if the state could simultaneously turn children against their parents, or neighbors against each other, or races against other races, then all that love turned into liability, making hostages of the emotionally afflicted.

"I saw you cut that banner down for us," Natalie said. "That was smart."

Quinceton kissed her forehead. "Thank you." There was a moment before they remembered where they were, and then they had to hurry out of the way of a long desk getting added to the mix.

"Alright," Quinceton said, still holding her. "We find my dad, and bounce fast as we can. You got anything else in the MOMA to care about?"

"Those Anti-Racist bastards?" Natalie didn't even seem to believe the question. "It won't be a waste of fire when it all burns to the ground."

"Makes it easy, then." Quinceton turned to the white guy building the barricade. "Hey, man, you seen a big Black guy with dyed pink hair up top? Named Horace, old guy in his fifties. You seen him?"

"I'm not sure, but maybe. I was up on the fourth floor earlier and I think I saw a guy like that up there, but that was a good thirty minutes ago."

"Okay, thanks. We find out anything, we'll tell you, especially if we can't find another exit."

"Good freakin' luck," the guy said. "No one here knows anything, so anything you find out is something." Bodies began to collect on the sec-ond-floor lobby.

A black-robed AAA/JJJ agent called up to the barricade, "You on the third floor—you can put the furniture down, and stop piling it up. The threat has been eliminated: Mumwaza is dead. Anti-Racism, the nonsense the Justice of Social Soldiers government used to reign—it's finished! All can be forgiven, de-whitened, and join our cause for true justice!"

Quinceton didn't wait for an answer, even if he might have learned what was in store for everyone under the de-whitening regime. This friction wouldn't have much time to simmer—he'd have to hurry.

With Natalie's hand in his, Quinceton cut more deeply into the third floor to find the rear staircase. It was full of hustle, with armed former Periphery Calm team members shuttling back and forth with anything that might block a bullet. The rooms all seemed the same: four big spray-painted art walls in a square or rectangle with rows of desks for the culture managers to pick the right imagery and political messaging for the masses.

Hurrying up the rear staircase, they soon arrived on the fourth floor, where Quinceton saw his father holding up the back end of a metal desk. The younger man rushed over to help turn the desk on its side and lay it beside the top of the rear staircase, limiting easy passage through yet another choke point. The fourth floor had less stuff to work with, or maybe it'd already been repurposed for the third-floor barricade.

"Welcome upstairs, son. It might not be the safest place on Earth, but I don't see any body-positive access, so it's pretty safe from our Knowing Leader."

"You haven't heard? Mumwaza got wiped out in the atrium." Quinceton could scarcely believe how little anybody knew about what had really happened, what was really going on, while they prepared for full resistance to an unknown end. Natalie had seen the coup, still wore the gown of a JSS-heavy date, and no one had even asked her for a word on anything.

"She was there," he added. "Dad, this is Natalie. I like her."

After a quick glance at Quinceton—Dad definitely approved of Natalie—he extended a big hand with a different sort of grin, one his son had never seen.

"Horace Rift," the old man said. "Too bad we couldn't meet under better times … meet and eat and not fight a revolution and all that, but someday soon, no doubt."

She took his hand. "I'd love that," she said. "Natalie Gutierrez. And you know, Quinceton helped distract the fools down there so I could get away." She paused, with an eye on her personal bodyguard. "I like him, too, I think."

Too much flattery, so Quinceton had to break it up. "Good thing the plan worked." The able-bodied sniper hadn't forgotten about the massive clusterfuck they'd willingly walked into, interrupting the pleasantries in a different, sour tone, but with a game face to back it up. "What's next? We cutting our cocks off to get in with Redgrave?"

"Easy, easy, son, there's a lady present. Don't forget the plan already worked, pretty much: the coup happened, and now the power vacuum sucks up all the weak bids for replacement authority. Within that destabilized environment—or because of the instability, finally out in the open—there is the opportunity for replacement without taking up a sword against the masses. This is the minimum amount of bloodshed: just limited to the figureheads and their loyalists, but severed from the people at large. We can save those people; we *are* saving those people. Whether we save ourselves or not, the fight is on now. The die is cast."

"Soldiers of fate and fortune," Quinceton said, offering the peak of his poetic memory. "But what's the plan now, exactly, Dad?"

"*Plan?* That's your favorite word. And anyway, you just saw it."

The scope of possibility from this point forward was almost too much to consider: anything, basically. The whole world had fallen apart by its own doing, and now all that was left was to get some safe distance from the funeral pyre so they didn't get scorched. There had never been much of a PLAN plan, but having lost the last semblance of a guiding North Star, Quinceton now missed it—the simplicity of knowing what should come next, even if it rarely happened on schedule, or even happened that way at all.

"If we get out of here, I know a place in the mountains that'd be comfortable for a while. It has good water, a cabin setup we could build on," Quinceton said, thinking out loud as armed rebels repurposed materials for a makeshift rampart downstairs. "If we get out of here, and we get to Placerville east of Sacramento, well, I think I could probably find it heading southwest, sorta, out of Placerville, from the school there." It was a peaceful memory. Maybe that's why he was getting stuck on it while the outside world clamored to get in.

"If we get out of here, we can all sip the finest bubbly over some T-bones," Dad answered, not following Quinceton into his realm of fantasy. "With Advi Pithawalla picking up the tab, no doubt. First, though, street exits: What'd you see down there?"

"The atrium is full of bodies and the AAA killers," Natalie said. "It's blocked for sure. I saw them collecting on the second floor—the lobby there under the barricade—and talking like they were going to stay. Talking like this takeover, and the people going upstairs ... yeah, they were talking like they expected it all was going to happen the whole time."

Quinceton wasn't going to let the word "plan" come out of his lips even one more time, and he saw a similar thought hit his father's brain too.

"Everyone got a plan," the old activist said. "You know anything else about what they're wanting, what they're talking about down there?"

"Real, hard facts or anything like that? Nope." Natalie shook her head. "But a group like that, with a leader who sees no more rivals, they'll want you to submit sooner or later. Whatever you want to hold out for is whatever spirit they'll want to break in you." Natalie had never looked so confident, and the elder Rift noticed it too. For a moment they all just looked at each other, exchanging a lot of thoughts, but with no one saying anything. If a single shot from downstairs hadn't echoed against the walls they would have held it for longer.

"Natalie, please get my son downstairs and get the hell out of here ... don't look back for nothing." The parent among them looked most worried, by far. "Quinceton, you, too, you hear me? A Harriet told us to keep the roof clear and protected, and once that's all set I'll come down and find you."

"The roof—why? How?" Quinceton stammered with some frustration. "How are you going to find us after all this blows up?" He was getting harsh flashbacks to the totally un-orchestrated scene in the atrium, where everything could have gone wrong all at once, and he especially didn't like the indefinite timeframe. Natalie squeezed his bicep to urge him on. Another few shots rang out downstairs, and they went unanswered. The next fight hadn't started yet. But it would soon.

"There'll be months of confusion no matter how this shakes out from here," the veteran parent said. "Challenges to government authority and responsibilities, reorganizing of the managerial elite … purges … it's just like last time. You can put that in stone. And with all that chaos, you think they'll worry about us? Or anyone who doesn't push for government power? Hell no. You visit the Clay anytime you wanna drop a word to me."

"Assuming I'm in the city, then yeah, easy enough."

"Even if it's a month or year from now, you guys get out safely and I'll come find you some day when it settles," Horace continued. "After this, they should all be easier to operate in, and don't forget, kids: We did it. We helped do this. All that JSS government bullshit, all those years? One botched award ceremony and it's done, and everyone saw it. So now our part ends, but it's on for others. We did that."

The "kids" nodded along as he spoke. Quinceton felt good about the pep talk, but quickly remembered that Natalie hadn't chosen any of this. "All we did won't mean much if Redgrave and his goons just take over like the JSS government did," Quinceton piped up. "Besides, you're thinking the wrong thing: We gotta figure a way out first. You get that the blockage on the third-floor landing over the lobby traps us up here as much as it holds them back, right? They can see and shoot from the lobby, you realize. The barricade won't stop people with enough motivation."

"That's right, son. Not much time now. Stay strong." Dad offered a fist bump and Quinceton met it; the elder Rift looked at his child an extra beat before releasing a long, deep sigh. "It's the world we're born into," Dad repeated from weeks, months, and years back. "And our fight is almost over." He turned away and faded into the upper floor.

It wasn't long before part of the commotion of the corridor banged into Quinceton's thigh. Whichever white guy carrying the offending chair or whatever didn't stop to apologize, and it would have been unnecessary to. In another time and place, or the same place yesterday, this could have been perceived as a career-advancing racial attack, but in the sober light of counterrevolution, it appeared to be just a clumsy white guy with a job to do.

"I should never have brought you up here," Quinceton told Natalie. All the people on this fourth floor had desperation on their faces, like they were all just prolonging the end, something the disguised AAA/JJJ agents downstairs didn't have to worry about seeing in each other.

"It was hero thinking," Quinceton continued. "I wanted to be, like, a hero, and save my dad, too, and bring everything together at the wrong time ... I'm sorry, Natalie."

"I know," she said. "And I love you for it ... cutting down that banner instead of just firing off like a fool. That small choice might've made all the difference." He moved in and covered her in a bear hug. His shoulders weren't so wide, but hers were much smaller.

"Thank you." Now was no time to think about love and such, but he appreciated her words all the same. She really got him, somehow.

Shots rang out from the pit of the building as a few former Periphery Calm members and escaping Elect scampered up from the third floor staircase.

"It's falling apart down there!" a womxn in reliever garb said. "Forget the barricade overlooking the lobby—it won't hold after they decide they want to storm it."

"Chaos!" a guy shouted in fancy-pants attire; they had been Elect as of maybe ten minutes ago. "Gotta fall back, and start a new barrier up here ... the top of the staircase, maybe?"

Quinceton grabbed the panicking person of privilege and clapped right in front of their nose. "Focus!" he yelled. "I know Redgrave, I know them all. What's happening down there?"

"He wants them to give up, he wants loyalty from everyone," the guy said, shaking his head. "But he can get through that barricade any time, I think."

Quinceton wanted to ask, "And then?" but knew it would have been wasted breath on this informant. "Yeah, he'd prefer followers and slaves to dead bodies," Quinceton agreed, then turned to Natalie. "I gotta meet this head-on, but maybe you're better off up here."

"Pshhht" was all she said. Quinceton took her at her word, clasping her hand again to sidestep the new clump of furniture being cobbled together at the top of the landing of level four.

Descending now required more dodging of people than traversing the crowded atrium before the show. The couple pushed against the current of hopeful evacuees, suspecting all the while that anyone who climbed past them was only venturing deeper into the guilt of enemy territory.

Quinceton heard Redgrave yelling before he reached the landing. "I don't *want* to break through!" Redgrave shrieked. "What I demand is for *you* to *disassemble* this mess you've created, and join me." He seemed to be far angrier now than he'd been during the ceremony but still deployed a lot of the vague, manipulative terms that the JSS government had used. "Without the establishment and acknowledgement of your own Justice, you will be hunted rather than kept; you will be outlaws, rather than your survival being an assumed responsibility of the state."

Before he'd even finished the threat, Quinceton had resolved never to use the word "justice" again now that it, like "Racism" and "white supremacy" previously, had been appropriated to simply apply pressure on any listener to agree with the larger power play being pushed.

A guy on the third-floor platform began to answer, but Quinceton cut him off with a determined look, his eyes doing most of the convincing.

"Redgrave!" Quinceton called out for all to hear, and hopefully go silent. "You won, totally, and for us all to see. What—this—now? Why? Why not let the people go?" It wasn't his best wording, but the looks he got from the nearby rebels were ones of respect.

There were a few figures Redgrave had to sidestep to see Quinceton's face, and the soldier gazing down from the third-floor platform stepped forward to assume ownership of his words. There was no cohesive leadership on Quinceton's side of the fence, no time to ask and locate other possible Liberati-leanings, but since they'd had the same instinct to separate from the AAA/JJJ rebels at the outbreak of conflict, they probably had more worldview in common than anyone else Quinceton was likely to stand beside, shoulder to shoulder.

"Quinceton? Is that you?" Redgrave seemed confused until they made eye contact, and then he relaxed. "Learning to use your tongue in new ways, aren't you, my boy?"

It was the kind of bait that was maybe worth caring about if you could, but the here and now put him next to Natalie, with Dad upstairs—he had much more to fight for than his pride. But without them in the mix, if he were alone with Redgrave … it would come cold, as best it can be served.

"I wouldn't go and say all that," Quinceton answered. "Still just a 'Blue Flame Special.' But a lot of shots were fired downstairs, right? So what're you and your people after here, now?"

"Oh, Quinceton," Redgrave moaned. "If you have to ask, I'm worried you didn't learn as much as I thought you did in Stockton." Eyeballs now gazed at Quinceton from many directions, including those on his side of the barricade. Redgrave saw the faces turn; he meant for them to. He knew how to use words to direct people's attention, and some bodies with it.

"That's right," Redgrave announced to the quieting crowd. "That skinny guy up there was at the Battle of South Lake, caught squatting with known Anti-Anti-Racist Liberati afterwards and sent to my Stockton DIE Camp. So, did you tell them why the JSS government ordered the suicide mission attack on the gates of Nevada?"

There was some chatter at this, there having been no previous admission that the Battle of South Lake had been doomed from the start. In all his casual inquiries, Quinceton had only been able to glean that the Battle of South Lake was a known disaster of cowardice and slaughter. But no one ever had any details about its original intent.

The voices were mostly on Quinceton's side of the barrier. "You were there, yeah?" a white girl asked him with curious eyes. "Did you see a tall half-Asian, half-white guy there? He was in the aquatic landing team. Did you see a guy like that?"

All Quinceton could do was shake his head as Redgrave waited with the crowd's attention in his palm.

"But the aquatic team, you did see them there?"

"Yeah, I did. And, hate saying it, but they got trapped and abandoned on the enemy side. I doubt any made it out alive." Quinceton's voice carried out to the crowd, confirming his presence in South Lake, and risking the possibility they'd believe however Redgrave wanted to frame it.

"That's right, few of the soldiers survived," Redgrave continued. "But you did, didn't you, Quinceton? And then, how much warning did you raise about the manipulations ordered from the Secure Spaces here? How much awareness have you raised about the BIPOC bodies so carelessly tossed into the charnel house of South Lake Tahoe? What have you done with what you've learned to help those around you?" Natalie was looking at Quinceton, too, but with a different face than the rest.

"What I really mean to ask is …" Redgrave said slowly, "why should any of us trust a single word you have to say?"

Blood pumped with fierce independence throughout Quinceton's body; he took a deep breath and exhaled on his own time. There was no cougar charging at him, no incoming shrapnel or any immediate reason to duck and cover. Redgrave had seized the first-floor atrium with a bloody coup, with force and surprise being sufficient to overthrow the hollow, performative virtue signaling of Anti-Racist government. But here, to advance past the second-floor lobby, he had veered from the field of battle to a test of wits, conviction, and above all, salesmanship.

"I mean, would anyone else like to know why formerly perfect Knowing Leader Mumwaza Q. Jumping Bull ordered the attack on South Lake Tahoe?" Redgrave kept going, not wanting to cede momentum. "Or why one of its few survivors has so selfishly kept silent about the massacre to protect himself, at the expense of each and every one of you?"

Murmurs of curiosity ebbed in from all directions, including Quinceton's third-floor landing. Natalie squeezed his hand, which helped hold his composure. He expected some revelations to come and tried to anticipate the spin he'd have to use to redirect.

"I did what I did because I'm one of them," Quinceton said. Having made no gesture to anyone specific, he felt the need to clarify. "We're all in the same boat. I had no idea why soldiers were *really* there in South Lake, because no one in the city ever *really* tells you what's what." Redgrave tried to interrupt, but Quinceton had the high ground and shouted over him. "In New California, it's the people against the power, and who here has had real power? And how come those in power don't even have to explain to the people what happened in the Battle of South Lake?"

It was the first time Quinceton had seen Redgrave stammer, and he loved the sight of it. He'd ignored the image of Redgrave going ballistic in the Raley's parking lot as accumulated failures coalesced into a total loss of control, but this was the same Redgrave returning for the rematch. In all that time in Stockton, there had never been another opportunity to challenge his neo-knowing borderline personality.

"Stop!" Redgrave shouted. "Hold your Anti-Anti-Racist tongue, or you'll be put down like a dog before you ever make it back to Stockton!"

The masked people on the lobby floor held their weapons at their sides like those on Quinceton's floor, watching, waiting. It had to be the first time any of them had seen anything like a public debate or discussion of truth on a rational, rather than identitarian, basis. God only knew what each individual reliever and AAA/JJJ agent was thinking at that precise moment when everything could flip, and suddenly they had a moment to choose and act for themselves.

"Ideas are more convincing than identities," Quinceton answered, looking at the people nearby. "So call me 'Liberati,' if you want, but that only means I'm a 'normal, thinking person.'" Quinceton felt strangely at ease holding court up here. People were really listening to him, even Juniper, who Quinceton noticed on the lower lobby floor gazing up at him. Juniper was paralyzed by something, but it wasn't fear; she seemed ever more curious to hear the next word.

There were people behind Quinceton now, people who gave him a little room to allow direct eye contact with others down below. They were all listening to him, not stopping him, and paying no heed to Redgrave's paroxysm of threats below. One of them was his father, Horace, sidestepping a few younger people from the rear hallway to the upper floors. The elder Rift heard Redgrave's shouts at his son and chuckled, nodding softly.

"Sounds like you got him on the ropes," Dad called out, voice projecting confidently from the stomach, interrupting the Chairperson's stammer and actually quieting him for a moment. "Wanna finish off the fucker?"

"It's a very important decision you're making," Redgrave called from below. The words were clear but his voice wavered, and everyone could hear it. "All of you, not just the dead men who want to speak for you—all of you. Look where you are. You're trapped in the top floors of a building from which there are no exits. Do you even understand what it means to stand on the other side of that barricade, to fight against Social Justice? Is that what you want to be remembered for? Being shot like an American or an Anti-Anti-Racist in order to stop human progress, the equal future we all want, Social Justice itself?"

There was the phrase that set Quinceton off. The phrase he'd conceded to so many times, but not once more.

"Your Social Justice is servitude!" Quinceton shouted from whatever perch he stood on, regardless of how long it could be defended. "And it all keeps us dependent on the state, which the JSS government uses to justify all their power and policy. All that talk about guaranteeing and giving you this and that? It was mostly so you wouldn't do it for yourselves, so you'd need government permission for everything, including your self-worth. So now, next, about Redgrave: Why in God's name are you seeing a better world coming from this slave driver?"

Most of the faces downstairs were still masked, but Juniper's wasn't. Judging from her face, and those nearby, Quinceton had said something very startling. If the JSS or AAA/JJJ government had the authority of God, then Quinceton had just proclaimed himself the Devil, but none of these faces saw him that way. Even the white people—or maybe the white people especially; Quinceton couldn't be sure—looked at him with true reverence, as though he alone could be the savior to free them from some mental captivity. He felt the temptation of power, and thought about former Knowing Leader Mumwaza Q. Jumping Bull and former-former Knowing Leader Kendaoi. Then he looked at Natalie.

The ousted politicians were just human, or human men, like he was. If he didn't have Natalie to think about, hadn't had Bones and Sarah to live with, or hadn't had Dad to steer him, well, he could just as easily have tried to take these trusting faces in his own self-serving direction.

"Perhaps you missed it, but the old definitions of 'diversity,' 'equity,' and 'inclusion' are lying on the floor down there, bleeding out," Redgrave said with menacing enunciation as he stepped forward to directly address his own people. "The JSS government sent over a hundred associates of known Anti-Anti-Racists to prove their loyalty at South Lake Tahoe. That's why it happened: The Knowers had human capital they didn't trust. It's been forever since there was a tangible victory over the Americans or white supremacy to celebrate, and Mumwaza Q. Jumping Bull would rather have had a good view of the water than a poster advertising his obesity and obsolescence. That's it—'Go fight and die for our new living spaces,' basically. And without me, the liberator of Stockton first and now all of New California, you would never know it. None of you would have the opportunity to 'de-whiten' and shed all history of racial humiliation for the chance at a noble future."

Redgrave paused the speech but stepped farther into the spotlight, soaking up the attention. "A wise person once said the moral arc of the universe is long, but bends toward justice. I am that arc, and that Social Justice. Monarchy gives way to aristocracy, aristocracy to capitalism and the self-replicating managerial class, and from there we got the JSS, the world's first Social Justice government. We saw its flaws, for sure, and its evolution was inevitable, but core convictions emphasizing equality of identity were finally realized as a responsibility of the state. Now, under my direction, the true meaning of Social Justice will be unearthed, tended, and nurtured in careful preparation for a final, permanent bloom. Now, with the opportunity to de-whiten, I've created the basis for a fully open, equitable world."

Few understood what Redgrave was really saying, or knew the wise man who had mentioned the moral arc of the universe. But Quinceton had read about the American King—Dr. Martin Luther, a guy who hadn't wanted to judge or be judged by race—and Quinceton definitely didn't see Redgrave as a fitting extension of the moral universe's arc. The young soldier really didn't want a new messiah in town, and if one were to get the job, Redgrave might've been his last pick in all of New California.

Quinceton wanted to challenge Redgrave on the rationale behind the Battle of South Lake especially, but he couldn't count on anyone else being there, or his having the right words to assert the reality he saw over Redgrave's practiced spin. But a universal human truism had been brewing in his mind ever since he took up reading—it seemed to be in every story of human identity, both triumph and failure, and all over Dr. King's writing and speeches—and yet he'd never seen Redgrave talk about it. *Why do we need race at all?*

"But why do they need to 'de-whiten' in order to shed history? Whose history? And what race? And whose opinion of that race? And what do they need you for, to sort out?" Quinceton sputtered at the end, as he didn't want to confuse his audience but probably was anyway. "What I'm asking is, why do we need an idea like 'race' at all? What does New California stand to win by dividing us into competing groups? Why do we all want to jostle and beg for government favoritism?"

"Fool!" Redgrave shouted back. Quinceton didn't answer. He didn't actually move—all the better to keep Redgrave talking. "There has never been identitarian peace among identity groups—never," he asserted. "The JSS government tried to introduce that potential, and learning from their unfortunate failures is why we, their successors, will succeed. And it begins with a wider tent, one big enough to fit everybody—*that,* I've already expanded with 'de-whitening.' It's just that simple: once we flatten the social privilege out of people, we can all live in equitable harmony."

It was all such a steaming pile of shit, Quinceton didn't even want to touch the statement. He didn't actually mean to laugh, but he did, and he wasn't the only one.

"They've had you cowed," Quinceton spoke directly to the people: the 'workers,' the 'relievers,' the 'patients,' the 'volunteers,' the 'Periphery Calm' team—whatever they'd been dubbed that day. "And they're hoping they still do. Redgrave is betting on it, but there's nothing to fear when you're together. Isolating each of you, making you feel alone in your unique, somehow 'privileged' identity, that is where that fear comes from: the fear of being excluded and exiled from the people around you, the fear of being a pariah. The fear of being alone." He glanced at Natalie, then back at the people on his floor and below.

"Who are *you*?" Redgrave shouted from below, voice rising. "Who the hell are you, *Quinceton*, to preach your truth to anyone and think it should be believed?" The overall loss of momentum from the atrium stage to this lobby floor had devastated the Redgrave brand into something like indignant jealousy. It wasn't an empowered look for an ambitious politician.

"There is no *'my truth'!* There's no more or less truth in a statement based on whoever makes it. Your Standpoint Theory is bunk, bunk that values 'identity' over reason and brains." There was an audible gasp from the lobby below, and perhaps relief around him on level three, but either way Quinceton wouldn't stop now. "Now that I think on it, the Standpoint Theory idea that 'I feel, therefore it is' has got to be one of the dumbest, most doomed, most obvious methods of controlling people the world has ever seen fail. *'Lived experience,'* my goddamn nutsack! Anyone with a brain worth using can see the social hierarchy Standpoint created overnight, and no one, no matter how dense or gullible, *no one* wants their thoughts and words to be limited by the feelings of other people with a more valued, but still arbitrary identity."

Quinceton saw Juniper listening intently at the base of the escalator on the lobby floor. Her maskless face on the AAA/JJJ agents' level amplified Quinceton's sense of communal encouragement. She almost looked like she wanted to hop on and join them all on the third floor landing. It struck him that just a few months ago, it had been Juniper asking Quinceton to help her get ahead with Redgrave at Stockton.

"So bold, Quinceton," Redgrave hissed. "So bold, you've become." He raised both arms in an exaggerated shrug, rotating for the crowd. "And now that you've forced this standoff, what now? What's the plan here, Quinceton?"

Of course there was no plan, or if there was one, this was it, more or less. The question reminded the young sniper of that which made Redgrave a threat: he could see other people's weaknesses and exploited them with ruthless exactitude. Lacking a plan had never really bothered any of the old Liberati, those who might have seen this standoff coming, like Dad, because an official plan could be intercepted and interrupted. But the complete disorganization left the top-floor resistance movement without a leader, or any way to pick one. Redgrave, whose career was little more than flipping from one self-righteous lily pad to another, would see the power vacuum at the outset. Being addressed—and ever more frequently eyeballed—as though he were some kind of Knowing Leader emphasized in the young sniper's mind that he was not.

"I speak only for myself," Quinceton announced to the room spread before him. He hoped he wasn't truly just speaking for himself, but a humble admission seemed appropriate. "And I've got no plan beyond backing basic humanity over political identities until my dying day."

"Death is eternal," Redgrave answered, quiet and cold. "And so is Social Justice."

"Feel like a victim or live like an equal," Quinceton retaliated with simple words.

It all played out in another moment when time seemed to slow, becoming impervious to memory. And it was Juniper who started it all.

The first bang happened and Redgrave clutched his ear, crumpling; Juniper, pistol smoking in her hand, too dumbfounded to fire a second shot; bodies of lobby agents piling on top of her, hands on her throat …

The next shot came from above, on Quinceton's level, and clipped an agent piling onto the Juniper scrum. Dad's heavy hand pressed down on Quinceton's dome, forcing the teenage boy to take cover and avoid the next salvo; Natalie already lay on her belly, as the old man had done the same for her.

"Hold tight!" Quinceton screamed at Natalie, but there was no way to hear him, with two hands clasped over her ears and the echo of explosions ringing at every level of the high-ceilinged space. He fumbled for his earplugs and fit one into his left ear, but didn't want to risk saving himself from deafness only to catch a stray bullet. So, he kept flat, rifle at his side, just watching, waiting.

Behind his feet, on one knee and steadying his breath, Dad was in the fight. His rifle might've shot once or twice in the same direction before he'd duck again, pause a beat, and retake position to find a new target.

"Lights out," he mouthed after one shot. Dad had seen enough violence in his New California days to enjoy delivering some of his own Social Justice, and only partly because it helped the cause. He really seemed to hate from the bottom of his being, and while Quinceton could easily forgive him for such rage, the son didn't want to carry that kind of fury forever.

But he wasn't going to sit around and let others fight his fight, either, so Quinceton reached for the rifle, peeked over the railing on half an elbow, and gasped at the carnage. Most of the AAA/JJJ agents below had little cover to use except the corpses of their own fallen comrades, and if it weren't for so many casualties on Quinceton's side, too, he might have seen it as hopeful. But really, the only way to justify this sacrifice now was to resist, to successfully hold out against the agent hordes—to survive, regroup, and thrive.

Quinceton took aim at a masked agent shooting at something near the barricade, exhaled, and fired. The bullet passed cleanly through the agent's face, ending their loyalties, confusion, and contribution to the identitarian hierarchy game in one practiced pull. He watched his target fall in something like a trance before realizing that the shot had drawn attention from below. There weren't that many resisters left shooting on the third floor, as many had fallen or dragged their wounded farther into the interior.

A clump of agents seemed to register Quinceton as an active shooter threat simultaneously, and as they rotated in his direction, he caught a momentary glimpse of Redgrave crouched in a ball behind his bodyguards. Not far away, alone and still, eyes staring at the ceiling, lay Juniper. Quinceton didn't have time to really look at the body, but he didn't see any blood pooling, not even a trickle. The red ring around her neck saddened him somehow. Even with all the death and despair of the evening, the fact that Juniper had been strangled to death, singled out for personal, intimate extermination, felt particularly infuriating. She had figured it all out in the end, and just in time to become (or remain) a sacrificial lamb in a brand new world.

Something fell on Quinceton's leg, and Dad groaned from behind; the old man had been hit in the upper bicep and dropped his rifle. The grimace on his face was painful to witness, and all the worse if the shot had been meant for Quinceton.

"Fall back!" Quinceton called to the few remaining resisters crouched behind the barricade. "Fall back to the fourth floor—tighter staircase, easier to defend. Hustle! Fall back!" The white guy he'd seen earlier on the barricade lay flat on his belly, pointing toward the lobby agents with one hand, then opening two palms to the ceiling in the universal clueless-ness signal. Quinceton nodded, mouthed "I GOT YOU," rolled twice to his right for better position, and sprang up with his rifle roaring fire.

The eruption of sound that sprang from the young sniper's vacillat-ing spray proved convincing enough on its own, as Quinceton couldn't be sure he hit anyone, but he had forced a few key enemies back into cover. The barricade guy, rifle slung over his shoulder, dragged two other fallen resisters, each by one arm. Quinceton kept firing, making sure to dot the lobby landscape with intermittent explosions, effectively pinning the en-emy down with the help of two other resisters who'd seen the retreat and had a few more bullets to spend defending it. Quinceton was going to say something to Natalie, but she was behind him now, pulling Dad to his feet en route to the central staircase.

"Go—I'll cover you!" one of the other upright resisters shouted. Quinceton wiggled backward across the floor, ducking behind a hallway wall that led deeper into the interior galleries and roadblocks. He fired off a few shots to let the last resisters know he could be counted on to cover for them in turn, but the enemies on the lobby floor had concealed themselves, like Redgrave, and didn't have the bloodthirst to clip fleeing resisters.

"To the staircase!" Quinceton shouted at them as the last resister passed by. It was a womxn with light skin and dark hair—she didn't look at all like Sarah, but Quinceton thought about his friend anyway. The womxn stopped maybe a dozen feet past Quinceton, fell to one knee, and used her scope to scan the horizon.

"Go!" she commanded, and together they retreated to the foot of the third-floor staircase. Dad leaned against the base railing, huddled with a few bleeding resisters, not looking up as he waved everyone through. A bramble of furniture and scattered metal faced them at the top of the stairs on the fourth-floor landing.

"Hurry!" someone reminded them from upstairs. "No time—hurry!"

The injured resisters seemed content to present their injuries to the oncoming AAA/JJJ agents in a plea for forgiveness, but they didn't know how bad it was in Stockton.

"You don't want to be hostages," Quinceton warned. He knelt, turning to offer his back and his sweat. "Hop on, and hold my rifle—who's first?"

An older resister tried to prevaricate, as though staying here to be captured was some kind of magnanimous act of self-sacrifice.

"Negative," Quinceton said with serene conviction. "You're all coming upstairs, like it or not. There's no chance of finding you again when it comes time to liberate the DIE Camps. No way Redgrave is letting resisters leave, no matter how injured."

"Okay," the older one said, a womxn in her fifties clutching her left knee. "I can limp up. Take one of the teens." She motioned to three young relievers pulled fresh from the rickshaw line.

"Which of you is hit worst?" Quinceton demanded. "No heroes, now. We gotta move."

Two of the kids pointed to the one in the middle, a Black boy doubled over on himself, the only one not paying attention.

"Can you get on my back?" The kid finally looked up, and in his grimace of agony Quinceton realized they were about the same age.

"It hurts to walk," the teen murmured. "Hurts to move, man."

"Hit in the stomach?"

The teen nodded.

"Alright, then, I'm carrying you." Quinceton hung the rifle around his neck and moved in with arms wide. "C'mon, man, this has gotta happen. Think of all the big asses you hauled around the city. This ain't shit. Someone, somewhere, owes you a lift now." He turned to Dad, who kept a hand over his arm wound, but otherwise watched in silence.

"You can get yourself up there, right?" Quinceton asked his father. The old man didn't answer; he just sort of shrugged in a half smile, which meant yes.

The teen relented as well, and Quinceton picked him up like a big heavy tray of Elect cutlery, laboring to keep his weight centered as he carried the former reliever up dozens and dozens of stairs. It was a long climb, but with adrenaline and all these eyes watching, it was easier than he'd expected, and when he arrived at the top, a path through the next bramble had already been cleared.

"Keep it open—these last few!" Quinceton didn't see whoever spoke, but the whole fourth-floor barricade seemed to watch the last retreating resisters coming up the staircase from the third. He had to duck, but Quinceton squeezed through the middle of the mess without banging anything critical. His father and the other walking wounded followed dutifully behind, with an eerie quiet filling the emptiness of the evacuated base at the bottom of the steps.

"They behind you? Redgrave and his goons?" Quinceton asked one of the last arrivals, the young womxn who reminded him of Sarah.

"I didn't see anything down there. Didn't hear anything useful, either." She shook her head, seeming to share the same worry. "But that doesn't mean they've giving up. They'll be here eventually, probably soon."

"If we can just shake them off Redgrave, break that link, then this is over," Quinceton said, trying to reassure them all. He wasn't even sure if he believed it himself—there was still no plan, obviously—but they all needed something to aim for.

"Defensive positions, take cover!" someone called out on their floor. "Wounded to the back, guns to the front! I hear them coming." The voice fell at the last words as the resisters watched the first line of bulletproof AAA/JJJ agents march in a row toward the foot of the staircase, four of them with black SWAT Mostly Peaceful Protest gear so thick, their shoulders touched each other and blocked the whole hallway. These black helmets, riot shields, and batons had to have been mothballed at the outset of the Defund Police/Liberate Jails movement, but as Redgrave knew where all the best bodies were buried, he could have saved such equipment for just the right time.

"We're through—close the barricade, lock it down!" Quinceton told the nearby survivors, helping them push the last few tables into place. The whole mess looked pretty makeshift compared to the Mostly Peaceful Protest armor, but it was about all they had.

Quinceton took position opposite the barricade, overlooking the battlefield staircase from the side. The first line of invaders—four black-clad agents progressing in lockstep—ascended from the bottom when the next identical wave formed into place. Reserves of AAA/JJJ agents were concealed underneath Quinceton's current landing, and he assumed there to be at least a couple dozen remaining to carry out Redgrave's commands.

And as for Stockton's Finest, the successful coup-plotter—he was nowhere to be seen but could be heard everywhere. In fact, it was the return of Redgrave's aggressive assertions that gave immediacy to the showdown they all expected.

"… goddamn murdering Racists and homophobes and white supremacists—all of them! Suit up and get in line, and don't stop decolonizing until you reach the fucking roof! Every single one of them! Social Justice t'day, Social Justice t'morrow, Social Justice fo-ever!"

"Conserve your ammo," someone on their side said. "Those shields and that armor, it's all bulletproof." The SWAT guys had their third line loaded on the staircase already and were closing in steadily, their front row almost halfway up.

"I have extra." Quinceton had almost forgotten the extra ammo bag that swayed from his belt.

"Even so, we're going to have to get creative." It was Dad's voice, still hopeful and steady as ever. "There's a better chance of breaking their spirit than killing them all anyway. Someone help me get behind that barricade."

Immediate agreement led to a reshuffling of positions, with a number of men crouching low behind the makeshift blockade. Quinceton could have joined in; they would have made room, and his first instinct was to back his father's play. But he was a trained sniper, and even Sarah had had wider shoulders than he did.

Quinceton crept along the low wall to choose a perch facing the staircase with a birds-eye view from above, overlooking the attack from an elevated rear. Shields and body armor weren't so useful when flanked from behind. From this height, it wasn't hard to see flesh in between protective plates.

"Hold!" Redgrave commanded from underneath Quinceton. The AAA/JJJ general hid well in the rear, obscured by his goons and the ceiling. But with his frontline halfway up the staircase, and the opposition poised to bomb the bejesus out of them with the crushing momentum of office tables and chairs, perhaps there was a moment to reconsider this costly incursion. Or maybe he just missed the spotlight.

"Before we claim additional life in our eternal crusade to rid the world of white supremacy, transphobia, and all other forms of identitarian bigotry, I beseech you, the resisters: Why? Why, truly, do you hide in the rafters, like rats pushed to the top mast of a sinking ship?"

The statement was met by stares behind the barricade that didn't look for Quinceton's approval. He was back to being a sniper—background protection, with the ability to decide life and death for his targets, assuming they didn't scope him first. The acoustics of the high ceilings and marble floors made it all the more important to keep voices low, and whatever the resisters on his side were deciding, Quinceton couldn't hear it. But that he would back it with lethal force, regardless of outcome, there was no doubt.

"... do you propose?" It was Dad's voice. He stood, presumably to face Redgrave man to man. "We've seen a lot of violence already, and I don't think any of us really know what it's all for. So now, you: Why do you want to get up here, and what do you want from us? If you can promise our freedom, and prove it by not bullshitting us even one more time, then okay, we'll throw down the weapons and give up."

Quinceton liked how simply his Dad spoke. It made Redgrave's opaque pronouncements all the more hollow and performative. It also forced Redgrave to think, or at least to pause, as they all waited for an answer to the most basic of questions—basically, "Can you not bullshit us just this once?" The front line of SWAT waited in the middle of the stairs, with two more rows behind them and untold reserves Quinceton couldn't see from his perch.

"I propose you drop this senseless revolt and join us. I propose you remember where you, a Black man, came from, and the hundreds of years that America—"

"*Heave!*" Dad shouted and the barricade lurched forward, propelled by however many sets of shoulders that would rather avalanche the enemy than carry another load of lies for their own safety.

Quinceton didn't wait for the first table to drop; he took aim at an AAA/JJJ stooge in the second row, saw a flash of neck skin, exhaled, and fired. The AAA/JJJ loyalist, as a traitor to all human freedom, fell forward on the steps as the first chair tumbled down the long, crowded flight of steps. Once again, the bang of one rifle served as the opening salvo to an organized, delineated, predictable clusterfuck.

For the briefest of moments, Quinceton could hear the scrape of office furniture being shoved over the marble of the fourth floor. As a long desk peered at the SWAT folk and then charged, many on the lower steps hopped the railing; the middle steps became a gauntlet of projectiles with a far steeper escape hatch.

This emerging no-man's-land forced an immediate fight-or-flight response from its trapped agents of conformity. Those who didn't bail pressed against the sides of the stairwell, some raising their weapons in desperation, but it was too late for most.

Though his first instinct after firing was to duck, having the enemy surrounded from above with an enfilade of steady fire significantly reduced the possibility of a coordinated response. At such times, some risk was worth it. The SWAT goons didn't make anything of the time God gave them, so they were the Devil's business now.

But when the first smoke canister went off on the fourth floor, Quinceton knew that their defenses wouldn't hold long. It was also an obvious volley to make by the enemy—being cut down on the stairwell assault was pretty wasteful, even for Redgrave. The smoke grenade would shroud the attack, blind the defense, and hinder anyone not wearing a mask.

"They're flanking us!" Quinceton heard someone shout from behind, somewhere in the far rear of the fourth floor. "They restarted the elevators! They'll hit us from behind!" Incoming fire sprang up from below, the barricade pretty much spent as projectiles covered for the stairwell invaders, Dad and Natalie on the other side, smoke billowing from the floor ... Quinceton couldn't see any position worth clinging to any longer.

"Upstairs!" he cupped his hand to mouth to shout across the vibrating stairwell. "Retreat upstairs! Natalie! You listening? Can you hear? Dad! Retreat!"

He couldn't see any faces in the smoke, but he recognized the voice.

"Follow us—this way!" It was Natalie. Quinceton dropped to his hands and knees and crawled back to his people below the fourth-floor guardrail. He had to weave through injured resisters, but there was no use trying to escape the bloody grime of combat.

He reached the end of the low protective wall toward Dad and saw the massive hole where the barricade had once been. There were a few resisters left firing from cover, but their defensive position had been spent in order to buy just this much time. The guy from downstairs, the white guy who'd helped Natalie get through the third-floor bramble, watched Quinceton with a resigned detachment from several feet away. His rifle lay limp in his lap as smoke canisters filled the air with the omen of another attack.

"Hey, wake up!" Quinceton shouted at him. His eyes darted around the clouded air, then fell back on Quinceton.

"We're dead," he answered weakly. "We took our shot. There is no plan."

"Didn't you hear?" Quinceton clapped in his face and shouted back with all the false confidence he could muster. "They got word out to Pithawalla! Only a matter of time before we're rescued. We just gotta find a position we can defend, hold out a little longer." There was a serious lack of credulity on the part of his fellow resister, but Quinceton pushed on with the hope his father had mentioned ever so briefly, and without much faith.

"They still remember us in America, they really do," he went on. "Pithawalla and his people, they're coming one day. Maybe not, like, in five minutes, but eventually. We're proving we're still worth it, that there's still plenty of people left here worth saving, and they'll see, somehow. You want to go out sitting here, pass away nice and easy, or you want to take your last shot fighting next to people caught in the same trap? Go out with a full-on 'Fuck You'?"

The guy looked at Quinceton with energized, believing eyes as the sniper hunted out a way to close him.

"Fight with us, brother."

The resister nodded.

A pause in gunfire filled the void when Quinceton stopped speaking, until the garbled sound of Redgrave's command voice trying to regroup invaded from downstairs. The white guy wiped one of his eyes, then the other, and kept nodding at Quinceton.

"I'm with you guys," he said. "Why the heck not? Here we go."

Some visibility cleared without new incoming smoke bombs, and across the hall, Dad lay against a wall with Natalie kneeling next to him. He still bled from his bicep but had been hit somewhere lower now, too, somewhere worse. Quinceton crawled over, the sounds and smells of human failure now muted to his senses.

"How bad is it?" he asked Natalie. Dad would probably downplay the hit, but she wouldn't.

"It's bleeding pretty bad," she said, her expression worried. "Maybe hit an artery in the leg."

"It was just a ricochet, I promise you." Dad attempted a brave face as he tried to stand, pushing against the wall to relieve weight on the leg, but it wasn't happening. Somewhere below, Redgrave was shouting over the commotion of another reorganization: "in cold blood" and "leaderless" were among the words Quinceton could actually decipher.

The wide-eyed white guy looked at Dad with dread, and it was impossible to blame him. Wounded were little more than liabilities from here on out. But it was the last family Quinceton had left, and life can't always be about practical concerns.

"Hey, man, need help here," Quinceton said. The guy knew who and what he was talking about. "Just help me lift him to the roof. We can set up a final defense there."

"Until Pithawalla and them come to the rescue," Dad hoped out loud. A couple of resisters crouching nearby heard these famous syllables, and more than just their heads perked up at the name. Dad noticed, and didn't waste the attention. "That's right!" he yelled down at Redgrave, voice echoing in the tall, slick gallery space. "We got Pithawalla incoming! That's the truth and freedom of the world, coming for your Neolithic asses! So tough with your SWAT plastic!"

They all heard him, upstairs and below. Everyone heard him. The resisters around him didn't have to believe every word to put faith in the promise of redemption. Hopefully, and with luck, they could be saved— they could be people again.

"What can I do?" It was the dutiful white guy, along for the ride now, but with an earnestness Redgrave could never inspire. "Like, how can I help?"

"Each one of you get under a shoulder," Natalie directed. "Give me your guns—you're going to have to carry him up at least one flight of steps as long as this one." She meant the steps nearby, the perilous ladder from third to fourth floor that now served as a warning to everybody, on both sides, and would have to be climbed again by all to the fifth floor and the roof above.

Horace Rift didn't try to protest as his son and the other resister bent to lift him from the ground, and actually helped the effort by leaning on his aids with their much younger legs. With hidden pain and zero complaints, the three men stood, Natalie kicking debris out of their path as the four resisters trudged to the foot of the next long staircase up.

Quinceton initially brightened to see so many resisters waiting at the bottom of the next flight, but recoiled at the increased responsibility required to include their unfortunate souls in some eventual escape. Even though he, Dad, and Natalie were rising farther and farther in the MOMA building, Quinceton hadn't forgotten the point of it all: to flee this madness with those he cared about. He couldn't help feeling some compassion for the other resisters, those who had found themselves trapped between a successful coup plot and a disorganized rabble for whom the word "plan" was a laughably absurd concept. Quinceton wanted them to survive, too, and that they were still breathing and looking to him for guidance made him feel that he should provide some.

"It's almost over now, guys," Quinceton said, voice calmer than he expected. "I can't make any promises, but word is that Pithawalla knows about us, and we've got to hold out somewhere he can reach from above, like the roof." The faces that peered back at him weren't putting much stock in a California refugee whose legend had shriveled to myth in recent years, so Quinceton considered a new tactic.

"I mean, we aren't doing so bad, right?" The question seemed to lift spirits far better than any Pithawalla pledge. "Just us, a clump of regular joes, in the middle of another bloody identity politics takeover, not wanting any of it. Don't you see? We are the sane people. That's our saving grace, right? To all who would attack us from here on out, we are the brave version of the JSS government servants, or the AAA/JJJ goons, or the happy, rich American Elect that preceded them. We are everybody, essentially, who ignores identity to see humanity—just that. Humanity."

There was a pause as the group absorbed the message.

"Did we break and run after the first shots, or the next fight in the lobby, or when we avalanched their SWAT?" Quinceton asked. "Hell no. We're together now, we're regular people. And maybe we're pulling this straight out of our asses, but we're regular people."

"And ended probably most of them no problem," an intense young Black womxn said as she refilled a clip with rifle rounds.

"I know we have no plan, but do they?" an older Latino asked. "Does Redgrave? If we knew his plan, we could plan around it."

"I think we can say for sure that this isn't going according to however he wanted it," Quinceton thought out loud. "Maybe the coup downstairs, taking out Mumwaza—*that* was the plan. And that part worked, probably even better than Redgrave and them planned it. But he didn't expect our resistance, and it seems to be driving him crazy. They took real losses in the lobby fight, and on the steps down there—"

Gunfire interrupted Quinceton, the sound reverberating from somewhere in the bowels of the building. Distracted by his speech, it took Quinceton a minute to add up the clue.

"That's not us, is it?" he asked, looking back down the hall from whence they'd come. A number of bystanders assured him in the negative.

"Yeah, that sounded like it came from way down below," Natalie confirmed. "I didn't see any resisters sticking around when we left."

"Okay, then music to our ears, maybe. With luck, there's some pissed off people in Redgrave's ranks, and with all those delicate suckers to manage, the inevitable infighting and platforming of de-centering stuff may have arrived early. This is good news, guys. They're coming, eventually, but we already knew that, and any shooting that isn't at us is a good sign. So let's not just sit here getting old and watching our hair fall out—to the roof, everybody!"

Some looked ready to cheer just then, and Natalie intercepted their team spirit with a well-timed "Shuuushhh!" Quinceton's father grinned softly at the scene, despite his wound.

"I'm ready, son, when y'all are," he said. "You got 'em oriented the right way, I think. Nothing else you can say to tell 'em what's what. So let's get to it."

"Word." It was all Quinceton had to say. The coachable white guy heard the exchange and was ready to help with lifting the old man. Dad stood with a grimace, doing his damnedest to soldier on stoically, but bleeding too much to pretend otherwise.

Quinceton knew the climb from the fourth to fifth floors was excruciating for his father, and a number of resisters passed them on the steps, usually with a word or two of encouragement. "You're almost there!" the

Latino man said when they were barely halfway up. "You don't need any-one. You got this." The guy stopped, waited, then hovered behind them, and looked ready to catch all three bodies should they fall backwards.

They were among the last of the surviving resisters to reach the fifth floor. When they did, the questions and scattered information started up before they had a chance to off-load Dad onto a bench, or even a decent piece of wall to slump against.

"They right behind you?" and "We're running low on nine millimeter" and "No first aid kits in any of the bathrooms" and "Do you see any sign of Pithawalla up here?"—it was all too much at once. Quinceton hadn't asked for this gig. He was just trying to get his people out in one piece while they still had some life left to spend.

"What do I look like, like I got a plan?" he asked back loud enough for them all to hear, still propping Dad up. "Past this point, I don't know my balls from my asshole. We're all just making do, however we can, with whatever we got, and I wouldn't expect any more stuff than what you're holding now. So someone, anyone, can you lead us to the roof? Everyone follow, help us fortify whatever we find up there, but there are no prom-ises. The hope of them burning out before they reach us is probably the best bet. They can't have too many loyal soldiers left, and Redgrave has to spend more and more of whatever credibility he has to keep them going."

"Let's hold out," some middle-aged Latina reliever said.

"A little longer is all we need," another worker added.

"I know a way to the roof," an elder white womxn announced. Her robes were Elect, but no one interrupted. "We may need to break a lock or two, but there's a way through the fifth floor."

"Go," Quinceton urged. "Lead on. We're behind you." Dad loomed heavily on his mind, and his frame seemed to gain weight with every pass-ing minute.

The womxn took them down a few hallways, still adorned with graph-ic JSS government art depicting violence from America's past. It was a fitting gauntlet of New California propaganda to withstand en route to their chosen demise at the hands of the coup-plotters, or to remember as they fought and figured a way to freedom. Either way, the Blacks he saw being whipped by Southern whites were not his only ancestors in the paintings and sculptures. The slave drivers were, too, just the other side of the same humanity—the side that excuses all acts of violence for their own security, employment, or sense of belonging. It wasn't all racial; it was just regrettably human. That was the common threat, and their shared path to salvation.

There was another loud bang from downstairs, then three more in short succession, and then the clear sound of Redgrave's voice, yelling in a frantic alto pitch. From the sound of it, and their distance from the voice, Quinceton hoped the AAA/JJJ faction leader was threatening someone from his own dwindling army. Perhaps, and with luck, Redgrave was struggling to keep all his SWAT goons pointed in the same direction.

Progress halted at a locked door with "ROOF ACCESS" written on it. As he was toward the rear of the refugee corridor, Quinceton was told that someone else had made off for a fireman hatchet or some other tool that could crack the lock, and that they should wait.

"Put me down," Dad asked, and they did. He slouched against a wall, breathing heavily. Quinceton wandered over to Natalie and the locked door, accepting reluctantly that there was nothing he could do to help crack it open. When he turned again, his father was shaking hands with his other carrier, who now sat on the floor cross-legged.

"Spencer," the white guy said. "I never really thought about it, to be honest with you. I've got family here in the city, and though it's a constant pain in the ass, my parents are too old and stubborn to immigrate anywhere." The guy caught a look from Dad, and the next time he spoke his tone added some defensiveness to it. "They don't buy into it, the JSS government or any of the victim and oppressor stuff, but you know, some people are just too set in their hometown."

"I hear you, Spencer," Dad said. "I'm Horace. You met my boy there— Quinceton's his name—and he knows a place up in the mountains, and we could always use some extra hands. You think about it, that's all I'm saying."

The guy sputtered in flattery as Quinceton heard metal against metal and turned to see the roof door crowbarred open. He checked to ensure it could open wide enough to fit the three of them through, and when his attention returned to his medic-evacuation detail, the white guy stuck his hand out in an assuming imposition, but somehow still friendly.

"Spencer," he said with a smile. "Your father was telling me about … well, I don't know, but let's finish this thing. And maybe after, we can team up, or you'll let me tag along for the cabins in the mountains." They shook hands.

"Yeah, man." Quinceton thought his words sounded welcoming enough, and was honestly kinda glad the guy could be coming with them. Assuming he'd bring his own lady, or that they could find others—he didn't know how long a friendship could last between two guys with only one Natalie around, and frankly didn't want to find out.

Lifting Dad to his feet again brought more attention to his wounds. His old man tried to play it cool, but he wouldn't last the night bleeding like this, from both his upper arm and somewhere on his leg. Whatever it was they were waiting for would have to happen soon.

Natalie held the roof door as wide as it would stretch as the three soldiers pressed through, stumbling over each other's feet as they climbed the steps. This last staircase wasn't nearly so long as the others, but it was far narrower, and when they finally reached the open-air top floor, Quinceton sagged to see so little of anything to hide and fight behind on their final battlefield.

At least it was deserted, save for a pair of those blue-eyed fist-sized insects, whose silent buzzing cleansed some anxiety from the downstairs ugliness. Then another few of the same bugs swooped in from the side of the building, as if they were coordinating to meet on the roof for a big party. But there wasn't time to worry about such small things.

"Sitting ducks," someone said, and they were right. There were a few vents, a boxy old air-conditioning unit that took up a lot of space in a corner, and no other obvious barricades to shoot behind. Quinceton couldn't hear anything from the interior, just the soft sound of the city breathing, in short distant howls and a low moaning from the gutters. The crowds of

MOMA Momalla Gala onlookers, likely bribed by some food handout to attend by some faceless JSS government official who now lay dead in the atrium, had dispersed long ago, and were no doubt spreading word that the city was considering new management, if not up for grabs entirely.

A black resister in reliever garb whom Quinceton recognized from downstairs burst through the roof door with a sharp "Yo!" The twenty or so remaining survivors waited for him to catch his breath, and as he did so, they heard a volley of gunfire from downstairs.

"Redgrave is rallying downstairs," he said, panting and looking around the small patch of turf and the twenty or so people packed onto it for a last stand. "And they'll be here in a couple minutes. This all we got?"

Plenty of bystanders answered in the affirmative, and as the group discussed ways to bar the door, Natalie appeared and found Quinceton's hand with hers. They wandered to the ledge and gazed east, across the bay toward the darkness of Oakland, where most lights had gone out long ago.

"You did really great down there," Natalie said, giving his knuckles a squeeze. "And you know, when you were covering the fourth floor staircase from the other side, well, your dad … he told me he was so proud of you."

"Yeah? What for?"

"He didn't tell me, exactly, but yeah really, he said it. I just wish you could have been there to hear it. But then if you had, I don't know if he still would have said it … boys, and their feelings, and talking about them …"

Quinceton listened but didn't know what to say, or what to do about any of it now. If he hadn't been sharing the experience with Dad and Natalie, he'd never have gotten this far. And if he hadn't met Sarah, then Bones, then Tinh and Mai, he might never have learned to see people for whoever they really were.

Quinceton searched for America with his eyes, knowing it was eons away, far beyond Tahoe—the farthest he'd been able to reach. He couldn't add any feelings to the equation; he hadn't seen enough of the world to know how he should feel about the pettiness and fragility of New California. All he felt was shame. Shame that they'd been able to hoodwink him for so long, shame that he'd played into it for a time, and shame for all the abuse that ghouls like Redgrave had already gotten away with. Justice for such social treason was linguistically impossible—what with "Social Justice" being among the first casualties of language—but now, in this final gasp, they had actually introduced the possibility of such a thing. Even at the cost of everything, and however brief, it was an achievement to cherish.

"What … are those lights in the sky?" someone said to Quinceton's right, looking over another side of the building.

"To the south!" another announced, and they all rushed to that side of the building, facing Los Angeles and Mexico.

And there they were: a string of lights weaving through the night in a choreographed arc of technological might. The dark towers of San Francisco's repurposed commerce buildings reflected far more dots than Quinceton appreciated at first, and as they approached the vertical obstacles of the city's tallest neighborhood, the shapes began to separate, casting light on each other and making the flying warships visible to all who'd collected on the top floor.

"They're helicopters!" Quinceton shouted to the rest, not trying to contain his elation. He could scarcely believe he could use the word "helicopter" in the present tense. It was one of many inventions requiring resources to function that New California couldn't reproduce—oil, in most cases, and certainly the common limitation on motorized transportation—so under the JSS government, they existed only in picture books and graveyards of metal. It seemed cosmically appropriate that the night the JSS was toppled he should see his first active helicopter in flight.

"Hey, no—don't shoot!" Dad was heated at some young guy, and Quinceton didn't blame him; anyone who would aim at their saviors deserved to go over the edge. But at least they didn't hear a shot go off. "Those are Pithawalla's choppers coming to save us. Holy hell, that's our goddamn air support! You all got that?"

"We can't anyway," the teenager answered sheepishly. "The triggers don't pull. I'm serious. Our guns don't work. Just aim anywhere and shoot if you want to prove me wrong."

Quinceton pointed his rifle at the bay and tried to fire, but the trigger wouldn't budge. Even adding his middle finger to his index finger couldn't generate the pressure to discharge. A few other voices confirmed their similarly fossilized weaponry.

"So what are we, sitting ducks now?" the teenager asked, his voice rising with worry. They could all hear commotion churning in the MOMA building. They weren't predominantly explosions anymore but the scrape of metal on marble, and a whole lot of yelling.

The helicopters fanned out behind the first, their leader painted black and slowing as it headed directly for their patch of roof. It rose and leveled itself, hovering some hundred feet above the now-defenseless survivors.

Quinceton stepped forward and cupped his hand to aim the sound at the door to the staircase. "Pithawalla's landing a warship on the roof!" he screamed with all his might. "Best watch out!"

"They can't hear you," Natalie reminded him. "They can't hear a thing from in there, not against that thing." She pointed to the helicopter, and Quinceton realized she was unquestionably correct.

The crowd had instinctually cleared the center of the roof for the chopper to land on, and as the other helicopters treaded water in a loose aerial circle overhead, Quinceton hustled to the edge for a better look. This first helicopter seemed much smaller than the others, and the doors opened mid-descent. Two camo-clad soldiers waved casually from the scene, seemingly at Quinceton himself.

"Hey!" he shouted back, not thinking about who could really hear. "We're about to be overrun by the goddamn Anti-Anti-Anti-Racists! They're right behind that door. Help us!"

The helicopter parked on the roof and the two soldiers disembarked, flanked by four more on the other side. Only two of them carried sidearms, shaped more like ovals than regular guns in a design he'd never seen before, and two were unarmed, showing their palms to the crowd in some kind of calming maneuver. The last two soldiers held small recording cameras, filming the curious encounter. One of the soldiers who had waved at Quinceton flipped up his visor, exposing a smiling light-skinned face, and stuck out his hand.

"Quinceton Rift, my man. Always wanted to meet you. Anyway, Redgrave and them, it's no sweat, dog. You just relax."

"What … my name … who are you?" Quinceton sputtered as he accepted the soldier's palm for a shake so weak it didn't really count. "And they're right behind that door! Are you even listening to me? They're armed and coming here … like, now!"

"You see those?" the soldier said, pointing to one of the oval weapons. "They have magnetic disruptors on them; that's why your guns don't shoot. So the new slave camp guy, Redgrave, you don't have to stress about his sticks and stones, man. You got it made now, Quinceton." The other soldiers had more success calming the remaining survivors, as some made for the helicopter and climbed in.

"Who are you? And how the hell do you know my name?"

"We're Americans. We've all been watching you for months now. You ever notice certain mechanical bugs and animals that always seemed like they're buzzing around windows and from above? That's how we keep tabs on you guys, so we'd know when to come back. And you did it, brother—here we are. Game over now. You won."

Natalie wandered over to listen as the first load of survivors made off in the full helicopter and another fixed to land in the same place.

"What is the game?" she asked. "And what were you waiting for? Who was waiting?"

"Hey, all fair questions," the soldier said, raising his voice so others nearby could hear too. "Pithawalla funded the beginning of this, for the moment when crazy California would burn out on its own steam and be ready to rejoin us. There's no sense coming in guns blazing, Nam-style, trying to wipe out everybody you actually wanna save. They always needed a Quinceton: a guy to disrupt the whole thing, to create the next power vacuum so when we arrive, the people are ready for a new mindset. One that doesn't pit everyone against each other, and so forth."

"So this is all a rescue mission?" Natalie asked. "You're here to save us, or you're here to set up a new government, and everything else?" There was banging against the roof door—it had to be Redgrave or his goons, but the threat seemed almost obsolete. Like the temptation to stop talking when you had something real to say just because you didn't officially have the race, lived experience, or venis to say it. Overhead, there was another one of those oversized bugs buzzing around.

"Not exactly," the soldier hesitated. "I mean, yes, we are here to rescue you—that's affirmative. The next government, though? They didn't tell me. I just know what everyone else knows about the power vacuum."

"I guess what I'm asking is," Natalie shouted, raising her voice and leaning forward, "who is in charge of you guys? Jumping Bull replaces Kendaoi, Redgrave replaces Jumping Bull, you replace Redgrave, but who are you? Is Pithawalla paying for all this just to replace Redgrave himself?"

The second full helicopter closed its doors and the rotators quickened, making speech near impossible. There was a chance for words in between the next one landing, but it wouldn't last too long.

"Look," the soldier said to Natalie, with Quinceton listening in, "I don't know more than they tell me, and I know Pithawalla's paying for a lot of it, but there's a whole other financing angle I can't possibly explain. Anyway, no one person is planning to take power any time soon, and it won't be Pithawalla—he's, like, ninety. And anyone from the outside would have no traction, I think, with the local population—they can't know how to speak to New Californians, not like you can. But the money—the money paying for this—most all the money is totally neutral."

He pointed to the insect above, nearly the size of a fist, that had stopped some eight feet above Quinceton. "Those, actually, pay for most of this, to be honest."

"W-what? How?" Quinceton stammered.

"I can explain all that later—it's not simple," the soldier answered. "And your Dad here, he needs help."

"Yeah, he really does." Spencer, the survivor who'd helped carry the old man up here, spoke directly to Quinceton. "And I gotta be real: I think they're legit. Yo, I think we take the life-saving rescue, y'know what I'm saying?" It was a convincing point, given the circumstances.

"But how do you know he's my father?" Quinceton demanded of the fancy new soldiers before even considering that they were both totally right about Dad. The old concerns—even the ones he still really, really cared about—seemed to dull in the presence of these alien people and their warships.

"We've been watching you since South Lake. There are millions of hidden cameras to record what goes on here, and then people choose which people to follow and what clips to keep and edit out. It's a television show, Quinceton, what we would call 'reality TV.' The biggest in the country, and you, bro, you're the star of the last six months!"

It was too much at one time. It didn't seem possible in a thousand different ways, none more discouraging than the idea that Quinceton was unique, important, or known outside his own small social circles and these scattered survivors.

"What … how do you record us without us knowing?"

"You know those big harmless bugs the size of a grapefruit? They're just disguised cameras to record stuff, typically outside the city. Here, there's plenty of old recording equipment to tap into, and places to hide anything else they need to see what's going down."

There was a loud slam against the roof door. Redgrave would meet his successors soon enough, and that was fine by Quinceton.

"You buying this?" he asked Natalie.

"Yeah, I really am," she said. "Look at all the power they have, and yet they don't use it to control us. The recording and paying for it don't make sense, but I think they might actually help us anyway. I'm not sure. But I think so."

"Let's get to it, son." Dad breathed slowly, but held on with intentional poise. "They sure ain't Anti-this-and-that centering the decentered centralization system of centered centralizing. Even if their words make no sense, their tools work, and they don't lead with their dumbest ideas—so at least you know they aren't from California. As good a reason as any to trust 'em."

As soon as Quinceton nodded to the skyship soldier, the guy called "Medic!" Another uniformed soldier with a red-and-white symbol on his chest hurried over with a different mechanical contraption about the size of a stray cat. In a flash, the thing was pulling lead from Dad's leg, dropping a flattened bullet on the blacktop roof next to them, and replacing the metal with white gauze and a bandage. It wasn't fixed, but it would hold through the evacuation.

Natalie picked up the discarded bullet fragment quickly. "A souvenir, from our time here," she said, taking Quinceton's hand once again. "Could be worth something in the big new world."

The soldiers offered to help carry the wounded Rift to the next escape chopper, but both Rifts turned them down. Spencer offered to carry the same shoulder he'd lifted to get the old man up here, but the roof wasn't so big, and the chopper was nearby.

"You get on, and we'll meet you there," Quinceton told him.

"And you know, Spencer, thanks for all you did for us down there," Dad said, his voice genuine.

"No problem," the survivor answered, not fully grasping the impact of Dad's words.

"No, really," Quinceton continued for his father. "You showed up for us, not knowing us, not having the same skin or God-knows-what identity. So, seriously, thank you."

Spencer nodded, and the deeper message seemed to register. He was a New Californian, too—he knew all the reasons why they were supposed to hate and distrust each other. He knew the challenge and rarity of transgressing such things.

"Yeah, well, glad you got us all here. Wasn't me, man." He smiled. "Catch you on the flip side. We'll all get food and joke on Redgrave and those JSS fools."

"Word," Quinceton agreed, giving him a fist bump. The dude turned and answered a boarding call to fill the last seats on the currently landed helicopter, but there would be another.

As he watched Spencer hand over his rifle and climb aboard, Quinceton felt certain they'd hang out again, and he also felt strangely confident they'd have a similar sense of humor, or at least see the same New California targets to laugh at. The rotors sped up, wind churning around them, and in a flash the great contraption lifted, reoriented itself midair, dipped its nose, and took off in a direction, likely south, for the great wasteland metropolis of Los Angeles.

There was more banging on the roof exit door, but whatever threat Redgrave posed seemed muted by all this advanced weaponry and the confidence that came with it.

Dad lurched to his feet with a companion boost to both his arms, and Quinceton helped manage one side of his weight as the next chopper dropped carefully into place. Only three survivors remained that Quinceton hadn't spoken to directly, and they waited as the wounded Rift eased onto a kind of flat stretcher inside the craft. The bandage would hold, just as this helicopter would fly. Whatever this new plan was, it would work because of the people behind it.

"All aboard?" a pilot called from the cockpit, then all sound was overwhelmed by the wind tunnel of choreographed slicing blades.

Except the roof door back to the MOMA didn't hold. It burst off in one more fateful blunder, all spiraling from the same megalomania. Redgrave's count of loyal followers had dwindled to six.

The chopper rocked as the wheels touched off, and in that moment Quinceton's eyes met Redgrave's once more. Some dynamic had changed, and not only because the ex-servant's burning fury had all but extinguished into a muted pity; it was the look on Redgrave's face that confirmed it. He glared from the Quinceton to the futuristic American soldiers, back to Quinceton, and to the helicopter, then to the other dancing lights in the sky, all foretelling the same, near-guaranteed outcome of this Earth-shaking SOMA MOMA Momalla Gala Massacre. No doubt Redgrave's entire universe had been contained within these walls just seconds earlier, everything of any import at his grasp and within reach so long as he could just appease those pesky last few holdouts … and now he looked like the guy who didn't get invited to the party, watching the last bus leave for infinite festivities.

"Wait!" he shouted at them in psychopathic envy. "Those are bigots you're saving! White supremacist sexist transphobic ableist Racists! All of you! Fire! Fire! *Fire!*"

At least two of the remaining AAA/JJJ agents raised automatic weapons and pressed down hard, but nothing happened. No bullets bypassed the American's magnetizers, and even though Quinceton's chopper had lifted off, it lingered just a bit longer to see this futile attempt thwarted in real time. Then, without sound or warning, every remaining stooge on the rooftop dropped their weapons, crouched into a ball, and waited for capture in the stillness of the fetal position.

"Remaining perps are in a body lock on the rooftop," a dark-skinned soldier said to his wrist, which no doubt carried word to every other ship in the squadron. "Delta team, intercept. Greyhawk 3 carrying wounded refugees, heading back to base. Medical team, standby. Debrief to follow." The soldier turned to Quinceton abruptly. "Actually, wait—you want to stick around to see them secure Redgrave before his date with The Hague?"

"I think you've earned at least that much," a female soldier said as she patched up Dad.

Quinceton gazed down at the rooftop, their helicopter waiting casually beside the scene as another descended in its place, this one with steel bars and some kind of cage in the rear. Redgrave could start getting used to living in a cell immediately, and The Hague didn't sound like a great roommate.

"That's all right," Quinceton balked at the offer. "I've seen enough. Let 'em take out the trash. We can keep going. My father, Natalie—we're done with this. I want to see what America looks like. Natalie and I got some living to do."

The male soldiers laughed. But Quinceton was dead serious.

"She seems very smart," the female medic replied, looking at Natalie. "And I hope you guys live a long, happy life together."

"If you can say no to about a million flawless women, then yeah, man, happy life together," the white soldier said, not to Quinceton.

"Yeah, brother," the dark solider said, leaning in. "Your avatar is already set up and has some army of women fighting to get at you the second you go digital. You're the star of the best reality TV show there ever was, or probably ever will be. You have more followers and a bigger fan list of influencers than the goddamn *president!* No joke, even if the president kinda is. You have no idea."

Nope, Quinceton surely did not, and he didn't even understand some of the words and phrases they'd used. But the difference was, these words weren't meant to constrict his free mind. Reality and the ability to think and speak openly about it mattered so much more than any vocabulary that had evolved to dictate truth and meaning and "Racism," or good and evil and all that, for other people.

As the helicopter soared over SOMA's MOMA building, with Redgrave facing handcuffs and all those Quinceton cared about heading for true American freedom, there would finally be social justice.

Printed in the USA
CPSIA information can be obtained
at www.ICGtesting.com
LVHW031913221223
767140LV00036B/1491/J